Welcome To

The Many-Colored Land

"Now, you travelers, listen! Any of you who think you'd like to escape, just think about the fossil zoo waiting bright-eyed and bushy-tailed. We got superlions and hyenas the size of grizzly bears. We got wild boars bigger'n oxen and mastodons that'll stomp you to death if they even catch sight of you. The creeks are full of pythons and crocs. The woods have poisonous spiders with bodies like peaches and fangs like gaboon vipers. You get away from the animals and the Firvulag will track you down and play devil-tunes on your mind until you go mad.

"It's bad out there, travelers! It's not the pretty Eden world they told you about in A.D. 2110."

"Gloomy? Feel out of place? Try the Pliocene; six million years in the past, no pollution, no taxes, equable climate. Climb into your Guderian Effect one-way time machine...it's an SF adventure novel on a grand scale."
Chicago Sun-Times

The Many-Colored Land

Volume I of The Saga of Pliocene Exile

Julian May

A Del Rey Book

BALLANTINE BOOKS • NEW YORK

A Del Rey Book
Published by Ballantine Books

ISBN 0-345-30989-8

This edition published by arrangement with Houghton Mifflin Company

Manufactured in the United States of America

First Ballantine Books Edition: July 1983

Cover art by Michael Whelan

For Tadeusz Maxim,
the noblest of them all

My heart is sore pained within me:
and the terrors of death are fallen upon me.

Fear and trembling have seized me:
and darkness has overwhelmed me

And I said: O that I had wings like a dove!
For then I would fly away and be at rest.

Lo, would I flee far away,
and live in the wilderness.

I would wait for him who will save me
from my cowardice and from the storm.

PSALM 55

CONTENTS

PROLOGUE

1

To confirm that it was indeed near death, the great vessel broke through into normal space with lingering slowness. The pain of the usually swift translation was prolonged as well, until the thousand, for all their strength, cursed and wept within their minds and became convinced that they would be trapped. It would be the gray limbo endlessly. That and pain.

But the Ship was doing its best. Sharing the agony of the passengers, it pushed and pried against the tough fabric of the superficies until there were flickers of black against the gray. The Ship and the people felt their anguish dim into a mere harmony of nearly musical vibrations that echoed, damped, and finally snapped off.

They hung in normal space, stars all around them.

The Ship had emerged in the shadow cone of a planet. For long moments, as the stunned travelers watched without knowing what they saw, the halo of pink atmosphere and the pearly wings of the eclipsed sun's corona gave an aureole to the black world. Then the Ship's ominous momentum carried them on; the chromosphere and the orange flames of the sun's limb burst forth, followed by its dazzling yellow substance.

The Ship curved in. The sunlit surface of the planet seemed

to roll open beneath them at their approach. It was a blue world with white clouds and snowy mountains and landmasses of ochre and red and gray-green—beyond doubt a world of compatible life. The Ship had succeeded.

Thagdal turned to the small woman at the directive console. Brede of the Two Faces shook her head. Dreary violet patterns on the motive display made plain that it had been the final effort of the Ship that brought them to this haven. They were fully in the grip of the system's gravity and no longer capable of inertialess locomotion.

Thagdal's mind and voice spoke. "Listen to me, remnant of battle companies. Our faithful craft has all but perished. It subsists only on mechanicals now and they will not serve much longer. We are on an impact trajectory and we must disembark before the hulk enters the lower atmosphere."

Emanations of sorrow, rage, and fear filled the dying Ship. Questions and reproaches threatened to stifle the mind of Thagdal until he touched the golden torc around his neck and forced them all to be silent.

"In the Name of the Goddess, hold! Our venture was a great gamble, with all minds turned against us. Brede is concerned that this place may not be the perfect refuge we had hoped for. Nevertheless, it is fully compatible, in a remote galaxy where none will dare to look for us. We are safe and have not had to use Spear or Sword. Brede and our Ship have done well to bring us here. Praise to their strength!"

The antiphon was raised dutifully. But sticking up out of the symmetry of it was a prickly thought:

Hymns be damned. Can we *survive* here?

Thagdal lashed back. "We will survive if Compassionate Tana wills, and even find the joy that has eluded us so long. But no thanks to you, Pallol! Shadow-sib! Ancient enemy! Trucebreaker! When we are delivered from this immediate peril you will answer to me!"

A certain amount of vulgar enmity swirled up to merge with Pallol's; but it was fogged by the dull-witted tone of mind that comes from the relief of terrible pain. Nobody else really wanted to fight now. Only the irrepressible Pallol was as game as ever.

Brede Shipspouse flowed soothingly over the impending shambles. "This Many-Colored Land will be a good place for us, my King. And *you* need have no fear, Pallol One-Eye. I have already sounded the planet—lightly, of course—and found no mental challenge. The dominant life-form dwells in speechless innocence and can be no threat to us for more than six million planetary orbits. Yet its germ plasm is indeed compatible for the nurturing and the service. With patience and skilled labor we will surely survive. Now let us go forth from here holding to our truce awhile longer. Let no one speak of vengeance, nor of mistrust of my beloved Spouse."

"Well said, Prescient Lady," came the thoughts and spoken words of the others. (Any dissenters were now keeping well submerged.)

Thagdal said, "The small flyers are waiting for us. As we depart, let all minds be raised in salute."

He went stomping from the control deck, golden hair and beard still crackling with squelched fury, white robes brushing over the now dulled metalloid of the decking. Eadone, Dionket, and Mayvar Kingmaker followed after, minds linked in the Song, fingers giving a farewell caress to the fast-cooling walls that had once thrummed with benevolent power. Little by little the others in various parts of the Ship took up the anthem until nearly all of them were in communion.

Flyers spurted away from the moribund vessel. More than forty birdlike machines pierced the atmosphere like glowing darts before decelerating abruptly and spreading their wings. One took the lead and the others formed a stately procession in its wake. They flew toward the world's largest landmass to await the calculated impact, came up from the south and crossed over the most distinctive feature of the planet—a vast, nearly dry sea basin, glittering with salt pans, which cut an irregular gash across the western reaches of the major continent. A snowy range made a barrier north of this Empty Sea. The flyers went beyond the mountains and hovered over the valley of a large eastward-flowing river, waiting.

The Ship entered on a westerly course, leaving a fiery trail as it ablated in the atmosphere. It swept the ground with a horrendous pressure wave that incinerated vegetation and altered the very minerals of the landscape below. Molten globules of green and brown glass showered the eastern highlands as the Ship's integument exploded away. The river waters vaporized from their bed.

Then came the impact—light-burst and heat-burst and sound-burst, as more than two thousand million tons of matter with a velocity of twenty-two kilometers per second inflicted its wound upon the world. The country rock metamorphosed; the substance of the Ship was all but consumed in the holocaust. Nearly a hundred cubic kilometers of planetary crust exploded upward and outward, the finer products rising in a black column to the stratosphere where the high thin winds spread them in a pall of mourning over much of the world.

The resultant crater was nearly thirty kilometers in diameter but not very deep, battered by tornadic storms engendered in the affronted atmosphere above the glowing ulcer in the land. The small flyers circled solemnly above it for many days, oblivious of the muddy hurricane as they waited for the earth-fires to cool. When the rain had done its work, the flyers departed for a long time.

They returned to the grave when their tasks were finally done and rested for a thousand years.

2

THE LITTLE RAMAPITHECUS WAS STUBBORN. SHE WAS CERTAIN that the baby must have gone into the tangle of maquis. His scent was there, distinct in spite of the heavy springtime perfume of heather, thyme, and gorse.

Uttering crooning calls, the ramapithecus forced her way into the ancient burned-over area, moving uphill. A lapwing, vivid yellow and black, gave a *peewit* cry and limped away, trailing one wing. The ramapithecus knew that this charade was intended to distract her from a nearby nest; but thoughts of bird-prey were far from her simple mind. All she wanted was her missing child.

She toiled up the overgrown slope, using a piece of tree branch to beat down the brush that impeded her. She was able to utilize this tool and a few others. Her brow was low, but her face was quite vertical, with a small, humanoid jaw. Her body, a little over a meter in height, was only slightly stooped, and clothed except for the face and palms in short brown fur.

She continued her crooning. It was a message not framed in words, which any young one of the species would recognize: "Here is Mother. Come to her and be safe and comforted."

The maquis thinned out as she reached the crest of the

height. Out in the open at last, she looked around and gave a low moan of fear. She stood on the edge of a monstrous basin containing a lake of deepest blue color. The rim curved away to the horizon on either hand, completely barren of vegetation along the narrow lip and down the steep slope to the water.

About twenty meters away from her stood a terrible bird. It was something like a fat heron but as tall as a pine tree and just as long, with wings, head, and tail drooping sadly to the ground. From its belly trailed a knobby appendage with climbing holds. The bird was hard, not made of flesh. It was layered in dust, crusted and scabbed with yellow and gray and orange lichen over what had once been a smooth black skin. Far along the rim of the astrobleme, in both directions, she could see other such birds standing widely spaced, all looking into the dark-mirrored depths.

The ramapithecus prepared to flee. Then she heard a familiar sound.

She gave a sharp hoot. Immediately, a tiny upside-down head popped out of an orifice in the belly of the nearby bird. The child chittered happily. His sounds had the meaning: "Welcome, Mother. This is fun! Look what is here!"

Exhausted, overcome by relief, her hands bloody from breaking through the thorns, the mother howled in fury at her offspring. Hastily, he came down the exit ladder of the flyer and scuttled up to her. She scooped him up and crushed him to her breast; then she put him down and cuffed the sides of his head, left-right, pouring out a torrent of indignant chatter.

Trying to placate her, he held out the thing he had found. It resembled a large ring, but was really two conjoined semi-circlets of twisted gold, thick as a finger and rounded, incised with tortuous little markings like the borings of gribbles in sea-logged wood.

The young ramapithecus grinned and snapped open two knobby ends of the ring. The other ends were held by a kind of pivoting hinge that allowed the halves to rotate and open wide. The child placed the ring around his neck, twisted it and snapped the catch shut. The golden torc gleamed against his tawny fur, much too large for him but alive with power nevertheless. Smiling still, he showed his mother what he was now able to do.

She shrieked.

The child leaped in dismay. He tripped over a rock and fell backward. Before he could recover, his mother was upon him, yanking the ring over his head so that the metal bruised his ears. And it hurt! The loss of it hurt worse than any pain he had ever known. He must get it back—

The mother screamed even louder as he tried to grab at the torc. Her voice echoed across the crater lake. She flung the golden thing as far away as she could, into a dense thicket of spiny gorse. The child wailed his broken-hearted protest, but she seized his arm and hauled him toward the path she had made through the maquis.

Well concealed and only slightly dented, the torc gleamed in the dappled shadows.

3

IN THE EARLY YEARS AFTER HUMANITY, WITH A LITTLE HELP from its friends, had set out to overrun the compatible stars, a professor of dynamic field-physics named Théo Guderian discovered the way into Exile. His researches, like those of so many other unorthodox but promising thinkers of the time, were sustained by a no-strings grant from the Human Polity of the Galactic Milieu.

Guderian lived on the Old World. Because science had so many other things to assimilate in those exciting times (and because Guderian's discovery seemed to have no practical application whatsoever in 2034), the publication of his culminating paper caused only a brief flutter in the dovecote of physical cosmology. But in spite of the prevailing air of indifference, a small number of workers from all six of the coadunate galactic races continued to be curious enough about Guderian's findings to seek him out in his modest home-cum-workshop outside of Lyon. Even as his health failed, the Professor received these visiting colleagues with courtesy and assured them that he would be honored to repeat his experiment for them if they would pardon the crudities of his apparatus, which he had removed to the cellar of his cottage after the Institute disclaimed further interest in it.

It took Madame Guderian some time to become resigned to

the exotic pilgrims from other stars. One had, after all, to preserve the social convenances by entertaining the guests. But there were difficulties! She overcame her aversion to the tall, androgynous Gi after much mental exercise, and one could always pretend that the Poltroyans were civilized gnomes. But she could never get used to the awesome Krondaku or the half-visible Lylmik, and one could only deplore the way that some of the less fastidious Simbiari dripped green on the carpet.

What was to be the last group of guests called just three days before Professor Guderian's terminal illness commenced. Madame opened the door to greet two outworld male humans (one alarmingly massive and the other quite ordinary), an urbane little Poltroyan wearing the gorgeous robes of a Full Elucidator, a two-and-a-half-meter Gi (mercifully with clothes on), and—sainte vierge!—no less than *three* Simbiari.

She welcomed them and put out extra ashtrays and waste-baskets.

Professor Guderian conducted the extraterrestrial visitors to the cellar of the large country cottage just as soon as the politenesses had been exchanged. "We will proceed at once to the demonstration, good friends. You will forgive me, but today I am a trifle fatigued."

"Most regrettable," said the solicitous Poltroyan. "Perhaps, my dear Professor, you would benefit from a rejuvenative course?"

"No, no," Guderian said with a smile. "One lifetime is quite enough for me. I feel I am most fortunate to have lived in the era of the Great Intervention, but I must confess that events now seem to be moving faster than my composure can tolerate. I look forward to the ultimate peace."

They passed through a metal-sheathed door into what was apparently a converted wine cellar. An area of stone paving some three meters square had been removed, leaving bare earth. Guderian's apparatus stood in the middle of it.

The old man rummaged for a moment in an antique oak cabinet near the door and came up with a small pile of reading-plaques, which he distributed to the scientists. "A précis of my theoretical considerations and diagrams of the device are contained in these booklets, which my wife has been kind enough to prepare for visitors. You must excuse the simplicity of the format. We have long since exhausted our major funding."

The others murmured sympathetically.

"Please stand here for the demonstration. You will observe that the device has certain affinities to the subspace translator and thus requires very little power input. My own modifications have been designed with a view toward phasing in residual magnetics contained in the local rock strata, together with the deeper contemporary fields being generated beneath the continental platform. These, interacting with the matrices of the translator fields, generate the singularity."

Guderian reached into the pocket of his work smock and took out a large carrot. With a Gallic shrug, he remarked, "Expedient, if somewhat ridiculous."

He placed the carrot on an ordinary wooden stool and carried it to the apparatus. Guderian's device rather resembled an old-fashioned latticework pergola or gazebo draped in vines. However, the frame was made of transparent vitreous material except for peculiar nodular components of dead black, and the "vines" were actually cables of colorful alloys that seemed to grow up from the cellar floor, creep in and out of the lattice in a disconcerting fashion, and abruptly disappear at a point just short of the ceiling.

When the stool and its carrot were in position, Guderian rejoined his guests and activated the device. There was no sound. The gazebo shimmered momentarily; then it seemed as if mirror panels sprang into existence, hiding the interior of the apparatus completely from view.

"You will understand that a certain waiting period is now in order," the old man said. "The carrot is almost always effective, but from time to time there are disappointments."

The seven visitors waited. The wide-shouldered human clutched his book-plaque in both hands but never let his eyes leave the gazebo. The other colonial, a placid type from some institute on Londinium, made a tactful examination of the control panel. The Gi and the Poltroyan read their booklets with equanimity. One of the younger Simbiari inadvertently let an emerald drop fall and made haste to scuff it into the cellar floor.

Numerals on the wall chronometer flickered past. Five minutes. Ten.

"We will see whether our game is afoot," the Professor said, with a wink at the man from Londinium.

The mirrored energy field snapped off. For the merest nanosecond, the startled scientists were aware of a pony-shaped creature standing inside the gazebo. It turned instantly to an articulated skeleton. As the bones fell, they disintegrated into grayish powder.

"Shit!" exclaimed the seven eminent scientists.

"Be calm, colleagues," said Guderian. "Such a dénouement is unfortunately inevitable. But we shall project a slow-motion holo so that our catch may be identified."

He switched on a concealed Tri-D projector and froze the action to reveal a small horselike animal with amiable black eyes, three-toed feet, and a russet coat marked with faint white stripes. Carrot greens stuck out of its mouth. The wooden stool was beside it.

"Hipparion gracile. A cosmopolitan species abundant during Earth's Pliocene Epoch."

Guderian let the projector run. The stool quietly dissolved. The hide and flesh of the little horse shriveled with dreadful slowness, peeling away from the skeleton and exploding into a cloud of dust, while the internal organs simultaneously swelled, shrank, and puffed into nothingness. The bones continued to stand upright, then tumbled in graceful slow arcs. Their first contact with the cellar floor reduced them to their component minerals.

The sensitive Gi let out a sigh and closed its great yellow eyes. The Londoner had turned pale, while the other human, from the rugged and morose world of Shqipni, chewed on his large brown mustache. The incontinent young Simb made haste to utilize a wastebasket.

"I have tried both plant and animal bait in my little trap," Guderian said. "Carrot or rabbit or mouse may make the trip to the Pliocene unharmed, but on the return journey, any living thing that is within the tau-field inevitably assumes the burden of more than six million years of earthly existence."

"And inorganic matter?" inquired the Skipetar.

"Of a certain density, of a certain crystalline structure— many specimens make the round trip in fairly good condition. I have even been successful in circumtranslating two forms of organic matter: amber and coal travel unscathed."

"But this is most intriguing!" said the Prime Contemplator of the Twenty-Sixth College of Simb. "The theory of temporal plication has been in our repository for some seventy thousand of your years, my worthy Guderian, but its demonstration eluded the best minds of the Galactic Milieu . . . until now. The fact that you, a human scientist, have been even partially successful where so many others have failed is surely one more confirmation of the unique abilities of the Children of Earth."

The sour-grape flavor of this speech was not lost on the Poltroyan. His ruby eyes twinkled as he said, "The Amalgam of Poltroy, unlike certain other coadunate races, never doubted that the Intervention was fully justified."

"For you and your Milieu, perhaps," said Guderian in a low voice. His dark eyes, pain-tinged behind rimless eyeglasses, showed a momentary bitterness. "But what of us? We have had to give up so much—our diverse languages, many of our social philosophies and religious dogmata, our so-called nonproductive lifestyles . . . our very human sovereignty, laughable though its loss must seem to the ancient intellects of the Galactic Milieu."

The man from Shqipni exclaimed, "How can you doubt the wisdom of it, Professor? We humans gave up a few cultural fripperies and gained energy sufficiency and unlimited lebensraum and membership in a galactic civilization! Now that we don't have to waste time and lives in mere survival, there'll be no holding humanity back! Our race is just beginning to fulfill its genetic potential—which may be greater than that of any other people!"

The Londoner winced.

The Prime Contemplator said suavely, "Ah, the proverbial human breeding capacity! How it does keep the gene pool roiled. One is reminded of the well-known reproductive superiority of the adolescent organism as compared to that of the mature individual whose plasm, while less prodigally broadcast, may nonetheless burgeon more prudently in the pursuit of genetic optima."

"Did you say mature?" sneered the Skipetar. "Or atrophied?"

"Colleagues! Colleagues!" exclaimed the diplomatic little Poltroyan. "We will weary Professor Guderian."

"No, it's all right," the old man said; but he looked gray and ill.

"The Gi hastened to change the subject. "Surely this effect

you have demonstrated would be a splendid tool for paleo-biology."

"I fear," Guderian replied, "that there is limited galactic interest in the extinct life-forms of Earth's Rhône-Saône Trough."

"Then you haven't been able to—er—tune the device for retrieval in other areas?" asked the Londoner.

"Alas, no, my dear Sanders. Nor have other workers been able to reproduce my experiment in other localities on Earth or on other worlds." Guderian tapped one of the plaque-books. "As I have pointed out, there is a problem in computing the subtleties of the geomagnetic input. This region of southern Europe has one of the more complex geomorphologies of the planet. Here in the Monts des Lyonnais and the Forez we have a foreland of the utmost antiquity cheek by jowl with recent volcanic intrusions. In nearby regions of the Massif Central we see even more clearly the workings of intracrustal metamor-phism, the anatexis engendered above one or more ascending asthenospheric diapirs. To the east lie the Alps with their stu-pendously folded nappes. South of here is the Mediterranean Basin with active subduction zones—which was, incidentally, in an extremely peculiar condition during the Lower Pliocene Epoch."

"So you're in a dead end, eh?" remarked the Skipetar. "Too bad Earth's Pliocene period wasn't all that interesting. Just a few million years marking time between the Miocene and the Ice Age. The shank of the Cenozoic, so to speak."

Guderian produced a small whiskbroom and dustpan and began to tidy up the gazebo. "It was a golden time, just before the dawn of rational humankind. A time of benevolent climate and flourishing plant and animal life. A vintage time, unspoiled and tranquil. An autumn before the terrible winter of the Pleis-tocene glaciation. Rousseau would have loved the Pliocene Epoch! Uninteresting? There are even today soul-weary people in this Galactic Milieu who would not share your evaluation."

The scientists exchanged glances.

"If only it weren't a one-way trip," said the man from Londinium.

Guderian was calm. "All of my efforts to change the facies of the singularity have been in vain. It is fixed in Pliocene time, in the uplands of this venerable river valley. And so we come to the heart of the matter at last! The great achievement of time-travel stands revealed as a mere scientific curiosity." Once more, the Gallic shrug.

"Future workers will profit from your pioneering effort," declared the Poltroyan. The others hurried to add appropriate felicitations.

"Enough, dear colleagues," Guderian laughed. "You have been most kind to visit an old man. And now we must go up to Madame, who awaits with refreshment. I bequeath to sharper minds the practical application of my peculiar little experiment."

He winked at the outworld humans and tipped the contents of the dustpan into the wastebasket. The ashes of the hipparion floated in little blobby islands on the green alien slime.

PART I

THE LEAVETAKING

1

BURNISHED TRUMPETS SOUNDED A FLOURISH. THE DUCAL PARty rode gaily out of the Château de Riom, horses prancing and curvetting as they had been trained, giving a show of spirit without imperiling the ladies in their chancy sidesaddles. Sunshine sparkled on the jeweled caparisons of the mounts, but it was the gorgeous riders who earned the crowd's applause.

Greenish-blue reflections from the festive scene on the monitor blackened Mercedes Lamballe's auburn hair and threw livid lights across her thin face. "The tourists draw lots to be in the procession of nobles," she explained to Grenfell. "It's more fun to be common, but try to tell them that. Of course the principals are all pros."

Jean, Duc de Berry, raised his arm to the cheering throng. He wore a long houppelande in his own heraldic blue, powdered with fleurs de lys. The dagged sleeves were turned back to show a rich lining of yellow brocade. The Duc's hosen were pure white, embroidered with golden spangles, and he wore golden spurs. At his side rode the Prince, Charles d'Orléans, his robes particolored in the royal scarlet, black, and white, his heavy golden baldric fringed with tinkling bells. Other nobles in the train, gaudy as a flock of spring warblers, followed after with the ladies.

"Isn't there a hazard?" Grenfell asked. "Horses with untrained riders? I should think you'd stick with robot mounts."

Lamballe said softly, "It has to be real. This *is* France, you know. The horses are specially bred for intelligence and stability."

In honor of the maying, the betrothed Princess Bonne and all her retinue were dressed in malachite-green silk. The noble maidens wore the quaint headdresses of the early fifteenth century, fretted gilt-wire confections threaded with jewels, rising up on their braided coiffures like kitten ears. The crépine of the Princess was even more outlandish, extending out from her temples in long golden horns with a white lawn veil draped over the wires.

"Cue the flower girls," said Gaston, from the other side of the control room.

Mercy Lamballe sat still, gazing at the brilliant picture with rapt intensity. The antennae of her comset made the strange headpiece of the medieval princess out on the château grounds look almost ordinary in comparison.

"Merce," the director repeated with gentle insistence. "The flower girls."

Slowly she reached out a hand, keying the marshaling channel.

Trumpets sounded again and the peasant crowd of tourists oohed. Dozens of dimpled little maids in short gowns of pink and white came running out of the orchard carrying baskets of apple blossoms. They romped along the road in front of the ducal procession strewing flowers, while flageolets and trombones struck up a lively air. Jugglers, acrobats, and a dancing bear joined the mob. The Princess blew kisses to the crowd, and the Duc distributed an occasional piece of largesse.

"Cue the courtiers," said Gaston.

The woman at the control console sat motionless. Bryan Grenfell could see drops of moisture on her brow, dampening the straying tendrils of auburn hair. Her mouth was tight.

"Mercy, what is it?" Grenfell whispered. "What's wrong?"

"Nothing," she said. Her voice was husky and strained. "Courtiers away, Gaston."

Three young men, also dressed in green, came galloping from the woods toward the procession of nobility, bearing armfuls of leafy sprigs. With much giggling, the ladies twined these into head-wreaths and crowned the chevaliers of their choice. The men reciprocated with dainty chaplets for the damsels, and they all resumed their ride toward the meadow where the maypole waited. Meanwhile, directed by Mercy's commands, barefoot girls and grinning youths distributed flowers and greenery to the slightly self-conscious crowd, crying: "Vert! Vert pour le mai!"

Right on cue, the Duc and his party began to sing along with the flutes:

> C'est le mai, c'est le mai,
> C'est le joli mois de mai!

"They're off pitch again," Gaston said in an exasperated voice. "Cue in the filler voices, Merce. And let's have the lark loops and a few yellow butterflies." He keyed for voice on the marshaling channel and exclaimed, "Eh, Minou! Get that clot out from in front of the Duc's horse. And watch the kid in red. Looks like he's twitching bells off the Prince's baldric."

Mercedes Lamballe brought up the auxiliary voices as ordered. The entire crowd joined in the song, having slept on it on the way from Charlemagne's Coronation. Mercy made birdsong fill the blossom-laden orchard and sent out signals that released the butterflies from their secret cages. Unbidden, she conjured up a scented breeze to cool the tourists from Aquitaine and Neustria and Blois and Foix and all the other "French" planets in the Galactic Milieu who had come, together with Francophiles and medievalists from scores of other worlds, to savor the glories of ancient Auvergne.

"They'll be getting warm now, Bry," she remarked to Grenfell. "The breeze will make them happier."

Bryan relaxed at the more normal tone in her voice. "I guess there are limits to the inconveniences they'll endure in the name of immersive cultural pageantry."

"We reproduce the past," Lamballe said, "as we would have *liked* it to be. The realities of medieval France are another trip altogether."

"We have stragglers, Merce." Gaston's hands flashed over the control panel in the preliminary choreography of the maypole suite. "I see two or three exotics in the bunch. Probably those comparative ethnologists from the Krondak world we were alerted about. Better bring over a troubadour to keep 'em happy until they catch up with the main group. These visiting firemen are apt to write snotty evaluations if you let 'em get bored."

"Some of us keep our objectivity," Grenfell said mildly.

The director snorted. "Well, *you're* not out there tramping through horseshit in fancy dress in the hot sun on a world with low subjective oxygen and double subjective gravity!... Merce? Dammit, kiddo, are you fuguing off again?"

Bryan rose from his seat and came to her, grave concern on his face. "Gaston—can't you see she's ill?"

"I'm not!" Mercy was sharp. "It's going to pass off in a minute or two. Troubadour away, Gaston."

The monitor zoomed in on a singer who bowed to the little knot of laggards, struck a chord on his lute, and began expertly herding the people toward the maypole area while soothing them with song. The piercing sweetness of his tenor filled the control room. He sang first in French, then in the Standard English of the Human Polity of the Galactic Milieu for those who weren't up to the archaic linguistics.

> Le temps a laissé son manteau
> De vent, de froidure et de pluie,
> Et s'est vestu de broderie
> De soleil luisant—cler et beau.
>
> Now time has put off its dark cloak
> Of gales and of frosts and of rain,
> And garbs itself in woven light,
> Bright sunshine of spring once again.

A genuine lark added its own coda to the minstrel's song. Mercy lowered her head and tears fell onto the console before her. That damn song. And springtime in the Auvergne. And the friggerty larks and retroevolved butterflies and manicured meadows and orchards crammed with gratified folk from faraway planets where the living was tough but the challenge was being met by all but the inevitable misfits who slubbed the beautiful growing tapestry of the Galactic Milieu.

Misfits like Mercy Lamballe.

"Beaucoup regrets, guys," she said with a rueful smile,

mopping her face with a tissue. "Wrong phase of the moon, I guess. Or the old Celtic rising. Bry, you just picked the wrong day to visit this crazy place. Sorry."

"All you Celts are bonkers." Gaston excused her with breezy kindness. "There's a Breton engineer over in the Sun King Pageant who told me he can only shoot his wad when he's doing it on a megalith. Come on, babe. Let's keep this show rolling."

On the screens, the maypole dancers twined their ribbons and pivoted in intricate patterns. The Duc de Berry and the other actors of his entourage permitted thrilled tourists to admire the indubitably real gems that adorned their costumes. Flutes piped, cornemuses wailed, hawkers peddled comfits and wine, shepherds let people pet their lambs, and the sun smiled down. All was well in la douce France, A.D. 1410, and so it would be for another six hours, through the tournament and culminating feast.

And then the weary tourists, 700 years removed from the medieval world of the Duc de Berry, would be whisked off in comfortable subway tubes to their next cultural immersion at Versailles. And Bryan Grenfell and Mercy Lamballe would go down to the orchard as evening fell to talk of sailing to Ajaccio together and to see how many of the butterflies had survived.

2

THE ALERT KLAXON HOOTED THROUGH THE READY ROOM OF Lisboa Power Grid's central staging.

"Well, hell, I was folding anyhow," big Georgina remarked. She hoisted the portable air-conditioning unit of her armor and clomped off to the waiting drill-rigs, helmet under her arm.

Stein Oleson slammed his cards down on the table. His beaker of booze went over and sluiced the meager pile of chips in front of him. "And me with a king-high tizz and the first decent pot all day! Damn lucky granny-banging trisomics!" He lurched to his feet, upsetting the reinforced chair, and stood swaying, two meters and fifteen cents' worth of ugly-handsome berserker. The reddened sclera of his eyeballs contrasted oddly with the bright blue irises. Oleson glared at the other players and bunched up his mailed servo-powered fists.

Hubert gave a deep guffaw. He could laugh, having come out on top. "Tough kitty! Simmer down, Stein. Sopping up all that mouthwash didn't help your game much."

The fourth cardplayer chimed in. "I told you to take it easy on the gargle, Steinie. And now lookit! We gotta go down, and you're half-plotzed again."

Oleson gave the man a look of murderous contempt. He shed the a/c walkaround, climbed into his own drill-rig, and began plugging himself in. "You keep your trap shut, Jango. Even blind drunk I can zap a truer bore than any scat-eatin' li'l Portugee sardine stroker."

"Oh, for God's sake," said Hubert. "Will you two quit?"

"You try teaming with an orry-eyed squarehead!" Jango said. He blew his nose in the Iberian fashion, over the neck-rim of his armor, then locked on his helmet.

Oleson sneered. "And you call *me* slob!"

The electronic voice of Georgina, the team leader, gave them the bad news as they went through the systems check. "We've lost the Cabo da Roca-Azores mainline bore 793 kloms out and the service tunnel, too. Class Three slippage and overthrust, but at least the fistula sealed. It looks like a long trick, children."

Stein Oleson powered up. His 180-ton rig rose thirty cents off the deck, slid out of its bay, and sashayed down the ramp, wagging its empennage like a slightly tipsy iron dinosaur.

"Madre de deus," growled Jango's voice. His machine came after Stein's, obeying the taxi regulation scrupulously. "He's a menace, Georgina. I'll be damned if I drill tandem with him. I'm telling you, I'll file a beef with the union! How'd *you* like to have a drunken numbwit the only thing between your ass and a bleb of red-hot basalt?"

Oleson's bellowed laughter clanged in all their ears. "Go ahead and file with the union, pussywillow! Then get yourself a job to fit your nerve. Like drilling holes in Swiss cheeses with your—"

"Will you cut that crap?" Georgina said wearily. "Hubey, you partner with Jango this shift and I'll go tandem with Stein."

"Now wait a minute, Georgina," Oleson began.

"It's settled, Stein." She cycled the airlock. "You and Big Mama against the world, Blue Eyes. And save your soul for Jesus if you don't sober up before we hit that break. Let's haul, children."

A massive gate, eleven meters high and nearly as thick, swung open to give them entry to the service tunnel that dived under the sea. Georgina had fed the coordinates of the break into the autohelms of their drill-rigs, so all they had to do for a while was relax, wiggle around in their armor, and maybe snuff up a euphoric or two while hurtling along at 500 kph toward a mess under the bottom of the Atlantic Ocean.

Stein Oleson raised the partial pressure of his oxygen and gave himself a jolt of aldetox and stimvim. Then he ordered the armor's meal unit to deliver a liter of raw egg and smoked herring purée, together with his favorite hair of the dog, akvavit.

There was a low muttering in his helmet receiver. "Damn atavistic cacafogo. Ought to mount a set of ox horns on his helmet and wrap his iron ass in a bearskin jockstrap."

Stein smiled in spite of himself. In his favorite fantasies he did imagine himself a Viking. Or, since he had both Norse and Swedish genes, perhaps a Varangian marauder slashing his way southward into ancient Russia. How wonderful it would be to answer insults with an axe or a sword, unfettered by the stupid constraints of civilization! To let the red anger flow as it was meant to, powering his great muscles for battle! To take strong blonde women who would first fight him off, then yield with sweet openness! He was born for a life like that.

But unfortunately for Stein Oleson, human cultural savagery was extinct in the Galactic Age, mourned only by a few ethnologists, and the subtleties of the new mental barbarians were beyond Stein's power to grasp. This exciting and dangerous job of his had been vouchsafed him by a compassionate computer, but his soul-hunger remained unsatisfied. He had never considered emigrating to the stars; on no human colony anywhere in the Galactic Milieu was there a primal Eden. The germ plasm of humanity was too valuable to fritter in neo-lithic backwaters. Each of the 783 new human worlds was completely civilized, bound by the ethics of the Concilium, and obligated to contribute toward the slowly coalescing Whole. People who hankered after their simpler roots had to be content with visiting the Old World's painstaking restorations of ancient cultural settings, or with the exquisitely orchestrated Immersive Pageants—almost, but not quite, authentic to the last detail—which let a person actively savor selected portions of his heritage.

Stein, who was born on the Old World, had gone to the Fjordland Saga when he was barely out of adolescence, traveling from Chicago Metro to Scandinavia with other vacationing students. He was ejected from the Longboat Invaders Pageant and heavily fined after leaping into the midst of a mock mêlée, chopping a hairy Norseman's arm off, and "rescuing" a kidnapped British maiden from rape. (The wounded actor was philosophical about his three months in the regeneration tank. "Just the hazards of the trade, kid," he had told his remorseful attacker.)

Some years later, after Stein had matured and found a certain release in his work, he had gone to the Saga pageants again. This time they seemed pathetic. Stein saw the happy outworld visitors from Trøndelag and Thule and Finnmark and all the other "Scandinavian" planets as a pack of silly costumed fools, waders in the shallows, nibblers, masturbators, pathetic chasers after lost identity.

"What will you do when you find out who you are, greatgrandchildren of test tubes?" he had screamed, fighting drunk at the Valhalla Feast. "Go back where you came from—to the new worlds the monsters gave you!" Then he had climbed up onto the Aesir's table and peed in the mead bowl.

They ejected and fined him again. And this time his credit card was pipped so that he was automatically turned away by every pageant box office...

The speeding drill-rigs raced beneath the continental slope, their headlights catching glints of pink, green, and white from the granite walls of the tunnel. Then the machines penetrated the dark basalt of the deep-ocean crust below the Tagus Abyssal Plain. Just three kilometers above their service tunnel were the waters of the sea; ten kilometers below lay the molten mantle.

As they drove two abreast through the lithosphere, the members of the team had the illusion of going down a gigantic ramp with sharp drops at regular intervals. The rigs would fly straight and level, then nose down sharply on a new straight path, only to repeat the maneuver a few moments later. The service tunnel was following the curvature of the Earth in a series of straight-line increments; it had to, because of the power-transmittal bore it served, a parallel tunnel with a diameter just great enough to admit a single drill-rig when there was a need for major repairs. In most parts of the complex undersea power system, service tunnels and bores were connected by adits every ten kloms, allowing the maintenance crews easy access; but if they had to, the drill-rigs could zap right through the rough rock walls of the service tunnel and mole their way to the bore from any angle.

Until the time when the alarm had run in Lisboa, the main-line bore between continental Europe and the extensive Azores mariculture farms had been lit with the glare of a photon beam. This ultimate answer to Earth's ancient energy-hunger originated at this time of day in the sunshine of the Serra da Estrela Tier 39 Collection Center northwest of Lisboa Metro. With its sister centers at Jiuquan, Akebono Platform, and Cedar Bluffs KA, it gathered and distributed solar energy to be used by consumers adjacent to the 39N parallel all around the globe. A complex of spidery stratotowers, secure against the forces of gravity and high above the weather, gathered light rays from the cloudless skies, arranged them into a coherent beam, and sent this to be distributed safely underground via a web of mainline and local feeder bores. A photon from the Portuguese (or Chinese or Pacific or Kansas) daylight would be directed on its way by means of plasma mirrors operating within the bores, and would reach the fog-bound folk in the farms of the North Atlantic before an eye could blink. The ocean farmers utilized the power for everything from submarine harvesters to electric blankets. Few of the consumers would bother to think where the energy came from.

Like all of Earth's subterranean power bores, Cabo da Roca-Azores was regularly patrolled by small robot crawlers and muckers. These could make minor repairs when the planetary crust shifted in a common Class One incident, not even interrupting the photon beam. Class Two damage was severe enough to cause an automatic shutdown. Perhaps a tremor would shift a segment of the bore slightly out of alignment, or damage one of the vital mirror stations. Crews from the surface would race to the scene of the disruption via the service tunnels, and the repairs were usually made very quickly.

But on this day, the tectonic adjustment had been rated at Class Three. The Despacho Fracture Zone had shrugged, and a web of minor faults in the suboceanic basalt had waggled in sympathy. Hot rock surrounding a three-kilometer section of the paired tunnels suddenly moved north-south, east-west, up-down, crumpling not only the power bore but the much larger service tunnel as well. As the mirror station vaporized in a very small thermonuclear flash, the searing photons of the beam burned undeflected for a microsecond before safety cutoff. The beam punched through the shattered bore wall and continued to burn a straight-arrow path westward through the crust until it broke through the sea floor. There was a steam explosion in the liquefied rock just as the beam died, which effectively sealed the fistula. But a large region that had formerly been fairly stable solid rock was now reduced to a shambles of rubble, cooked oceanic ooze, and slowly cooling pockets of molten lava.

A bypass restored power to the Azores within one second after the break. Until the repairs were made, the islands would take most of their energy from the Tier 38 Collection Center northwest of Lorca in Spain, via Gibraltar-Madeira. Drill crews from both ends of the damaged bore segment would get to clean up the mess, rebuild the mirror, and spin reinforcement sleeves for the tunnels passing through the new zone of instability.

Then there would be light once again.

"Lisbong leader, this is Ponta Del Three-Alfa coming up on Klom Seven-Niner-Seven, c'mon."

"Lisbong Sixteen-Echo gotcha, Ponta Del," said Georgina. "We're at Seven-Eight-Zip and rolling . . . Seven-Eight-Five . . . Seven-Niner-Zip . . . and at the fall, Seven-Niner-Two. You guys gonna take the fistula?"

"Affirm, Lisbong, with one unit on the bore for linkup. Long time no see, Georgina, but we gotta stop meeting like this! Put your best zapper on the mainline rebore, sweetie. She gonna be a sneako rascal, c'mon."

"Have no fear, Ponta Del. See you in a short, Larry lovie. Sixteen-Echo gone."

Stein Oleson gritted his teeth and gripped the twin joy sticks of his rig. He knew he was the best shot Lisboa had. Nobody could zap a truer bore than he could. Lava blisters, magnetic anoms—nothing ever threw him off the true. He got ready to blast.

"Hubert, get on that mainline rebore," Georgina said.

Humiliation and rage twisted Stein's guts. A nauseous blend of bile and herring rose in his throat. He swallowed. He breathed. He waited.

"Jango, you follow Hubey with the sleeve-spinning until you hit the mirror. Then get on that. Steinie, let's you and me open up this service tunnel."

"Right you are, Georgina," Stein said quietly. He thumbed

the stud on his right stick. A greenish-white ray blazed out of the rig's nose. Slowly, the two big machines began to cut through the fall of steaming black rock while little robot muckers scuttled about hauling the debris away.

3

THE ENTIRE VOORHEES CLAN HAD TAKEN TO DEEP SPACE ALmost immediately after the Great Intervention. It was to be expected of the descendants of New Amsterdam skippers and four generations of U.S. Navy airmen; a yearning for far horizons was programmed into the Voorhees genes.

Richard Voorhees and his older sibs Farnum and Evelyn were born on Assawompset, one of the longest-settled "American" worlds, where their parents were based with the Fourteenth Fleet. Far and Evvie carried on the family tradition—line officers both, she commanding a diplomatic courier, he the exec on one of the asteroid-sized colonization transports. Both had served with distinction during the brief Metapsychic Rebellion of the 'Eighties, a credit to the family name, to the service, and to humanity at large.

Then there was Richard.

He also went to the stars, but not in government service. The structured military life was repellent to him and he was excessively xenophobic as well. Members of the five exotic races were common visitors at Assawompset Sector Base, and Richard had hated and feared them from the time he was a toddler. Later, in school, he found a rationalization for the dread as he read about the half-century preceding the Intervention on Old Earth, when more and more frequent probings by the eager anthropologists of the Milieu had disturbed and sometimes terrified humanity. The Krondaku had been guilty of particularly tactless experimentation; and crews from certain Simbiari worlds had even descended to mischief-making among the natives when overcome by ennui during long surveillance tours.

The Galactic Concilium had dealt sternly with such transgressions, which were fortunately few. Nevertheless a remnant of the old "alien invasion" psychosis persisted in human folklore even after the Intervention had opened the way to the stars. Mild manifestations of xenophobia were rather common among human colonists; but not many people carried their prejudice as far as Richard Voorhees.

Fanned by feelings of personal inadequacy, the irrational fears of the child matured into full-blown hatred in the grown man. Richard rejected Milieu service and turned instead to a career as a commercial spacer. There he could pick and choose his shipmates and the ports he visited. Farnum and Evelyn tried to be understanding of their brother's problem; but Richard knew all too well that the Fleet officers secretly looked down upon him.

"Our brother the trader," they would say, and laugh. "Well, it's not quite as bad as being a pirate!"

Richard had to pretend to be a good sport about the jibing for more than twenty years, while he worked his way up from spacehand to mate to hired skipper to owner-operator. The day came at last when he could stand at the dock at Bedford Starport and admire the quarter-klom sleekness of CSS Wolverton Mountain, rejoicing that she was his own. The ship had been a VIP speedster, equipped with the most powerful superluminal translator as well as oversized inertialess drivers for slower-than-light travel. Voorhees had the passenger accommodations ripped out and converted her to full-auto express cargo, because that was where the real money was.

He let it be known that there was no journey too long or too dangerous for him to dare, no risk he was not prepared to undertake in the delivery of a rare or desperately needed load anywhere in the galaxy. And the clients came.

In the years that followed, Richard Voorhees made the appalling Hub run eight times before the precarious colonies there were abandoned. He burned out four sets of upsilon energy-field crystals and nearly fused his own nervous system on a record-breaking run to Hercules Cluster. He carried drugs and life-saving equipment and parts to fix vital machinery. He expedited samples of ores and cultures and suspect organisms from outlying human colonies to the vast laboratories of the Old World. He was able to prevent a eugenic catastrophe on Bafut by rushing in replacement sperm. He had given mild gratification to a dying tycoon by speeding one precious bottle of Jack Daniel's from Earth to the faraway Cumberland System. He had toted just about everything but the serum to Nome and the message to Garcia.

Richard Voorhees became rich and a little famous, underwent rejuvenation, acquired a taste for antique aeroplanes, rare Earth vintages, gourmet goodies, and dancing women, grew a big black mustache, and told his distinguished older brother and sister to go screw themselves.

And then, on a certain day in 2110, Richard sowed the seed of his own ruin.

He was alone as usual on the bridge of Wolverton Mountain, deep in the gray negation of subspace, going balls-up for the isolated Orissa system 1870 light-years south of the Galactic Plane. His cargo was a large and intricate temple of Jagannath, including sacred images and rolling stock, intended to replace a religious complex that had been accidentally destroyed on the Hindu-settled planet. Old World artisans, using tools and ancient patterns now unavailable to their colonial kin, had crafted a perfect replica; but they had taken much too long doing it. Voorhees' contract specified that he had to get the temple and its statuary to Orissa within seventeen days, before the local celebration of Rath Yatra, when the god's effigy was scheduled to be transported in solemn procession from the temple to a summer dwelling. If the ship arrived late and the faithful had to commemorate their holy days without the sacred edifice and images, the shipping fee would be halved. And it was a very large fee.

Voorhees had been confident of meeting the deadline. He programmed the tightest hyperspatial catenary, made sure he had extra dope for the pain of breaking through the superficies on short leash, and settled down to play chess with the guidance computer and trade gossip with the ship's other systems. Wolverton Mountain was completely automated except for her skipper; but Richard had sufficient vestigial social tendencies to program all of the robotics with individual identities and voices, together with input from the scandal sheets of his favorite worlds, jokes, and sycophantic chatter. It helped to pass the time.

"Communications to bridge," said a winsome contralto, interrupting Richard's attack on the computer's queen.

"Voorhees here. What is it, Lily darling?"

"We've intercepted a contemporaneous subspace distress signal," the system said. "A Poltroyan research vessel is dead in the matrix with translator trouble. Navigation is plotting its pseudolocus."

Damn grinning little dwarfs! Probably poking around in their usual busybody way and all the while letting the u-crystals deteriorate without proper maintenance.

"Navigation to bridge."

"Yes, Fred?"

"That vessel in distress is damn near our catenary, Captain. They're lucky. This slice of the hype doesn't get much traffic."

Richard's fist closed around a chess pawn and squeezed. So now he could go nursemaid the little buggers. And kiss half his commission goodbye, like as not. It would probably take several subjective days to make repairs, considering the fumble-fingeredness of the Poltroyans and the fact that Wolverton Mountain carried only three robot excursion engineers. If it was a shipful of humans in distress, there'd be no question of heaving to. But exotics!

"I've acknowledged receipt of the distress signal," Lily said. "The Poltroyan vessel is in a state of life-system deterioration. They've been trapped for some time, Skipper."

Oh, hell. He was only two days out of Orissa. The Poltroons could certainly hang on for a few days longer. He could catch them on the flip-flop.

"Attention all systems. Carry on original subspace vector. Communications, cease all external transmissions. Lily, I want you to erase from the log that distress signal and all subsequent inter- and intraship communications up to the sound of my mark. Ready? *Mark*."

Richard Voorhees made his delivery in time and collected

the entire fee from the grateful worshipers of Jagannath.

A Lylmik Fleet cruiser rendered assistance to the Poltroyans at about the same time that Voorhees docked on Orissa. The Poltroyans had less than fifteen hours of oxygen remaining in their life-support system when the rescuers arrived.

The Poltroyans turned their recording of Voorhees' initial response to the distress signal over to the Sector Magistratum. When Richard returned to Assawompset, he was placed under arrest on suspicion of violating the Galactic Altruism Statutes, Section 24: "Ethical Obligations of Deep-Space Vessels."

After being convicted of the charge, Richard Voorhees was fined a stupendous sum that wiped out most of his assets. Wolverton Mountain was confiscated and her skipper proscribed from engaging in any aspect of astrogation or interstellar commerce for the rest of his natural lives.

"I think I'll visit the Old World," Richard told his solicitor after the whole thing was over. "They say you can't beat it as a place to blow your brains out."

4

FELICE LANDRY SAT ERECT IN THE SADDLE ON THE BACK OF her three-ton verrul, stun-gun cradled in her right arm. She bowed her head in acknowledgment of the cheers. There were nearly fifty thousand fans in the arena for the big game—a splendid turnout for a small planet such as Acadie.

Landry nudged the verrul into a complicated routine of dressage. The hideous beast, resembling a stilt-legged rhino with a ceratopsian neck frill and wicked glowing eyes, minced in and out of the bodies without stepping on a single one. Of all the players on the green-and-white sawdust grid, Landry was the only one still mounted and conscious.

Other verruls in the sideline pens behind the burladero added their trumpeting to the crowd's applause. With casual skill, Felice had her mount pick up the scarlet ring with its nose horn. Then she sent the animal galloping toward the now un-defended Whitewing goal, even though there was no longer any need for speed.

"Lan-*dree*! Lan-*dree*!" screamed the spectators.

It seemed that the young girl and the beast would crash into the cavernous scoop at the end of the field. But just before they were upon it, Landry gave the verrul a sharp crossrein and an unspoken command. The creature wheeled full about, tossing its monstrous head, which was nearly as long as the girl's body. The ring went sailing through the air and entered the scoop dead center. The goal signal lit up and blared in triumph.

"Lan-*DREEE*!"

She held her gun high and shouted back at the mob. Shock waves of orgasm surged through her. For a long minute she could not see, nor did she hear the single deep peal from the referee's bell that marked the end of the game.

As her senses cleared, she condescended to smile at the leaping, gesticulating throng. Celebrate my victory, people-children-lovers. Call my name. But do not press.

"Lan-*dree*! Lan-*dree*! Lan-*dree*!"

A ref came trotting up with the championship banner hanging at the end of a long lance. She holstered the stun-gun, took the flag, and raised it up. She and the verrul made a slow circuit of the arena, both of them nodding to the deafening plaudits of Greenhammer and Whitewing fans alike.

There had never been such a season. Never such a championship game. Never before the coming of Felice Landry.

The sports-mad people of "Canadian" Acadie took their ring-hockey very seriously. At first, they had resented Landry for daring to play the dangerous game. Then they had devoured her. Short, slightly built but preternaturally strong of mind and body, with an uncanny ability to control the evil-tempered verrul mounts, Felice had vanquished male players of talent and experience to become a sports idol in her first professional season. She played both offense and defense; her lightning-fast stun coups became a legend; she herself had never fallen.

In this, the last match of the championship series, she had scored eight goals—a new record. With all of her teammates downed in the final period, she had singlehandedly fought off Whitewing's last-ditch assault on the Greenhammer goal. Four stubborn giants of the Whitewing team had bitten the dust before she triumphed and went on to score that last go-to-hell goal.

Applaud. Adore. Tell me I am your queen-mistress-victim. Only stay back.

She guided the verrul toward the players' exit, fragile on the back of the monstrous animal. She wore an iridescent green

kilt, and green head plumes on the back-tilted helmet. The once
buoyant frizz of her platinum hair now straggled in limp ropes
against the shiny black leather of her skimpy hoplite-style cuir
bouilli armor.

"Lan-*dree*! Lan-*dree*!"

I have poured myself and discharged myself for you, slaves-
eaters-violators. Now let me go.

Small medical carts were scuttling through the passageway
toward the arena to bring in the stunned. Felice had to keep
firm control of the nervous verrul as she moved toward the
Greenhammer ramp. Suddenly there were people all around
her—assistants, trainers, verrul grooms, second-string bench-
warmers, gofers, and hangers-on. They raised a ragged cheer
of greeting and congratulation, tinged with overfamiliarity. The
heroine among her own.

She gave a tight, regal smile. Someone took the bridle of
the verrul and soothed it with a bucket of feed.

"Felice! Felice, baby!" Coach Megowan, hot from the observation booth and still trailing game-plan tapes like a person
caught in an old-time ticker tape parade, came pounding down
from the upper level of the arena. "You were unbelievable,
lovie! Glorious! Pyrotechnic! Kaleidoscopic!"

"Here you go, Coach," she said, leaning down from the
saddle and passing him the banner. "Our first pennant. But not
our last."

The jostling partisans began to shout. "You tell the world,
Felice! Say again, sweetie-baby!" The verrul gave a warning
growl.

Landry extended a graceful black-gauntleted arm toward the
coach. Megowan yelled for somebody to bring a dismounting
platform. Grooms steadied the animal while the girl allowed
the coach to hand her down.

Adulation-joy-pain-nausea. The burden. The need.

She slipped off her Grecian helm with its tall green feathers
and handed it to a worshipful female trainer. One of her fellow
players, a massive reserve guard, was emboldened by the frenzy
of victory.

"Give us a big wet smack, Landry!" he giggled, gathering
her in before she could sidestep.

An instant later he was spread-eagled against the corridor
wall. Felice laughed. A beat later, the others joined in. "Some

other time, Benny precious!" Her eyes, brown and very large, met those of the other athlete. He felt as though something had taken him by the throat.

The girl, the coach, and most of the crowd passed on, heading for the dressing rooms where the reporters were waiting. Only the importunate guard was left behind, sliding slowly down the wall to sit, panting quietly, feet stuck out and arms limp at his sides. A medic driving a meat wagon found him there a few minutes later and helped him to his feet.

"Jeez, guy . . . and you weren't even in the game!"

With a sheepish scowl, Benny admitted what had happened.

The medical attendant wagged his head in amazement. "You had a lotta nerve making a pass. Sweet-face that she is, that little broad scares me shitless!"

The guard nodded, brooding. "You know? She *likes* shooting the guys down. I mean, she actually gets her bang from it. Only you can see she'd just as soon the poor sods was dead as snoozing. You grab? She's a freak! A gorgeous, talent-loaded, champion bitch-kitty freak."

The medic made a face. "Why else would a woman play this crazy game? Come on, hero. I'll give you a lift to the infirmary. We've got just the thing for that wonky feeling in your tummy."

The guard climbed onto the cart beside a snoring casualty. "Seventeen years old! Can you imagine what she's gonna be like when she grows up?"

"Jocks like you shouldn't have an imagination. It gets in the way of the game-plan." The medic gunned the cart down the corridor toward the sound of distant laughter and shouting.

Outside in the arena, the cheering had stopped.

5

"TRY AGAIN, ELIZABETH."

She concentrated all of her mind's strength on the projective sense, what there was left of it. Hyperventilating and with heart racing, she strained until she seemed to be floating free of the chair.

Project from the plaque in front of you:

SMILE-GREETING. TO YOU KWONG CHUN-MEI THERAPIST FROM ELIZABETH ORME FARSPEAKER. IF I HAD THE WINGS OF AN ANGEL OVER THESE PRISON WALLS I WOULD FLY. ENDS.

"Try again, Elizabeth."

She did. Again and again and again. Send that ironic little message that she had chosen herself. (A sense of humor is evidence of personality integration.) Send it. Send it.

The door to the booth opened and Kwong came in at last. "I'm sorry, Elizabeth, but I still don't get a flicker."

"Not even the smile?"

"I'm sorry. Not yet. There are no images at all—only the simple carrier. Look, dear, why don't we wrap it up for today? The vital-signs monitor has you in the yellow. You really need more rest, more time to heal. You're trying too hard."

Elizabeth Orme leaned back and pressed her fingers to her aching temples. "Why do we keep up the pretense, Chun-Mei? We know there is slightly better than zip probability that I'll ever function as a metapsychic again. The tank did a beautiful job of putting me back together after the accident. No scars, no aberrations. I'm a fine, normal, healthy specimen of female humanity. Normal. And that's all, folks."

"Elizabeth—" The therapist's eyes were filled with compassion. "Give yourself a chance. It was almost a complete neocortical regeneration. We don't understand why you didn't regain your metafunctions together with your other mental faculties, but given time and work, you may very well recover."

"No one with my sort of injury ever has."

"No," came the reluctant admission. "But there *is* hope and we must keep trying to get through. You're still one of us, Elizabeth. We want you operant again no matter how long it takes. But you must keep trying."

Keep trying to teach a blind woman to see the three full moons of Denali. Keep trying to teach a deaf woman to appreciate Bach, or a tongueless one to sing Bellini. Oh, yes.

"You're a good friend, Chun-Mei, and God knows you've worked hard with me. But it would be healthier if I just accepted the loss. After all, think of the billions of ordinary people who live happy and fulfilling lives without any metapsychic functions at all. I simply must adapt to a new perspective."

Give up the memory of the mind's angel wings lost. Be happy inside the prison walls of my own skull. Forget the beautiful Unity, the synergy, the exultant bridging from world to world, the never-afraid warmth of companion souls, the joy of leading child-metas to full operancy. Forget the dead identity of dead Lawrence. Oh, yes.

Kwong hesitated. "Why don't you follow Czarneki's advice and take a good long vacation on some warm peaceful world? Tuamotu. Riviera. Tamiami. Even Old Earth! When you return we can begin again with simple pictorials."

"That might be just the thing for me, Chun-Mei." But the slight emphasis wasn't lost on the therapist, whose lips tightened in concern. Kwong did not speak, fearing to cause even deeper pain.

Elizabeth put on her fur-lined cloak and peered through the drapes covering the office window. "Good grief, just look how the storm has picked up! I'd be a fool not to grab at a chance to escape this Denali winter. I hope my poor egg will start. It was the only one in the transport pool this morning and it's very nearly ready for the scrap heap."

Like its driver.

The therapist followed Elizabeth Orme to the door and placed one hand on her shoulder in impulsive empathy. Projecting peace. Projecting hope. "You're not to lose courage. You owe it to yourself and to the entire metacommunity to keep on trying. Your place is with us."

Elizabeth smiled. It was a tranquil face with only a few fine lines about the corners of the eyes, stigmata of deep emotion subsequent to the regeneration that had restored her broken forty-four-year-old body to the perfection of young adulthood. As easily as a crayfish grows new limbs, she had grown new cells to replace smashed arms and rib cage and pelvis, lungs and heart and abdominal organs, shattered bone and gray matter of her skull and forebrain. The regeneration had been virtually perfect, so the doctors had said. Oh, yes.

She gave the therapist's hand a gentle squeeze. "Goodbye, Chun-Mei. Until the next time."

Never, never again.

She went out into the snow, ankle-deep already. The illuminated office windows of the Denali Institute of Metapsychology made squarish golden patterns on the white quadrangle. Frank, the custodian, gave her a wave as he plied a shovel along the walk. The melting system must have broken down again. Good old Denali.

She would not be coming back to the Institute where she had worked for so many years—first as a student, then as counseling farspeaker and redactor, finally as patient. The continuing pain of deprivation was more than her sanity could bear, and Elizabeth was basically a practical woman. It was time for something completely different.

Filled with purpose, clutching the hood of her cloak closely about her head, she headed for the egg park. As was her custom now, she moved her lips as she prayed.

"Blessed Diamond Mask, guide me on my way to Exile."

6

ADMITTING THE HUMAN RACE TO THE GALACTIC MILIEU IN advance of its sociopolitical maturation had been risky.

Even after the first metaphysic human threat to Milieu security had been put down by the venerated Jack and Illusio, there persisted stubborn evidence of humanity's original sin.

People such as Aiken Drum.

Aiken was one of those peculiar personalities who drive behavior modification specialists to distraction. He was normally chromosomed. His brain was undamaged, undiseased, and of superior intelligence quotient. It was crammed with latent metafunctions that might, in due time, be coaxed into operancy. His childhood nurturing on the newly founded colony of Dalriada was no different from that of the other thirty thousand nonborns who were engendered from the sperm and ova of carefully selected Scottish forebears.

But Aiken had been different from the rest of the hatch. He was a natural crook.

Despite the love of surrogate parents, the devotion of skilled teachers, and the inevitable corrective courses administered almost continuously throughout his stormy adolescence, Aiken stubbornly clung to his destined path of knavery. He stole. He lied. He cheated when he felt he could get away with it. He took joy in breaking the rules and was contemptuous of peers with normal psychosocial orientation.

"The subject Aiken Drum," summarized his personality inventory, "displays a fundamental dysfunction in the imaginative sense. He is essentially flawed in his ability to perceive the social and personal consequences of his own actions and is self-centered to a deleterious degree. He has proved resistant to all techniques of moral impression."

But Aiken Drum was charming. And Aiken Drum had a roguish sense of humor. And Aiken Drum, for all his rascal ways, was a natural leader. He was clever with his hands and ingenious in dreaming up new ways to outrage the established order, so his contemporaries tended to view him as a shadow hero. Even Dalriada's adults, harried by the awesome task of raising an entire generation of test-tube colonists to populate an empty new world, had to laugh at some of his enormities.

When Aiken Drum was twelve, his Ecology Corps crew was charged with the cleanup of a putrefying cetacean carcass that had washed up on the beach of the planet's fourth-largest settlement. Saner heads among the children voted for bulldozing the twenty-ton mess into the sand above high-tide level. But Aiken convinced them to try a more spectacular means of disposal. So they had blown up the dead whale with plastic explosive of Aiken's concoction. Fist-sized gouts of stinking flesh showered the entire town, including a visiting delegation of Milieu dignitaries.

When Aiken Drum was thirteen, he had worked with a crew of civil engineers, diverting the course of a small waterfall so that it would help feed the newly completed Old Man of the Mountain Reservoir. Late one night, Aiken and a gang of young confederates stole quantities of cement and conduit and modified the rocks at the rim of the falls. Dawn on Dalriada revealed a passable simulacrum of gigantic male urogenital organs, taking a leak into the reservoir forty meters below.

When Aiken Drum was fourteen, he stowed his small body away on a luxury liner bound for Caledonia. The passengers were victimized by thefts of jewelry, but monitors showed that no human thief had entered their rooms. A search of the cargo deck revealed the young stowaway and the radio-controlled robot "mouse" he had sent foraging, programmed to sniff out precious metals and gemstones that the boy calmly admitted he planned to fence in New Glasgow.

They sent him home, of course, and the behaviorists had still another shot at redirecting Aiken's errant steps toward the narrow road of virtue. But the conditioning never took.

"He breaks your heart," one psychologist admitted to another. "You can't help but like the kid, and he's got a brilliantly inventive mind in that troll bod of his. But what the hell are we going to do with him? The Galactic Milieu just has no niche for Till Eulenspiegel!"

They tried redirecting his narcissism into comedic entertainment, but his fellow troupers nearly lynched him when he queered their acts with practical jokes. They tried to harness his mechanical ability, but he used the engineering school facilities to build outlaw black boxes that gave illegal access to half the computerized credit systems in the Sector. They tried metaphysic deep-redact and deprivation conditioning multiphase electroshock and narcotherapy and old-time religion.

Aiken Drum's wickedness triumphed over all.

And so, when he reached an unrepentant twenty-first birthday, Aiken Drum was confronted with a multiple-choice question, the answer to which would shape his future:

> *As a confirmed recidivist, counterproductive to the ultimate harmony of the Galactic Milieu, which of these options do you choose?*
> *a. Permanent incarceration in Dalriada Correctional Institution*
> *b. Psychosurgical implant of a docilization unit*
> *c. Euthanasia*

"None of the above," said Aiken Drum. "I choose Exile."

7

SISTER ANNAMARIA ROCCARO FIRST MET CLAUDE WHEN HE brought his dying wife to the Oregon Cascade Hospice.

Both of the old people had been salvage exopaleontologists—Claude Majewski specializing macrofossils and Genevieve Logan in micros. They had been married for more than ninety years and one rejuvenation, and together they had surveyed the extinct life-forms of more than twoscore planets colonized by humanity. But Genevieve had grown weary at last and refused a third lifetime, and Claude had concurred in her decision, as he had throughout most of their time together. They stayed in harness as long as possible, then spent a few declining years in their cottage on the Pacific Coast of Old World North America.

Claude never thought about the inevitable end until it was upon them. He had a vague notion that they would someday drift off quietly together in their sleep. The reality, of course, was less tidy. Claude's Polish peasant body proved in the end to have a much greater staying power than that of his Afroamerican wife. The time came when Genevieve had to go to the Hospice with Claude accompanying her. They were welcomed by Sister Roccaro, a tall and open-faced woman, who took personal charge of the physical and spiritual consolation of the dying scientist and her husband.

Genevieve, riddled with osteoporosis, partly paralyzed and dulled by a series of small strokes, was a long time passing. She may have been aware of her husband's efforts to comfort her, but she gave very little evidence of it. Suffering no pain, she spent her days sedated in a dreamy reverie or in sleep. Sister Roccaro found that more and more of her professional efforts were devoted to dealing with Claude, who was frustrated and deeply depressed by his wife's slow drift toward life's end.

The old man was still physically sturdy at the age of one hundred and thirty-three, so the nun often took him walking in the mountains. They tramped the misty evergreen forests of the Cascade Range and fished for trout in streams running off the Mount Hood glaciers. They checklisted birds and wild-flowers as high summer came on, climbed the flanks of Hood, and spent hot afternoons sitting in the shade on the mountainside without speaking, for Majewski was unable or unwilling to verbalize his grief.

One morning in the early July of 2110, Genevieve Logan began to sink quickly. She and Claude could only touch one another now, since she could no longer see or hear or speak. When the sickroom monitor showed that the old woman's brain had ceased to function, the Sister celebrated the Mass of Departure and gave the last anointing. Claude turned off the machines himself and sat beside the bed, holding Genevieve's skeletal brown hand until the warmth left it.

Sister Roccaro gently pressed the wrinkled coffee-colored lids down over the dead scientist's eyes. "Would you like to stay with her awhile, Claude?"

The old man smiled absently. "She's not here, Amerie. Would you walk with me if no one else needs you for a while? It's still early. I think I'd like to talk."

So they put on boots and went out again to the mountain, the trip via egg taking only a few minutes. Parking at Cloud Cap, they ascended Cooper Spur by an easy trail and came to a halt below Tie-In Rock, on a ridge at the 2800-meter level. They found a comfortable place to sit and took out canteens and lunches. Just below was Hood's Eliot Glacier. To the north, beyond the Columbia River Gorge, were Mount Adams and distant Rainier, both snow-crowned like Hood. The symmetrical cone of Mount St. Helens, to the west downriver, sent up a gray plume of smoke and volcanic steam.

Majewski said, "Pretty up here, isn't it? When Gen and I were kids, St. Helens was cold. They were still logging the forests. Dams blocked the Columbia, so the salmon had to climb upstream on fish ladders. Port Oregon Metro was still called Portland and Fort Vancouver. And there was a little smog, and some overcrowding if you wanted to live where the jobs were. But all in all, life was pretty good out here, even in the bad old days when St. Helens erupted. It was only toward the very end, before the Intervention when the world was running out of energy and the technoeconomy collapsing, that this Pacific Northwest country started to share some of the griefs of the rest of the world."

He pointed eastward, toward the dry canyons and the high-desert scrub of the old lava plateau beyond the Cascades.

"Out there lie the John Day fossil beds. Gen and I did our first collecting there when we were students. Maybe thirty or forty million years ago, that desert was a lush meadowland with forested hills. It had a big population of mammals— rhinos, horses, camels, oreodonts—we call them cookie monsters—and even giant dogs and sabertooth cats. Then one day the volcanoes began to erupt. They spread a deep blanket of ash and debris all over these eastern plains. The plants were buried and the streams and lakes were poisoned. There were pyroclastic flows—kind of a fiery cloud made of gas and ash and bits of lava, racing along faster than a hundred-fifty kloms an hour."

He slowly unwrapped a sandwich, bit, and chewed. The nun said nothing. She took off her bandanna head scarf and used it to wipe the sweat from her wide brow.

"No matter how fast or how far those poor animals ran, they couldn't escape. They were buried in the layers of ash. And then the vulcanism stopped. Rain washed away the poisons and the plants came back. After a while, the animals returned, too, and repopulated the land. But the good life didn't last. The volcanoes erupted again, and there were more showers of ashes. It happened over and over again throughout the next fifteen million years or so. The killing and the repopulating, the shower of death and the return of life. Layer after layer of fossils and ashes were laid down out there. The John Day formation is more than half a klom thick—and there are similar formations above and below it."

As the old man spoke, the nun sat staring at the tableland to the east. A pair of giant condors circled slowly in a thermal. Below them, a tight formation of nine egg-shaped flying craft wafted slowly along the course of an invisible canyon.

"The ash beds were capped with thick lava. Then, after more millions of years, rivers cut down through the rock and into the ash layers below. Gen and I found fossils along the watercourses—not just bones and teeth, but even leaf-prints and whole flowers pressed into the finer layers of ash. The records of a whole series of vanished worlds. Very poignant. At night, she and I would make love under the desert stars and look at the Milky Way in Sagittarius. We'd wonder how the constellations had looked to all those extinct animals. And how much longer poor old mankind could hang on before it was buried in its own ash bed, waiting for paleontologists from Sagittarius to come dig *us* up after another thirty million years."

He chuckled. "Melodrama. One of the hazards of digging fossils in a romantic setting." He ate the rest of his sandwich and drank from the canteen. Then he said, "Genevieve," and was quiet for a long time.

"Were you shocked by the Intervention?" Sister Roccaro asked at last. "Some of the older people I've counseled seemed almost disappointed that humanity was spared its just ecological deserts."

"It was tough on the Schadenfreude crowd," Majewski agreed, grinning. "The ones who viewed humankind as a sort of plague organism spoiling what might otherwise have been a pretty good planet. But paleontologists tend to take a long view of life. Some creatures survive, some become extinct. But no matter how great the ecological disaster, the paradox called life keeps on defying entropy and trying to perfect itself. Hard times just seem to help evolution. The Pleistocene Ice Age and pluvials could have killed off all the plant-eating hominids. But instead, the rough climate and the vegetation changes seem to have encouraged some of our ancestors to become meat eaters. And if you eat meat, you don't have to spend so much time hunting food. You can sit down and learn to think."

"Once upon a time, hunter-killer was better?"

"Hunter doesn't equate with murderer. I don't buy the totally depraved ape-man picture that some ethologists postulate for human ancestry. There was goodness and altruism in our hominid forebears just as there's good in most people today."

"But evil is real," said the nun. "Call it egocentrism or malignant aggression or original sin or whatever. It's there. Eden's gone."

"Isn't biblical Eden an ambivalent symbol? It seems to me that the myth simply shows us that self-awareness and intelligence are perilous. And they can be deadly. But consider the alternative to the Tree of Knowledge. Would anyone want innocence at such a price? Not me, Amerie. We really wouldn't want to give back that bite of apple. Even our aggressive instincts and stubborn pride helped make us rulers of the Earth."

"And one day . . . maybe of the galaxy?"

Claude gave a short laugh. "God knows we used to argue long enough about that notion when the Gi and the Poltroyans cooperated with us on salvage digs. The consensus seems to be that despite our hubris and pushiness, we humans have incredible potential—which justified the Intervention before we got ourselves too screwed up. On the other hand, the trouble we caused during the metapsychic flap back in the 'Eighties makes you wonder whether we haven't simply transferred our talent for spoiling to a cosmic stage instead of just a planetary one."

They ate some oranges and after a time Claude said, "Whatever happens, I'm glad that I lived to reach the stars, and I'm glad that Gen and I met and worked with other thinking beings of goodwill. It's over now, but it was a wonderful adventure."

"How did Genevieve feel about your travels?"

"She was more strongly tied to Earth, even though she enjoyed the outworld journeyings. She insisted on keeping a home here in the Pacific Northwest, where we had been raised. If we had been able to have children, she might never have agreed to leave. But she was a sickle-cell carrier, and the technique for modifying the genetic codon was developed after Gen had passed optimal child-bearing age. Later on, when we were ready for rejuvenation, our parenting instincts were pretty well atrophied, and there was so much work to do. So we just kept on doing it together. For ninety-four years . . ."

"Claude." Sister Roccaro reached out her hand to him. A light breeze stirred her short curly hair. "Do you realize that you're healed?"

"I knew it would happen. After Gen was dead. It was only her going that was so bad. You see, we'd talked it all out months ago, when she was still in control of her faculties, and did a lot of commiserating and accepting and emotional purging. But she still had to go, and I had to watch and wait while the person I loved more than my own life slipped farther and farther away but was never quite gone. Now that she's dead, I'm functional again. I just ask myself what in the world I'm going to do?"

"I had to answer the same question," the nun said carefully.

Majewski gave a start, then studied her face as though he had never seen it before. "Amerie, child. You've spent your life consoling needy people, serving the dying and their mourners. And you still have to ask a question like that?"

"I'm not a child, Claude. I'm a thirty-seven-year-old woman and I've worked at the Hospice for fifteen of those years. The job . . . has not been easy. I'm burnt out. I had decided that you and Genevieve would be my last clients. My superiors have concurred with my decision to leave the order."

Shocked beyond words, the old man stared at her. She continued, "I found myself becoming isolated, consumed by the emotions of the people I was trying to help. There's been a shriveling of faith, too, Claude." She gave a small shrug. "The kind of thing that people in the religious life are all too likely to suffer. A sensible scientific type like you would probably laugh—"

"I'd never laugh at you, Amerie. And if you really think I'm sensible, maybe I can help you."

She rose up and slapped gritty rock dust off her jeans. "It's time for us to get off this mountain. It'll take at least two hours to walk back down to the egg."

"And on the way," he insisted, "you're going to tell me about your problem and your plans for the future."

Annamaria Roccaro regarded the very old man with amused exasperation. "Doctor Majewski, you're a retired bone digger—not a spiritual counselor."

"You're going to tell me anyhow. In case you don't know

it, there's nothing more stubborn in the Galactic Milieu than a Polack who's set his mind to something. And I'm a lot more stubborn than a lot of other Polacks because I've had more time to practice. And besides that," he added slyly, "you would never have mentioned your problem at all if you hadn't wanted to talk it over with me. Come on. Let's get walking."

He set off slowly down the trail and she followed. They tramped along in silence for at least ten minutes before she began to speak.

"When I was a little girl, my religious heroes weren't the Galactic Age saints. I could never identify with Père Teilhard or Saint Jack the Bodiless or Illusio Diamond Mask. I liked the really old-timey mystics: Simeon Stylites, Anthony the Hermit, Dame Julian of Norwich. But today, that kind of solitary commitment to penitence is contrary to the Church's new vision of human energetics. We're supposed to chart our individual journey toward perfection within a unity of human and divine love."

Claude grimaced at her over his shoulder. "You lost me, child."

"Stripped of the jargon, it means that charitable activity is in; solitary mysticism is out. Our Galactic Age is too busy for anchoresses or hermits. That way of life is supposed to be selfish, escapist, masochistic, and counter to the Church's social evolution."

"But you don't think so—is that it, Amerie? You want to go off and fast and contemplate in some lonesome spot and suffer and attain enlightenment."

"Don't you laugh at me, Claude. I tried to get into a monastery . . . the Cistercians, Poor Clares, Carmelites. And they took one look at my psychosocial profile and told me to get lost. Counseling, they advised! Not even the Zen-Brigittines would give me a chance! But I finally discovered that there *is* one place where an old-fashioned solitary mystic wouldn't be out of place. Have you ever heard of Exile?"

"What paleobiologist hasn't?"

"You may know that there's been a sort of underground railroad to it for a good many years. But you may not know that use of the timeportal was given official Milieu sanction four years ago in response to an increasing demand. All kinds of people have gone into Exile after undergoing a survival regimen. People from every imaginable educational background and profession, from Earth and from the human colonies. All of those time-travelers have one thing in common: They want to go on living, but they can't function any longer in this complex, structured world of galactic civilization."

"And this is what you've chosen?"

"My application was accepted more than a month ago."

They came to a tricky scree slope, the remnant of an old avalanche, and concentrated on traversing it safely. When they reached the other side they rested for a moment. The sun beat down hotly. The retroevolved condors were gone.

"Amerie," the old man said, "it would be very interesting to see fossil bones with flesh on them."

She elevated an eyebrow. "Isn't this notion a trifle impulsive?"

"Maybe I've nothing better to do. Seeing Pliocene animals alive would be an interesting windup to a long career in paleobiology. And the day-to-day survival aspects wouldn't pose any problems for me. If there's one thing you learn out in the field, it's roughing it in comfort. Maybe I could kind of help you get your hermitage set up. That is—if you wouldn't think I was too great a temptation to your vows."

She went into gales of laughter, then stopped and said, "Claude! You're *worried* about me. You think I'll get eaten by a sabertooth tiger or trampled by mastodons."

"Dammit, Amerie! Do you know what you're letting yourself in for? Just because you climb a few tame mountains and catch stocked trout in Oregon you think you can be a female Francis of Assisi in a howling wilderness!" He looked away, scowling. "God knows what kind of human dregs are wandering around there. I don't want to cramp your style, child. I could just keep an eye on things. Bring you food and such. Even those old mystics let the faithful bring 'em offerings, you know. Amerie—don't you understand? I wouldn't want anything to spoil your dream."

Abruptly, she threw her arms around him, then stepped back smiling, and for an instant he saw her not in jeans, plaid shirt, and bandanna, but robed in white homespun with a rope knotted about her waist. "Doctor Majewski, I would be honored to have you as a protector. You may very well be a temptation. But I'll be steadfast and resist your allure, even though I love you very much."

"That's settled, then. We'd better get on down and arrange for Genevieve's requiem without delay. We'll take her ashes with us to France and bury her in the Pliocene. Gen would have liked that."

8

THE WIDOW OF PROFESSOR THÉO GUDERIAN HAD BEEN AS-
tounded when the first time-tripper appeared at the gate of the
cottage on the slope of the Monts du Lyonnais.

It happened in the year 2041, early in June. She was working
in her rose garden, snipping deadheads from the splendid standards of Mme. A. Meilland and wondering how she would be
able to pay the death duties, when a stocky male hiker with a
dachshund came striding up the dusty road from Saint-Antoine-
des-Vignes. The man knew where he was going. He stopped
precisely in front of the gate and waited for her to approach.
The little dog sat down one step behind her master's left heel.

"Good evening, Monsieur," she said in Standard English,
folding her secateurs and slipping them into the pocket of her
black salopette.

"Citizen Angélique Montmagny?"

"I prefer the older form of address. But yes, I am she."

He bowed formally. "Madame Guderian! Permit me to present myself. Richter, Karl Josef. I am by profession a poet and
my home has been up to now in Frankfurt. I am here, chère
Madame, to discuss with you a business proposal concerning
the experimental apparatus of your late husband."

"I regret that I am no longer able to demonstrate the device." Madame pursed her lips. The fine beak of her aquiline nose lifted proudly. Her small black eyes sparkled with unshed tears. "Indeed, I am shortly going to have it dismantled so that the more valuable components can be sold."

"You must not! You must not!" cried Richter, taking hold of the top of the gate.

Madame took a step backward and stared at him in aston- ishment. He was moon-faced, with pale protuberant eyes and thick reddish brows, now hoisted in dismay. Expensively dressed as for a strenuous walking tour, he wore a large rucksack. To it were lashed a violin case, a lethal-looking dural catapult, and a golfer's umbrella. The stolid dachshund guarded a large parcel of paged books, carefully wrapped in plass and equipped with straps and a carrying handle.

Gaining control of his emotions, Richter said, "Forgive me, Madame. But you must not destroy this so-wonderful achieve- ment of your late husband! It would be a sacrilege."

"Nevertheless, there are the death duties," said Madame. "You spoke of business, Monsieur. But you should know that many journalists have already written about my husband's work—"

"I," said Richter with a faint moue of distaste, "am not a journalist. I am a poet! And I hope you will consider my proposal most seriously." He unzipped a side compartment of the pack and removed a leather cardcase, from which he ex- tracted a small blue rectangle. He held this out to Madame. "Evidence of my bona fides."

The blue card was a sight draft on the Bank of Lyon entitling the bearer to collect an extraordinary amount of money.

Madame Guderian unlatched the gate. "Please enter, M. Richter. One trusts the little dog is well mannered."

Richter picked up his package of books and smiled thinly. "Schatzi is more civilized than most humans."

They sat on a stone bench below a bee-loud arch of Soleil d'Or and Richter explained to the widow why he had come. He had learned of Guderian's time-gate at a publisher's cocktail party in Frankfurt and decided that very evening to sell every- thing that he owned and hasten to Lyon.

"It is very simple, Madame. I wish to pass through this time-portal and live permanently amid the prehistoric simplicity of the Pliocene Epoch. The peaceable kingdom! Locus amoenus! The Forest of Arden! The sanctuary of innocence! The halcyon land unwatered by human tears!" He paused and tapped the blue card still in her hand. "And I am willing to pay handsomely for my passage."

A madman! Madame fingered the secateurs deep in her pocket. "The time-gate," she said carefully, "opens in but a single direction. There is no return. And we have no detailed knowledge of what lies on the other side in the Pliocene land. It was never possible to circumtranslate Tri-D cameras or other types of recording equipment."

"The fauna of the epoch is well known, Madame, as is the climate. A prudent person need have nothing to fear. And you, gnädige Frau, must suffer no qualms of conscience in permitting me to use the portal. I am self-sufficient and well able to look after myself in a wilderness. I have selected my equipment with care, and for companionship there is my faithful Schatzi. Don't hesitate, I beg of you! Let me pass through tonight. Now!"

A madman indeed, but perhaps one that Providence had sent!

She remonstrated with him for some time while the sky darkened to indigo and the nightingales began to sing. Richter parried all of her objections. He had no family to miss him. He had told no one of his intentions, so there would be no inquiries made of her. No one had observed him walking on the lonely road from the village. She would be rendering him a blessing, fulfilling for him what had once been an impossible dream of Arcady. He was not committing suicide, he was merely entering a new, more tranquil life. But if she refused him, his Seelenqual would leave him only the grimmest alternative. And there was the money . . .

"C'est entendu," Madame said at last. "Please accompany me."

She led him down into the cellar and threw on the lights. There stood the gazebo with its cables, just as poor Théo had left it. The poet gave a joyous cry and rushed to the apparatus, tears running down his round cheeks.

"At last!"

The dachshund trotted sedately after her master. Madame picked up the parcel of books and placed it inside the lattice.

"Quickly, Madame! Quickly!" Richter clasped his hands in a paroxysm of exaltation.

"Listen to me," she said sharply. "When you have been translated, you must immediately remove yourself from the point of your arrival. Walk three or four meters away and take the dog with you. Is this clear? Otherwise you will be snatched back into the present day as a dead man and crumble to dust."

"I understand! Vite, Madame, vite! Quickly!"

Trembling, she moved to the simple control panel and activated the time-portal. The mirrored force fields sprang up, and the poet's voice was silenced as if by a broken teleview connection. The old woman sank down on her knees and recited the Angelic Salutation three times, then got up and switched off the power.

The mirrors vanished. The gazebo was empty.

Madame Guderian let a great sigh escape her lips. Then she thriftily turned out the cellar lights and mounted the stairs, fingering the small slip of blue plass tucked securely in her pocket.

After Karl Josef Richter, there were others.

The very first gratuity allowed Madame to pay the inheritance tax and discharge all of her other debts. Some months later, after her mind had been fully opened to the time-gate's profitmaking potential by the coming of other visitors, she let it be known that she was establishing a quiet auberge for walking tourists. She purchased land adjoining her cottage and had a handsome guesthouse built. The rose gardens were expanded and several of her relatives drafted to assist with domestic duties. To the astonishment of skeptical neighbors, the inn prospered.

Not all of the guests who entered chez Guderian were seen to leave. But the point was moot, since Madame invariably required payment in advance.

Some years passed. Madame underwent rejuvenation and displayed an austere chic in her second lifetime. In the valley below the inn, the most ancient urban center in France also underwent graceful transition, as did all of the metropolitan centers of Old Earth in those middle years of the twenty-first century. Every trace of the ugly, ecologically destructive technology was gradually obliterated from the great city at the confluence of the Rhône and Saône. Necessary manufacturing establishments, service and transit systems were relocated in underground infrastructures. As the surplus population of Lyon was siphoned off to the new planets, empty slums and dreary suburbs faded into meadows and forest reserves, dotted here and there with garden villages or efficient habitat complexes. Lyon's historic structures, representing every century for the more than 2000 years of its lifetime, were refurbished and displayed like jewels in appropriate natural settings. Laboratories, offices, hotels, and commercial enterprises were tucked into recycled buildings or disguised to harmonize with the ambiance of nearby monuments. Plaisances and boulevards replaced the hideous concrete autoroutes. Amusement sites, picturesque alleys of small shops, and cultural foundations multiplied as colonials began returning to the Old World from the far-flung stars, seeking their ethnic heritage.

Other types of seekers also came to Lyon. These found their way to the inn in the western foothills, now called l'Auberge du Portail, where Madame Guderian personally made them welcome.

In those early years, when she still regarded the time-portal as a business venture, Madame set up simple criteria for her clientèle. Would-be timefarers had to spend at least two days with her at the auberge while she and her computer checked civil status and psychosocial profile. She would send no one through the gate who was a fugitive from justice, who was seriously deranged, or who had not attained twenty-eight years of age (for the great step demanded full maturity). She would permit no one to carry modern weaponry or coercive devices back to the Pliocene. Only the simplest solar-powered or sealed-pack machines might be taken. Persons obviously unprepared for survival in a primeval wilderness were dismissed and told to return upon acquiring suitable skills.

After thinking deeply on the matter, Madame made a further condition for women candidates. They must renounce their fertility.

"Attendez!" she would snap at the stunned female applicant in her unreconstructed Gallic way. "Consider the inescapable lot of womankind in a primitive world. Her destiny is to bear child after child until her body is worn out, submitting all the while to the whims of her male overlord. It is true that we modern women have complete control of our bodies as well as the ability to defend ourselves from outrage. But what of the daughters who might be born to you in the ancient epoch? You will not possess the technology to transfer your reproductive freedom to them. And with the return of the old biological pattern comes also the return of the old subservient mind-set. When your daughters matured, they would surely be enslaved. Would you consign a loved child to such a fate?"

There was also the matter of paradox.

The notion that time-travelers might disrupt the present world by meddling with the past had seriously troubled Madame Guderian for many weeks after the departure of Karl Josef Richter. She had concluded at last that such a paradox must be impossible, since the past is already manifest in the present, with the continuum sustained in the loving hands of le bon dieu.

On the other hand, one ought not to take chances.

Human beings, even the rejuvenated and highly educated people of the Coadunate Galactic Age, could have little impact on the Pliocene or any subsequent time period if they were restrained from reproducing. Given the social advantage to female travelers, the decision to demand the renouncing of motherhood as a condition of transport was confirmed in Madame's mind.

She would say to the protestors: "One realizes that it is unfair, that it sacrifices a portion of your feminine nature. Do I not understand? I, whose two dear children died before reaching adulthood? But you must accept that this world you seek to enter is not one of life. It is a refuge of misfits, a death surrogate, a rejection of normal human destiny. Ainsi, if you pass into this Exile, the consequences must rest upon you alone. If life's force is still urgent within you, then you should remain here. Only those who are bereaved of all joy in this present world may take refuge in the shadows of the past."

After hearing this somber speech, the women applicants would ponder and at last agree—or else depart from the auberge, never to return. Male time-travelers came to outnumber the female by nearly four to one. Madame was not greatly surprised.

The existence of the time-gate came to the attention of local authorities some three years after the Auberge du Portail commenced operation, when there was an unfortunate incident involving a refused applicant. But Madame's high-powered Lyon solicitors were able to prove that the enterprise violated no local or galactic statute: It was licensed as a public accommodation, a common carrier, a psychosocial counseling service, and a travel agency. From time to time thereafter, certain local government bodies made stabs at suppression or regulation. They always failed because there were no precedents . . . and besides, the time-gate was useful.

"I do a work of mercy," Madame Guderian told one investigatory panel. "It is a work that would have been incomprehensible scarcely one hundred years ago, but now, in this Galactic Age, it is a blessing. One need only study the dossiers of the pathetic ones themselves to see that they are out of place in the swift-paced modern world. There have always been such persons, psychosocial anachronisms, unsuited to the age in which they were born. Until the time-portal, these had no hope of altering their fate."

"Are you so confident, Madame," a commissioner asked, "that this time-portal leads to a better world?"

"It leads to a different and simpler world, at any rate, Citizen Commissioner," she retorted. "That seems sufficient to my clients."

The auberge kept careful records of those who passed through the Pliocene gate and these would later be fascinating fodder for statisticians. For example, the travelers tended to be highly literate, intelligent, socially unconventional, and aesthetically sophisticated. Above all they were romantic. They were mostly citizens of the Old World rather than of the colonial planets. Many of the timefarers had earned their living in the professions, in science, technology, or other high disciplines. An ethnic assay of the travelers showed significant numbers of Anglo-Saxons, Celts, Germans, Slavs, Latins, Native Americans, Arabs, Turks and other Central Asiatics, and Japanese. There were few African blacks but numbers of Afroamericans. Inuit and Polynesian people were attracted by the Pliocene world; Chinese and Indo-Dravidians were not. Fewer agnostics than believers chose to abandon the present; but the devout time-travelers were often fanatics or conservatives disillusioned about modern religious trends, particularly the Milieu dicta that proscribed revolutionary socialism, jihads, or any style of theocracy. Many nonreligious, but few orthodox, Jews were tempted to escape to the past; a disproportionate number of Muslims and Catholics wanted to make the trip.

The psychoprofiles of the travelers showed that a significant percentage of the applicants was highly aggressive. Small-time ex-convicts were common clients, but the more formidable reformed evildoers apparently preferred the contemporary scene. There was a small but persistent trickle of broken-hearted lovers, both homophile and heterosexual. As was to be expected, many of the applicants were narcissistic and addicted to fantasy. These people were apt to appear at the auberge in the guise of Tarzan or Crusoe or Pocahontas or Rima, or else costumed as throwbacks to every conceivable Old World era and culture.

Some, like Richter, outfitted themselves for the journey with Spartan pragmatism. Others wanted to bring along "desert island" treasures such as whole libraries of old-fashioned paged books, musical instruments and recordings, elaborate armories, or wardrobes. The more practical gathered together livestock, seeds, and tools for homesteading in the style of the Swiss Family Robinson. Collectors and naturalists brought their paraphernalia. Writers came equipped with goose quills and flagons of sepia ink—or the latest in voicewriters with reams of durofilm sheets and book-plaque transcribers. The frivolous cherished delicacies of food and drink and psychoactive chemicals.

Madame did her utmost to accommodate the impedimenta, given the physical restriction of the gazebo's volume, which was roughly six cubic meters. She urged the travelers to consider pooling their resources, and sometimes this was done. (The Gypsies, the Amish, the Russian Old Believers, and the Inuit were particularly shrewd in such matters.) But given the idiosyncratic nature of the timefarers, many preferred to be completely independent of fellow humans, while others ignored practicalities in favor of romantic ideals or precious fetishes.

Madame saw to it that each person had the minimal survival necessities, and extra shipments of medical supplies were regularly sent through the gate. Beyond that, one could only trust in Providence.

For nearly sixty-five years and throughout two rejuvenations, Angélique Guderian personally supervised the psychosocial evaluation of her clients and their eventual dispatch to the Pliocene. As the uneasy cupidity of her early years was finally submerged in compassion for those she served, the fees for passage became highly negotiable and were often waived. The number of prospective travelers increased steadily, and there came to be a long waiting list. By the turn of the twenty-second century, more than ninety thousand fugitives had passed through the time-portal to an unknown fate.

In 2106, Madame Guderian herself entered the Pliocene world called Exile—alone, dressed in her gardening clothes, carrying a simple rucksack and a bundle of cuttings from her favorite roses. Since she had always despised the Standard English of the Milieu as an insult to her French heritage, the note she left said:

"Plus qu'il n'en faut."

The Human Polity of the Galactic Concilium was not willing to accept this "more than enough" judgment however; the time-portal obviously filled a need as a glory hole for inconvenient aberrants. Organized in a humane and somewhat more efficient manner, it was allowed to continue in operation. There was no advertisement of the service, and referrals were kept discreetly professional.

The ethical dilemma of permitting persons to exile themselves to the Pliocene was tabled. Study confirmed that no time-paradox was possible. As for the fate of the travelers, they were all doomed in one way or another anyhow.

9

ALL THE WAY BACK TO EARTH FROM BREVON-SU-MIRI-kon, Bryan Grenfell planned the way he would do it. He would call Mercy from Unst Starport just as soon as he got through the decon and remind her that she had agreed to go sailing with him. They could meet at Cannes on Friday evening, which would allow him time to drop off the conference data at the CAS in London and pick up some clothes and the boat from his flat. Fair weather was scheduled for the next three days, so they could cruise easily to Corse on even Sardegna.

In some secluded cove, with moonlight on the Mediterranean and soft music playing, he would nail her.

"This is your Captain speaking. We are five minutes from reentry into normal space above the planet Earth. There will be a momentary discomfort as we pass through the superficies, which may inconvenience sensitive persons. Please do not hesitate to call your flight attendant if you require an anodyne, and remember that your satisfaction is our prime directive. Thank you for traveling United."

Grenfell leaned toward the com. "Glendessarry and Evian." When the drink appeared he tossed it off, closed his eyes, and thought of Mercy. Those sad sea-colored eyes, ringed by the dark lashes. The hair of cedarwood red framing her pale high-boned cheeks. Her body, almost as thin as a child's but tall and elegant in a long gown of leaf-green with trailing darker ribbons. He could hear her voice, lilting and resonant, as they walked in the apple orchard that evening after the medieval pageant.

"There is no such thing as love at first sight, Bryan. There's only sex at first sight. And if my scrawny charms inflame you, then let's lie together, because you're a sweet man and I'm in need of comfort. But don't talk about love."

He had, though. He couldn't help it. Realizing the illogic of the thing, observing himself from afar with a chagrined detachment but still unable to control the situation, he knew he loved her from the first moment they met. Carefully, he had tried to explain without appearing a complete ass. She had only laughed and pulled him down onto the petal-strewn lawn. Their passion had delighted them both but brought him no true release. He was caught by her. He would have to share her life forever or go in misery apart.

Only one day with her! One day before he had to travel to the important meeting on the Poltroyan planet. She had wanted him to stay, suggesting the sailing holiday, but he, duty-bound, had put her off. Imbecile! She might have needed him. How could he have left her alone?

Only one day...

Bryan's old friend Gaston Deschamps, encountered fortuitously in a Paris restaurant, had invited him to kill some empty hours observing the Fête d'Auvergne from behind the scenes. Gaston, the pageant director, had called it a droll exercise in applied ethnology. And so it had been—until the introduction.

"Now we will return to those thrilling days d'antan," Gaston had proclaimed after giving him the fifty-pence tour of the village and the château. The director had led the way to a high tower, thrown open the door to the elaborate pageant control room, and she had been sitting there.

"You must meet my fellow wonder-worker, the associate director of the Fête, and the most medieval lady now alive in the Galactic Milieu... Mademoiselle Mercedes Lamballe!"

She had looked up from her console and smiled, piercing him to the heart...

"This is your Captain speaking. We are now reentering

normal space above the planet Earth. The procedure will take only two seconds, so please bear with us during the brief period of mild discomfort."

Zang.

Toothextractionhammeredthumbwhangedfunnybone.

Zung.

"Thank you for your patience, ladies and gentlemen and distinguished passengers of other sexes. We will be landing at Unst Starport in the beautiful Shetland Islands of Earth at exactly 1500 hours Planet Mean Time."

Grenfell mopped his high brow and ordered another drink. This time, he sipped. Unbidden, an ancient song began unreeling in his mind, and he smiled because the song was so like Mercy.

> There is a lady sweet and kind
> Was never face so pleased my mind.
> I did but see her passing by,
> And yet I love her till I die.

He would take the tube to Nice and egg on to Cannes. She would be waiting for him at the quay of that peaceful old town, perhaps wearing a green playsuit. Her eyes would have that expression of gentle melancholy and be green or gray, changeable as the sea and as deep. He would stagger up with his dufflebag and a fitted picnic hamper full of food and drink (champagne, Stilton, gooseliver sausage, sweet butter, long loaves, oranges, black cherries), and he would trip over his feet and she would smile at last.

He would take out the boat and make the small boys at the slip stand back. (There were always small boys now that families had rediscovered the quiet Côte d'Azur.) He would attach the thin tube of the tiny inflator and throw the wadded packet of silver-and-black decamole film into the water. Slowly, slowly as the boys gaped, the eight-meter sloop would grow: bulb keels, hull, decks, furniture fixed below, cabin, cockpit, railings, mast. Then he would produce the separate pieces—rudder and tiller, stabilizer, boom with sails still furled, lines, deck seats, lockers, buckets, bedding and all—born miraculously of taut decamole and compressed air. Dockside dispensers would fill the keels and stabilizers with mercury and ballast the rest of the boat and its fittings with distilled water, adding mass to the rigid microstructure of the decamole. He would rent the auxiliary, the lamps, pumps, navigear, the gooseneck, CQR anchor, and other hardware, pay off the harbormaster and bribe the small boys not to spit over the quayside into the cockpit.

She would board. He would cast off. With a fresh breeze, it would be up sail for Ajaccio! And somehow, in the next days, he would get her to agree to marry him.

I did but see her passing by...

When the starship landed in the beautiful Shetlands it was six degrees Celsius and blowing a dreary northeast gale. Mercedes Lamballe's teleview number responded with a SUBSCRIBER CANCELED SERVICE notice.

In a panic, Grenfell finally got hold of Gaston Deschamps. The pageant director was evasive, then angry, then apologetic. "The fact is, Bry, the damn woman's chucked it. Must have been the day after you went offworld two months ago. Left us flat—and the busiest time of the season, too."

"But where, Gaston? Where's she gone?"

On the view screen, Deschamps let his gaze slide away. "Through that damn time-portal into Exile. I'm sick about it, Bry. She had everything to live for. A bit off her bonk, of course, but none of us suspected she was that far gone. It's a damn shame. She had the best feel for the medieval of anyone I've ever known."

"I see. Thanks for telling me. I'm very sorry."

He broke the connection and sat in the teleview kiosk, a middle-aged anthropologist of some reputation, mild-faced, conservatively dressed, holding a portfolio full of Proceedings of the Fifteenth Galactic Conference on Culture Theory. Two Simbiari who had come in on the same ship with him waited patiently outside for some minutes before tapping on the kiosk door, leaving little green smears on the window.

And yet I love her...

Bryan Grenfell held up on apologetic finger to the Simbiari and turned back to the teleview. He touched the # stall.

"Information for what city, please?"

"Lyon," he said.

...Till I die.

*   *   *

Bryan posted the data to the CAS and picked up his own egg in London. Even though he could have done the research just as easily at home, he took off for France that same afternoon. Installing himself in the Galaxie-Lyon, he ordered a supper of grilled langouste, orange soufflée, and Chablis, and immediately began to search the literature.

The library unit in his room displayed a depressingly long list of books, theses, and articles on the Guderian time-portal. He thought about skipping over those cataloged under Physics and Paleobiology and concentrating on the Psychoanalogy and Psychosociology entries; but this seemed unworthy of her, so he poked his card into the slot and resignedly ordered the entire collection. The machine spat out enough thin plaque-books to pave the large hotel room six times over. He sorted them methodically and began to assimilate, projecting some, reading others, sleep-soaking the most tedious. Three days later he fed the books back into the unit. He checked out of the hotel and requested his egg, then went up to the roof to wait for it. The corpus he had just absorbed sloshed about in his mind without form or structure. He knew he was subconsciously rejecting it and its implications, but the realization was no great help.

Broken hearts healed and memories of vanished love faded away, even of this strange love whose like he had never known before. He realized that this had to be true. Measured judgment, consideration of the scary data he had stuffed himself with, common sense uncharged with emotion told him what he must do. Sensibly do.

Oh, Mercy. Oh, my dear. The uttermost part of the galaxy is nearer than you are, my lady passing by. And yet. And yet.

10

ONLY GEORGINA HAD BEEN SORRY TO HEAR THAT STEIN WAS going. They had got gloriously drunk together on his last day in Lisboa and she'd said, "How'd you like to do it in a volcano?" And he had muttered fondly that she was a crazy fat broad, but she assured him that she knew a guy who would, for suitable consideration, look the other way while they took a research deep-driller out of Messina, where there was this adit that led right into the main chamber of Stromboli.

So what the hell, they egged on over and the guy did let them get away with it. So what if it cost six kilobux? It was seismic down there in the surging lava with colored gas bubbles oozing slowly up the observation window like a bunch of jellyfish in a bowl of incandescent tomato soup.

"Oh, Georgina," he had moaned in the postcoital triste. "Come with me."

She rolled over on the padded floor of the driller cockpit, white flesh turned to scarlet and black by the glare outside, and gave the weeping giant mother-comfort from her melon-sized breasts.

"Steinie. Lovie. I've got three beautiful children and with my genetic quotient I can have three more if I want them. I'm happy as a clam at high tide playing with my kids and torching busted bores and loving up any man who isn't afraid I'll eat him alive. Steinie, what do I need with Exile? This is my kind of world. Exploding in three million directions all at once! Earthlings increasing and multiplying in every nook of the galaxy and the race evolving into something fantastic practically before your eyes. You know that one of my kids is coming out meta? It's happening all over the place now. Human biology is evolving right along with human culture for the first time since the Old Stone Age. I couldn't miss it, lovie. Not friggerty likely."

He broke away and knuckled out tears, disgusted with himself. "You better hope I didn't plant anything in your potato patch then, kid. I don't think my genes'd meet your standards."

She took his face in both hands and kissed him. "I know why you have to go, Blue Eyes. But I've also seen your PS profile. The squiggles in it have nothing to do with heredity, whatever you may think. Given another nurturing situation, you would have turned out fine, laddie."

"Animal. He called me a murdering little animal," Stein whispered.

She rocked him again. "He was hurt terribly when she died, and he couldn't know you understood what he was saying. Try to forgive him, Steinie. Try to forgive yourself."

The deep-driller began to lurch violently as massive eructations of gas rose from Stromboli's guts. They decided to get the hell out of there before the sigma-field heat shields gave way, and burrowed out of the lava chamber via an extinct underwater vent. When they finally emerged on the floor of the Mediterranean west of the island, the driller's hull clanged and pinged with the sounds of rocks falling through the water.

They rose to the surface and came into a night of mad melodrama. Stromboli was in eruption, farting red and yellow fire clouds and glowing chunks of lava that arched like skyrockets before quenching themselves in the sea.

"Holy petard," said Georgina. "Did we do that?"

Stein grinned at her owlishly as the driller rocked on steaming waves. "You wanna try for continental drift?" he asked, reaching for her.

11

RICHARD VOORHEES TOOK THE EXPRESS TUBE FROM UNST TO Paris to Lyon, then rented a Hertz egg for the last part of his journey. His earlier notion of eating and drinking and screwing his way across Europe and then jumping off an Alp had been modified when a fellow passenger on the liner from Assa-wompset happened to mention the odd Earth phenomenon of Exile.

That, Richard knew instantly, was just the kind of reprieve he needed. A new start on a primitive world full of human beings with no rules. Nothing to bug you but the occasional prehistoric monster. No green Leakie-Freakies, no dwarf Polliwogs, no obscene Gi, no glaring Krondaku making you feel like your nightmares just came true, and *especially* no Lylmik.

He started pulling the strings as soon as he got out of decon and was able to get to a teleview. Most Exile candidates applied months in advance through their local PS counselors and took all the tests before they ever left home. But Voorhees, the old operator, knew that there had to be a way of expediting matters. The magic passkey had come via a big Earthside corporation for which he had done a delicate job less than a year ago. It was to the advantage of both the corporation and the ex-spacer that he exit the here and now as soon as possible; and so with scarcely any arm-twisting at all, the outfit's VP-Operations agreed to use his good offices to convince the people at the auberge to let Richard take abbreviated tests right there at the starport, then proceed directly to Go.

This evening, however, as he glided out of the Rhône Valley toward the Monts du Lyonnais, he still admitted to a few qualms. He landed at Saint-Antoine-des-Vignes just a few kilometers from the inn and decided to have one last meal on free turf. The August sun had dropped behind the Col de la Luère and the resolutely quaint village drowsed in leftover heat. The café was small but it was also dim and cool and not, thank God, too cutesy atmospheric for comfort. As he ambled in, he noted approvingly that the Tri-D was off, the musicbox played only a subdued, jangling tune, and the smells of food were incredibly appealing.

A young couple and two older men, locals by the look of their agrigarb, sat at window tables wolfing large plates of sausage and bowls of salad. On a stool at the bar sat a huge blond man in a glossy suit of midnight nebulin. He was eating a whole chicken prepared with some pinkish sauce and washing it down with beer from a two-liter pewter tankard. After hesitating for a moment, Richard went and took another stool.

The big fellow nodded, grunted, and kept feeding his face. From the kitchen came the proprietor, a jolly pot-bellied man with a heroic aquiline nose. He beamed a welcome to Voorhees, spotting him as an offworlder immediately.

"I have heard," Richard said carefully, "that the food in this part of Earth is never prepared with synthetics."

The host said, "We'd sooner gastrectomize than insult our bellies with algiprote or biocake or any of the rest of that crapdiddle. Ask any gorf in the place."

"Say again, Louie!" cackled one of the oldsters at the window, hoisting a dripping hunk of sausage on his fork.

The proprietor leaned on the counter with hands palm down. "This France of ours has seen a lot of change. Our people are scattered over the galaxy. Our French language is dead. Our country is an industrial beehive underground and a history buff's Disneyland on top. But three things remain unchanged and immortal—our cheeses, our wines, and our cuisine! Now, I can see that you've come a long way." The man's eyelid drooped in a ponderous wink. "Like this other guest here, maybe you still have a ways to go. So if you're looking for a really cosmic meal—well, we're a modest house, but our cooking and our cellar are four-star *if* you can pay for it."

Richard sighed. "I trust you. Do it to me."

"An apéritif, then, which we have chilled and ready! Dom Pérignon 2100. Savor it while I bring you a selection of whimsies to whet your appetite."

"Is that champagne?" the chicken muncher asked. "In that little bitty bottle?"

Richard nodded. "Where I come from, a split of this will set you back three centibux."

"No shit? How far out you be, guy?"

"Assawompset. The old Assawomp-hole of the universe, we call it. But don't *you* try."

Stein chortled around his chicken. "I never fight with a guy till I meet him formal."

The host brought a napkin with two small pastries and a little silver dish full of white steaming lumps. "Brioche de foie gras, croustade de ris de veau à la financière, and quenelles de brochet au beurre d'écrevisses. Eat! Enjoy!" He swept out.

"Financier, huh?" muttered Richard. "There's a good epitaph." He ate the pastries. One was like a cream puff stuffed with delicious spiced liver. The other seemed to be a fluted tart shell filled with bits of meat, mushrooms, and unidentifiable tidbits in Madeira sauce. The dish with white sauce consisted of delicate fish dumplings.

"This is delicious—but what am I eating?" he asked the host, who had emerged to take the credit cards of the local diners.

"The brioche is filled with goose liver pâté. The tart has a slice of truffle, braised veal sweetbread, and a garnish of tiny chicken dumplings, cock's combs, and kidneys in wine sauce. The pike dumplings are served in creamy crayfish butter."

"Good God," said Richard.

"I have an outstanding vintage coming up with the main course. But first, grilled baby lamb filet with little vegetables, and to set it off, a splendid young Fumé from the Château du Nozet."

Richard ate and sipped, sipped and ate. Finally the host returned with a small chicken like that which Stein had lately devoured. "The specialty of the house—Poularde Diva! The most adolescent of young pullets, stuffed with rice, truffles, and foie gras, poached and coated with paprika suprême sauce. To accompany it, a magnificent Château Grillet."

"You're kidding!" Richard exclaimed.

"It never leaves the planet Earth," the host assured him solemnly. "It rarely leaves France. Get this behind your uvula, guy, and your stomach'll think you died and went to heaven." Once again he whirled out.

Stein gaped. "My chicken tasted good," he ventured. "But I ate it with Tuborg."

"To each his own," Richard said. After a long pause for attending to business, he wiped pink sauce off his mustache and said, "You figure somebody on the other side of the gate will know how to brew up some good booze?"

Stein's eyes narrowed. "How you know I'm goin' over?"

"Because you couldn't look less like some colonial gorf visiting the Old Country. You ever thought about where your next bucket of suds is coming from in the Pliocene?"

"Christ!" exclaimed Stein.

"Now me, I'm a wine freak. As much as I could be, dragging my ass all over the Milky Way. I was a spacer. I got busted. I don't wanta talk about it. You can call me Richard. Not Rick. Not Dick. Richard."

"I'm Steinie." The big driller thought for a minute. "The stuff they sent me about this Exile told how they let you sleep-learn any simple technology you think would be useful in the other world. I don't remember if it was on the list, but I bet I could cram brewing easy. And the hard sauce—you can make that outa just about anything. Only tricky bit would be the condensation column, and you could whip that up outa copper-film decamole and hide it in your hollow tooth if they didn't wanta let you in with it on the up. You with your wine, though, you might have a problem. Don't they use special grapes and stuff?"

"Don't they fuggin' ever," said Richard gloomily, squinting through the glass of Grillet. "I suppose the soil would be different back then, too. But you might be able to come up with something halfway decent. Let's see. Grapevine cuttings of course, and definitely yeast cultures, or you'd end up with moose pee for sure. And you'd have to know how to make some kind of bottles. What did they use before glass and plass?"

"Little brown jugs?" Stein suggested.

"Right. Ceramic. And I think you can make bottles outa leather if you heat and mold it in water—Christ! Will you listen to me? The hung spacer carving out a new career as a grape-squash moonshiner."

"Could you get a recipe for akvavit?" Stein was wistful. "It's just neat alcohol with a little caraway seed. I'll buy all you can make." He did a double take. "Buy? I mean barter, or something . . . Shit. You think there'll be *anything* civilized waiting for us?"

"They've had nearly seventy years to work on it."

"I guess it all depends," Stein said hesitantly.

Richard grunted. "I know what you're thinking. It all depends on what the rest of the fruitcakes have been up to all this time. Have they got a little pioneer paradise going, or do they spend their time scratching fleas and carving each other's tripes out?"

The host came up with a dirty old bottle, which he cradled like a precious child. "And here . . . the climax! But it'll cost you. Château d'Yquem '83, the famous Lost Vintage of the Metapsychic Rebellion year."

Richard's face, furrowed with old pain, was suddenly transformed. He studied the tattered label with reverence. "Could it still be alive?"

"As God wills," shrugged mon hôte. "Four point five kilobux the bottle."

Stein's mouth dropped. Richard nodded and the host began to draw the cork.

"Jeez, Richard, can I hit you for a little taste? I'll pay if you want. But I never had anything that cost so much."

"Landlord—three glasses! We will all drink to my toast."

The host sniffed the cork hopefully, gave a beatific smile, then poured three half-glasses of golden-brown liquid that sparkled like topaz in the lantern light.

Richard lifted his glass to the other two.

> A man may kiss his trull goodbye.
> A rose may kiss the butterfly.
> A wine may kiss the crystal glass.
> But you, my friends, may kiss mine ass!

The ex-spacer and the café proprietor closed their eyes and sampled the wine. Stein tossed his down in one gulp, grinned, and said, "Hey! It tastes like flowers! But not much sock to it, is there?"

Richard winced. "Bring my buddy here a crock of eau de vie. You'll like that, Steinie. Sort of akvavit without the seeds . . . You and I, landlord, will continue to bless our tonsils with the Sauternes."

So the evening wore on, and Voorhees and Oleson told each other edited versions of the sad stories of their lives while the proprietor of the café clucked in sympathy and kept refilling his own glass. A second bottle of Yquem was called for and then a third. After a while, Stein bashfully told them what Georgina's *other* farewell presents had been. His new friends demanded that he model them; so he went out into the darkened egg park, got the stuff from the boot, and stalked back into the café resplendent in a wolfskin kilt, a wide leather collar and belt studded with gold and amber, a bronze Viksø helmet, and a big steel-bladed battle-axe.

Richard toasted the Viking with the last of the Château d'Yquem, which he chugalugged from the bottle.

Stein said, "The horns on the helmet were really like ceremonial, Georgina said. Vikings didn't wear 'em in battle. So these are demountable."

Richard giggled. "You look perfek, Steinie ole rascal! Jus' perfek! Bring on th' mashtodons 'n' dinosaurs 'n' whatall. All they hafta do's look at you and they'll piss blue." His face changed. "Why din' I bring a costume? Ever'body goes back in time needs a costume. Why din' I think? Now I'll hafta go through the time-gate in fuggin' civvies. Never did have no class, Voorhees, dumb damn Dutchman. No fuggin' class never."

"Aw, don' be sad, Richard," begged the café man. "You don' wanna spoil yer meal 'n' lovely wine." His beady eyes lit with an expression of drunken craft. "Got it! There's guy in Lyon runs the flickin' opera. Comes up here 'n' eats himself shtooperuss. An' this guy's au ciel du cochon over one kinda wine, 'n' I gotta whole case you c'd use t'bribe 'em if y'could stan' the tab. They got any kinda costume y'd want at the opera. Merde alors, it's not even two hunnerd hours yet! Guy might not even be'n bed! What say?"

Stein whacked his new buddy on the back and Voorhees clutched the edge of the bar. "Come on, Richard! I'll pop for halvsies!"

"I c'd call the guy up ri' now," said the smirking host. "Bet he'd meetcha at the oper'house."

So they did work it out, and in the end Stein piloted the egg with the half-conscious Richard and a case of Château Mouton-Rothschild '95 down to the Cours Lafayette of sleeping Lyon, where a furtive figure guided them into the parking subway and then through a maze of turned-off walkways to the opera's backstage rooms and costumery.

"That one," Richard said at last, pointing.

"So! Der fliegende Holländer!" said the impresario. "Never would have pegged you for that one, guy."

He helped Richard to put on the seventeenth-century garb, which included a rich black doublet with slashed sleeves and a wide lace collar, black breeches, funnel-top boots that folded over, a short cape, and a wide-brimmed hat with a black plume.

"By damn, that's more like it!" Stein whacked Richard on the back. "You make a pretty good pirate. So that's what you're like deep down inside, huh? A reg'lar fuckin' Blackbeard?"

"Black *Mushtash*," said Voorhees. He collapsed, out cold.

Stein paid off the impresario, flew them back to the darkened café to transfer Richard's luggage from the rented egg, and then hopped it for l'Auberge du Portail. By the time they got there, the ex-spacer had revived.

"Let's have another drink," Stein suggested. "Try my oh-dee-vee."

Richard took a swallow of the raw spirit. "Not mush bouquet . . . but con*sider*'ble authority!"

The two costumed roisterers went singing through the rose garden and pounded on the oaken door of the inn with the blunt side of Stein's battle-axe.

The staff responded unperturbed. They were used to having clients arrive in a more or less fuddled condition. Six powerful attendants took charge of the Viking and Black Mustache, and in no time at all they were snoring between lavender-scented sheets.

12

FELICE LANDRY AND THE PSYCHOSOCIAL COUNSELOR STROLLED into the flagged courtyard of the auberge, down an open passage, and into an office that looked out at the fountain and flowers. The room had been copied from the study of a fifteenth-century abbess. The stone fireplace with its bogus coat of arms had a huge bouquet of scarlet gladioli fanned between dog-headed andirons.

"You've come such a long way, Citizen Landry," said the Counselor. "It's a pity that your application has encountered such difficulties."

He leaned back in the carved chair, forming a church-and-steeple with his fingers. He had a pointed nose, a perpetual half-smile, and tightly curled black hair with a flashy white blaze in front. His eyes were wary. He had read her profile. Still, she looked docile enough in that gray-blue gown, twisting her poor little fingers in anxiety.

Kindly, he said, "You see, Felice, you're really very young to be contemplating such a serious step. As you may know, the first custodian of the time-portal"—he nodded to an oil portrait of the sainted Madame that hung above the fireplace—"set a minimum age of twenty-eight years for her clients. Now, we may agree today that Angélique Guderian's restriction was arbitrary, based upon antiquated Thomistic notions of psychomaturation. But nevertheless, the basic principle does remain quite valid. Fully formed judgment is essential for life-and-death decisions. And you are eighteen. I'm sure you are far more mature than most persons of your age, but nevertheless, it would be prudent to wait a few more years before opting for Exile. There *is* no return, Felice."

I am harmless and afraid and small. I am in your power and I need your help so badly and would be so grateful. "You've studied my profile, Counselor Shonkwiler. I'm rather a mess."

"Yes, yes, but that can be treated, Citizen!" He leaned forward and took her cool hand. "We have so many more facilities here on Earth than were available on your home planet. Acadie is so remote! It's hardly to be expected that the counselors out there would have the latest therapy techniques. But you could go to Vienna or New York or Wuhan, and the top people would certainly be able to smooth out your little SM problem and the male-envious hyperaggression. There would be only the smallest bit of personality derangement. You would be quite as good as new when the course of treatment was finished."

The melting and submissive brown eyes began to brim up. "I'm sure you have only my best interests at heart, Counselor Shonkwiler. But you must try to understand." Pity, aid, empathize, condescend to help the pathetic little one! "I prefer to remain the way I am. That's why I've refused treatment. The thought of other persons manipulating my mind—changing it—fills me with the most dreadful fear. I just couldn't permit it!"

I wouldn't permit it.

The counselor moistened his lips and suddenly realized that he was stroking her hand. He gave a start, dropped it, and said, "Well, your psychosocial problems wouldn't ordinarily preclude transfer into Exile. But besides your youth, there is the second matter. As you are aware, the Concilium does not permit persons having operant metapsychic powers to pass into Exile. They are too valuable to the Milieu. Now, your tests show that you are possessed of *latent* metafunctions with coercive, psychokinetic, and psyhocreative potentials of extremely high magnitude. No doubt these were partly responsible for your success as a professional athlete."

She showed a smile of regret, then slowly dropped her head so that the now limp platinum hair curtained her face. "That's all over now. They wouldn't have me any longer."

"Quite so," said Shonkwiler. "But if your psychosocial problems were successfully dealt with, it *might* be possible for the people at the MP Institute to bring up your latent abilities to operant status. Think what that would mean! You would become one of the elite of the Milieu—a person of vast influence—a literal world shaker! What a noble career you might have, spending yourself in service to a grateful galaxy. You might even aspire to a role in the Concilium!"

"Oh, I could never think of doing that. It's frightening to think of all those minds . . . Besides, I could never give up being what I am. There *must* be a way for me to pass through the time-portal, even if I am underage. You must help me find the way, Counselor!"

He hesitated. "The recidivist clause might have been invoked if the unfortunate MacSweeny and Barstow had elected to press charges. There is no age restriction for recidivists."

"I should have thought of that myself!" Her smile of relief was dazzling. "Then it's all so simple!"

She rose and came around to Shonkwiler's side of the desk. Still smiling, she took both his shoulders in her cool little hands, pressed with the thumbs, and snapped his collarbones.

13

CICADAS BUZZED IN THE BRANCHES OF THE OLD PLANE TREES that shaded the dining terrace. The scent of mignonette distilled from the gardens in the noontime heat and mingled with the perfume of the roses. Elizabeth Orme toyed with her fruit salad and drank minted iced tea while she marveled over the list that slowly glided over the surface of the plaque-book before her.

"Will you listen to these vocations, Aiken? Architect, Daub-and-Wattle. Architect, Log. Architect, Unmortared Stone. Bamboo Artificer. (I didn't know bamboo grew in Europe during the Pliocene!) Baker. Balloonist. Basketmaker. Beekeeper. Brewer. Candle and Rushlight Maker. Ceramicist. Charcoalburner. Cheesemaker. Dompteur (-euse)...What in the world is that, do you suppose?"

Aiken Drum's black eyes flashed. He leapt to his feet, reddish golliwog hair abristle, and cracked an imaginary whip. "Hah, sabertooth kittycat! Down, sirrah! So you defy the commands of your master? Roll over! Fetch!... Not the ringmaster, you fewkin' fool!"

Several of the nearby lunchers gawked. Elizabeth laughed. "Of course. Wild-animal tamers would be very useful in the Pliocene. Some of those large antelopes and things would be valuable if they could be domesticated. Still, I wouldn't want to tackle a mastodon or rhino on the strength of a quickie sleep-course in the art."

"Oh, the people here will do better than that for you, candy-doll. What happens is, you sleep-soak a very basic education in neolithic technology and general survival. Then you'll at least have the wits to dig a latrine that won't swallow you whole, and you'll know what Pliocene fruits aren't going to send you pushing up the daisies. After you sop up the basics, you pick one or more of the japes on that little list to specialize in. They give you a detailed sleeper on it, and lab work, and reference plaques for the tricky bits."

"H'mm," she mused.

"I imagine they try to steer you into a field that isn't already overcrowded. I mean, the folks on the other side of the gate would be apt to get testy if you sent 'em eighty-three lutanists and a taffy puller, when what they really wanted was somebody who knew how to make soap."

"You know, that's not really so funny, Aiken. If there is any kind of organized society on the other side, they'd be entirely dependent on the gate operators to send suitably trained people. Because the women timefarers are sterile, there'd be no young apprentices to replace workers who died or just wandered away. If your settlement lost its cheesemaker, you'd just have to eat crud and whey until another one popped through the gate."

Drum finished his iced tea and began to chew the cubes. "Things can't be too shabby in Exile. People have been going through since 2041. The vocational guidance thing hasn't been perking for anything like that long—just the last four years or so—but the older inmates of the nut-loft must have got *something* going." He thought for a minute. "Figure that most of the ones who went through were macroimmune and maybe even rejuvenated, since that was perfected in the early 'Forties. Barring the expected attrition from accidents, getting eaten by monsters, emigration to the Pliocene Antipodes, or just plain human bloody-mindedness, there ought to be quite a crowd still knocking around. Eighty, ninety thou easy. And like as not with a barter-style economy operating. Most of the time-travelers were damn intelligent."

"And crackers," said Elizabeth Orme, "even as thee and me."

She made an unobtrusive gesture toward an adjoining table, where a great blond man in a Viking outfit drank beer with a saturnine, well-used wayfarer in floppy seaboots and a ruffled black shirt.

Aiken rolled his eyeballs, looking more gnomish than ever. "Do you think that's weird? Wait till you see my rig-out, lovie!"

"Don't tell me. A Highland lad with bagpipe and tartan and a sporran full of exploding joints."

"Pissy patoot, woman. You certainly were telling the truth when you said your mind-reading powers were washed up. Ah-ah-ah! Don't plead with me! It's going to be a big surprise. What I *will* tell you now is my chosen vocation for the Land of No Return. I am going to be a Jack-of-all-trades. Scottish-style Connecticut Yankee in King Arthur's Court! . . . And how about you, my beautiful burned-out brain-bender?"

Elizabeth's smile was dreamy. "I don't think I'll take a new persona. I'll just stay me—maybe in red denim—and wear my farspeaker's ring with one of Blessed Illusio's diamonds in remembrance of times past. As for the vocation—" She speeded up the book so that the list of occupations raced past, then turned back to the beginning. Her brow furrowed in concentration. "I'll need more than one trade. Basketmaker, Charcoalburner, Tanner. Put them all together, add one more that begins with B . . . and guess my new profession, Aiken Drum."

"Balls o' brass, woman," he howled, slapped a hand on the table delightedly. The Viking and the pirate stared in mild surprise. "A balloonist! Oh, you lovely lady. You'll soar again in one way or another, won't you, Elizabeth?"

There was a soft chime. A disembodied woman's voice said, "Candidates in Group Green, we would be most pleased if you would join Counselor Mishima in the Petit Salon, where a most interesting orientation program has been arranged for you . . . Candidates in Group Yellow—"

"Green. That's us," said Aiken. The pair of them drifted into the main building of the inn, all whitewashed stone, dark heavy beams, and priceless objects of art. The Petit Salon was a cozy air-conditioned chamber furnished with brocaded armchairs, fantastically carved armoires, and a faded tapestry of a virgin and her unicorn. This was the first time that the group, which was destined to pass through the time-portal in a body after five days' training, had come together. Elizabeth studied her fellow misfits and tried to guess what exigencies had driven them to choose Exile.

Waiting for them in the otherwise empty room was a lovely pale-haired child in a simple black cheongasm. Her chair was separated from the others by a couple of meters. One of her slender wrists was fastened to the heavy chair arm by a delicate silver chain.

The pirate and the Viking glanced in, looking bashful and truculent because nobody else was yet in costume. They clomped forward and sat down precisely in the center of the row of seats. Another pair that seemed acquainted entered without speaking—a milkmaid-hale woman with curly brown hair, wearing a white coverall, and a stocky man who appeared to be middle-aged, having a snub nose, Slavic cheekbones, and corded hairy forearms that looked able to throttle an ox. A quasi-academic personage in an antique Harris jacket arrived last of all, carrying a briefcase. He looked so self-possessed that Elizabeth found it impossible to imagine what his problem might be.

Counselor Mishima, tall and sleek, came in beaming and nodding. He expressed his delight at their presence and hoped they would enjoy the introduction to Pliocene geography and ecology that he was pleased to present at this time.

"We have among us a distinguished person far more knowledgeable in paleoecology than I," the counselor said, bowing low to the Slavic type. "I would appreciate his interrupting me should my little lecture require correction or embellishment."

Well, that explains *him*, Elizabeth thought. A retired paleontologist bent on touring the fossil zoo. And the dolly on the leash is a recidivist whacko, a few stripes blacker than poor Aiken, no doubt. The boys in fancy dress are your obvious anachronistic losers. But who is the White Lady? And the Thinking Man who wears tweeds in August?

The room light faded and the tapestry rose to reveal a large holograph screen. There was music. (Lord Jesus, thought Elizabeth. Not Stravinsky!) The screen went from black to living Tri-D color in an orbiter's view of Pliocene Earth, six million years—give or take a few—backward in time.

In a long shot, it looked pretty familiar. But then the lens zoomed in.

Mishima said, "The continents, you will observe, are in their approximate modern positions. However, their outlines have an unfamiliar aspect, primarily because shallow epicontinental seas still covered some areas, while others, now lying underwater, were then dry land."

The globe rotated slowly and stopped when Europe was well positioned. The lens zoomed in closer and closer.

"You will all be furnished with a set of durofilm maps—small-scale for the entire Lower Pliocene Earth, one-to-seven-million of Europe, and one-to-one-million of France. Should you plan an excursion to other parts of the world or simply have an interest in them, we will do our utmost to provide you with suitable maps or marine charts."

"How accurate will they be?" asked the pirate.

"Extremely so, we believe." Mishima's response was smooth. "The Pliocene being one of the most recent geological epochs, our computers have been able to map its topography with an accuracy that must approach eighty-two percent. The areas most speculatively derived include fine details of the littoral, minor watercourses, and certain aspects of the Mediterranean Basin."

He began to show them closeup views of different areas, all in vivid relief and supplemented by an outline overlay of the modern landform.

"The British Isles are fused into a single very large mass, Albion, which is probably joined by a narrow isthmus to Normandy. The Low Country area is submerged by the Anversian Sea, as is northwestern Germany. Fennoscandia is an unbroken unit, as yet unsundered by the Baltic. Poland and Russia are strewn with swamps and lakes—some quite large. Another great body of fresh water lies southwest of the Vosges in France, and there are large Alpine lakes . . ."

To the east, the land looked almost completely unfamiliar. A brackish lagoon, the Pannonian Basin, covered Hungary and drained through the Iron Gate and the Dacian Strait to a shallow remnant of the once dominant Tethys Sea, also called Lac Mer. This spread swampy lagoons and salt water far into Central

Asia and northward to the iceless Boreal Ocean. In years to come, only the Aral and the Caspian Seas would remain as souvenirs of the vanished Tethys.

"Note also that the Euxinic Basin, which will someday become the Black Sea, is also fresh water. It is fed by the towering ranges of Caucasia, Anatolia, and the Helvetides to the west. A vast swamp occupies the area of the modern Sea of Marmara. Below this is Lake Levant, roughly corresponding to the Aegean Sea of today."

"The Med looks pretty mixed up to me," the Viking observed. "In my line of work I had to know something about the crazy geology of that region. It seems to me you gotta be doing a whole lotta guessing to come up with that layout there."

Mishima acknowledged the point. "There are problems connected with the chronology of the successive Mediterranean inundations. We believe this configuration is most plausible for the early Pliocene. Please observe that the now vanished peninsula of Balearis juts eastward from Spain. There is a single narrow island in place of modern Corse and Sardegna. Italy during that time has only its Apennine spine above sea level, together with an unstable southern area called Tyrrhenis, which once was much larger but now is sinking."

He gave them a closer view of western Europe.

"This is the region that should be of immediate interest to you. The Rhône-Saône Trough contains a great river, draining swamps north of Switzerland and the large Lac de Bresse. The lower Rhône Valley of Pliocene times was probably invaded by the Mediterranean. Many of the volcanoes in the Massif Central were active, and there was also vulcanism in Germany, Spain, central Italy, and in the subsiding Tyrrhenian area. Farther north in France, we see that Brittany is an island separated from the mainland by the narrow Strait of Redon. The Atlantic forms a deep embayment southward into Anjou. Part of Gascony is also inundated by the sea."

"But Bordeaux seems to be all right, thank God," said the pirate.

Mishima chuckled. "Ah! Another connoisseur! You will be delighted to know, Citizen, that a number of other timefarers expressed a wish to settle in the Bordeaux area. They have carried with them certain portable apparatus and cuttings of many different grapes . . . Incidentally, Citizens, such information as we have about these earlier time-travelers is available from our computer at your convenience. And if you wish to have other information—for example, data on religious or ethnic groups, or on the kinds of books, art matériel, or other cultural items known to have been translated—please do not hesitate to request it."

The academic type in the tweed jacket asked, "Will the computer give information on individual persons?"

Aha! thought Elizabeth.

"The usual statistics, similar to those in your own dossiers, are available on those persons who have already passed through. It is also possible to obtain information on the items taken as baggage and the traveler's destination in the Pliocene world, if stated."

"Thank you."

"If there are no further questions—?" Mishima nodded to Felice, who had raised a languid hand.

"Is it true that none of these travelers took any weapons with them?"

"No *modern* weapons were allowed by Madame Guderian, and we have followed her wise dictum. No zappers, no stunguns, no atomics, no sonic disruptors, no solar-powered blasters, no gases, no gunpowder-based weapons. No psychocoercive drugs or devices. However, many kinds of primitive weaponry from different eras and cultures have been taken into the Pliocene."

Landry nodded. Her face was void of expression. Elizabeth tried, without realizing what she was doing, to throw a redactive probe into her, but of course it was useless. Nevertheless, the ex-metapsychic was amazed when the young woman turned her head and stared directly at her for a long minute before looking back at the screen.

She couldn't have felt anything, Elizabeth told herself. There was nothing to feel. And even if the carrier went out, there's no way she could have known that it was me. Was there?

Counselor Mishima said, "Let us briefly note some of the names that have been given to the geographical features. Then we will survey the plant and animal life of the so-called Pontian Facies of Lower Pliocene times . . ."

14

JUST AS SOON AS THE LECTURE ENDED, GRENFELL HURRIED TO his room and the computer terminal, which was housed in a renaissance credence of wormy fruitwood. He requested the data in permanent durofilm sheets, not really knowing what to expect. What did emerge was pathetically meager—but it unexpectedly included a full-length color portrait, probably taken just prior to her passing through the gate.

Mercy Lamballe was wearing a cowled cloak of deep reddish brown that concealed most of her auburn hair and made dark pits of her eyes. Her face was white and strained. The dress was long, simply cut, of Nile green with a trimming of gold embroidery about the neck, wrists, and hem. Her narrow waist was held in a girdle of some dark color, from which hung a purse and a small scabbard with unidentifiable instruments in it. She wore gold bracelets and a gold necklace, both with purple stones. A large brocaded valise sat beside her. She carried a covered basket and a leather case that looked as though it held a small harp.

She was accompanied by a huge white dog wearing a spiked collar, and four sheep.

He stared at the picture for some time, memorizing it while his eyes stung. Then he read her tersely summarized dossier:

LAMBALLE, MERCEDES SIOBHAN 8-∅49-333-∅32-421F. B: St.-Brieuc 48:31N, ∅2:45W, FrEu, Sol-3 (Earth), 15-5-2∅82, d. Georges Bradford Lamballe 3-946-2∅2-664-117 & Siobhan Maeve O'Connell 3-429-697-551-418. Sb:∅. M:∅. D:∅. C:∅. Phy: H17∅cm, W46kg, Sfr1, Hrd2, Egn4, DMmole Rscap. Men: 1A+146(+3B2), PSA+5+4.2+3.∅-∅.7+6.1, MPQ-.∅79(L) +28+6+133+468+1. MedHist:NSI, NST, NSS (Supp1). PsyHist: AlienRefr-4 (non-dis), Fug-5 (non-dis), MDep-2 (.25 dis UT) (Supp2). Ed: BA Paris 21∅2, MA(Anthr) Oxon 21∅3, PhD (FrMedHis) Paris 21∅4, DLH(CeltFL) Dublin 21∅5. Emp: ImPag Eire (T4-T1) ∅5-∅8;(DirAsst3-2) ∅8-∅9. ImPag France (DirAsst1) ∅91∅. Res: 25a Hab Cygne, Riom 45:54N, ∅3:∅7E, FrEu, Sol-3. CivSt:★1★A-∅∅1∅. CrRt:A-∅1-3. Lic: E3, Tv, Ts, E1Tc2, Dg.

REMARKS: Ent: 1∅-5-211∅. VocOpt: Dyer, Sheep Husb, Smallholder, Weaver, Wool Tech. PersInv: (Supp3). Dest: NS Attmt: NS.

TRANS: 15-5-211∅   REF: J. D. Evans GC2

SUPPLEMENT 3	*Personal Inventory, Lamballe, M. S.*
Clothing:	Gown, silk, grn emb-Au. Gown, silk, w embr+grn. Gown, polchro, blk emb-Ag-myl. Scarves, silk, 3. Cloak, repelvel, terracotta. Smalls, silk, asst w, 3sts. Hose, silk, w, 3pr. Shoes, low, leather, 2pr. Belt, leather. Purse, leather. Chatelaine, leather + scissors, knife, file, comb, stylus, fork, spoon.
Baggage:	Survival Unit A-6★. Smallholder Unit F-1★. Sheep Kit OV-1★. Fleck, Music, 5Ku, w/AVP (Supp4). Fleck, Library, 1∅Ku, w/AVP (Supp5). Decamole appl: spin-wheel, hand-

spindle, carder, loom L4H, dye-tub.
Valise, leather-brocade. Basket,
esparto, cov. Necklace, Au & amethyst. Bracelets, Au & amethyst,
3. Ring, Au & pearl. Mirror, Ag,
1∅cm. Noteplaque, 1Ku. Sewkit S-
1★. Harp, gilt carved sycamore
wood, Celtic, w/case, leather. Harp
strings & pegs, asst spare. Fife,
open, Ag.

Plants:

Strawberry "Hautbois Supérieur
12e," 1∅∅ pts. Hemp (Cannabis
s. sinsemilla) 15 ctgs. CulHb Unit
CH-1★. SmGrain Unit SG-1★. Misc
seed pkts: Bluebell (Campanula
bellardi), Indigo (Indigofera tincto-
ria), Madder (Rubia tinctorum), Pea
"Mangetout."

Animals:

Chien des Pyrénées, "Bidarray's
Deirdre Stella-Polaris" (1F,
pr4M + 4F). Sheep, Rambouillet ×
Débouillet (3F @ pr2F; 1M).

. . . .

There was more—the supplements with details of her medical and psychiatric history, the library supplements listing her
music and books. He skimmed these, then returned to the
poignant inventory and the portrait.

Will I find you again, Mercy in your silken gown and golden
jewelry, with your harp and your fife and your strawberries
and bluebells? Where will you go to tend your pregnant sheep?
(Dest: NS.) Will I find you alone, except for loyal Deirdre and
her pups, as you've always lived? (Attmt: NS.) Will you welcome me and teach me the songs of old Languedoc or old
Ireland, or will your heartswound still be too deep for me to
fill? (MDep-2, .25 dis UT.)

What did you find on the other side of the time-portal when
you stepped through on your birthday, beginning your twenty-
ninth year of life six million years before you were born? And

why am I leaving this bravest of all new worlds for a constricting unknown? What's in the dark that I'm so afraid of finding/not finding?

Beguiled my heart, I know not why. And yet I love her till I die.

15

CLAUDE MAJEWSKI OPENED HIS EYES, WIPED THE RHEUM OUT of them with a tissue, and removed the earplug that had been teaching him while he slept how to mortise wind beams into the rafters of a log cabin. His left arm was full of pins and needles and his feet were cold. Damn crocky old circulation shot to hell. As he kneaded the blood back into the muscles, he reflected that he would miss the luxury of the auberge's goosedown pillows, liquicelle mattress, and real muslin sheets. He hoped the survival kit they would test today had a decent camp bed.

He padded across the sunny room to the bath. Here the compassion of Madame Guderian was made manifest in black-and-white marble and golden plumbing, in thick towels, perfumed soap and toiletries by Chanel, in sauna and sunlamp and la Masseuse ready to cradle the clients of the inn in soothing elegance after sobering lessons in la vie sauvage.

Some poor timefarers struggling to endure the Pliocene world would remember the last days at the auberge for French cooking, soft beds, and precious works of art. But Majewski knew that his fondest memories would be of the sybaritic john. The warm padded seat that welcomed his spindly shanks! The tissue, like perforated rabbit fur! He harked back to some of the primitive conveniences he and Gen had suffered on boondock planets—portacans with broken heating units; noisome stone and wood tillyhouses full of lurking critters; rough two-holers over flooded trenches; even one ghastly night of storms on Lusatia when he had squatted on a log and *then* discovered that it harbored little mitey monstrosities.

O blessed sanitary plumbing! If no one else invented a Pliocene water closet, Claude intended to give it an earnest shot.

He had a cool perfumed shower, cleaned his teeth (third set, good as new), made a face at himself in the Louis XIV mirror. Not too decrepit. A casual appraisal might judge his age to be late fiftyish. He was vain about his Polish green eyes and striking thatch of waved silver hair, the result of having the male-pattern baldness codons erased from his genetic heritage on the last rejuv. But thank God he'd depilated the rest of his pelt! Characters like that pirate who prized facial hair might have another song to sing in a primitive world—especially a warm and buggy one like Pontian Europe. The old paleobiologist had noted with grim humor that yesterday's lectures and clever animated movies on Pliocene ecology had barely mentioned the insects and other invertebrate denizens. It was more dramatic to show vast herds of hipparions and graceful gazelles being harried by scarcely less graceful cheetahs; or machairodont lions sinking their long canines into bellowing hoe-tuskers.

Claude went back into the bedroom and asked room service to send coffee and croissants. Since this second day was to feature simple survival techniques, he put on the clothing he planned to wear through the gate. Experience had made his choice of kit easy: fishnet underwear, old-fashioned bush shirt and pants made of the best Egyptian long-staple cotton, socks of Orcadian wool with fat left in, and indestructible boots from Etruria. He had brought along his old backpack even though the auberge stood ready to furnish all equipment. It contained his poncho of breathable grintlaskin and an Orcadian sweater. And in one zip compartment was a beautiful Zakopane box, all carved and ornamented wood. Gen's box. It hardly weighed a thing.

As he breakfasted, he studied the program for the day's

activities. Introduction to Survival Unit A-6*. Shelter and Fire. Minimizing Environmental Hazards (ho ho). Orienteering. Fishing and Trapping.

He sighed, drank the perfect coffee, and munched a flaky bread roll. It was going to be a long day.

16

SISTER ANNAMARIA ROCCARO HAD DONE A FAIR BIT OF CAMP-
ing, but the expensive new decamole equipment contained in
Unit A-6* was a delight and a revelation to her.

She and the other members of Group Green had first gone
to class, where a hearty woman instructor briefed them; then
they had paired up and descended to a cavern carved out of
the living rock 200 meters below the cellars of the auberge.
They were let loose into a sunny meadow with a winding stream
and told to become acquainted with their survival gear.

The simulated sun felt hot, even though the reset of their
body thermostats was progressing apace. After she and Felice
had hiked a short distance, Amerie decided that she would have
to forego the sandals that had been her first choice for Pliocene
footgear. They were suitably monastic and airy, but they also
admitted twigs and small stones. Short buskins or even modern
boots would be better for cross-country travel. She also decided
that the white doeskin habit was overwarm, even with detach-
able sleeves. Homespun would be better. She could have a
doeskin scapular, cowl, and cloak to keep off the weather.

"Aren't you hot in that outfit, Felice?" she asked her companion. Landry was wearing the green-and-black ring-hockey

uniform, which was evidently her choice for the Pliocene.

"It suits me," the girl said. "I'm used to working in it, and my planet was much warmer than Earth. That doeskin looks very high-priestess, Amerie. I like it."

The nun felt strangely flustered. Felice looked so incongruous in her warrior's cuirass and greaves and that Grecian helm with its brave green feathers perched on the back of her head. Stein and Richard had started to tease her when she appeared in the costume that morning; but for some reason, they had broken off almost immediately.

"Shall we camp here?" the nun suggested. A large cork oak grew beside the brook, shading a flat surface that looked like a good place to set up the cabin. The two women shed their packs, and Amerie extracted the fist-sized inflator from hers and studied it. Their instructor had said that the sealed power supply would be good for about twenty years. "Here are two nozzles, one to blow things up and the other to deflate. It says: IMPERATIVE TO SHEATH UNUSED NOZZLE."

"Try my cabin-pak." Felice held out a wad about the size of a sandwich. "I can't believe it'll grow into a four-by-four house."

Sister Roccaro fixed the dangling flat tube of the pak to the inflator, then pressed the activating stud. Compressed air began to spurt into the wad, turning it into a large silvery square. The two women positioned the cabin properly, then watched it grow. The floor thickened to about nine centimeters and became quite rigid as air filled the complex micropore structural web between the layers of film. The walls, somewhat thicker for insulation, grew up, complete with transparent zipable windows and interior screen-curtains. A steeply gabled silvery roof that overhung the doorway inflated last of all.

Felice peered inside the doorless entry. "Look. The floor has sprouted fixed furniture."

There were bunks for two with semidetached pillows, a table, shelves, and at the rear a silvery box with a pipe leading to the roof. Felice read aloud: "BALLAST STOVE WITH SAND OR UNIT WILL COMPRESS UPON COOLING . . . This material must be nearly impossible to destroy!" She reached behind her left greave and produced a glittering little gold-handled dirk. "Can't puncture it, either."

"What a pity they've made it to degrade in twenty years. Still, we should be at one with our environment by then."

Large bucket-shaped hollows in each corner of the cabin had to be ballasted with stones, earth, water, or whatever else was to hand. A very small pocket near the door yielded up a whole handful of pill-sized wads that were to be inflated separately, then weighted with sand or with water. The latter could be injected into the interstitial area by means of a simple collapsible bulb siphon. The pills grew into a cabin door, chairs, cooking gear (with the sand-ballast note), filamentous rugs and blankets, and other miscellany. Less than ten minutes after they had begun to set up camp, the women were relaxing in a fully equipped cabin.

"I can hardly believe it," Sister Roccaro marveled, rapping on the walls. "It feels quite solid. But if there were any wind, the whole cabin would blow away like a bubble unless you weighted it down."

"Even wood is mostly thin air and water," said Felice with a shrug. "This decamole just seems to reproduce the structurally reinforced shell of a thing and let you add mass. Wonder how the stuff compensates for heat and pressure changes? Some kind of valves, I suppose. You'd obviously have to guy this house in a high wind, though, even if you filled most of the wall hollows with water or dirt. But it sure beats a tent. It even has ventilators!"

"Shall we inflate the boat or the minishelter or the bridge sections?"

"They were optional. Now that I've seen how decamole works, I'll take the rest of the equipment on faith." Felice crossed her legs and pulled off her gauntlets slowly. She was seated at the small table. "Faith. That's your game, isn't it?"

The nun sat down. "In a way. Technically, I intend to become an anchoress, a kind of religious hermit. It's a calling that's completely obsolete in the Milieu, but it used to have its fans in the Dark Ages."

"What in the world will you be doing? Just praying up a storm all day long?"

Amerie laughed. "Part of the night, too. I intend to bring back the Latin Divine Office. It's an ancient cycle of daily prayers. Matins starts it off at midnight. Then there's Lauds at dawn. During the daytime there are prayers for the old First, Third, Sixth, and Ninth Hours. Then Vespers or Evensong at sunset, and Compline before going to bed. The Office is a collection of psalms and scripture readings and hymns and special prayers that reflected centuries of religious tradition. I think it's a terrible pity that no one prays it any more in the primitive form."

"And you just keep saying this Office all the time?"

"Good grief, no. The individual hours aren't that long. I'll also celebrate the Mass and do penance and deep meditation with a little Zen. And when I'm hoeing weeds or doing other chores there's the Rosary. It's almost like a mantra if you do it the old way. Very calming."

Felice stared at her with well-deep eyes. "It sounds very strange. And lonely, too. Doesn't it frighten you, planning to live all alone with nobody but your God?"

"Dear old Claude says he'll maintain me in style, but I'm not too sure I can take him seriously. If he does supply me with some food, I may be able to handcraft some items in my spare time that we can barter."

"Claude!" Landry was contemptuous. "He's been around, that old man. He's not a complete case like those two machos in fancy dress, but I caught him looking at me in a fishy way."

"You can't blame people for looking at you. You're very beautiful. I've heard you were a great sports star on your home world."

The girl's lip curled in a grim little smile. "Acadie. I was the best ring-hockey player of all time. But they were afraid of me. In the end, the other players—the men—refused to come up against me. They made all kinds of trouble. Finally, I was barred from the game when two players claimed I had deliberately tried to do them serious injury."

"Had you?"

Felice lowered her gaze. She was twisting the fingers of her gloves and a flush was rising from her neck into her cheeks. "Maybe. I think I did. They were so hateful." She raised her pointed chin in defiance, the hoplite helmet pushed to the back of her head giving her the look of a miniature Pallas Athene. "They never wanted me as a woman, you know. All they wanted was to hurt me, to spoil me. They were jealous of my strength, and afraid. People have always been afraid of me, even when I was just a child. Can you imagine what that was like?"

"Oh, Felice." Amerie hesitated. "How—how did you ever begin playing that brutal game?"

"I was good with animals. My parents were soil scientists and they were always moving around on field expeditions. Newly opened lands, still full of wildlife. When the local kids in the area would snub me, I'd just get myself some pets for friends. Small creatures at first—then larger and more dangerous kinds. And there were some beauties on Acadie, I can tell you! Finally, when I was fifteen, I tamed a verrul. It's something like a very large Earth rhinoceros. A local animal dealer wanted to buy him for ring-hockey training. I'd never paid much attention to the game before, but I did after I sold the beast. I woke up to the fact that there was a big-money business that might be perfect for my special talents."

"But to break into a professional sport when you were only a young girl—"

"I told my parents I wanted to become an apprentice verrul trainer and groom. They didn't mind. I had always been excess baggage. They just made me finish school and let me go. They said, 'Be happy, baby.'"

She paused and stared at Amerie without expression. "I was a groom only until the team manager saw how I could control the animals. That's the secret of playing the game, you see. The verrul has to make the goals and maneuver to keep you from getting stunned by the short-range weapons the players carry. I played in the preseason as a novelty, to give the Greenhammer box office a hype. The team had been in the cellar for three years running. When they saw that I was more than a publicity gimmick they put me onto the first string in the season opener. I whipped the other clowns on the team into such a froth trying to outdo me that we won the bloody game. And all the rest . . . and the pennant, too."

"Wonderful!"

"It should have been. But I had no friends. I was too different from the rest of the players. Too freakish. And in the second year . . . when they really began to hate me and I knew they would force me out, I—I—"

She pounded both fists on the table and her child's face twisted in anguish. Amerie waited for the tears, but there were none; the briefly revealed hurt was masked almost as soon as it had showed itself. Sitting across the table, Felice relaxed, smiling at the other woman.

"I'm going to be a huntress, you know. On the other side. I could take care of you much better than the old man, Amerie."

The nun rose up, blood pounding in her temples. She turned away from Felice and walked out of the cabin.

"I think we need each other," the girl said.

17

My dear Varya,

We have completed our little games of survival and craftsmanship now, and our bodies are fully acclimated to the tropical
world that was Pliocene Earth. There remain only a Last Supper
and a good night's sleep before passage through the time-portal
at dawn. The apparatus is inside a quiant cottage in the gardens
of the auberge, and you can't imagine a more incongruous site
for the gate into another world. One looks in vain for the sign
above the doorway saying, PER ME SI VA TRA LA PERDUTA GENTE,
but the feeling is there all the same.

After five days of working together (more like a holiday
camp than basic training, you must understand), the eight of
us in Group Green have achieved shaky competence in our
chosen fields of primitive technology and a faith in our ability
to cope that is probably dangerously inflated. Few of the others
seem to appreciate the potential hazard that we might face from
our predecessors into Exile. My fellow Greenies are more inclined to worry about being stamped upon by mammoths or
bitten by python-sized vipers than to anticipate a hostile human

reception committee greedily awaiting the day's grab bag of well-heeled wayfarers.

You and I know that the time-gate arrivals would certainly have been ritualized in some manner by the people on the other side. What the ritual will be is another matter. We can hardly expect to be treated as casual commuters, but whether we shall encounter welcome or exploitation is impossible to fathom. The literature offers certain speculative scenarios that make my flesh crawl. Personnel at the auberge are careful to present a neutral face while at the same time reinforcing our childhood self-defensive training. We will pass through the portal in two groups of four persons, with larger pieces of baggage following. This, I feel, is designed to give us a certain safety in numbers—although the momentary pain and disorientation of ordinary subspace translation will probably affect time-travelers as well, putting us at a tactical disadvantage for the first minute following our arrival in the Pliocene.

Your amused speculations upon my new vocation in the primitive world were much appreciated. However, since the last dinosaurs perished at least 60 million years before the Pliocene Epoch, there will be little call for sweeping up after them! So much for your visions of me as an antediluvian fertilizer tycoon. Prosaically enough, my new job is to be little more than an extension of my erstwhile hobby of sailing. I shall fish for a living and ply the seas on my Quest, and perhaps undertake the odd bit of trade if the occasion presents. The sloop was far too sophisticated a vessel to take to the Pliocene, so I traded her in for a smaller trimaran that can be ballasted with water and sand instead of mercury. If need be, I can whip up a very simple craft from scratch materials as well. We are furnished with toolheads of a gemlike glassy material, vitredur, which stays eversharp and is virtually indestructable for some 200 years, after which it degrades, like decamole. Besides the shipwright's kit, I am equipped with the auberge's survival gear (very impressive) and what they call a Smallholder Unit— tools and decamole appliances for setting up light housekeeping on a subsistence farm, together with a few packets of seeds and a large fleck library with a raft of "how-to" books on every subject from animal husbandry to zymurgy.

The latter, by the way, is the vocation of choice for our Viking. He also confided to me that if there should be a demand for swashbuckling mercenary warriors, he might combine the two trades.

The individual whom I dubbed the Pirate also plans to get involved with alcoholic beverages—wines and brandies, that is. He and the Viking are now the straightest of friends, spending their off-hours tossing down the most expensive spirits that the auberge can supply and speculating on the quality of female consolation that might be available in the By-and-By. (Group Green itself has lean pickings. Besides the Nun, our female members include a sinister Virgin Huntress who seems to have wreaked mayhem or worse on one of the auberge counselors in order to qualify as a recidivist, and an extremely cautious ex-Meta Lady who is, at the moment at least, content to remain just one of the boys.)

Last night we had a fascinating glimpse into the background of the Pirate. His brother and sister turned up unexpectedly to say adieu and turned out to be Fleet line officers of the most impressive stripe. The poor P was very discomfited and the ex-Meta Lady speculates that he must be a cashiered spacer himself. He's a competent sort if you don't mind grouches. I worked with him for a few hours in the Small Boat Handling exercise, which he wanted to cram, and he seemed to have a natural flair for messing about in the water.

Most of the others in Group Green seem to be alone in the world. The Nun received a long conference call from her religious sistren in North America bidding her bon voyage. And earlier today she met with a Franciscan Brother in full conventual fig, no doubt hearing her last confession or whatever. (The friar drove one of those souped-up Gambini eggs with the heat dissipation fins, not the patient gray donkey you might have anticipated from memoirs of Il Poverello.) The Nun was a medic and psychological counselor by profession and plans to retire to a hermitage. I hope the poor woman isn't counting on ministering angels such as the Old Paleontologist overmuch. He's a fine chap with a penchant for carpentry, but I dare say the ex-Meta is right when she pegs him as a death-wisher.

I concur with your analysis of the Little Joker. There must have been some valid square-peg reason for him to be thrown off his home world, but it's a pity that his wild talents couldn't be harnessed for the Milieu. Poor little nonborn. He's endeared himself to the rest of us Greenies—not only for his ghastly sense of humor, but also for his fantastic ability to make something out of nothing. He has assembled a large collection of vitredur toolheads that need only be equipped with shafts or handles to be operational. You get the feeling that after this boy has been in the Pliocene for a week or two, the Industrial Revolution will be raging. He has a whole forge lashup in decamole for his village blacksmith and rustic mechanician acts, and has acquired a plaqueful of geological survey charts to clue him in on metal ores in the unlikely event that none of the other Exiles has gone in heavily for prospecting.

You may be interested in the peculiar social structure of Group Green. The foundress of the auberge was a practical psychologist of no mean ability and realized quite early on that her clients would need support from fellow travelers in order to maximize survival potential beyond the gate. On the other hand, they would tend to be far too eccentric to stand for any of the more obvious schemes of imposed organization. So Madame Guderian fell back on the old "put 'em through hell together and they'll end up buddies" shtick—which you must admit is apt to induce feelings of solidarity in all but the most sociopathic. (And it did, too, with the obvious exception.)

During each day's Group activities we have spent the most strenuous sessions working together, often thrust into outlandish situations where we were forced to cooperate with one another in order to complete a difficult task quickly and well. For example, we bridged a thirty-meter pond full of alligators in one lesson; captured, butchered, and "utilized" an elk in another; and defended ourselves against hostile human stalkers in a third. Ironically, the most accomplished primitive in the Group is the Old Paleontologist, who seems to have knocked about the wilder shores of Galactica for more than a century while gleaning fossil bones.

We are known to each other by first names only, and we may divulge such details of our background as we choose or don't choose. As you may imagine, this leaves a wide margin for parlor psychoanalysis—with the ex-Meta Lady as head gamesmistress. She had me taped as a Questing Lover after the first day, and I'm afraid that she anticipates a melancholy end to my masculine Evangeline-fixe, since she keeps trying to distract me with speculations on rôle playing among the auberge clientèle, the political implications of Exile, and other anthropological amusements.

Do you think I'm doomed, too, Varya? *I* don't, you know.

Late this afternoon I got a call from London, and it was Kaplan and Djibutunji and Hildebrand and Catherwood, bless their bones, telling me goodbye. Aunt Helen sent a note, but she is really nearly gaga now, since declining rejuv.

Your dear letter was in this morning's post. I don't have to tell you how much I appreciate your agreeing to carry on with the liaison committee. It's the one work I really hated to leave unfinished. There is still the ultimate correlation of the pre-Rebellion mazeway material, but I feel that Alicia and Adalberto have that pretty well in hand.

And so I come at last to the farewell, Varya, and I wish I could be eloquent and memorable instead of just my stodgy self. The gaudiness of the act will have to speak for me. Whatever you do, don't mourn. My only hope of happiness lies on the other side of the Exile gate and I must risk going after it. Remember the years we shared as lovers and colleagues and friends and know that I'm glad they happened. Joy and light to you, my Very Dear.

Forever,
BRY

18

WHEN THE LAST SUPPER, WITH ITS CRAZY SMÖRGÅSBORD OF requested dishes, was finally over, the eight members of Group Green took their drinks out onto the terrace, where they instinctively gathered apart from the other guests. Even though it was only half after twenty, the sky over Lyon had turned black as the scheduled weekly storm built up in the north. Pink flashes silhouetted approaching thunderheads.

"Feel the static buildup!" Elizabeth exclaimed. "Even with my metafunctions out, the ionization before a really big storm always gets to me. Every sense sharpens. I begin to feel so clever I can barely contain myself! Capacitor Earth is charging and so am I, and in just a minute or two I'll be able to zap mountains!"

She faced into the strengthening wind, long hair streaming and red denim jumpsuit clinging to her body. The first subsonics of distant thunder curdled the air.

Felice affected a languid tone. "Were you able to move mountains before?"

"Not really. The larger psychokinetic powers are really very rare among metas—almost as rare as genuine creativity. My PK ability was only good for a few parlor tricks. What I specialized in was farspeaking, the glorified telepathy function. It should really be called farsensing because it includes a species of sight as well as hearing. I was also highly operant in redaction, which is the therapeutic and analytical power that most lay persons call mind-alteration. My husband had similar faculties. We worked as a team training the minds of very young children in the first difficult steps toward metapsychic Unity."

"They wanted *me* to go to a redactor," Felice said, her voice thrilling with loathing. "I told them I'd rather die. I don't know how you meta people can stand rummaging around in others' brains. Or always having some other meta able to read your own secret thoughts. It would be horrible never to be alone. Never to be able to hide. I'd go mad."

Elizabeth said gently, "It wasn't like that at all. As far as metas reading each other . . . there are many different levels to the mind. Modes, we call them. You can farspeak to many people on the declamatory mode, or speak at short range to a group on the conversational mode. Then there's the intimate mode, that only one person can receive from you. And beneath that are many other conscious and unconscious layers that can be screened off by means of mental techniques that all metapsychics learn when they're very young. We have our private thoughts, just as you do. Most of our telepathic communication is nothing more than a kind of voiceless speech and image projection. You can compare it to electronic audiovisuals— without the eletromagnetic radiation."

Felice said, "Deep redactors can get into a person's innermost thoughts."

"True. But with them, there is almost always a doctor-patient relationship appertaining. The patient gives conscious permission for the scrutiny. Even then, a dysfunction may be so strongly programmed that the therapist is powerless to get behind it—no matter how much the patient may be willing to cooperate."

"Yeah," said Stein. He tilted his great mug of beer, holding it before his face.

Felice persisted. "I *know* that metas can read secret thoughts. Sometimes the coach of our team would bring in redactors to work on guys in slumps. Metas could always spot the ones who'd lost their nerve. You can't tell me those poor bastards would deliberately let the shrinks find out something that'd get them fired!"

Elizabeth said, "An untrained person, a nonmeta, gives away information in subverbal ways without being aware of it. Think of it as mental mumbling. Haven't you ever stood next to a person who was talking to himself, muttering under his breath? When a person is frightened or angry or trying very hard to work out a problem or even sexually aroused, the thoughts become . . . loud. Even nonmetas can sometimes pick up the vibes — the mind-pictures or subvocal speech or emotional surges. The better the redactor, the better he is at making sense out of the crazy mishmash that human brains broadcast."

Bryan asked, "Is there any way an ordinary person can shut out a mind reader?"

"Of course. It's possible to stymie superficial snooping rather easily. Just keep a firm grip on your mental broadcasting. If you think someone is really digging, think of some neutral image like a big black square. Or do some simple exercise when you're not speaking out loud. Count one-two-three-four, over and over. Or sing some dumb song. That'll block out all but the best redactor."

"I'm glad you can't read *my* mind now, lovie," Aiken Drum put in. "You'd fall into a quagmire of sheer funk. I'm so scared about going through this time-gate that my red corpuscles have gone puce! I tried to back out. I even told the counselor I'd reform if they'd let me stay here! But nobody'd believe me."

"I can't think why," Bryan said.

A reddish bolt of lightning reached from cloud to cloud above the hills; but the sound, when it came, was muffled and unsatisfying, a beat from a dead tympanum.

Aiken asked Elizabeth, "How did the ballooning work out, sweets?"

"I crammed the theory of building one from native materials — tanning fishskins for the envelope and weaving a basket and plaiting cordage from bark fibers. But I did my practicing in one of these." She took a package the size of two large bricks from her shoulder bag. "It blows up five storeys tall, double-walled and semidirigible. Bright red, like my suit. I have a power source to inject hot air. Of course, the power won't last for more than a few flight-weeks, so eventually I'll have to shift to charcoal. Making that's a mess. But it's the only ancient fuel that's suitable—unless I can find some coal."

"No sweat, doll-eyes," Aiken said. "Stick with me and my mineral maps."

Stein laughed contemptuously. "And how you gonna mine the stuff? Draft Snow White and the Seven Dwarfs? The nearest coal's gotta be a hundred kloms north, around Le Creusot or Montceau, and way to hell and gone underground. Even if you reach the stuff without blasting, how you gonna tote it around to where it'll do you some good?"

"So I'll need a week or two to work out the fewkin' details!" Aiken shot back.

"There would be other coal deposits much nearer," Claude Majewski said. "Those modern maps of yours are deceptive, Aiken. They show the strata and deposits as they exist today, in the twenty-second century—not as they were six million years ago. There used to be little limnic coal basins all over the Massif Central and a really large deposit at Saint-Étienne, but they were all worked out late in the twentieth century. Go back to the Pliocene and you'll probably find easy pickings just a few kloms south of here. Find some near a volcano, and you might luck out with natural coke!"

"Better hold off establishing Pliocene Mining, Unlimited, until you eyeball the territory," Richard advised Aiken with a sour grimace. "The local honchos might have their own ideas about us helping ourselves to the natural resources."

"Entirely possible," Bryan agreed.

"We could convince them to let us have a piece of the action," said Felice. She smiled. "In one way or another."

The nun said, "We could also try to avoid conflict by going to an unsettled area."

"I don't think that's Felice's style," Aiken said. "She's looking forward to a little fun and games—aren't you, babe?"

Landry's pale frizzy hair was standing out from her head in a charged cloud. She was wearing the simple cheongsam again. "Whatever I'm looking forward to, I'll find. Right now all I want is another drink. Anybody coming with me?" She strolled back into the auberge, followed by Stein and Richard.

"Somebody should tell those two they're wasting their time," the old man muttered.

"Poor Felice," Amerie said. "What an ironic name for her, when she's so dreadfully unhappy. That aggressive pose is just another form of armor, like the hockey uniform."

"And underneath she's just crying for love?" Elizabeth inquired, her eyes nearly shut and a faint smile on her lips. "Be careful, Sister. That one's standing in the need of prayer, all right. But she's more of a black hole than a black sheep."

"Those eyes eat you alive," Aiken said. "Something damned inhuman is moving around in there."

"Not even normally homophilic," Majewski said. "But I'll certainly grant you the damned."

"That's a cruel and cynical thing to say, Claude!" exclaimed the nun. "You don't know anything of the girl's background, any of the things that have maimed her spirit. You talk as though she were some monster—when all she is, is a pathetic proud child who has never learned how to love." She took a deep breath. "I'm a medic as well as a nun. One of my vows is to help the suffering. I don't know if I can help Felice, but I'm certainly going to try."

A gust of wind lifted Amerie's veil and she clutched it impatiently with one strong hand. "Don't stay up too late, guys. Tomorrow's creeping up on us." She hurried off the terrace and disappeared into the darkened garden.

"Could be it's the nunnie who'll need the prayers," Aiken said, giggling.

"You shut up!" barked Claude. Then he said, "Sorry, son. But you want to watch that smartass mouth of yours. We're going to have enough trouble without your adding to it." He looked at the sky as a prolonged and powerful bolt of lightning descended over the eastern hills. Ground-strokes rose up to meet it and there was a grumble of thunder. "Here comes the storm. I'm going to bed, too. What I want to know is, who the hell ordered the omens for this outfit?"

The old man stomped away, leaving Elizabeth, Aiken, and Bryan staring after him. Three successive thunderbolts gave him a ridiculously theatrical exit; but none of the people still on the terrace was smiling any more.

"I never told you, Aiken," Elizabeth ventured at last, "how much I like your costume. You were right. It's the most spectacular one in the whole auberge."

The little man began snapping his fingers and clacking his heels like a flamenco dancer, turning and posing. Lightning shone on his loose-fitting garment. What seemed to be cloth of gold was actually a costly fabric woven from the byssus threads of Franconian mollusks, famed throughout the galaxy for beauty and toughness. All up and down the arms and legs of the suit were small flapped and fastened pockets; pockets covered the breast area and the shoulders and hips and there was a very large pocket on the back with an opening on the bottom. Aiken's golden boots had pockets. His belt had pockets. Even his golden hat, with the brim tipped up jauntily on the right side, had a band full of tiny pockets. And every pocket, large or small, bulged with some tool or instrument or compressed decamole appliance. Aiken Drum was a walking hardware shop incarnate as a golden idol.

"King Arthur would dub you Sir Boss at first sight," Elizabeth said, explaining to Bryan: "He plans to set himself up as a Pliocene Connecticut Yankee."

"You wouldn't have to bother with Twain's solar eclipse to gain attention," the anthropologist conceded. "The suit alone is enough to overawe the peasantry. But isn't it rather conspicuous if you want to spy out the land?"

"This big pocket on my back has a chameleon poncho."

Bryan laughed. "Merlin won't have a prayer."

Aiken watched the Lyon city lights dim and disappear as the approaching storm curtained the valley with rain. "The Connecticut Yankee had to contend against Merlin in the story, didn't he? Modern technology versus sorcery. Science against the superstition of the Dark Ages. I can't remember too much about the book. Read it when I was about thirteen there on Dalriada and I know I was disappointed with Twain for wasting so much space on half-baked philosophy instead of action. How did it end? You know—I've forgotten! Think I'll go hit the computer for a plaque of the thing for bedtime reading." He gave Bryan and Elizabeth a wink. "But I may decide to aim higher than Sir Boss!"

He slipped off into the auberge.

"And then there were two," Bryan said.

Elizabeth was finishing her Rémy Martin. She reminded him in many ways of Varya—calm, incisively intelligent, but with the shutters always closed. She projected cool comradeship and not the slightest jot of sex.

"You won't be staying with Group Green for long, will you, Bry?" she remarked. "The rest of us have built a dependence in these five days. But not you."

"You don't miss much. Are you sure your metafunctions are really gone?"

"Not gone," she said. "But they might as well be. I've dropped into what we call the latent state because of brain damage. My functions are still there, but inaccessible, walled up in the right half of my brain. Some persons are born latent— with the walls. Others are born operant, as we say, and their mind-powers are available to them, especially if they receive proper training from infancy. It's closely analogous to the acquisition of language by babies. My work back on Denali involved a good deal of that kind of training. Very rarely, we were even able to coax latents into operancy. But my own case is different. I have just a few teaspoonsful of my original cerebrum left. The rest is regenerated. The leavening was enough for a resoul job, and a specialist restored my memories. But for some unknown reason, metapsychic operancy seldom survives a really spectacular brain trauma."

"What happened, if you don't mind my asking?"

"My husband and I were caught in a tornado while we were egging on Denali. It's a sweet little world, with some of the galaxy's worst weather. Lawrence was killed outright. I was broken to bits but ultimately restored. Except for the MP functions."

"And is losing them so unbearable—" he began, then cursed and apologized.

But she was calm, as always. "It's nearly impossible for a nonmeta to understand the loss. Think of going deaf, dumb, blind. Think of being paralyzed and numb all over. Think of losing your sex organs, of becoming hideously disfigured. Put all of the anguish together and it's still not enough, once you've known the other thing and then lost it . . . But you've lost something, too, haven't you, Bry? Maybe you can understand something of the way I feel."

"Lost some*thing*. Perhaps it does make more sense to say it that way. God knows there's no logic to the way I feel about Mercy."

"Where will you look for her? If the others in the Pliocene don't know where she's gone?"

"All I have is an instinct. I'll try Armorica first because of her Breton ancestry. And then Albion—the Britain that will be. I'll need the boat because there's a question whether the Channel was dry land at the precise period we'll be living in. Sea level seems to have fluctuated in an odd way at the beginning of the Pliocene. But I'll find Mercy somehow, no matter where she's gone."

And what will I find in my beautiful balloon, Elizabeth wondered. And what will it matter? Will the Exile world be any less empty than this one?

Perhaps if she and Lawrence had wanted children...but that would have compromised the work, and so they had agreed to forego them, finding love fulfillment in each other, mating for life as almost all metapsychics did, knowing that when one had inevitably gone there would still be the Unity, the billion-fold mind-embrace of the Galactic Milieu.

Or there would have been...

The first large drops of rain made a rataplan on the leaves of the plane trees. Blue-white flashes lit the whole valley and the thunder seemed to shake the mountain roots. Bryan grabbed Elizabeth's hand and pulled her through the porte-fenêtre into the main salon a few seconds before the real downpour began.

19

THE PREDAWN WAS CHILLY, WITH GRAY CLOUDS SCUDDING southward as though late for an appointment at the Mediterranean. The Rhône Valley brimmed with mist. A small log fire had been lit in the main salon and it was there that the members of Group Green gathered after breakfasting in their rooms. Each person carried the materials for a new life and dressed for the rôle chosen. (Their extra baggage had preceded them to the time-gate staging area: Claude's case of Wybrowa, Bryan's Scotch, Richard's supplies of spices and yeasts and sodium bisulfite, Stein's keg, Elizabeth's liqueur chocolates, and Amerie's large painting of Saint Sebastian.) Richard and Stein whispered together as they stared at the weak flames. Amerie, a half-smile on her lips, fingered the beads of a large wooden rosary that hung from her belt. The others stood apart, waiting.

At precisely five hundred hours, Counselor Mishima came down the broad staircase from the mezzanine and bid them a solemn good-morning.

"Please accompany me."

They picked up their things and followed in single file out of the salon, across the terrace, and into the sodden garden, where the flagstones were still puddled with rain and the blossoms on the rose-standards hung torn and battered from the storm.

The balconies of the main guesthouse overlooked the garden. Up above, dim faces behind glass doors were watching them—just as they themselves had watched other dawn processions of eight time-travelers led by a single counselor. They had seen Gypsies and Cossacks and desert nomads and voortrekkers, Polynesians with feathered capes and warriors with crossbows, swords, and assegais; there had been Bavarian hikers in lederhosen, bearded white-robed prophets, shaven-headed Oriental votaries, sunbonneted American pioneers, cowboys, fetishists costumed in pathetic grotesquery, and sensible-looking people wearing levis or tropical gear. The travelers in the early morning parades had moved through the garden to an old cottage shaded by mulberry trees, its white stucco and half-timbering shrouded in climbing vines. Madame Guderian's lace curtains still hung at the windows and her pink and white geraniums bloomed in earthenware pots beside the large front door. The eight guests and the counselor would enter the cottage and the door would close behind them. After half an hour had elapsed, the counselor alone would emerge.

Bryan Grenfell stood behind Counselor Mishima as he unlocked the Guderian cottage with an old-fashioned brass key. A large ginger cat sat in the dry shelter of the shrubbery, watching the group with a sardonic golden eye. Grenfell nodded to it as he passed inside. You've seen a lot of us go this way, haven't you, Monsieur le Chat? And how many of them by now felt as used and foolish and tired as I do—but still too stubborn to turn back? Here I go, in my pragmatic tropical kit with a haversack full of simple necessities and high-protein food, armed with a steel-tipped walking stick and a small throwing knife hidden beneath the sleeve of my left forearm, and Mercy's dear picture and dossier in my breast pocket. Here I go into the deep cellar . . .

Stein Oleson had to duck his head passing through the door and walk with caution through the hall lest he brush against

Madame's tall clock with its wagging brass pendulum, or knock some fragile bibelot from its place on the wall, or catch the curling horns of his Viking helmet on the little crystal chandelier. Stein was finding it more and more difficult to keep silent. Something was expanding inside of him that demanded to cry out, to roar, to vent a great gust of laughter that would make all the rest of the group shrink away from him as from the door of a suddenly opened furnace. He felt his manhood coming alive beneath the wolfskin kilt, his feet itching to leap and trample, his arm muscles tensing to swing the battle-axe or brandish the vitredur-tipped spear he had added to his armory. Soon! Soon! The tangle in his guts would come free, the fire in his blood would power him to heroism, and the joy would be so huge that he would damn near die with the swallowing of it . . .

Richard Voorhees followed Stein carefully down into the cellar. His heavy, folded-over seaboots were awkward on the worn steps. He had a suspicion that he would have to switch to the more comfortable athletic shoes in his backpack once they had passed through the gate and done a first reconnaissance on the other side. Practicalities first, then rôle playing! The secret of success, he told himself, would lie in a swift assessment of the local power structure, covert appeal to the have-nots, and establishment of a suitable base. Once he got the distillery operating (with Stein, and maybe Landry, to keep the locals from muscling in), he'd be on a sound economic footing and ready to jockey for political influence. He smiled in anticipation and carefully adjusted the hipband of the backpack so that it would not wrinkle the skirts of his doublet. Didn't some of those old sea rovers set themselves up as virtual kings in early America? Jean Lafitte, Bloody Morgan, even old Blackbeard himself? And how do you like Richard Voorhees for King of Barataria? He chuckled out loud at the thought, completely forgetting that his costume had not really belonged to an operatic buccaneer, but to a different kind of seafarer altogether . . .

Felice Landry watched Counselor Mishima manipulate the elaborate lock mechanism of the cellar door. It swung ponderously open and they entered the old wine-keep, dark and musty and with a faint overscent of ozone. She stared at the gazebo, that unlikely gate to freedom, and clutched her new arbalest to her black-armored bosom. She was trembling, nauseated, exerting all her willpower to keep from disgracing herself in this ultimate moment. For the first time since early childhood, her eyes, within the T-shaped Grecian helmet opening, were sticky-lashed with tears . . .

"We will translate you in groups of four, as I have already explained," said Counselor Mishima. "Your extra baggage will follow after an interval of five minutes, so be prepared to retrieve it from the tau-field area. And now, if the first people will position themselves—"

Elizabeth Orme watched without emotion as Bryan, Stein, Richard, and Felice crowded closely into the latticed booth and stood motionless. All of them, she thought, have made their plans except me. They have their goals—touching or comical or mad. But I'll be content to drift through the Exile world in my scarlet balloon, looking down on all the people and the animals, listening to wind and the cry of birds, smelling pollen, resin from the forest, smoke from wildfire on the grassland. I'll come to earth only when I feel that the Earth is real again and I am. If we ever can be . . .

Mirrored walls sprang up as Mishima threw the switch. The four people in the gazebo were on their way. Aiken Drum, his golden suit glittering with a hundred reflections from the cellar lights, stepped forward impulsively.

"Damn! So that's all there is to it? Not even enough power drain to dim the lamps!" He studied the vinelike cables that seemed to grow out of the packed soil of the floor and disappear somewhere short of the vaulted ceiling. Mishima warned him to touch nothing, and Aiken gave him a reassuring gesture. But he had to get a close look. The glassy framework was shot through with faintly moving patterns hovering at the edge of visibility. The black bodies of the lattice-nodes each enclosed a tiny point of unwinking light that seemed to be shining at a great distance.

"How long does it take for people to get from here to there?" Aiken asked. "Or should I say from now till then?"

"The translation is in theory instantaneous," replied Mishima. "We maintain the field for some minutes in order to enable a safe exit. And I may say that never once, in the four years that the Human Polity has carried on the work of Madame Guderian, has there been an accident to time-travelers."

Aiken said, "Counselor, I'd like to take one more thing with me into Exile. Can you give me a description and diagram of this device?"

Without a word, Mishima opened the oaken cabinet and took out a small plaque-book. It was obvious that other travelers had made the same request. Aiken kissed the plaque triumphantly and stowed it in a large pocket below the right knee of his shining suit.

Mishima stepped to the control console and switched off the field. The mirror-walls winked out. The gazebo was empty.

"They have passed safely through the portal. Now the rest of you may enter."

Claude Majewski hefted his twenty-kilo pack and was the first inside. Old Man, you're crazy, he said to himself—then smiled because he could hear Gen saying it. On a sudden impulse, he opened the pack compartment that held the carved and inlaid box from the Polish mountains and took it out. Is there really a Pliocene world beyond this gate, Black Girl? Or is it a hoax after all, and do we step out of the glass cage into death? Oh, Gen, go with me. Wherever . . .

Sister Annamaria Roccaro was the last to get into position, smiling in apology as she crowded next to Aiken Drum and felt the hard tools in his pockets pressing through the sleeves and skirts of her habit. Aiken was nearly a head shorter than the sturdy nun, almost as small as Felice but in no way as vulnerable. He'd survive, would Aiken Drum. May the rest of us as well! And now, Mother of God, hear my archaic prayer: Salve Regina, mater misericordiae; vita, dulcedo, et spes nostra, salve. Ad te clamamus, exsules, filii Hevae. Ad te suspiramus, gementes et flentes in hac lacrimarum valle. Eia ergo, advocata nostra, illos tuos misericordes oculos ad nos converte. Et Jesum, benedictum fructum ventris tui, nobis post hoc exilium ostende—

Mishima threw the switch.

There was pain of translation and a momentous snap hurtling them into the gray limbo. They hung without breath or heartbeat, each one screaming alone into silence. And then they felt sudden warmth and opened their eyes to a blinding dazzle of green and blue. Hands were pulling them, voices urging them to step forward out of the shimmering area that had been the gazebo, to step down a little, to come out quickly before the field reversed itself, to enter into Exile.

PART II

THE INITIATION

1

"Come along, sport, come along now. Step down a little. We're the guardians of the time-portal. We're here to help you. Come on. You're feeling zonked-out right now, but that'll pass away right quick. Just relax and come along. You made it safe to Exile. You're safe—you hear me, cob? Come on now. We're all going along to Castle Gateway. You can relax there. We'll have a nice yabber and answer all your questions. Come on."

As the pain receded and his wits phased in again, Bryan was at first aware only of the nagging voice and brilliant light. Such an ordinary twangy voice! Such an extraordinary light! He was conscious of somebody holding him by the right wrist and upper arm, a blurred figure he couldn't quite focus on. Another someone seemed to be vacuuming dust off his clothes with a hand-held machine. Then he was being forced to walk and he looked at his feet and saw them quite clearly, shod in a pair of pigskin boots with crinkled soles, moving first over damp granite, then on thick sod with grass that had been mowed or cropped short. He was stepping on small daisylike flowers. A butterfly with zebra stripes and long swallowtails hung motionless on a dew-spangled weed.

"Wait," he mumbled. "Stop." The insistent tugging left off

and he was able to stand still and look about him. The newly risen sun shone over a wide expanse of green tableland going golden in its higher, drier reaches. Tanzania? Nebraska? Dorubezh?

France.

Nearer, there were rounded boulders of crystalline rock. They had been used to mark the sides of a path that led back to a peculiar, indistinct block hanging in the air like a heat mirage. Men dressed alike in white tunics and pants with blue cords about the waist were gathered around Richard and Stein and Felice. Several more guardians stood waiting for the other members of Group Green to arrive. The wavering force field winked out. Bryan insisted upon standing still until it reappeared with four more human figures, which the guardians hastened to lead into open ground.

"All safe, sport. You can come along with me now. The rest'll all be tagging along."

Bryan discovered that the ordinary voice belonged to a skinny, deeply tanned man with grayish-blond hair and a long nose bent to one side. He had a prominent larynx and wore a twisted necklet of dark metal, about as thick and as round as a finger, incised with intricate little markings, and fastened in the front with a knoblike catch. His tunic, apparently of finely spun wool, had a streak of dried food down the front. For some reason, this reassured Bryan. He did not resist when the man began pulling him along the path again.

They were ascending a small hill a couple of hundred meters from the time-portal area. As the anthropologist's mind cleared, he was excited to see a stone fortress of considerable size perched on the eminence, facing east. It did not resemble the fairytale châteaux of France, but rather the simpler castles of his English homeland. Except for the absence of a moat, it was something like Bodiam in Sussex. When they came closer, Bryan saw that there was an outer ringwall of rough masonry about twice the height of a man. Inside this, beyond an encircling space that formed an outer ward, was a four-sided bailey, a hollow square without a central keep, with towers at the corners and a great barbican at the entrance. Above the gate was the effigy of a bearded human face, crafted in yellow metal. When they came close to the outer wall, Bryan heard an eerie howling.

"Right through here, cob," said the guide reassuringly. "Don't pay no mind to the amphicyons."

They went into a passage that led through the outer ward to the portcullis of the barbican. On either side were stout wooden grilles. A dozen huge creatures galloped clumsily up to the bars and began slavering and snarling.

"Interesting watchdogs," Bryan said unsteadily.

The guide kept hustling him along. "Too right! Primitive canids. Bear-dogs we call 'em. They weigh about three hundred kilos and eat anything that bloody well doesn't eat them first. When we have to secure the fortress, we just lift these grilles and give the beasts access to the whole outer ward."

Inside the large barbican structure was a corridor that branched right and left, leading to peripheral rooms behind the massive curtain-wall. The guide led Bryan up an open stairway to the second level. Here the corridors were whitewashed and there were handsome brass sconces with containers of oil ready to be lighted at nightfall. Deeply bayed windows giving onto the inner court let daylight into the hall.

"We got a small reception room for each of you," the guardian said. "Sit down and rest and have some tucker if you like." He threw open a heavy wooden door and led the way into a chamber that measured about four by four. It was carpeted with a thick wool rug in shades of brown and gray and furnished with surprisingly well crafted chairs and benches of turned wood. Some had corded seats and backs, while others were padded with black woolen cushions. On a low table were ceramic pitchers containing hot and cold liquids, drinking tumblers, a bowl of purple plums and small cherries, and a plateful of seedcakes.

The guide helped Bryan unfasten his backpack. "There's facilities through that curtained door. Some new arrivals feel the need. A chap from the interview committee will come to you in about ten minutes. Meanwhile, just live it cool."

He went out and closed the door.

Bryan walked to an embrasured window in the exterior wall and gazed at the landscape through an ornamental brass grating. He could see amphicyons prowling in the narrow space below. Beyond the outer wall was the pathway and the rock outcropping with its four cornerstones that marked the position of the time-portal. Shading his eyes against the rising sun, he saw the savanna undulating gently toward the Rhône Valley. A small herd of four-footed animals grazed in the far distance. A bird sang an intricate song. Somewhere in the castle, the sound of human laughter echoed briefly.

Bryan Grenfell sighed. So this was the Pliocene!

He began examining his surroundings, his mind automatically filing away the homely details that could tell an anthropologist so much about the culture of a new world. Walls of mortared stone, whitewashed (casein?), with stained oak framing around the doorways and shutters for the glassless window. The convenience had a smaller louvered slit in the wall for ventilation. Its toilet was a simple hole in the masonry reminiscent of the medieval garderobes to be found in English castles. It sported a wooden seat and a nicely carved lid, and had a box of green leaves mounted on the wall beside it. For washup there was a ceramic basin and laver (thrown stoneware, slip-decorated, salt-glazed). The soap was fine-grained, properly aged, and scented with some herb. The hand towel resembled coarse linen.

He strolled back to the reception room. The food laid out on the table added its data to the mass. Bryan ate a cherry, putting the large pit neatly into an empty dish and noting that the flesh was meager but sweet. Probably the original European bird cherry or some close relative. The tiny plums also seemed to be wild. If any time-travelers had brought budwood from improved stonefruits, the resulting trees might have been too susceptible to Pliocene insects and diseases to survive without chemical protection. He wondered about wine grapes and strawberries but seemed to recall that both were rather resistant, and so there was a fair chance that Richard would have his wine and Mercy her strawberries and cream...

The cold drink tasted of citrus, and the steaming pitcher turned out to contain hot coffee. Agnostic though he was, Bryan sent up a prayer of thanks for the latter. The seedcakes had a firm texture and a faint aroma of honey. They had been baked properly and decorated with hazelnuts on top. The cookie plate was incised with a simple motif and had a handsome sang de boeuf glaze.

There was a light tapping on the door. The brass latch lifted to admit a mild-looking older man with a neatly trimmed mustache and imperial. He smiled tentatively and sidled in when

Bryan gave him a friendly murmur. He wore a blue tunic with a white cord about the waist and had the same necklet of dark metal as the guardians had worn. He seemed ill at ease and perched on the very edge of a bench.

"My name is Tully. I'm a member of the interview committee. If you wouldn't mind—I mean, we can probably help you find your way about and all if you'd tell us just a little about yourself and your plans. Not to pry, you understand! But if we could know just a little of your background and about the trade you've learned, it would help ever so much. I mean, we could tell you which places have need of your—uh—talents if you're interested in settling down. And if you don't want to settle down, perhaps you have questions you'd like to ask *me*. I'm here to help you, do you see?"

He's afraid of me, Bryan realized in amazement. And then he thought of the kind of persons who might come through the gate—persons such as Stein and Felice, for example—who might react to the initial disorientation and culture-shock with violence, and decided that Tully had every reason to be cautious in his initial encounter with new arrivals. He probably rated combat pay. To soothe the man, Bryan leaned back easily in one of the chairs and munched on a seedcake.

"These are very good. Made with oats, are they? And sesame? It's reassuring to be greeted with civilized food. An excellent psychological maneuver on your part."

Tully gave a delighted little laugh. "Oh, do you think so? We've tried hard to make Castle Gateway a welcoming environment, but some of the arrivals are deeply stressed and we sometimes have difficulty calming them."

"I felt a bit wonky at first, but I'm fine now. Don't look so anxious, man! I'm harmless. And I'll answer any reasonable questions."

"Splendid!" The interviewer smiled his relief. He took out a small sheet of writing material (paper? vellum?) from a belt pouch, together with an ordinary twenty-second-century pen. "Your name and former occupation?"

"Bryan Grenfell. I was a cultural anthropologist specializing in the analysis of certain kinds of social conflict. I'm most interested in studying your society here, even though I'm not too sanguine about the possibility of publishing my work."

Tully chuckled in appreciation. "Fascinating, Bryan! You

know, there have been *very* few members of your profession to come through the gate. You'll certainly want to go on to the capital and talk to the people there. They'd be most interested in you. You could provide unique insights!"

Bryan looked surprised. "I'm equipped to earn my living as a fisherman or coastal trader. I never thought my academic credentials would be appreciated in the Pliocene."

"But we aren't savages!" Tully protested. "Your scientific talents will very likely prove invaluable to—um—administrative persons, who'll welcome your advice."

"So you do have a structured society."

"Very simple, very simple," the man said hurriedly. "But I'm sure you'll find it worthy of careful study."

"I've already begun on that, you know." Bryan watched Tully's meticulously barbered face. "This building, for instance, has been well designed for security. I'm most interested in knowing what you secure against."

"Oh—there are several kinds of animals that are quite dangerous. The giant hyenas, the machairodus sabercats—"

"But this castle seems more suited to defense against human aggression."

The interviewer fingered his neck-ring. His eyes darted here and there and finally fixed Bryan with a sincere expression. "Well, of course there *are* unstable personalities coming through the portal, and even though we try very hard to assimilate everyone, we have an inevitable problem with the really serious misfits. But you need have no fear, Bryan, because you and the rest of your party are quite safe here with us. Actually, the—um—disturbed element tends to hide away in the mountains and in other remote places. Please don't worry. You'll find that the high-culture persons have complete ascendancy here in Exile. Everyday life is as tranquil as it can be in a—um—*aboriginal* environment."

"How nice of you."

Tully nibbled on the end of his pen. "For our records—that is, it would be helpful if we knew just exactly what kind of equipment you've brought with you."

"To be put into the common store?"

Tully was shocked. "Oh, nothing like that, I assure you. All travelers *must* retain the tools of their trade in order to survive and be useful members of society, mustn't they? If you'd rather not discuss the matter, I won't press. But sometimes people come through with extraordinary books or plants or other things that could be of great benefit to everyone, and if these persons would consent to share, the quality of life for all would be enhanced." He smiled winningly and poised the pen.

"Aside from a trimaran sailing craft and the fishing gear, I have nothing special. A voicewriter with a plaque-converter for the sheets. A rather large library of books and music. A case of Scotch that seems to have gone astray . . ."

"And your traveling companions?"

Bryan said easily, "I think you'd better let them speak for themselves."

"Oh, certainly. I only thought I'd . . . well, yes." Tully put away his writing materials and flashed another bright smile. "Now, then! You must have some questions you would like to ask *me*!"

"Just a few for now. What is your total population?"

"Well, we hardly keep accurate census figures, you understand, but I think a reasonable estimate would be about fifty thousand human souls."

"Strange, I would have guessed more. Do you suffer from disease?"

"Oh, hardly at all. Our ordinary macroimmunization and genetically engineered resistances seem to protect us very well here in the Pliocene, although the very earliest travelers didn't enjoy the full-spectrum coverage of those who have come to Exile within the last thirty years or so. And of course those who were lately rejuvenated can expect a much longer life span than those who were treated with the earlier technology. But most of our—um—attrition has come from accidents." He nodded soberly. "We have physicians, of course. And certain medications are regularly sent through the time-portal. But we cannot regenerate persons suffering really serious trauma. And this world may be said to be civilized, but it is hardly *tame*, if you take my meaning."

"I understand. Just one other question for now." Grenfell reached into his breast pocket and took out the color picture of Mercedes Lamballe. "Can you tell me where I might find this woman? She arrived here in mid-June of this year."

The interviewer took the picture and studied it with widening eyes. He finally said, "I think—you will find she has gone to our capital city in the south. I remember her very well. She made a most vivid impression on all of us. In view of her unusual talents, she was invited to—um—go down and assist with administration."

Bryan frowned. "What unusual talents?"

In some haste, Tully said, "Our society is quite different from that of the Galactic Milieu, Bryan. Our needs are special. All of this will be made clear to you later, when you get a more complete overview from people in the capital. From a professional standpoint, you have some intriguing investigations awaiting you."

Tully rose. "Have a little more refreshment now. Another person would like to interview you in a short while, and then you can rejoin your companions. I'll come for you in about half an hour, shall I?"

Smiling again, he slipped out the door. Bryan waited for a few moments, then got up and tried the latch. It wouldn't budge. He was locked in.

He looked around the room for his iron-shod walking stick. It was nowhere to be found. He rolled up his sleeve to check on the little throwing knife in its scabbard. He was not surprised to find that the leather sheath was empty. Had his introductory "vacuum cleaning" been a frisk with a metal detector?

Well, well, he said to himself. So *this* is the Pliocene!

He sat down again to wait.

2

RICHARD VOORHEES HAD RECOGNIZED THE PSYCHIC DISORIEN-
tation of the time-portal as a variant of that experienced by
humans every time that starships passed from the normal universe into the quasi-dimensional gray subspace during superluminal travel. However, the "snap" of temporal translation
was prolonged many times longer than that of hyperspace cross-
over. Richard had also noted peculiar differences in the texture
of the gray limbo. There was a dimly perceived rotation about
consecutive axes; a compression (was everything, every atom
in the universe, subtly smaller 6 million years in the past?); a
quality to the gray that was less fluid and more frangible (did
one swim through space and smash through time?); a sense of
diminishing life-force all about him that would fit in nicely
with certain philosophers' notions of the essence of the Milieu.

When Richard dropped through the air a short distance and
landed on the granite outcropping of Exile, he was in control
of himself almost immediately, as every starship's master had
to be after spatial translation. Pushing aside the eager hands of
a guardian, he exited from the tau-field under his own power
and did a fast eyeball scan while the guide murmured inanities.

Just as Counselor Mishima had promised, the Pliocene Rhône

Valley was much more narrow, and the country on this western flank, where the auberge would one day stand on a wooded hillside, was now flatter and less dissected by streams. It was, in fact, a plateau, rising slightly to the south. He spotted the castle. On the skyline behind it, smoking in the early sunlight, were two titanic snow-clad volcanoes. The northerly one would be Mont-Dore; the larger cone to the south, the Cantal.

There was grass. There were rabbity critters crouching motionless, pretending to be rocks. Off in a hollow was a grove of trees. Did the little apelike ramapithecines roam those woods?

Guardians were leading Bryan, Stein, and Felice up the path toward the castle. Other men in white helped the second group from the time-gate area. Who was in charge of the place? Some Pliocene baron? Was there an aristocracy here? Would he, Richard, be able to elbow his way into it? His mind tossed up question after question, fizzing with a youthful enthusiasm that astounded and delighted him. He recognized what was happening. It was a belated reprise of the spacer's favorite malady—the New Planetfall Eagers. Anyone who ranged widely throughout the galaxy and endured the boredom of subspace gray was likely (if not too jaded) to work himself into a lather of anticipation over the imminent landing upon a hitherto unvisited world. Would the air smell good? Would the ions vitalize or poop? Would the vegetation and animals delight or disgust the eye? Would the local food ditto the tastebuds? Would the people be successful and sprightly or beaten down by hardship? Would the ladies screw if you asked them to?

He whistled a few notes of the bawdy old ballad through his teeth. Only then did he become aware of the anxious voice and the plucking at his sleeve.

"Come along, sir. Your friends have gone on to Castle Gateway. We've gotta get along, too. You'll want to rest and refresh yourself and like as not ask some questions."

The guardian was a dark-haired man, well built but rather raw-boned, with the spurious youthfulness and overwise eyes of a fairly recent rejuvenate. Richard took in the dark metal necklet and the white tunic that was probably a lot more comfortable in this tropical climate than Richard's own black velvet and heavy broadcloth.

"Just let me look around a little, guy," Richard said, but

the man kept tugging at him. To avoid argument, Richard began to move along the path leading to the castle.

"That's a nice commanding position you've got there, guy. Is that mound artificial? What do you do for a water supply up here? How far to the nearest town?"

"Easy on, traveler! Just you come along with me. The interview committeeman will be able to answer your questions better than I can."

"Well, at least tell me the prospects for local gash. I mean— back in the present—or the future or whatever the hell you call it here—we were told that the male-female ratio here was about four—to one. I wanta tell you that almost turned me off from coming over! If it wasn't for certain pressing circumstances, I might not have come to Exile at all! So how is it really? You have women up at the castle?"

The man replied austerely, "We're hosting a number of female travelers, and the Lady Epone is temporarily in residence. No women live permanently at Castle Gateway."

"So where do you guys get it? Is there a village or a town for weekend passes or whatever?"

In a matter-of-fact manner the man said, "Many of the castle staff are homophile or autoerotic. The rest are serviced by traveling entertainers from Roniah or Burask. There are no small villages in this area, only widely separated cities and plantations. Those of us who serve at the castle are happy to remain there. We're well rewarded for our work." He fingered his necklet with a small smile, then redoubled his effort to rush the new arrival along.

"Sounds like a real organized setup," said Richard in a dubious tone.

"You've come into a wonderful world. You're going to be very happy here once you've learned a little about our ways . . . Don't mind the bear-dogs. We keep them for security. They can't get at us."

They hurried through the outer ward and into the barbican, where the guardian tried to steer Richard up the stairway. But the ex-spacer pulled away, saying, "Be right back! Gotta take a look at this fascinating place!"

"But you can't—" exclaimed the guardian.

But he did. Clutching his plumed hat, Richard broke into

a run that was only slightly slowed by the weight of his back-pack. He went clattering over the flagstones into the deep interior of the gatehouse, dodging around corners at random until he emerged into the large inner courtyard of the castle. This early in the morning, the area was deeply shadowed, surrounded on four sides by the two-storey hollow wall with its corner towers and battlements. The courtyard was nearly eighty meters square. At its center was a fountain with trees planted around it in stone boxes. More trees grew at regular intervals around the perimeter. One entire side of the yard was taken up by a large double corral neatly walled in perforated stone. Half of it contained several score large quadruped animals of a type Richard had never seen before. The other half of the corral seemed to be empty.

Hearing the voices of pursuers, Richard dodged into a kind of cloister that ran around the other three sides of the inner ward. He ran for a short distance, then turned into a side corridor. It was a dead end. But on either side were doors leading into apartments within the great hollow wall.

He opened the first righthand door, slipped inside, and closed the door behind him.

The room was black. He stood perfectly still, catching his breath, gratified to hear the sound of running feet grow louder, then fade away. For the moment, he had escaped. He fumbled in one pocket of his backpack for a light. Before he could switch it on, he heard a faint sound. He stood immobile. A line of radiance had sprung into being across the darkened room. Someone was opening another door with infinite slow-ness and the illumination from the inner chamber swept toward him in a widening beam until he was caught.

Silhouetted in the doorway was a very tall woman. She was dressed in a filmy sleeveless gown that seemed almost invisible. Richard could not see her face but he knew she had to be beautiful.

"Lady Epone," he said, not knowing why.

"You may come in."

He had never heard such a voice. Its musical sweetness held an unmistakable promise that set him on fire. He dropped his pack and came toward her, a figure dressed entirely in black drawn by her bright allure. As she went slowly into the inner chamber, he followed. Dozens of lamps hung from the ceiling, reflecting off draperies of shimmering gold and white gauze that curtained a vast bed.

The woman held out her arms. Her loose gown was of pale blue, unbelted, with long yellow panels floating from the shoulders like misty wings. She wore a golden circlet about her neck and a golden diadem on her blonde hair. The hair hung nearly to her waist and so, if Richard's eyes didn't deceive him, did her incredibly pendulous breasts beneath the gossamer fabric.

She stood nearly half a meter taller than he did. Looking down with unhuman glowing eyes, she said, "Come closer."

He felt the room turn. And the eyes shone more brilliantly and soft skin caressed him until he was drawn into an abyss of joy so intense that it must destroy him. She cried, "Can you? Can you?"

He tried. And he could not.

The sweet breath of light turned into a whirlwind then, screeching and cursing and tearing at him, not at his body but at something cringing apologetically behind his eyes, worthless and deserving to be punished. Torn out, held up to ridicule, flung down and trodden upon, hammered by blasts of hatred, the shapeless thing shrank into a smaller and smaller mass until it was a blot of utter insignificance, finally vanishing in the white blaze of pain.

Richard woke.

A man in a blue tunic knelt at his feet, fumbling with his ankles. Richard was clamped into a heavy chair, seated in a small room with walls of unadorned gray limestone blocks. The Lady Epone was standing in front of him, her eyes flat and jade-colored, her mouth curved in a smile of contempt.

"He's ready, Lady."

"Thank you, Jean-Paul. The headpiece, if you please."

The man brought a simple silver coronet with five points and placed it on Richard's head. Epone turned to a construction on a table beside the chair, which Richard had mistaken for some kind of elaborate jeweled metallic sculpture. The apparatus glowed faintly in its crystalline parts, the multicolored lights waxing and waning in what was evidently some malfunction. Epone gave the largest prism, a pinkish thing the size of a fist, an impatient flick with thumb and forefinger.

"Ah, bah! Will nothing function in this cursed place? There!
Now we will begin."

She folded her arms and inclined her gaze on Richard. "What
is your given name?"

"Go to hell," he muttered.

A tremendous throb of agony seemed to lift the top of his
skull.

"Please speak only to answer my questions. Obey my orders
at once. Do you understand?"

Sagging against the chair clamps, he whispered, "Yes."

"What is your given name?"

"Richard."

"Close your eyes, Richard. Without speaking, I wish you
to send out the word *help*."

Sweet Jesus, that was an easy one! Help!

A man's voice said, "Minus six farspeak."

"Open your eyes, Richard," commanded Epone. "Now I
want you to listen carefully. Here is a dagger." She drew a
silver blade from somewhere within her draperies and held it
toward him on both open hands. The palms had only a few
faint lines in their milky softness. "Force me to plunge the
dagger into my heart, Richard. Revenge yourself on me. Destroy me by my own hand. Kill me, Richard."

He tried! He willed the death of the monstrous bitch. He
tried.

"Minus two point five coerce," said the minion standing
behind the chair.

Epone said, "Concentrate on what I am saying to you, Richard. Your life and your future here in Exile depend upon what
you do in this room." She cast the dagger down onto the table,
less than a meter away from his pinioned right arm. "Make the
knife rise up, Richard. Send it at me! Drive it into my eyes!
Do it, Richard!"

There was a terrible eagerness in her tone this time, and he
tried desperately to oblige her. He knew now what was happening. They were testing him for latent metafunctions—this
one psychokinesis. But he could have told them—

"Minus seven PK."

She leaned close to him, fragrant, lovely. "Burn me, Richard. Bring up flames from your mind and let them blacken and

cook and turn to ash this body that you will never know because you are not a man but a poor worm without sex or sensibility. Burn me!"

But he was the one who burned. Tears coursed down his cheeks and caught in his mustache. He tried to spit at her but his mouth was clotted and his tongue swollen. He twisted his head because his eyes would not close to shut out the blue and primrose coolness of her cruelty.

"Plus two point five create."

"Interesting, but not good enough, of course. Rest for a moment now, Richard. Think of your companions upstairs. One by one they will come to this room as so many others have come, and I will get to know them as I know you. And some will serve the Tanu in this way and others in that, but all *will* serve, save a few blessed ones who will find that the gate into Exile is the door into paradise after all . . . You have one last chance. Come into my mind. Feel me. Probe me, take me to bits and reassemble me in a more compliant image." She bent closer and closer toward him until the flawless skin of her face was only a few handsbreadth from his own. No pores, no creases on that face. Only pinpoint pupils in the nephrite eyes. But beauty! Vile and tantalizing beauty of incredible age.

Richard strained against the clamps of the chair. His mind screamed.

I hate you and violate you and diminish you and cover you with excrement! And I call you *dead*! I call you *rotted*! I call you writhing in pain everlasting, stretched on the rack of the superficies until the exhalation of the universe dies and space falls in upon itself . . .

"Minus one redact."

Richard fell forward. The coronet dropped from his head to strike the stone flags with a bell tone of finality.

"You've failed again, Richard," Epone said in a bored voice. "Inventory his possessions, Jean-Paul. Then put him in with the others for the northern caravan to Finiah."

3

ELIZABETH ORME WAS SO DAZED BY THE SHOCK OF THE translation that she scarcely felt the guiding hands that urged her up the pathway toward the castle. Someone relieved her of her pack and she was glad. The soothing mumble of the guide's voice carried her back to another time of pain and fear long ago. She had felt herself awakening in a cushioning womb of warm solution where she had been regenerating for nine months in a web of tubes and wires and monitoring devices. Her eyes blinded, her skin deprived of tactile sensation by the long immersion in amniotic fluid, she could nevertheless hear a gentle human voice that calmed her fear, told her she was whole again and shortly to be freed.

"Lawrence?" she whimpered. "Are you all right?"

"Come along now, missy. Just come along. You're safe now and you're among friends. We're all going up to Castle Gateway and you'll be able to relax there. Just keep on walking like a good girl."

Strange howls of maddened animals. Open the eyes in horror and shut them again. *Where is this place?*

"Castle Gateway, in the world you call Exile. Take it easy, missy. The amphicyons can't get us. Just up these stairs now and we'll have you lying down for a nice rest. Here we go."

Opening doors and a small room with—what? Hands were pressing her to sit down, to lie down. Someone lifted her feet and arranged a pillow under her head.

Don't go away! Don't leave me here alone!

"I'll be back in just a few minutes with the healer, missy. We won't let anything happen to *you*, bank on that! You're a very special lady. Relax now while I get somebody to help you. Washroom behind that curtain."

When the door closed she lay motionless until a surge of nausea rose in her gorge. Struggling up, she lurched into the washroom and vomited into the basin. An excruciating pain lanced her brain and she nearly collapsed. Leaning against the whitened stone wall, she gasped for breath. The nausea receded and so, more slowly, did the agony in her head. She became aware of someone else entering the room, two persons speaking, arms supporting her, the rim of a thick cup pressed to her lips.

I don't want anything.

"Drink this, Elizabeth. It will help you."

Open. Swallow. There. Good. Now sit again.

A voice, deep and honey-rich. "Thank you, Kosta. I'll take care of her now. You may leave us."

"Yes, Lord." Sound of door closing.

Elizabeth clutched the arms of her chair, waiting for the pain to come back. When it didn't, she let herself relax and slowly opened her eyes. She was sitting at a low table that held a few dishes of food and drink. Across from her, standing beside a high window, was an extraordinary man. He was robed in white and scarlet and wore a heavy belt of linked squares of gold set with red and milk-white gemstones. Around his neck was a golden torc, thick twisted strands with an ornamented catch in front. His fingers, holding a stoneware cup with the medicine, were oddly long, with prominent joints. She wondered vaguely how he had managed to slip on the many rings that gleamed in the morning sunlight. The man had blond shoulder-length hair cut in a fringe above his eyes, which were very pale blue, seemingly without pupils, and sunken deep into bony orbits. His face was beautiful despite the fine webwork of lines at the corners of his smiling mouth.

He was nearly two and a half meters tall.

Oh, God. Who are you? What is this place? I thought I was going back in time to Pliocene Earth. But this is not . . . this can't be . . .

"Oh, but it is." His voice, with a musical lilt, was kind. "My name is Creyn. You are indeed in the time-epoch known as Pliocene and on the planet Earth—which some call Exile and others the Many-Colored Land. You've been disoriented by your passage through the time-portal—perhaps more seriously than the rest of your companions. But that's understandable. I've given you a mild strengthening draft that will restore you. In a few minutes, if you please, we'll talk. Your friends are being interviewed now by people of our staff who welcome all new arrivals. They're resting in rooms like this one, having a bit of food and drink and asking questions that we're doing our best to answer. The guardians of the gate alerted me to your distress. They were also able to perceive that you are a most unusual traveler, which is why I am interviewing you myself . . ."

Elizabeth had closed her eyes again as the man droned easily on. Peace and relief permeated her mind. So there really is a Land of Exile! And I've really managed to come into it safely. Now I can forget what I've lost. I can build a new life.

She opened her eyes wide. The tall man's smile had become ironic.

"Your life will certainly be new," he agreed. "But what is lost?"

You . . . can hear me.

Yes.

She leaped to her feet, drew breath, cried out in a shattering scream. Vocalization of ecstasy. Life found restored renewed. Gratitude.

Softly! she told herself. Draw back from the pinnacle. Gently. After that first mad interior leap, go cautiously. Reach out at the simplest possible mode, at wide wide focus, for you are weak with rebirth.

I/we rejoice with you Elizabeth.

Creyn. You permit shallowquestion?

Shrug.

Elizabeth slipped clumsily beneath the surface of his smile, where a neat reticulation of data waited passively for her study. But the deeper layers were shielded by warning hardness. She snatched up the proffered information and got out quickly. Her throat had gone dry and her heart pounded with the shock of the assimilation. Gently! Gently. Two mental blows within a few minutes on her raw tenderness. Suspend heal allow self-redaction. He cannot read deeply or far. But coerce yes. Redact yes moststrongly. Other abilities? No data.

She spoke out loud at last in a calm voice. "Creyn, you are not a human being and you are not a true operant metapsychic. These two things contradict my experience, so that I am confused. In the world I come from, only persons with operant metapsychic powers are able to communicate in purely mental speech. And only six races in all our galaxy possess the genes for metability. You belong to none of them. May I probe deeper to learn more about you?"

"I regret that I cannot permit it at this time. Later there will be suitable opportunities for us to . . . get to know one another."

"Are there many of your people here?"

"A sufficient number."

In the split second that he replied she hurled a redactive deep-probe with all her strength right between his pale-blue eyes. It bounced and shattered. She had to cry out with the violence of the rebound, and the man named Creyn laughed.

Elizabeth. That was most impolite. And it won't work.

Shame. "It was an impulse, a social error I apologize for. In our world, no metapsychic would dream of probing without invitation unless placed in a threat situation. I don't know what came over me."

"You've been discomposed by the portal."

Wonderful dreadful pitiless one-way portal! "It's more than that," she said, sinking back into the chair. She did a swift tour of her mental defenses. Up and fairly secure, rawness crusting over, familiar patterns reasserting.

"Back on the other side," she said, "I suffered a serious brain injury. My metafunctions were obliterated in the regeneration process. It was thought that the loss was permanent. Otherwise"—she gave it mental underlining—"I never would have been allowed to cross into Exile. Nor would I have wanted to come."

We are most fortunate. Welcome from allTanu.

"You've had no other operant metas come through?"

"A group of nearly one hundred arrived abruptly some twenty-seven years ago. I'm sorry to say they were unable to adapt to our local conditions." *Cautioncaution. Wallup.*

Elizabeth nodded. "They would have been fugitive rebels. It was a sad time for our Galactic Milieu . . . Are all of them dead, then? Am I the only operant in Exile?"

Perhaps not for long.

She braced herself on the table, rose and walked closer to him. His amiable expression changed. "It is not our custom to enter lightly into another's private space. I request you in courtesy to withdraw."

Polite regret. "I simply wanted to look at your golden collar. Would you take it off so that I can examine it? It seems to be a remarkable piece of craftsmanship."

Horrors! "I'm sorry, Elizabeth. The golden torc bears a weight of religious symbolism among us. We wear it as long as we live."

"I think I understand." She began to smile.

PROBE.

Elizabeth laughed aloud. *Now you must apologize Creyn!*

Chagrin unease. Regrets Elizabeth. You will take some getting used to.

She turned away. "What will become of me?"

"You'll go to our capital city, rich Muriah on the White Silver Plain. It lies in the south of this Many-Colored Land. We'll have a wonderful welcome for you there among the Tanu, Elizabeth."

She spun around and met his eyes. "Those that you rule. Will they welcome me, too?"

Caution. "They will love you as they love us. Try to suspend judgment on us until you have all of the data. I know that there are aspects of your situation that trouble you now. But have patience. You are in no danger."

"What happens to my friends? The people who came through the time-portal with me?"

"Some of them will be coming to the capital. Others have already indicated that they prefer to go elsewhere. We'll find good places for all of them. They'll be happy."

Happy ruled? Unfree?

"We do rule, Elizabeth, but kindly. You'll see. Don't judge until you see what we've done with this world. It was nothing, and we've transformed it—just this little corner—into something marvelous."

It was too much . . . her head began to throb again and vertigo came. She dropped back into the soft cushions of the bench. "Where—where did you come from? I know every sentient race in our Milieu six million years into the future—coadunate and non. There is no people resembling you—except for humans. And I'm certain you're not of our genus. Your mental pattern is different."

Differences similarities parallels starwhirlpools in countless numbers to the uttermost limit.

"I see. No one in my future time has managed intergalactic travel. We have not yet been able to supersede the pain barrier of the necessary translation. It rises geometrically with the increase in distance."

Mitigant.

"How interesting. If it were only possible to transmit information about that back through the portal."

"We can discuss this later, Elizabeth. In the capital. There are other possibilities even more intriguing that will be made clear to you in Muriah." Distraction. He fingered his gold necklet and at once there was a tapping on the door. A nervous little man in blue stepped into the room and saluted Creyn by placing his fingers to his forehead. The Tanu gave a regal gesture of acknowledgment.

"Elizabeth, this is Tully, one of our trusted interviewers. He's been talking to your companions, discussing their plans for the future and answering their questions."

"Have all of them recovered from the passage?" she asked. "I'd like to see them. Talk to them."

"In good time, Lady," said Tully. "All of your friends are safe and in good hands. You mustn't worry. Some of them will be going south with you, while others have chosen to travel to another city in the north. They feel their talents will be appreciated more up there. You'll be interested to know that caravans will be leaving here this very evening, going in both directions."

"I see." But did she? Her thoughts were muddled again. She threw a tentative query at Creyn, which he parried neatly.

Trust in me Elizabeth. All will be well.

She turned back to the little interviewer. "I want to be sure of saying goodbye to those of my friends who are going north."

"Certainly, Lady. It will be arranged." The little man put a hand to his necklet and Elizabeth looked at it closely. It seemed identical to the one worn by Creyn except for the dark color of the metal.

Creyn. I want to put thisone to the question.

Disdain. He is under ourprotection. Would you distress him in prematureattempts to satisfy curiosity? Questioning would distress him verymuch. Perhaps permanent harm. He has little data. But do asyouwish with him.

"Thank you for telling me about my friends, Tully," she said in a gentle tone.

The man in blue looked relieved. "Then I'll just run along to the next interview, shall I? I imagine Lord Creyn has already answered all of your questions about—um—*general* matters."

"Not quite all." She reached for pitcher and glass and poured some of the cold drink. "But I expect he will, in time."

4

NO SOONER HAD THE BLUE-CLAD INTERROGATOR LEFT THE room than Aiken Drum was testing the wooden door, discovering that it was locked, and doing something about it.

He used the tough glassy needle of a leatherworking fid to probe the slot where the brass latchbar came through until he was able to lift a concealed pawl that was preventing the notched bar from moving. Opening the door carefully, he saw the device on the other side that activated the locking mechanism. A tiny stone from the floor served to jam it.

He pulled the door shut and went creeping down the hallway, passing other closed rooms where he assumed his comrades from Group Green were incarcerated. He wouldn't let them out yet; not until he looked things over to see how he might take advantage of this strange situation. There was something powerful as well as peculiar at work here in the Pliocene, and it was obvious that it would take more than the simple-minded schemes of Stein and Richard to con the local yokels.

. . . Look out!

He darted into one of the deep window bays that overlooked the castle's inner courtyard. Whipping out his chameleon poncho, he hunkered down in the shadows and tried to blend inconspicuously into the stone floor.

Four sturdy guardians, led by a man in blue, went dashing down the corridor in the direction from which Aiken had come. They never looked in his direction and in a moment the reason became apparent.

There was a roar of rage in the distance and a muffled crash. Heavy blows began to ring against the inner side of one of the reception room doors. Aiken peered from his alcove in time to see the group of castle lackeys cringe away from the first door at the head of the stairway. Even from his viewpoint more than ten meters away, Aiken could see the slabs of thick oak tremble from the force of rhythmic smashes.

The guardian in blue paused outside the door and fingered his torc in an agony of apprehension. The four other men gaped as their leader screeched, "You let him keep the iron axe? You stupid *turds*!"

"But, Master Tully, we put enough soporific in his beer to stun a mastodon!"

"But not enough to even slow down this Viking maniac, that's obvious!" Tully hissed. The door vibrated with a particularly mighty blow and the point of Stein's axe blade showed momentarily through broken wood before it was pulled back. "He'll be out of there in minutes! Salim, run for Lord Creyn. We'll need a *very* large gray torc. Alert Castellan Pitkin and the security squad, too. Kelolo, bring more guardians with a net. And tell Fritz to close the portcullis in case he gets away down the stairway. Hurry! If we can net this bastard as he breaks through we might just *salvage* this crock of shit!"

The two guardians raced off in opposite directions. Aiken shrank back into the shadows. Good old Steinie. Somehow he'd seen through the façade of phony goodwill and decided to take direct action. Drugged beer! Good God—suppose the coffee had been doped, too? He hadn't taken more than half a cup, though. And he'd tried to play the game their way when Tully interviewed him. He felt certain he had put himself over as a potentially useful but harmless little clown-handyman. Maybe they only drugged the big, dangerous-looking types.

"Hurry, hurry, hurry *up*, you fools!" Tully wailed. "He's breaking out!"

This time Aiken didn't dare look. But he heard a triumphant bellow and a squawk of splintering wood.

"I'll teach you to lock me in!" Stein's voice called out.

"Wait till I get my hands on that little white-bellied prick who juiced my beer! *Yah! Yah! Yah!*"

A very tall figure dressed in scarlet and white went striding past Aiken's refuge, trailed by a jangling squad of warriors, all human, wearing domed kettle-helmets and heavy coats of yellowish scale-armor.

"Lord Creyn!" came Tully's voice. "I've sent for the net and more men . . . Oh, thank Tana! They're here!"

Lying flat on the floor under the poncho, Aiken wormed over the stones until he had a good view down the corridor. Stein, yelling with each blow of the axe, had enlarged the hole in the door until it was nearly large enough to permit his escape. The people from the castle had regained their discipline with the coming of Creyn and stood waiting.

Six armored men had a strong net deployed on the floor. Two more soldiers poised on either side of the disintegrating door with clubs as thick as a man's arm and studded with rounded metal knobs. The unarmed guardians fell back in a protective line before the towering form of Creyn.

"Hee-*yah*!" cried Stein, kicking the last obstructing pieces of oak from the opening. His horned Viking helmet popped out for an eyeblink and then withdrew for the charge.

He emerged with a leap that carried him nearly to the opposite side of the broad corridor, beyond reach of the net and into the midst of the guardians gathered about their awesome master. Men in white flung themselves at the berserker with despairing screams. Stein hewed at them, both hands swinging the battle-axe in short vicious arcs that sheared through flesh and bone and sent pathetic severed things bouncing from walls and along the floor, fountaining crimson as they rolled. The armored soldiers clubbed at him without effect and tried to seize his arms while he kept chopping at the barrier of living and dead men separating him from Creyn. In some way, Stein knew very well who his principle enemy was.

"I'll get you!" the Viking roared.

Creyn's robes showed scarcely any white now. He stood impassively against the wall, fingering the golden ring about his throat. One soldier finally snatched the horned helmet from Stein's head while another swung a club, catching the giant at the back of the neck with a force that would have crushed the bones of a less heroic vertebral column. For three long seconds, the Viking stood like a grotesque statue, his axe raised within easy striking distance of Creyn's head. Then Stein's fingers loosened. The weapon went tumbling down behind his back. His knees bent slowly and his head fell onto his breast as the net was belatedly flung over him.

One of the warriors drew a short bronze sword and rushed forward, eyes glittering. Before he could strike, he halted as though paralyzed. Another soldier pried the blade from his hand.

"No one is to harm this one," the Tanu overlord said. He moved through the shambles until he could look down upon Stein's unconscious body. Kneeling on the gory flags, Creyn held out his hand for the short sword and used it to cut the meshes covering Stein's head. Then he took a gray metal torc from a large pouch at his belt and fitted it about the fallen rock driller's neck.

"He is harmless now. You may remove the net. Take him to a fresh reception room and clean him up so that I may treat his wounds. He'll be most welcome in the capital."

Rising, Creyn beckoned for a pair of soldiers to accompany him. All three of them made bloody footprints as they walked toward Aiken's hiding place, slowed, and stopped.

"Come out," Creyn said.

"Oh, well!" Aiken gave him a grin as he scrambled to his feet. He flourished his hat in a mock salute and bowed from the waist. Before he realized what was happening, Creyn bent down and snapped something around his neck.

Oh, Christ, Aiken thought. Not me, too!

You are a completely different breed of cat, Aiken Drum, and bound for more sophisticated amusements than your muscular friend.

Aiken craned his head to look into the wintry eyes far above him. The Tanu's hair that had been so sleek and shining was clotted now with the blood of men who had died defending him—died unwillingly, from the sound of their hopeless screams, freed from the symbol and source of their bondage only at the moment that Stein's blade severed their heads from their bodies.

"I suppose you can do what you like with us, once you've put on these fewkin' dog collars," Aiken said bitterly, touching the thing about his own throat. It was warm. For one fraction of a second he felt a flash of pleasure born in his loins go racing along his nerves like lightning through wires before it exited his body through tingling fingers and toes.

What the *hell*!

Did you like that? It's only a sample of what we can give you. But our greatest gift will be the fulfillment of your own potential, freeing you even as you serve us.

The way these poor sods served? Headless trunks piled limbs awash in blood?

Amusement. Your own torc is silver and not gray. As befits a latent metapsychic made operant. You're going to enjoy the Pliocene very much, my lad.

"Well, I'll be damned!" Aiken exclaimed aloud. Delight. *Delight. DELIGHT!* "How many of the functions am I strong in?"

Find out for yourself.

A built-in master control mechanism in the collar for you guys I presume.

What do you think?

Aiken gave a crooked grin. "Better than gray, less than gold. Tell you what. I'll take it!" He folded his poncho carefully and stowed it back into his lumbar pouch. "What next, Chief?"

"We'll let you wait in a fresh reception room for now. One with a more effective lock. In a few hours, you'll be leaving for our capital city, Muriah. Don't be apprehensive. Life here in Exile can be very pleasant."

As long as I know who's boss?

Affirm.

The guards hustled Aiken Drum through a door. He called over his shoulder, "Have one of your flunkies bring me a good stiff drink, will you, Chief? All this fighting raises a terrible thirst in a man."

Creyn had to laugh. "It will be done." Then the guards slammed the door and barred it.

5

AMERIE HAD HEARD THE SOUNDS OF FIGHTING IN THE CORRIDOR outside and pressed her ear to the boards of the locked door to confirm her suspicions. It had to be Stein or Felice. Could one of them have been driven insane by the shock of the translation? Or was there a good reason for the violent outburst?

She tore open her backpack and rummaged in the Small-holder Unit for the small plass envelope holding the cord-saw. Dragging one of the benches over to the window, she tucked her skirts into her rope belt and jumped up.

Cut halfway through the upper bars of the brass grille on the inside! Cut all of the way through the bottom bars, then lever the whole thing outward with the top of another bench after I smash it apart! I could unbraid the rug and make a rope out of the wool—but wait! The decamole bridge sections would work—two for a ladder and the third to cross over the area with those damn bear-dogs—

"Oh, Sister. What are you *doing*?"

She whirled around, hampered by both index fingers being engaged in the rings of the cord-saw. Tully and a burly guardian stood at the open door. The little interviewer's tunic was covered with dark stains.

"Please come down, Sister. What a dreadfully reckless thing

to think of! And all so unnecessary. Believe me, you are in no danger."

Amerie locked eyes with him, then stepped down, resigned. The big guardian held out his hand for the saw and she gave it to him without a word. He tucked it into one of the pockets of her pack and said, "I'll carry this for you, Sister."

Tully said, "We are having to expedite our usual interview program because of a most regrettable accident. So if you will accompany Shubash and me—"

"I heard sounds of fighting," she said. "Who was hurt? Was it Felice?" She strode to the open door and looked out into the corridor. "Merciful God!"

Guardians had removed the dead and injured, and cleanup crews were sluicing the walls and floor with big buckets of water; but traces of mayhem were still sickeningly apparent.

"What have you done?" Amerie cried.

"The blood is that of our own people." Tully was somber. "It was shed by your companion, Stein. He, by the way, is unhurt except for bruises. But five of our men are dead and seven others seriously injured."

"Oh, Lord. How did it happen?"

"I'm sorry to say that Stein went berserk. It must have been a delayed reaction to the temporal translation. Passage through the time-portal sometimes triggers deeply buried psychic explosives. We try to protect both the travelers and ourselves by confining new arrivals to these reception rooms for a while during the recovery period—which is why *your* door was locked."

"I'm sorry about your people," she told him with sincere regret. "Steinie is—strange—but a dear man when you get to know him. What will happen to him now?"

Tully fingered his gray collar. "We who guard the gateway have our duty and at times it is a heavy one. Your friend has received treatment that should preclude another attack. He won't be punished any more than a sick man is punished for his illness . . . Now, Sister, we must hurry you along to the next phase of our interview. The Lady Epone requires your assistance."

They passed through the dreadful hallway and down the stairs to a small office on the other side of the barbican. Felice

Landry was waiting alone, seated in an ordinary cushioned chair beside a table that held a metal sculpture all studded with jewels. The two men conducted Amerie inside and withdrew, closing the door.

"Felice! Stein has—"

"I know," the athlete interrupted in a whisper. She put one gloved finger to her lips, then sat silent, holding her emerald-plumed leather helmet demurely in her lap. With her hair standing out from her head and her enormous brown eyes wide, she looked like a pretty child waiting to be forced onstage for some sinister theatrical performance.

The door opened and Epone glided in. Amerie stared at the immensely tall figure in astonishment.

"Another sentient race?" the nun blurted out. "Here?"

Epone inclined her majestic head. "I will explain it to you shortly, Sister. Everything will be clarified in good time. For now, I require your assistance in gaining the confidence of your young companion for a simple test of mental abilities." She picked up a silver coronet from the table and approached Felice with it.

"No! No! I told you, I won't let you!" the girl shrieked. "And if you try to force me, it won't register. I know all about these rotten mind tricks!"

Epone appealed to Amerie. "Her fears are irrational. All of the newly arrived timefarers consent to the test for latent met-abilities. If we discover that you possess them, we have the technology to bring them up to operancy so that you and all of the community may enjoy their benefits."

"You want to *probe* me," Felice spat out.

"Certainly not. The test is a simple calibration."

Amerie suggested, "Perhaps if you tested me first. I'm quite sure that my own MP latencies are minimal. But it would probably reassure Felice if she could see just what happens in the test."

"An excellent idea," Epone said, smiling.

Amerie took Felice's hand and raised her from the chair. She could feel the trembling fingers even through the leather glove, but the emotion hidden in those unfathomable eyes was something much different from fear. The nun spoke soothingly. "Stand there, Felice. You can watch while I go through this, and then if the idea still distresses you, I'm sure this lady will respect your personal convictions." She turned to Epone. "Won't you?"

"I assure you, I mean you no harm," the Tanu woman replied. "And as Felice has said, the test will not give proper results unless the subject cooperates. Please be seated, Sister."

Amerie unfastened the pin that held her black veil, then slipped off the soft white wimple that had covered her hair. Epone set the silver coronet on the nun's brown curls.

"First we will test the farsensing function. If you would, Sister, wtihout speaking, attempt to tell me *greetings*."

Amerie squeezed her eyes shut. One point of the coronet acquired a faint violet spark.

"Minus seven. Very weak. Now for the coercive faculty. Sister, exert all of your willpower upon me. Force me to close my eyes."

Amerie glowered in concentration. Another point of the coronet grew a somewhat more intense bluish spark.

"Minus three. Stronger, but still far below the potentially useful range. Now let us test psychokinesis. Try very hard, Sister. Levitate yourself in your chair just one centimeter above the floor."

The resultant rosy-gold spark was hardly visible and the chair stayed firmly on the flagstones.

"Ah, a pity. Minus eight. Relax now, Sister. In testing the creative function, we will ask you to spin an illusion for us. Close your eyes and visualize a common object—perhaps your shoe!—suspended in midair before you. *Will* this object to appear before us. Try hard!"

A greenish spark like a miniature star. And—was it really there?—the faintest phantasm of a hiking boot.

"Do you see, Felice?" the Tanu exclaimed. "Plus three point five!"

Amerie's eyes popped open and the illusion vanished. "Do you mean I actually did it?"

"The coronet artificially enhances your natural creativity, converting it from latent to operant. Unfortunately, your psychic potential in the faculty is so low as to be virtually useless, even with maximum gain."

"It figures," said the nun. "Veni creator spiritus. Don't call me, I'll call you."

"There is one more test, for the MP function that is to us

most important of all." Epone manipulated the crystalline device, which had begun to flicker. When the glow in the jewels had steadied, she said, "Look into my eyes, Sister. Look beneath them, into my mind if you are able to. Can you perceive what is hidden there? Can you analyze it? Collate its scattered bits back to coherency? Heal its wounds and scars and voids of pain? Try. Try!"

Oh, poor one. You want to let me, don't you? But . . . strong, too strong. Looking out at me beating on transparent walls so strong and now darkening darkening. Black.

A red spark had flared for a brief moment, a microscopic nova. It dimmed to near invisibility. Epone sighed.

"Minus seven ultimate redact. I would have given much— but enough." She removed the coronet and turned to Felice with a kindly expression. "Will you permit me to test you now, child?"

Felice whispered, "I can't. Please don't make me do it."

"We can wait until later, in Finiah," Epone said. "Very likely you are a normal human woman, as your friend is. But even for you, without metafaculties, we can offer a world of happiness and fulfillment. All women enjoy a privileged position in the Many-Colored Land because so few pass through the time-portal. You will be cherished."

Amerie paused in the act of restoring her headdress and said, "You should know from a study of our customs that some of our priests are consecrated virgins. I'm one. And Felice is not heterosexually oriented."

Epone said, "That is a pity. But given time, you will adjust to the new status and be happy."

Felice stepped forward and spoke very quietly. "Do you mean to tell us that women are sexually subservient to men here in Exile?"

Epone's lips curved upward. "What is subservience and what is fulfillment? It is feminine nature to be the vessel yearning to be filled, to be the nurturer and sustainer, to spend the self in giving care to the beloved other. When that destiny is denied, there can only be a void, weeping and rage . . . as I and so many other women of my race know only too well. We of the Tanu came here long ago from a galaxy at the farthest limits of Earth's visibility, exiles driven forth because we refused to modify our lifestyle according to principles abhorrent to us. In many ways, this planet has been an ideal refuge. But its atmosphere fails to screen out certain particles that are detrimental to our reproductive capacity. Tanu women produce healthy children rarely and with great difficulty. Nevertheless we are vowed to racial survival. We prayed through the hopeless centuries and at length Mother Tana answered us."

A dawning realization came to Amerie. Felice showed no emotion. The nun said, "All of the human women going through the time-gate have been sterilized."

"By reversible salpingotomy," said the serene exotic.

Amerie sprang to her feet. "Even if you undo it, the genetics—"

"—are compatible. Our Ship, who brought us here (blessed be its memory), chose this galaxy and this world for the perfect compatibility of the germ plasm. It was expected that aeons would have to ensue before we achieved full reproductive potential, even using the native life-form you call ramapithecine as a nurturer of the zygote. But we live so very long! And we have such power! So we endured until the miracle occurred and the time-portal opened and began sending you to us. Sister, you and Felice are young and healthy. You will cooperate, as others of your sex have done, because the rewards are great and the punishments insupportable."

"Fuck you!" said the nun.

Epone walked to the door. "The interview is at an end. You will both prepare for the caravan journey to Finiah. It is a beautiful city on the Proto-Rhine, near the site of your future Freiburg. Humans of goodwill live happily there, served by our good little ramas so that they are relieved of all drudgery. You will learn contentment, believe me." She went out and softly closed the door.

Amerie turned to Felice. "The bastards! The rotten bastards!"

"Don't worry, Amerie," said the athlete. "She didn't test me. *That's* the important thing. I kept smearing pathetic whinings over my thoughts all of the time that she was near me, so if she could read me at all, she probably believes I'm nothing but a poor little leather gal."

"What are you going to do? Try to escape?"

Felice's dark eyes glowed and she laughed out loud. "More. I'm going to take 'em. The whole goddamned lot."

6

THERE WERE BENCHES UNDER THE TREES OF THE WALLED COMpound, but Claude Majewski chose to sit on the pavement in the shade of the animal-pen partition where he could watch the living-fossil beasts and brood. He turned the carved Zakopane box over and over in his big hands.

A fine end to your frivolity, Old Man. Sold down the river in your one hundred and thirty-third year! And all because of a crazy whimsical gesture. Oh, you Polacks always were romantic fools!

Is that why you loved me, Black Girl?

The really humiliating aspect was that it had taken Claude so long to figure the thing out. Didn't he welcome the first friendly contact, the attractive sitting room with the food (and the john), all nicely calculated to soothe the frightened old poop after the stress of translation? Wasn't Tully genial and harmless, drawing him out and flattering him and dishing the codswallop about the great life of peace and happiness they would all enjoy in Exile? (All right, Tully *had* overdone it just a little.) And the first sight of Epone had all but stupefied him, the unexpected presence of an exotic on Pliocene Earth numbing his natural prudence while she measured him, found him wanting, and dismissed him.

Even when the armed guards led him politely across the courtyard he had been docile as a lamb . . . until the last minute when they took away his pack, opened the gate, and pushed him into the people pen.

"Easy does it, traveler," one guard had said. "You'll get your pack back later if you behave yourself. Make trouble, and we have the means to subdue you. Try to escape and you join the bear-dogs for dinner."

Claude had stood there with his mouth open until a sane-looking fellow prisoner in Alpine climbing kit came over and led him into the shade. After an hour or so, Claude's pack was returned by a guard. Any equipment that might have aided in escape had been removed. He was told that the vitredur woodworking tools would be returned to him when he was "safe" in Finiah.

After the first shock had passed off, Claude explored the people pen. It was actually a large and well-shaded yard with ornamental walls of pierced stonework more than three meters high, patrolled by guards. An indoor extension led to a fairly comfortable dormitory and a washroom. The compound held eight women and thirty-three men. Claude recognized most of them from having watched their early morning march through the auberge gardens to the Guderian cottage. They represented approximately one week's bag of timefarers, with the missing ones presumed to have been sorted out by Epone's test and shunted to some alternate destiny.

Claude soon discovered that the only one of his comrades from Group Green in the pen was Richard. He lay in an ominous sleep on one of the dormitory bunks. He would not awaken when the old man shook him by the shoulder.

"We've a few others like him," said the Alpine climber. His face was long, weathered, and finely wrinkled with the indeterminate middle-aged look of decaying rejuvenation. He had humorous gray eyes and ash-colored hair beneath his Tyrolean hat. "Some people just seem to drop out of it, poor devils. Still, they're better off than the lizzy who hanged himself day before yesterday. You lot today are the last of the week's consignment. Tonight we'll move out. Just be glad you haven't had to stick it out here for six days like some of us."

"Did any try to escape?" Claude asked.

"A few before I came. A Cossack named Prischchepa from my group. Three Polynesians yesterday. The bear-dogs even ate their feathered cloaks. Pity. Do you like recorder music? I feel like a bit of Purcell. Name's Basil Wimborne, by the way."

He sat down on a vacant bunk, took out a wooden flute, and began to play a plaintive melody. The old man recalled that Bryan had often whistled snatches of it. Claude listened for a few minutes, then wandered back outside.

Other time-travelers were reacting to their imprisonment according to their individual psychology. An aging artist bent over a sketch pad. Side by side under a tree sat a young couple dressed as Yankee pioneers, caressing one another in oblivious passion. Five Gypsy men argued conspiratorially and practiced close-combat lunges with invisible knives. A perspiring middle-aged male in a rabbit-trimmed toga and kidskin domino kept demanding that the guards give him back his discipline. Two Japanese ronin, sans swords but otherwise attired in handsome fourteenth-century armor, were playing goban with a decamole board. A lovely woman veiled in rainbow chiffon resolved her tensions in dance; the guards outside had to keep discouraging her from climbing up the walls and leaping into space like a billowy butterfly, crying, "Paris—adieu!" In a shady spot sat an Australoid black man in a crisp white shirt, riding breeches, and elastic-sided boots; the four tiny speakers of his music library were arranged about him, endlessly alternating "Der Erlkönig" with an antique cut of Will Bradley's "Celery Stalks at Midnight." A fellow dressed in jester's motley juggled three silver balls with persistent lack of skill before an audience of an elderly woman and her Shih-Tzu puppy, which never tired of chasing the balls. Perhaps the most pathetic of the prisoners was a tall robust man with a ginger beard and hollow eyes, beautifully accoutered in imitation chainmail and a medieval knight's silken surtout emblazoned with a golden lion. He strode about the compound in a frenzy of agitation, peering through the holes in the wall and crying, "Aslan! Aslan! Where are you now that we need you? Save us from la belle dame sans merci!"

Claude decided that he was up a very shitty creek indeed. For some perverse reason he felt almost pleased with himself.

He picked up a fallen leafy twig and poked it through one

of the ornamental apertures into the adjacent animal corral.

"Here, boy. Here, boy."

One of the creatures on the other side of the wall pricked its tufted, horselike ears and ambled over for a taste. Claude watched it in delight as it first nipped off the leaves with tiny cropping teeth, then champed the woody parts with its strong molars. When the tidbit was swallowed, the animal gave him a look that plainly reproached his lack of generosity, so he got it more leaves.

It was a chalicothere, a member of one of the most peculiar and fascinating families of Cenozoic mammals. Its body was massive and deep-chested, nearly three meters long and with a horselike neck and head that testified to its perissodactyl affinities. Its front legs were somewhat longer than the hind ones and at least twice as stout as those of a draft horse. Instead of terminating in hoofs, the feet bore three toes ending in huge semiretractile claws. The inner ones on the front feet were nearly the size of a human hand, with the others only half as large. The chalicothere's body was clothed in a short hairy coat of bluish gray, dotted with white spots about the withers, flanks, and hindquarters. Its tail was rudimentary, but the creature did boast a fine mane of long black hair, a black streak down the spine, and flashy black featherings at the fetlocks. The intelligent eyes were set a bit farther forward on the skull than those of a horse and were fringed with heavy black lashes that the beast batted fetchingly. It wore a leather bridle and was thoroughly domesticated. The corral held at least sixty of the animals, most of them dapple-gray, with occasional white or sorrel individuals.

The Pliocene sun ascended over the barbican and finally shone directly into the courtyard, driving all but the most hardy prisoners into the relative coolness of the stone dormitory. A surprisingly decent noon meal of bayleaf-seasoned stew, fruit, and wine punch was served. Claude again tried vainly to awaken Richard and finally stowed the pirate's food under his bunk. After lunch most of the prisoners retired for a siesta, but Claude went back outside to pace his digestion into submission and speculate on his fate.

About two hours later, stablehands dressed in gray began toting in large baskets of gnarled tubers and fat roots resembling mangelwurzels. They dumped these into troughs for the animals. While the chalicotheres were feeding, the men mucked out the pen with big twig brooms and wooden shovels, dumped the manure into wheeled carts, and trundled it off toward the corridor leading to the castle's postern gate. Two of the hands stayed behind with a portable pump apparatus, which they immersed in the central fountain. While one man pumped a stirrup, the other unreeled a stiff canvas hose with which he washed the floor of the corral, the excess water draining off into gutters. When the pavement was clean, he turned the spray onto the feeding animals. They uttered whickers and squeals of delight.

The old paleontologist nodded with satisfaction. Water lovers. Root eaters. So chalicotheres *were* denizens of the damp semitropical forest or muddy river bottomlands. And they did use their claws to dig for roots. A minor mystery of paleobiology was solved—for him, at least. But were the prisoners actually going to have to ride such archaic steeds? The beasts wouldn't be as fast as horses, but they looked as though they had a lot of endurance. And their gait—! Claude winced. If one of those creatures cantered with him aboard, his old knees and hip joints were going to shatter like antique Christmas-tree ornaments.

A sound in the shadowed cloister caught his attention. Soldiers were leading two new prisoners to the back door of the compound, which opened into the dormitory. Claude saw a waving green plume and a glimpse of black and white. Felice and Amerie!

He hurried inside and was standing there as the two women were led into the prison. One guard put down their packs, which he had carried, and said in a friendly fashion, "Won't be long to wait now. Better get something to eat from the leftovers on the table over there."

The knight errant came running over to them with a tragic expression. "Is Aslan on his way? Have you seen him, good Sister? Perhaps this warrior-maid is of his entourage! Aslan must come or we be doomed!"

"Oh, piss off," muttered Felice.

Claude took the knight by one mailed elbow and led him to a bunk near the other door. "Stay here and watch for Aslan." The man nodded solemnly and sat down. Somewhere in the dimness, another prisoner was weeping. The Alpinist was playing "Greensleeves" on his recorder.

When Claude returned to his friends, he found Felice rooting in her pack and cursing. "All missing! The arbalest, my skinning knives, the ropes—just about every damn thing I might have used to get us out of here!"

"You might as well forget it," Claude told her. "If you resort to violence, they'll collar you. That fellow playing the flute told me about a prisoner who went bonkers and attacked a mess attendant. Soldiers clubbed him down and put one of those gray metal neck-rings on him. When he stopped screaming and recovered his senses, he was as mild as milk. Couldn't get the collar off, either."

Felice swore more eloquently. "Are they planning to collar us all, then?"

Claude glanced around, but nobody was paying the slightest attention to them. "Evidently not. As nearly as I can judge, the gray collars are a crude type of psychoregulator, probably linked to the golden ones worn by the Lady Epone and other exotics. Not all of the castle personnel wear collars. Soldiers and guardians do, and straw bosses like the worthy Tully. But the stablehands don't have collars, and neither do the mess attendants."

"Not in sensitive enough positions?" suggested the nun.

"Or maybe the hardware is in short supply," Claude said.

Felice frowned. "That could be. It would need a sophisticated technology to manufacture things like that. And so far, this outfit looks damn Mickey Mouse. Did you see how that mind calibrator kept fritzing out? And no running water in those reception rooms."

"They didn't bother to take any of my pharmaceuticals," said Amerie. "The collars must protect the guards from any drugging we might be tempted to try. Handy gadgets. No slave overseer should be without some."

"They may not need to collar people to keep them down," Claude said, grim. He gestured at the dormitory's listless inmates. "Just look at this crew! A few lively ones tried to escape and they were fed to the bear-dogs. I think that most folks falling into a nightmare like this are so traumatized that they just float for a while and hope things won't get worse. The guards are cheerful and spin yarns about the good life waiting

for us. The food's not bad. Wouldn't *you* just take it easy and
see what develops, instead of fighting it?"

"No," said Felice.

Amerie added, "The women's expectations aren't quite so
rosy, Claude." She told him tersely of their interview with
Epone, and of the origins and reproductive predicament of the
exotic race. "So while *you* may be able to live peacefully
building log cabins, Claude, Felice and I are going to be turned
into broodmares."

"Damn them!" whispered the old man. "*Damn* them!" He
stared at his big hands, still strong, but blotched with liver
spots and corded with blue veins. "I wouldn't be worth a fart
in a teacup in any real dustup. What we really need is Stein."

"They took him," Amerie said, and explained how Tully
told her that the Viking had been "treated" to prevent further
trouble. They all knew what that had to mean.

"Are any of the others here?" Felice asked.

"Just Richard," said the old man. "But he's been asleep
ever since I was put in here this morning. I couldn't wake him,
either. Maybe you ought to take a look at him, Amerie."

The nun took her pack and followed Claude to Richard's
bunk. It was surrounded by empty beds for a reason that was
easily apparent. The sleeping man had soiled himself. His arms
were folded tightly over his breast and his knees were drawn
up nearly to his chin.

Amerie lifted one eyelid, then took his pulse. "Jesus, he's
close to catatonic. What could they have done to him?"

She searched in her pack and came up with a minidoser,
which she pressed to Richard's temple. As the bulblet collapsed
and the powerful drug entered the unconscious man's blood-
stream, he gave a faint moan.

"There's a chance this might bring him around if he's not
too far gone," the nun said. "Meanwhile, will you guys help
me clean him up?"

"Right," said Felice, starting to shuck her armor. "His pack's
here. He ought to have other clothes."

"I'll get water," Claude said. He headed for the washroom,
where there was a stone tank supplied by a conduit from the
fountain. He filled a wooden bucket and brought soap and
quantities of rough towels. As he sloshed back between the
bunks, one of the Gypsies eyed him.

"You help your friend, old man. But maybe he's better off the way he is. Useless to them!"

A woman with a hairless head clutched at him. She wore wrinkled yellow robes and her Oriental face was ravaged by scars, an unusual sight. Perhaps they were part of her religious devotion. "We wanted to be free," she croaked. "But these monsters from another galaxy will enslave us. And the worst of it is, they look *human*."

Claude pulled away from her. Trying to ignore other cries and whispers, he made his way to Richard's bed.

"I gave him another shot," Amerie said grimly. "It'll bring him around or kill him. Damn—if only we could give him a sugar drip."

The knight gave a shout. "They're starting to saddle the faerie steeds! We'll soon be on our way to Narnia!"

"See what's going on, Claude," Felice ordered.

He pushed through others who were hurrying outside and managed to get close to the perforated wall nearest the central court. Stablehands were leading pairs of chalicotheres from the corral to ranks of hitching rails across the yard. More servitors brought out piles of tack and started placing pads on the animals' backs. To one side, eight of the beasts were segregated for special treatment, their bronze-studded harness and other equipment marking them as soldiers' mounts.

An amused voice at Claude's shoulder said, "Don't seem to think we'll need much guarding on the trip, do they?" It was Basil, the Alpine hiker, watching the proceedings with interest. "Ah! There's the explanation. Catch the clever modification of the stirrups?"

Bronze chains dangled from them. They were padded with narrow leather sleeves and would probably hang loosely enough about the ankle to be only minimally uncomfortable when fastened.

The saddling took some time and the sun westered behind the castle. It was obvious that they were scheduled for a night march in order to avoid the daytime heat on the savanna. A squad of four troopers led by an officer wearing a short blue cloak came marching to the compound gate and unbarred it. The soldiers were attired in light bronze kettle-helmets and piece-armor, worn over tan shirts and shorts. They were armed with intricately pulleyed compound bows, bronze short swords, and vitredur lances. As the soldiers entered the pen, the prisoners fell back. The officer addressed the crowd in a matter-of-fact voice.

"All you travelers! It's nearly time to move out of here. I'm your caravan leader, Captal Waldemar. We're gonna get to know each other pretty good in the next week or so. I know you've had a hard time, some of you, staying in this hot compound while you waited for the contingent to be complete. But things will be better soon. We're on our way north to the city of Finiah, where you'll be making your home. It's a good place. A lot cooler than here. The journey is about four hundred kilometers and it will take us about six days. We'll go by night for two days here in the hot country, then switch to day travel when we hit the Hercynian Forest.

"Now, you travelers, listen! Don't give me any trouble and you'll get good food at stations along the way. Fuck up and you'll be short-rationed. Make me really unhappy and you won't eat at all. Any of you travelers who think you'd like to escape, just think about the fossil zoo waiting bright-eyed and bushy-tailed for stragglers on foot. We got sabertooth cats like superlions and hyenas the size of grizzly bears. We got wild boars bigger'n oxen that take a human leg off with one bite. We got rhinos and mastodons that'll stomp you to death if they even catch sight of you. And the deinotheriums, the hoe-tusker elephants, they like to use people for cute tug-o'-war games and then dance on the pieces! They only stand four or five meters at the shoulder, by the way. You escape the big buggers and you can get nailed by the small fry. The creeks are full of pythons and crocs. The woods have poisonous spiders with bodies like peaches and fangs like gaboon vipers. You get away from the animals and the Firvulag will track you down and play devil-tunes on your mind until you go mad or die from the horrors.

"It's bad out there, travelers! It's not the pretty Eden world they told you about in A.D. 2110. But nobody has to worry if they stick with the caravan. You're gonna ride those critters that you been looking at in the pen next door. They're chalicotheres, kind of a distant relative of the horse, and we call 'em chalikos. They're smart and they like people, and with those claws they have, nothing messes with 'em much. Be nice to your chaliko. He's transportation and a bodyguard in one package . . .

"Now, in case any of you travelers feel like riding off into the tall timber—forget it. These torcs, these necklets that us soldiers wear, they let us keep complete control of the chalikos. You leave the driving to us. And we'll also have trained amphicyons ranging along the flanks of the caravan. Those beardogs know that any rider who tries to light out is fair meat. So live cool and we'll all have a good ride.

"Right! Now I want you to get your stuff together. You can either transfer your things from packs into saddlebags or just lash your rig behind the cantle of the saddle. I understand two of you have pet animals with you. We'll have pannier baskets that they can ride in. The guy that brought the pregnant goat . . . your animal will have to stay here until the weekly trade and supply caravan brings it on. Most of your proscribed tools and weapons and the bulky stuff taken from you when you first arrived will be carried on our pack animals. You may get most of the things back eventually, if you behave.

"Everything clear? Right! I want all of you lined up here, two by two and ready to ride, in half an hour. When you hear a big bell ring, you know you got just five minutes to line up or it's your ass. That's *all*!"

He turned on his heel and marched out with his detail following. They didn't even bother to bar the gate.

Murmuring, the prisoners began shuffling back inside to gather their belongings. Claude reflected that night travel was another demoralizing factor calculated to stifle notions of escape, as were the inflated descriptions of Pliocene fauna. Spiders as big as peaches forsooth! Next it would be the Giant Rat of Sumatra! On the other hand, the amphicyons were a real enough menace. He wondered how fast they could run on those primitive digitigrade feet. And what in the world were the horrendous Firvulag?

Across the yard another party under guard was emerging from the gatehouse. Hostlers cut out six animals from the main remuda and led them to a mounting platform. Claude saw one slim figure in gold lamé being helped aboard a saddled chaliko, and there was another standing by in a scarlet jumpsuit and a third—

"Aiken!" the old man shouted. "Elizabeth! It's me! Claude!"

The figure in red began to remonstrate with another blue-caped captal of the guard. The arguing got louder and louder and finally Elizabeth stamped her foot and the man shrugged. She broke from the group and ran across the courtyard, the officer following at leisure. She pulled open the people-pen gate and threw herself into the white-haired paleontologist's arms.

"Kiss me," she whispered breathlessly. "You're supposed to be my lover."

He folded her to his breast while the soldier eyed him with interested speculation. Elizabeth said, "They're sending us to the capital, Muriah. My metafunctions are returning, Claude! I'm going to do my best to get away. If I do, I'll try to help you all, somehow."

"That's enough now, Lady," said the solider. "I don't care what Lord Creyn told you. You've got to get ready to ride."

"Goodbye, Claude." She gave him a real kiss, full on the lips, before she was hurried back across the courtyard and helped onto her mount. One of the soldiers fastened the slender chains about her ankles.

Claude raised one hand. "Goodbye, Elizabeth."

From a covered area beyond the main animal pen came a majestic figure riding a snow-white chaliko with scarlet and silver trappings. The captal saluted. Then he and two soldiers swung into their saddles. A command rang out.

"All ready! Portcullis up!"

The file of ten riders went slowly into the arched passage of the barbican. There was a distant excited howling from the bear-dogs. The last prisoner in line turned to wave at Claude before he disappeared into the shadowed opening.

And goodbye to you, Bryan, thought the old man. I hope you find your Mercy. One way or another.

He went back into the dormitory to help with Richard, feeling old and weary and not at all pleased with himself any more.

7

THE PARTY OF TEN FORMED UP TO RIDE TWO BY TWO AS SOON
as they had quit Castle Gateway. Creyn and his captal led and
the two soldiers followed behind the small group of prisoners.
The sun was just down and they traveled eastward into the
dusk, down the gradual slope of the plateau toward the twilit
Rhône-Saône Valley.

Elizabeth sat easily in her saddle, eyes closed and hands
clasped on the pommel while the reins lay free. It was fortunate
that the chaliko did not require guidance from its rider; because
Elizabeth was fully occupied in listening.

Listen . . . but be unaware of the sounds made by the mounts
plodding over soft earth. Do not hear the crickets, the frogs
tuning up in the misty swales scattered in the hollows of the
tableland. Be deaf to the birds' evensong, the distant yelping
of hyaenids emerging for the night's hunt, the murmuring voices
of companion riders. Listen not with the ears but with the newly
recovered metapsychic farsensing faculty.

Reach out afar, afar. Search for other minds like your own,
other speakers, other please-God *truepeople*. (Shame on you
for that, arrogant sickee, but be forgiven just this once.)

Listen, listen! The reborn ultrasense is not yet fully operant, and yet there are things to be heard. Here in the party: the guarded exotic consciousness of Creyn in converse with his captal, dark-minded Zdenko, the two concealed behind a torc-generated screen easily breached; but forebear, since they would be aware of the penetration. Pass over Aiken and the other silver-torc prisoners, the man Raimo and the woman Sukey, their infantile mental babblings as grating as the efforts of fledgling violinists importuning the ears of a cranky virtuoso. Ignore the gray-torced guards and poor unconscious Stein, and Bryan with his brain still unfettered except by chains of his own forging. Leave them all and journey afar.

Listen back at the castle where another exotic voice is—yes—singing. Lesser notes of silver and gray respond in dim echoing of the golden tone. Listen ahead, closer to the great river, to a complex alien mutter: exultation, impatience, anticipated dark joy, cruelty. (Drop *that* horrid thing until later.) Listen farther east, north, northwest, and south. Perceive other concentrations, golden amorphous clots betokening the presence of still more of the artificially enhanced exotic minds, their thoughts too numerous and unfocused for your convalescent mind to sort, their harmonies and occasional peaks of power so strange, yet so achingly familiar in their resemblance to the metapsychic networks of the dear lost Milieu.

Listen to the anomalies! Soft gibberings and puerile thrusts. Other unhuman minds—unaugmented by torcs, perhaps genuinely operant? What? Who? Where? Data inconclusive, but there are many. Listen to faint traceries of dread-patterns and pain-patterns and resignation-loss-patterns coming from God knew where or what. Shrink back. Press past them and beyond, listening. Listening.

That! A fleeting contact from the north that winks out in a spasm of apprehension as soon as you touch it. Tanu? Enhanced human farspeaker. Call out, but receive no response. Project friendship and need, but hear no answer . . . Perhaps you imagined it after all.

Listen afar, afar. Sound the entire Exile world. Are any of you here, sisters and brothers of the mind? Do any farsense in the uniquely human mode that the exotics cannot know? Answer Elizabeth Orme farspeaker redactor searcher hoper prayer! Answer . . .

Planet aureole. Emanations of lower life-forms. Mental whispers from normal humanity. The jabber of the Tanu and their torced minions. An ambiguous murmur from the other side of the world, evanescent as a remembered dream. Is it real or reverberate? Imagination or reality? Track it, lose it. Hover despairingly and know that it never was. The Earth is mute.

Go out beyond the world-halo and perceive the diapason roar of the hidden sun and the thinner arpeggios of stars near and distant, tingling with their own planets and life. No metapsychic humanity? Then call to the ancient-in-your-day Lylmik race, frail artisans of mental prodigies . . . but they do not yet exist. Call to the Krondaku, brothers-mental despite their fearsome bodies . . . but they, too, are a race still in embryo, as are the Gi, the Poltroyans, and the rude Simbiari. The living universe is uncoadunate, mind still chained to matter. The Milieu is in its childhood and Blessed Diamond Mask unborn. There is no one to answer.

Elizabeth withdrew.

Her eyes beheld her own hands, the diamond ring symbolic of her profession faintly luminous, mocking. Banal mental images lapped and splattered her. The wide-open subvocalization of the soldier Billy, brooding over the aging but available charms of a female tavern keeper at a place called Roniah. The other guard, Seung Kyu, preoccupied with a wager he plans to make upon some contest, the outcome of which might now be modified by the participation of Stein. The captal broadcasting pain waves from a boil in his armpit that is aggravated by the bronze breastplate of his light armor. Stein seemingly asleep, calmed by his gray torc. Aiken and the woman named Sukey weaving a crude but effective screen over some mental shenanigans. Creyn now deep in verbal conversation with the anthropologist, discussing the evolution of Tanu society since the opening of the time-portal.

Elizabeth wove a shield behind which she could mourn, impervious as the diamond of her future patron saint. And when it was finished she let the bitter sorrow and rage blaze up. She wept for the irony of having fled from loneliness and bereavement, only to encounter it transformed and fresh. Cocooned, wrapped in the fire of loss, she drifted. Her face was as tranquil as that of a statue in the bright light of the Pliocene stars, her mind as inaccessible as they.

"...the Ship had no way of knowing that this sun was shortly to enter into a prolonged period of instability, triggered by a nearby supernova. Within a hundred years of our arrival, only one conceptus in thirty survived until term. Of those that were born, only about half were normal. We live long, by human standards, but we faced extinction unless the disaster could somehow be ameliorated."

"You couldn't simply pack up and leave?"

"Our Ship was a living organism. It died heroically when it brought us to Earth, making an intergalactic leap unprecedented in the history of our race... No, we could not leave. We had to find another solution. The Ship and its Spouse had chosen Earth for us because of a basic compatibility between our plasma and that of the highest native life-form, the ramapithecines. This enabled us to dominate them with our torc technology—"

"To enslave them, you mean?"

"Why use such a pejorative term, Bryan? Did your people speak of enslaving chimpanzees or whales? The ramas are scarcely more sentient. Or would you have had us live in a Stone Age culture? We came here voluntarily in order to follow an ancient lifestyle no longer permissible on the worlds of our galaxy. But we hardly desired to subsist on roots and berries or live in caves."

"Perish the thought. So you made the ramas your servants and went your merry way until the sun went spotty. And then your genetic engineers found a new use for the ramas, I presume."

"Don't equate our technology with your own, Bryan. At this late stage of our racial life we are very poor engineers— genetic, or otherwise. All we were able to do was utilize the rama females as planting beds for our fertilized ova. It increased our reproductive rate only slightly and was a lame expedient at best. You can see how the arrival of human time-travelers— genetically compatible and virtually immune to the effects of the radiation—would seem providential to us."

"Oh, very. Still, you have to admit that the advantages are mostly one-sided."

"Are you so certain of that? Recall what kind of misfit human beings make the decision to come to Exile. We Tanu have a great deal to offer them. Better things than they ever dreamed possible, if they possess latent metafunctions. And we really ask so little in return."

Something came jabbing Elizabeth.

Stop that.

Jabjabjab.

Go away.

Jab. Jabjab. Come out help I've screwed it.

Stop small pecking childmind Aiken.

JAB!

Vexing insect swat you Aiken! Bother someone else.

JabscratchPOUND. Dammit Elizabeth she's going to bollix up STEIN.

Slowly, Elizabeth turned in her saddle and stared at the rider next to her. Aiken's mind nattered on as she brought into focus a womanform in dark flowing robes. Sukey. A tense face with plump cheeks and a button nose. Indigo eyes set too closely together for beauty, glazed with panic.

Elizabeth went into her without invitation and grasped the situation in an instant, leaving Aiken and the late-arriving Creyn to watch from outside in helpless impotence. Sukey was in the grip of Stein's enraged mind, her sanity almost overwhelmed by the mental power of the wounded man. It was plain what had happened. Sukey was a potentially strong latent redactor and her new silver torc had made the metafunction operant. Egged on by Aiken, she had tested her ability by snooping into Stein, intrigued by the apparent helplessness of the sleeping giant. The young woman had slipped in beneath the low-level neural bath generated by the gray torc, which Creyn had set up to soothe the berserker and block out residual pain from his healing injuries. Under this lid, Sukey had seen the pitiful state of Stein's subconscious mind—the old psychic ulcerations, the newly torn rents in his self-esteem, all gurging about in a maelstrom of suppressed violence.

The tempter had whispered to Sukey, and her innate compassion had responded. She had begun a hopelessly incompetent redact operation on Stein, confident that she could help him; but the brute resident in the pain-filled Viking soul had reared up and attacked her for her meddling. Now both Sukey and Stein were caught in a fearsome conflict of psychoenergies. If the antagonism were not promptly resolved, the outcome could be total personality disjunction for Stein and imbecility for the woman.

Elizabeth sent one blazing thought to Creyn. She dove in and folded the great wings of her own redactability about the frenzied pair. The young womanmind was flung unceremoniously out, to be fielded by Creyn, who let Sukey down easily and then watched with a respect tinged by some other emotion as the mischief was undone.

Elizabeth wove restraints, stopped the psychic whirlpool, calmed the heaving pit of fury. She plucked away the jerry-built mind-alteration structure confected by Sukey, with its naive and impudent drainage channels that were too puny for true catharsis. She bore Stein's damaged ego up with loving force while melting the edges of the wounds and pressing the torn parts back so that healing could begin. Even the older psychic abcesses swelled and burst and vented some of their poison through her. Humiliation and rejection diminished. The father-monster shrank toward pathetic humanity and the mother-lover lost some of her vesture of fantasy. Stein-Awakened looked into Elizabeth's mirror of healing and cried out. He rested.

Elizabeth emerged.

The party of riders had come to a halt, crowding closely around Elizabeth and her mount. She shivered in the sultry evening air. Creyn took his own soft scarlet-and-white cloak and draped it about her shoulders.

"It was magnificent, Elizabeth. None of us—not even Lord Dionket, our greatest—could have done better. They are both safe."

"It still isn't complete," she forced herself to say. "I can't finalize him. His will is very strong and he resists. This took—all I have now."

Creyn touched the circle of gold about his neck. "I can deepen the neural envelope generated by his gray torc. Tonight, when we reach Roniah, we will be able to do more for him. He will recover in a few days."

Stein, who had not once moved during the metapsychic imbroglio, uttered a vast sigh. The two soldiers dismounted and came to adjust his saddle cantle so that it became a high supporting backrest.

"There's no danger of his falling now," Creyn said. "We'll make him more comfortable later. Now we had better ride on."

Bryan demanded, "Will somebody tell me what the hell is going on?" Lacking a torc, he had missed a great deal of the byplay, which had been telepathic.

A stocky man with tow-colored hair and a vaguely Oriental cast to his features pointed a finger at Aiken Drum. "Ask that one. He started it."

Aiken grinned and twiddled his silver torc. Several white moths appeared suddenly out of the darkness and began orbiting Sukey's head in a crazy halo. "Just a little do-goodery gone baddery!"

"Stop that," Creyn commanded. The moths flew away. The tall Tanu addressed Aiken in a tone of veiled menace. "Sukey was the agent, but it is obvious that *you* were the instigator. You amused yourself by placing your friend and this inexperienced woman in mortal danger."

Aiken's golliwog face was unrepentant. "Ah. She seemed strong enough. Nobody forced her to mess with him."

Sukey spoke up. Her voice had a ring of stubborn self-righteousness. "I was only trying to help. He was in desperate need! None of the rest of you seemed to care!"

Creyn said with asperity, "This was not the time or the place to undertake a difficult redaction. Stein would have been treated in good time."

"Let me get this straight," said Bryan. "She tried to alter his mind?"

"She tried to heal him," Elizabeth said. "I suppose Aiken urged her to try out her new metabilities, just as he's been testing his own. But she couldn't handle it."

"Stop talking about me as though I were a child!" Sukey exclaimed. "So I bit off more than I could chew. But I meant well!"

There was a harsh laugh from the towhead, whose silver torc was nearly concealed by a plaid flannel shirt. He wore heavy twill trousers and woodsman's boots with lug soles. "You meant well! Some day that'll be humanity's epitaph! Even that damned Madame Guderian meant well when she let people pass into this hell-world."

Creyn said, "It will be hell for you only if you make it so, Raimo. Now we must ride on. Elizabeth—if you feel able, would you help Sukey to understand something of her new power? At least advise her of the limitations she must accept for now."

"I suppose I had better."

Aiken rode close to scowling Sukey and patted her shoulder in a brotherly fashion. "There now, sweets. The past mistress of mindbendery will give you a flash course, and then you can work on *me*! I guarantee not to gobble you alive. We'll have lots of fun while you straighten out the kinks in my poor little evil soul!"

Elizabeth's mind reached out and gave Aiken a tweak that made him squawk out loud. "Enough of you, my lad. Go practice working your will on bats or hedgehogs or something."

"I'll give you bats," Aiken promised darkly. He urged his mount forward along the wide track, and the cavalcade began to move once more.

Elizabeth opened to Sukey, gentling the woman's fear and discomfiture.

I would like to help you. Little mindsister. Be at ease. Yes?

(Bloody-minded stubborn chagrin breaking down slowly.) Oh why not. I did make a terriblehash of it.

All over now. Relax. Let me know you...

Sue-Gwen Davies, aged twenty-seven, born and raised on the last of the Old World orbital colonies. A former juvenile officer full of sturdy empathy and maternal concern for her wretched young clients. The adolescents of the satellite had mounted an insurrection, rebelling against the unnatural life chosen for them by technocratic idealist grandparents, and the Milieu had belatedly ruled that the colony must be disbanded. Sukey Davies had rejoiced even as her job became redundant. She had no loyalty to the satellite, no philosophical commitment to the experiment that had become obsolete at the very moment that the Great Intervention commenced. All of Sukey's working hours had been spent trying to cope with children who stubbornly resisted the conditioning necessary for life in an orbiting beehive.

When the satellite colony was terminated, Sukey came down to Earth—that world seen below for so many aching years. Paradise and peace existed down there. She was sure of it!

Earth was Eden. But the real promised land was not to be found on Earth's manicured, busy continents.

It was inside the planet.

Elizabeth came up short. Sukey's mind was moderately intelligent, strong-willed, kindly, latent in high redactability and moderate farsense. But Sukey Davies was also firmly convinced that the planet Earth was hollow! Old-fashioned microfiche books smuggled onto the satellite by bored eccentrics and cultists had introduced her to the ideas of Bender and Giannini and Palmer and Bernard and Souza. Sukey had been enthralled by the notion of a hollow Earth lit by a small central sun, a land of tranquillity and invincible goodness, peopled by dwarfish gentlefolk possessing all wisdom and delight. Had not the ancients told tales of subterranean Asar, Avalon, the Elysian Fields, Ratmansu, and Ultima Thule? Even Buddhist Agharta was supposed to be connected by tunnels to the lamaseries of Tibet. These dreams seemed not at all outré to Sukey, the inhabitant of the inside surface of a twenty-kilometer-long spinning cylinder in space. It was logical that Earth be hollow, too.

So Sukey came down to the Old World, where people smiled as she explained what she was looking for. Quite a few helped relieve her of her severance pay as she pursued her quest. There were not, she discovered from expensive personal inspection, mirage-shielded polar apertures leading to the planetary interior, as claimed by some of the old writers; nor was she able to gain entrance to the underworld via the purported caves in Xizang. Finally she had gone to Brazil, where one author said there was a tunnel to Agharta located in the remote Serra do Roncador. An old Murcego Indian, sensing an additional gratuity, told her that the tunnel had indeed once existed; but unfortunately it had been closed by an earthquake "many thousands" of years in the past.

Sukey had pondered this pronouncement for three tearful weeks before concluding that she would surely be able to find the way into the hollow Earth by traveling back into time. She had dressed herself in robes reflecting her Welsh heritage and come eagerly to the Pliocene, where—

Creyn says *his* people founded the paradise!

Oh Sukey.

Yesyes! And I powerfulhealer can belong! Creyn's promise!

Calm. You can become metapractitioner of stature. But not instantly. Much much to learn dear. Trustlistenfollow *then* act.

Want/need to. Poor Stein! Other poorones I can help. Feeling them all around us do you feel too? . . .

Elizabeth withdrew from the fidgeting immaturity of Sukey's mind and cast about. There *was* something. Something completely alien to her experience that had only glimmered on the fringes of her perception earlier in the evening. What was it? The enigma would not resolve itself into a mental image she could identify. Not yet. And so Elizabeth put the problem aside and returned to the task of instructing Sukey. The job was a difficult one that would keep her busy for quite some time, for which thanks be to God.

8

BOUND FOR THE RIVER RHÔNE, THE PARTY RODE FOR THREE
more hours into the deepening night and coolness, coming
down from the plateau via a steep trail with precarious switch-
backs into a forest so thick that the bright light of the stars was
blocked out. The two soldiers ignited tall flambeaux; one man
rode in the van and the other at the rear. They continued their
eastward progress while eerie shadows seemed to follow them
among the massive gnarled trees.

"Spooky, isn't it?" Aiken inquired of Raimo, who was now
riding beside him. "Can't you just imagine these big old cork
oaks and chestnuts reaching out to grab you?"

"You talk like an idiot," the other man growled. "I worked
in deep forests for twenty years in the B.C. Megapod Reserve.
Ain't nothing spooky about trees."

Aiken was unabashed. "So that's why the lumberjack outfit.
But if you know trees, you must know that botanists credit
them with a primitive self-awareness. Don't you think that the
older the plant, the more attuned to the Milieu it must be? Just
look at these trees along here. Don't tell me they had hardwoods
eight-ten meters across on the Earth we knew! Why, these
babies must be thousands of years older than any tree on Old

Earth. Just reach out to 'em! Use that silver torc of yours for something besides an Adam's apple warmer. Ancient trees . . . evil trees! Can't you feel the bad vibes in this forest? They could resent our coming here. They might sense that in a few million years, humans like us'll destroy 'em! Maybe the trees hate us!"

"I think," said Raimo with slow malevolence, "that you're trying to make a fool outa me like you did with Sukey. Don't!"

Aiken felt himself hoisted up from his saddle. His chained ankles caught him like a victim on a rack. Higher and higher he rose, until he was suspended dangerously close to the branches overhanging the trail.

"Hey! It was only a joke and that *hurts*!"

Raimo began to chuckle and increased the tension still more.

Squeeze. Pummel the glacial mind-grip of the Finno-Canadian and make him let go, let go, let go!

With a crash that made the startled chaliko squeal, Aiken plummeted back into his saddle. Creyn turned around and said, "You have a penchant for cruelty that will have to be curbed, Raimo Hakkinen."

"I wonder if all your kind would think so?" inquired the former woodsman in an insolent tone. "Anyhow, you can make this little shit stop bugging me. Tree-spooks!"

Aiken protested, "A lot of old-time cultures believed that trees had special powers. Didn't they, Bryan?"

The anthropologist was amused. "Oh, yes. Tree cults were almost universal in the ancient world of the future. The Druids had an entire alphabet for divination based on trees and shrubs. It was apparently a relic of a more widespread tree-centered religion that derived from utmost antiquity. Scandinavians revered a mighty ash-tree named Yggdrasil. Greeks dedicated the ash to the sea-god Poseidon. Birches were sacred among the Romans. The rowan was a Celtic and Greek symbol of power over death. The hawthorn was associated with sex orgies and the month of May—and so was the apple. Oak trees were cult objects all over preliterate Europe. For some reason, oaks are especially vulnerable to lightning, so the ancients connected the tree with the thunder-god. Greeks, Romans, Gaulish Celts, the British, Teutons, Lithuanians, Slavs—they all held the oak to be sacred. The folklore of almost all European countries featured supernatural beings that dwelt in special trees or haunted the deep woods. The Macedonians had dryads and the Styrians had vilyas and the Germans had seligen Fräulein and the French had their dames vertes. All woodland sprites. Scandinavian people believed in them, too, but I've forgotten the name they gave them—"

"Skogsnufvar," said Raimo unexpectedly. "My grandfather told me. He was from the Åland Islands, where the people spoke Swedish. Full of dumb fairytales."

"Nothing like ethnic pride!" chortled Aiken. And that brought on another row, as the forester lashed out again with his enhanced PK function and Aiken fought back with his coercive power, trying to make Raimo ram his own forefinger down his throat.

At last Creyn cried, "Omnipotent Tana, enough!" Both men groaned, clutched at their silver torcs, and subsided like a pair of whipped schoolboys, silent but unrepentant.

Raimo pulled a large silver flask from his pack and began nursing from it. Aiken curled his lip. The forester said, "Hudson's Bay Company Demerara, one-fifty-one proof. Grownups only. Eat your heart out."

Elizabeth's cool voice requested, "Tell us about the Skogsnufvar, Bryan. Such an awful name. Were they beautiful?"

"Oh, yes. Long flowing hair, seductive bodies—and tails! They were your standard archetypal anima-female menace, luring men into the deep woods in order to sleep with them. And ever after, the poor chaps were completely in the power of the elf-women. A man who tried to leave would sicken and die, or else go mad. Victims of the Skogsnufvar were written about well into the twentieth century in Sweden."

Sukey said, "Welsh folklore had such creatures, too. But they lived in lakes, not forests. They were called the Gwragedd Annwn and they came up to dance on the water in the misty moonlight and lured travelers into their underwater palaces."

"It's a common folkloric theme," Bryan said. "The symbolism is easily grasped. Still—one has to feel a bit sorry for the poor male elves. They seem to have missed out on a lot of good dirty fun."

Most of the humans laughed, including the guards.

"Are there any parallel legends among your people, Creyn?" the anthropologist asked. "Or didn't your culture produce tales of enchantment?"

"There was no need," the Tanu replied in a repressive tone.

An odd notion occurred to Elizabeth. She attempted to slide a microprobe through Creyn's screen without triggering his awareness.

Ah Elizabeth don't. These petty aggressions games idle scrabblings for superiority.

(Innocent incredulity scorncolored taunt.)

Nonsense. I am oldtired civilized of goodwill to you and yours even ultimately crushable. But others mykind not. Beware Elizabeth. Reject not Tanu lightly. Remember puffin.

Puffin?

Childpoem your folk from humaneducator among us long deceased. Lonelybird only one of kind ate fishes bewailed solitude. Friendship proffered by fishes if bird refrained devouring. Deal accepted mealhabits changed. Fishes only game in town for puffin.

As you Tanu are for me?

Affirm Elizapuffinbeth.

She burst out laughing and Bryan and the other humans looked at her in blank astonishment.

"Somebody," Aiken remarked, "has been whispering behind our minds. Are you going to let us in on the joke, lovie?"

"The joke's on me, Aiken." Elizabeth turned to Creyn. "We'll have a truce. For now."

The exotic man inclined his head. "Then permit me to change the subject. We are approaching the bottomlands of the river, where we'll have our night's rest in the city of Roniah. Tomorrow we shall resume our journey in a more agreeable fashion—by boat. We should arrive in the capital city of Muriah in less than five days, if the winds are right."

"Sailboats on a turbulent river like the Rhône?" Bryan said, aghast. "Or—is it calmer here in the Pliocene?"

"You'll have to judge for yourself, of course. However, our boats are quite different from those you may have been accustomed to. We Tanu are not fond of water travel. But with the coming of humanity, safe and efficient boats were designed and river commerce became extensive. We now use boats not only for passenger travel but also to ship vital commodities from the north—especially from Finiah and from Goriah in the area you call Brittany—to the southern regions where the climate is more to our taste."

"I've brought a sailboat with me," the anthropologist said.

"Will I be permitted to use it? I'd like to visit your Finiah and Goriah."

"As you'll see, upstream travel is generally not feasible. We rely on caravans for that, using either chalikos or larger beasts of burden called hellads—a species of short-necked giraffe. In the course of your researches you will doubtless make visits to several of our population centers."

"Without a torc on him?" Raimo interjected. "You'd trust him?"

Creyn laughed. "We have something he wants."

Bryan flinched; but he knew better than to rise to the bait. He only said, "These vital commodities you ship. I suppose they include mostly foodstuffs?"

"To some extent. But this Many-Colored Land is literally overflowing with meat and drink for the taking."

"Minerals then. Gold and silver. Copper and tin. Iron."

"Not iron. It is unnecessary in our rather simple techno-economy. The Tanu worlds have traditionally relied on varieties of unbreakable glass in those applications where humanity utilized iron. It is interesting that in recent years you, too, have come to appreciate the versatile material."

"Vitredur, yes. Still, your fighting men seem to prefer the traditional bronze in their armor and weapons."

Creyn laughed quietly. "In the earliest days of the time-portal it was considered wise to restrict human warriors in that way. Now, when the restriction has become obsolete, humans continue to cling to the metal. We permit a bronze technology to flourish among your people where it does not conflict with our own needs. We Tanu are a tolerant race. We were self-sufficient before humans began to arrive and we are by no means dependent upon humanity for slave labor—"

Elizabeth's thought loomed large: OTHER THAN REPRODUCTIVE ENSLAVEMENT.

"—since the tedious and difficult work such as mining and agriculture and comfort maintenance is undertaken by ramas in all but the most isolated settlements."

"These ramas," Aiken broke in. "How come there weren't any back at the castle to do the dirty work?"

"They have a certain psychic fragility and require a tranquil environment if they are to function with minimal supervision. At Castle Gateway there is inevitable stress—"

Raimo gave a derisive grunt.

Bryan asked, "How are the creatures controlled?"

"They wear a much simplified modification of the gray torc. But you must not press me to explain these matters now. Please wait until later, in Muriah."

They rode into an area where the trees were not so thickly clustered, among giant crags at the base of a sparsely forested ridge. Up where the crest met the starry sky was a glow of colored light.

"Is that the town up there?" Sukey inquired.

"Can't be," Raimo said contemptuously. "Look at the thing move!"

They reined in their chalikos and watched the glow resolve into a thin skein of luminescence that twisted in and out of the distant silhouettes of trees at considerable speed. The light was a blend of many hues, basically golden but with knots that flared blue, green, red, and even purple in a panoply of sparkling commotion, wild and urgent.

"Ah!" Creyn said. "The Hunt. If they come this way you'll see a fine sight."

"It looks like a giant rainbow glowworm racing up there," Sukey breathed. "How lovely!"

"The Tanu at play?" Bryan asked.

Sukey uttered a disappointed cry. "Oh—they've gone over the ridge. What a shame! Tell us what the Hunt is, Lord Creyn."

The exotic man's face was grave in the starlight. "One of the great traditions of our people. You'll see it again, many times. I'll let you discover for yourselves what it is."

"And if we're good," Aiken put in impudently, "do we get to join in?"

"Possibly," Creyn replied. "It is not to every human's taste— nor even to every Tanu's. But you . . . yes, I think perhaps the Hunt would appeal to your particular sporting instinct, Aiken Drum."

And for an instant, the healer's emotional tone was plain for Elizabeth to read: disgust, mingled with an age-old sense of despair.

9

RICHARD SAW FLAMES.

They were moving toward him or he was moving toward them and they were vivid orange and resin-smoky, rising tall into a wavering queue in the nearly windless dark.

He saw that it was a pile of burning brush the size of a small hut, crackling and hissing but throwing no sparks, seeming to draw abreast of him, pass him by and recede, disappearing at last behind a grove of black trees that had crept up unseen in the night but now stood backlighted by the bonfire's glow.

It hurt his neck to look back. He let his head loll forward. There was something bulky just in front of him that had long hair and moved rhythmically. It was very strange! He himself was rocking, firmly supported in some kind of seat that held him upright. His legs were thrust forward at an angle, the calves resting on unseen supports, feet braced against wide treads. His arms, clad in the familiar sleeves of a master spacer's coverall, rested in his lap.

181

A funny kind of starship, he mused, with a hairy control console. And the environmental must be on the fritz because the temperature was nearly thirty and there was dust in the air and a peculiar smell.

Trees? And a bonfire? He looked around and saw stars— not the proper colored stars you see in deep space, but little twinkling specks. Far away, in the black below the starry bowl, was another small exclamation point of fire.

"Richard? Are you awake? Would you like some water?"

Well! Would you look at who was flying the righthand seat of this crate? None other than the old bone hunter! Would have thought he was too creako to qualify. But then you don't need much finesse to fly on the ground...

"Richard, if I pass you the canteen, can you hold on to it?"

Smells of animals, pungent vegetation, leather. Sounds of creaking harness, brisk clumping feet, huffing exhalations, something yipping in the distance, and the voice of the persistent old man beside him.

"Don't want water," said Richard.

"Amerie said you'd need it when you woke up. You're dehydrated. Come on, son."

He took a closer look at Claude there in the darkness. The old man's figure was illuminated by starlight; he was astride a huge horse-like creature that was loping easily along. Damnedest thing! *He* was riding one, too! There were the reins draped over the pommell of a saddle right in front of him below the hairy control console—neck—of the critter. And it was trotting straight and level without any guidance at all.

Richard tried to pull his feet up and discovered that his ankles were fastened somehow to the stirrups. And he wasn't wearing his seaboots, and someone had exchanged his opera costume for the spacer's coverall with the four stripes on the sleeves that he had stuffed into the bottom of his pack, and he had an imperial grand champion hangover.

"Claude," he groaned. "You got any booze?"

"You can't have any, boy. Not until the drug Amerie shot into you wears off. Here. Take the water."

Richard had to lean far out to grasp the canteen and the starry sky lurched. If his ankles had not been fastened, he would have fallen from the saddle.

"Jesus, I been chewed up and spit out, Claude. Where the hell are we? And what's this thing I'm riding?"

"We're about four hours out from the castle, riding due north and parallel to the Saône River. As near as I can judge, you're riding a nice large specimen of Chalicotherium goldfussi, which the locals call a chaliko, not a calico. The beasts travel a pretty fair clip here on the plateau, maybe fifteen or sixteen kloms an hour. But we lost time fording creeks around a little swamp, so I guess we might be thirty kloms above Lyon. If there was a Lyon."

Richard cursed. "Bound where, for God's sake?"

"Some Pliocene metropolis called Finiah. From what they told us, it's on the Proto-Rhine about in the position of Freiburg. We get there in six days."

Richard drank some of the water and discovered he was very thirsty. He could remember nothing beyond the welcoming smile on Epone's face as he followed her into the dazzling inner chamber of the castle. He tried to marshal his wits, but all he could rake up were tattered dreams in which his brother and sister seemed to urge him to get up or he'd be late for school. And the penalty for that would be cruising the gray limbo forever and ever, searching for a lost planet where Epone would be waiting.

After a while, he asked, "What happened to me?"

"We aren't sure," Claude temporized. "You know, don't you, that there were exotics in the castle?"

"I remember a tall woman," Richard muttered. "I think she did something to me."

"Whatever it was, you were out for hours. Amerie got you semiconscious so that you'd be able to move out with the rest of us in the caravan. We thought you'd prefer that to being left behind alone."

"Christ, yes." Richard took slow swallows of water, leaned back, and watched the sky for a long time. There were a hell of a lot of stars, and pearly streaks of luminescent cloud toward the zenith. As the caravan began descending a long downhill slope, he could see that he and the old man were near the tail end of a long double file of riders. Now that his eyes worked properly again, he discerned other dark shapes coursing along both sides of the column with awkward humping strides.

"What the devil are those things out there?"

"Amphicyons riding herd on us. We have a guard of five soldiers, too, but they hardly ever bother to check up. There are two bringing up the rear and three in front with the Exalted Lady."

"The *who*?"

"Epone herself. She comes from Finiah. These exotics—they're called Tanu, by the way—seem to have widely scattered settlements, each with a central urban area and satellite supporting plantations. My guess is that humans function as slaves or serfs, with some exceptional types enjoying special privileges. Evidently the Tanu cities take turns collecting a week's worth of time-travelers at Castle Gateway, minus the specials who get siphoned off to the capital and the unlucky ones who are killed trying to escape."

"We *aren't* special, I take it."

"Just part of the grunt-pack. Amerie and Felice are in the caravan, too. But the four other Greenies were sifted out and sent south to the big time. Group Green seems to have been unusual in having so many taken. There were only two other people sent to the capital from the rest of the week's contingent."

As they rode along, the old man told Richard as much as he could about the day's events and the presumed fate of Aiken, Elizabeth, Bryan, and Stein. He also summarized Waldemar's little speech and reluctantly told of the future in store for the women of the party.

The ex-spacer ventured a few questions, then fell silent. Too bad about the nun going to an exotic harem. She'd been decent to him. On the other hand, that stuck-up Ice Queen of an Elizabeth needed a good stoking. And Felice, that sly little bitch—! Richard had offered her a harmless little suggestion back at the auberge and she'd sent him up like a holiday firework. Damn teasing little snatch! He hoped the exotics had peckers like baseball bats. It would serve her right. Might even make a real woman out of her.

The caravan moved steadily down the incline, heading a little east of north now and coming closer to the river. The beacon fire was their landmark. Claude had told him that similar fires were spaced about two kloms apart all the way from the castle. A scouting party must be riding in advance of the caravan along the track, torching the waiting piles of brush if all was well.

"I think I see a building down there," Claude said. "Maybe it's the place where we stop for a break."

Richard sure as hell hoped so. He had drunk too much water.

From the head of the column came the silvery notes of a horn sounding a three-toned call. This was echoed distantly. After a few minutes had passed, a dozen or so tiny pinpricks of fire emerged from the vicinity of the downslope bonfire and approached the caravan in a sinuous line: riders carrying torches, coming to escort them.

By the time the groups converged, Claude and Richard could see that the last beacon fire burned outside of a walled enclosure resembling an ancient American plains fort. It stood on a bluff above a tree-crowded watercourse that must drain into the Saône. The caravan halted momentarily, and Lady Epone and Waldemar went forward to greet the escort party. In the torchlight, Richard unconcernedly admired the stately Tanu woman, who was riding a white chalicothere of exceptional size and wearing a dark-blue hooded cloak that floated behind her.

After a moment's conference, two of the soldiers from the fort rode off to one side and in some manner called in the pack of amphicyons. The bear-dogs were led away on a side path while the rest of the escort fell in beside the caravan for the last part of the journey. A gate in the palisade opened and they rode inside, two by two. Then, in what was to become a familiar procedure, the prisoners had their mounts tethered to posts in front of double troughs of feed and water. At the left of each chaliko was a dismounting block. After the soldiers unlocked their chains, the muscle-sore travelers descended and gathered in an untidy group while Waldemar addressed them once again.

"All you travelers! We'll rest here for one hour, then go on until early morning, another eight hours." Everybody groaned. "Latrines in the small building behind you, get your food and drink in the bigger building next door. Anybody sick or gotta complaint, see me. Be ready to remount when you hear the horn. Nobody comes into the area beyond the hitching rail. That's *all*."

Epone, who was still on chalikoback, guided her beast delicately through the throng until she loomed over Richard.

"I'm glad to see you're recovering."

He gave her a quizzical look. "I'm just dandy. And it's nice to know you're a lady who cares about the health of her livestock."

She threw her head back and laughed, cascades of sound like the deep strumming of a harp. Her partially hidden hair gleamed in the torchlight. "It really *is* too bad about you," she said. "You've certainly got more spirit than that silly medievalist."

She turned her animal away, rode to the opposite side of the compound, and was helped out of the saddle by obsequious men in white tunics.

"What was that all about?" inquired Amerie, who had come up with Felice.

Richard glowered. "How the fuck should I know?" He went tottering off toward the latrine.

Felice watched him go. "Are all your patients this grateful?"

The nun laughed. "He's coming along just fine. You know they're on the mend when they bite your head off."

"He's nothing but a stupid weakling."

"I think you're wrong about that," Amerie said. But Felice only snorted and went off to the mess hall. Later, when the two women and Claude were eating cheese and cold meat and maize bread, Richard came and apologized.

"Think nothing of it," the nun sad. "Sit down with us. We've got something to talk over with you."

Richard's eyes narrowed. "Yeah?"

Claude said softly, "Felice has a plan for escape. But there are problems."

"No shit?" the pirate guffawed.

The little ring-hockey player took Richard's hand and squeezed. His eyes bulged and he pressed his lips together. "Less noise," Felice said. "The problem isn't in the escape itself, but in the aftermath. They've taken our maps and compasses. Claude has a general knowledge of this part of Europe from his paleontology studies more than a hundred years ago, but that won't help us if we can't orient ourselves while we're on the run. Can you help us? Did you study the large-scale map of Pliocene France when we were back at the auberge?"

She dropped his hand and Richard stared at the whitened

flesh, then threw her a glance of pure venom. "Hell, no. I figured there'd be plenty of time for that once we arrived. I brought a self-compensating compass, a computer sextant, all the charts I'd need. But I suppose all the stuff was confiscated. The only route I looked at was the one west to the Atlantic—to Bordeaux."

Felice grunted in disgust. Claude persisted in a peaceable tone, "We know you must be experienced in navigation, son. There's got to be some way we can orient ourselves. Can you locate the Pliocene polestar for us? That would be a big help."

"So would a frigate of the Fleet Air Arm," Richard grumbled. "Or Robin Hood and his merry men."

Felice reached out for him again and he dodged back hastily. "Can you do it, Richard?" she asked. "Or are those stripes on your sleeves for good conduct?"

"This isn't my home planet, dykey-doll! And the noctilucent clouds don't make the job any easier."

"A lot of vulcanism," Claude said. "Dust in the upper atmosphere. But the moon has set and there aren't any ordinary clouds. Do you think you'd be able to get a fix as the glowing patches come and go?"

"I might," Richard muttered. "But why the hell I should bother beats me . . . What I want to know is, what happened to my pirate outfit? Who put this coverall on me?"

"It was there," Felice said sweetly, "and you needed it. Badly. So we obliged. Anything to help out a friend."

Claude hurried to say, "You got all messed up in some fight you were in back at the castle. I just cleaned you up a bit and washed your other clothes. They're hanging on the back of your saddle. Should be dry by now."

Richard looked suspiciously at the smirking Felice, then thanked the old man. But a fight? Had he been in a fight? And who had been laughing at him with lofty contempt? A woman with drowning-pool eyes. But not Felice . . .

Amerie said, "Please try for the polestar if you feel well enough to manage it. We only have one more night of travel on this high north road. Then we'll be angling off every which way and traveling in the daytime. Richard, it's important."

"Okay, okay," he grouched. "I don't suppose any of you Earthworms knows the latitude of Lyon."

"About forty-five north, I think," said Claude. "Around the

same as my boyhood home in Oregon, anyhow, from the way I remember the sky over the auberge. Too bad we don't have Stein. He'd know."

"A rough guess is good enough," Richard said.

The nun lifted her head. The sound of a horn came from outside in the fort's yard. "Well, here we go again, Group. Good luck, Richard."

"Megathanks, Sister. If we follow any escape plan *this* kid dreams up, we're gonna need it."

They rode on through the night, traveling from beacon to beacon along the plateau trail with the river valley at their right and the scattered small volcanoes of the Limagne giving an occasional ruby pulse in the southwest. Constellations totally unfamiliar to the Earth natives of the twenty-second century crowded the sky of Exile. Many of those stars were the same ones that would be visible in the planet's future; but their differing galactic orbits had twisted the familiar star patterns all out of recognition. There were stars in the Pliocene sky that were destined to die before the time of the Galactic Milieu; others that Milieu people would know were at this time still dark in their dustcloud wombs.

Richard viewed the Pliocene heavens with nonchalance. He'd seen an awful lot of different skies. Given plenty of time and a fixed base for observation, finding the local Polaris would be a snap, even with eyeball instrumentation alone. It was only the fact that they were moving on animal-back, and the need for a quick fix, that made the thing a bit tricky.

Now. *If* the old fossil-flicker was right about the rough latitude, and *if* they were on a near-northerly course on this trail as Claude thought they'd have to be, given the lay of the land, *then* the polestar should be about halfway between the horizon and the zenith somewhere in . . . there.

He had picked up a couple of stiff twigs from the litter back at the fort and now bound them together into a cross-sight with a hair from his mount's mane. Each stalk was twice as long as his hand. He hoped the field wouldn't be too limited.

Adjusting his position in the saddle to minimize the effect of the chaliko's rocking gait, he memorized the constellations that had to be roughly circumpolar. Then he held the cross-sight at arm's length and aligned the vertical axis with the straight track ahead (analog: two upright chaliko ears) and centered it on a likely star he had tentatively selected. He carefully noted the positions of five other bright stars within the quadrants of his sight and then relaxed. Three hours from now, when planetary rotation had made those six stars seem to change position slightly, he'd take another sighting. His near-photographic memory would do an angular comparison within the field of the cross-sight, and with luck he would be able to discern the imaginary hub in the sky about which all those stars were turning. The hub would be the pole. It might or might not have a star on it or near it that could be dubbed Pliocene Polaris.

He would center the cross-sight anew on this point in the sky and try to verify the pole's position before dawn with a two-hour shot. Failing that, he would check it tomorrow night with a good long time interval for maximum rotation.

Richard set his wrist chronometer's alarm for 0300, glad that he hadn't followed the impulse to throw the thing away back in Madame Guderian's rose garden on that rainy morning when he had abandoned his universe . . .

Less than twenty hours ago.

10

EVEN THOUGH HE HAD BEEN PARTIALLY BREIFED BY CREYN ON
what to expect, Bryan found the reality of the riverside city of
Roniah nearly overwhelming. The party of riders came suddenly upon the place after wending their way through a dark
canyon where the guards' torches barely illuminated a narrow
trail cut in buff sandstone. The caravan emerged onto a knoll
overlooking the confluence of the Saône and the Rhône and
saw the town below on the west bank, just south of the snout
of forested crags where the two great rivers joined.

Roniah was built on a rise adjacent to the water. Twisting
around the hill's base was an earthen rampart crowned by a
thick fortified wall. All along the top of this, glittering like
lavish strings of orange beads, were closely spaced little fires.
High, square watchtowers jutted out from the wall every hundred
meters or so, and these, too, were outlined in pricks of fire all
along their crenellated battlements, around the windows, and
even up and down the corners and angles of the walls. A
massive city gate had almost every detail of its architecture
picked out in small lamps. Leading to the gate was a colonnaded
avenue half a kilometer long, every column of which was
capped with a huge flaming torch. The midway was flanked
with spangled geometrical patterns that might have been lamp-

bordered lawns or flowerbeds planted in parterre designs.

From the caravan's vantage point above the town, Bryan could see that Roniah was uncrowded, its mostly small houses laid out along wide curving streets. Since it was well past midnight, most of the dwellings showed no window lights; but along the edges of the roofs were little dots of fire; and the parapets that fronted the houses were also illuminated by thousands of the evenly spaced lamps. Closer to the riverside were a number of larger structures bearing slender towers of varying heights. The walls and major features of these buildings were outlined in light as elaborately as the city gate was—but instead of oil-lamp orange, the façades glowed with blue, bright green, aquamarine, and amber. Many of the towers had their windows ablaze.

"It's like fairyland," breathed Sukey. "All those little sparkling lights!"

"Each inhabitant is obligated to contribute to urban illumination by maintaining the lamps of his own house," Creyn said. "The common fuel is olive oil, which is extremely plentiful. The taller Tanu dwellings are lit by more sophisticated lamps energized by accumulations of surplus metapsychic emanations."

They rode down, following the track until it merged with a road paved in granite setts that widened to nearly eighty meters as it approached the avenue of fire-topped columns. Between the great pillars stood neat frameworks of bamboo arranged in aisles, separated by dark shrubbery and clusters of palm trees. Creyn explained that booths for a market were set up in this exterior garden every month, featuring the goods of local artisans as well as luxury products of all kinds brought in by caravans. Once a year there was also a Great Fair, which attracted people from all over western Europe.

"You have no daily market for foods, then?" Bryan asked.

"Meat is the great diet staple," Creyn replied. "Professional hunters, all human, bring in large quantities of game to the plantations in the more northerly reaches of both the Saône and Rhône. It is sent downstream daily to the town provisioners on barges, together with grain, fruit, and other produce from the farms, such as olive oil and wine. Most of the food processing is done at the plantations by rama workers. In years gone by, our own people supervised the plantations. Now almost all of them are overseen by humans."

"And you see no potential hazard in such an arrangement?" Bryan asked.

Creyn smiled, the flickering lights striking sparks from his deep-set eyes. "No hazard at all. The humans engaged in critical occupations all wear the torc. But try to understand that coercion is seldom necessary. For all but the most deeply disturbed of your people, the world of Exile is a happy one."

"Even for the women?" Elizabeth inquired.

The unperturbed Tanu said, "Even the lowliest nonmeta women of the commonalty are completely free from drudgery. They may engage in the occupations of their choice or live in indolence. They may even pleasure themselves as they will with human lovers. The only restriction is that their children must be by us. The more fortunate humans possessing genetic codons for metafunction enjoy a privileged position. They are welcomed into our society as probationary equals. In the fullness of time, those who have proved their loyalty to the Tanu may exchange their silver torcs for gold."

"Both men and women?" Aiken asked, his lips twitching.

"Both men and women. I'm sure you can appreciate our reproductive strategy. We not only strengthen our line against the effects of the local radiation but also incorporate your genes for latent and operant metability. Ultimately, we may hope to evolve fully operant metapsychics"—he nodded at Elizabeth—"even as you will have done six million years from now. We will then be freed from the limitation of the golden torcs."

Elizabeth said, "Quite a grand design. How do you reconcile it with the reality of this planet's future . . . with no Tanu?"

Creyn smiled. "The Goddess wreaks as she wills. Six million years is a long time. I think we Tanu will be grateful to settle for a small portion of it to call our own."

They approached closer to the great gate, which was twelve or thirteen meters wide and almost twice as high, fashioned of titanic balks of timber heavily reinforced with bronze plates.

"Not much action outside here at night, is there?" Aiken commented.

"There are wild animals and other dangers," Creyn said. "The night is not a time for humans to be abroad unless they are going about the business of the Tanu."

"Interesting," Bryan said. "These city walls and the rampart must be effective against almost any kind of night prowlers. They're certainly overelaborate as a protection from animal menaces. Or even aggression from outlaw humans—and I understand there are some here and there."

"Oh, yes," Creyn admitted, with a dismissing wave of his hand. "Little more than a minor nuisance."

"Then what purpose do the fortifications really serve?"

"There are always," Creyn said, "the Firvulag."

They came to a halt immediately in front of the gate. Above its arch was the same golden mask emblem that had adorned the entrance to Castle Gateway. Captal Zdenek, accompanied by one torch-bearing soldier, rode to a shadowed niche and detached a stout chain that dangled from the soffit of the overhanging archway. The chain had a ball of metal-caged stone on the end that measured a good half-meter in diameter. Zdenek rode out a short distance holding the ball and then turned, took aim, and let it swing back toward the gate in a pendulum arc. It struck a blackened bronze lens set into the timbered valve and there was a deep-throated *boom*, as from a huge Old World church bell. Even as the soldier caught the returning ball and put it back into its niche, the ponderous gate began to swing open.

Creyn rode forward alone, rising above the saddle to his full height so that his scarlet and white robes streamed back in the breeze rushing from the widening aperture. He cried out three words in an exotic tongue, simultaneously transmitting a complex mental image that the torc-wearing humans and Elizabeth were unable to decipher.

Two squads of human soldiers with crested helmets stood at attention on either side of the open entrance. The engraved plates and scales of their ceremonial bronze armor gleamed like gold in the light of countless flaming lamps. Beyond the gate, lining the otherwise deserted street for almost an entire block on both sides, were the ramas. Each small ape wore a metal collar and a blue and gold tabard. Each held a wand of some glassy material tipped with a blue or an amber light.

Creyn and his retinue passed between the ranks of ramapithecines, and the little animals turned and pattered alongside the chalikos, escorting the riders through the streets of the sleeping town. At one plaza, where the waters of a large fountain splashed onto floating lanterns, Captal Zdenek saluted Creyn and rode off toward a dim barracks with the soldiers Billy and Seung Kyu, their night's work at an end. The timefarers gaped at the houses, dark except for the myriad twinkling oil lamps along every roof gutter, garden wall, and balustrade. Exile architecture in the human quarter was a mélange of mortared stonework, half-timbering, and quasi-biblical mudplaster, with thick walls for coolness, tiled roofs, vine-hung loggias deep in shadow, and small patios planted with palms, laurels, and aromatic cinnamon trees.

"Munchkin Tudor," Bryan decided. Humanity had retained its sense of humor in spite of the six-million-year banishment.

They saw no people at all; but here and there other child-sized ramas, wearing tabards of differing colors, went about mysterious errands, pushing little covered carts. Once, in an oddly reassuring incident, an unmistakable Siamese cat streaked across the main avenue and disappeared into the open window of a house.

The chaliko riders neared a complex of larger buildings close to the river. These were constructed of a material resembling white marble and set off from the rest of the town by an ornamental wall breached at intervals by wide stairways. The parapet at the top was decorated with planter-urns spilling flowers. In place of the homely town lamps of ceramic or metal fretwork, torchères like great silver candlesticks lit the precincts of the Tanu. The dwellings were hung with chains of faceted glass lanterns, their blue and green and amber making an eerie contrast to the friendly warmth of the oil lamps on the streets of the outer town. There were a few familiar touches: waterlilies in tiled pools, climbing yellow roses supported on delicate trellises of marble filigree, a nightingale, wakened by the sound of their passage, that uttered a few sleepy notes.

They passed into a courtyard hemmed by ornate frosty buildings. Here a large door was suddenly flung open and golden radiance streamed forth, catching them by surprise. As the ramas stood solemnly by, human servitors came rushing out to take the bridles of the chalikos, unlock the ankle chains of the prisoners, and help them to dismount.

Then came the Tanu—twenty or thirty of them, laughing and calling out greetings to Creyn in the exotic tongue and chattering in animated exuberance over the time-travelers in musical Standard English. The Tanu wore thin flowing gowns and robes of vivid tropical colors, together with fantastic jewelry—wide yoke-collars all gemmed and enameled, with brocaded and jeweled ribbons dangling front and rear. The women had wired headdresses all hung with gemstones. Here and there among the lofty exotics were a few smaller human figures, just as gaudily dressed, but wearing silver torcs instead of the Tanu gold. Bryan studied these privileged humans with interest. They seemed to be socially integrated with the taller ruling race and just as anxious to make the acquaintance of the overawed prisoners.

Among the arrivals, only Aiken was completely at ease. With his pocketed suit flashing like liquid metal, he fairly hopped about the courtyard, making mocking obeisance to the laughing Tanu ladies, most of whom were nearly a third taller than he was. Bryan stood apart from the others and watched. The Tanu nobles were solicitous of the comfort of the prisoners, joking over the incongruity of the situation, somehow managing to make the newly met exiles feel wanted and welcome. Bryan had no doubt that mental speech was flying about as fervidly as the vocal sort. He wondered what kind of psychic stimulant might be operating at the lower levels of consciousness to make even sullen Raimo and the aloof Elizabeth slowly unbend and join in the conviviality.

"We don't want you to feel left out, Bryan."

The anthropologist turned and saw a slender exotic male garbed in a simple blue robe smiling at him. He had a handsome but sunken-eyed visage, lined about the mouth as Creyn's was. Bryan wondered whether this might be a sign of extreme age among these inhumanly youthful-looking people. The man's hair was of the palest ivory and he wore a narrow coronet of a material resembling blue glass.

"Permit me to welcome you. I am your host, Bormol, like yourself a student of culture. How eagerly we have awaited the arrival of another trained analyst! The last anthropologist who came to us arrived nearly thirty years ago and he was unfortunately in frail health. And we need your insights so urgently! We have so much to learn about the interaction of our two races if this Exile society is to flourish to our mutual advantage. The science of your Galactic Milieu can teach us the things we must know in order to survive. Come—we have good food and drink waiting for you and your friends inside. Share with us some of your first impressions of our Many-Colored Land. Give us your initial reactions!"

Bryan managed a rueful laugh. "You flatter me, Lord Bormol. And overwhelm me. I'm damned if I can make head or tail of your world as yet. After all, I've only just arrived. And excuse me, but I'm so tired out after this bloody shocking day that I'm ready to drop in my tracks."

"Forgive me. I'd completely forgotten you're without a torc. The mental refreshment that our people have been lavishing over your companions hasn't affected you. If you wish, we can—"

"No, thank you!"

Creyn came up and smiled ironically at the anthropologist's sudden alarm. "Bryan would prefer to do his work without the consolations of the torc . . . in fact, he has made this a condition of cooperation."

"You don't have to coerce me," Bryan said testily.

"Don't misunderstand!" Bormol appeared pained. He gestured at the gaudy throng, now leading the other prisoners inside with every evidence of good fellowship. "Are your friends being coerced? The torc isn't a symbol of bondage but of union."

Bryan felt a surge of anger and dreadful weariness erupt in him. His voice remained calm. "I know you mean well. But there are many of us humans—one might say most of us in my world of the future, most of the *normal* members of humanity—who would rather die than submit to your torc. In spite of all its consolations. Now you must excuse me. I'm sorry to disappoint you, but I'm not up to any learned discussions right now. I'd like to go to bed."

Bormol bowed his head. One of the human servants came running up with Bryan's pack. "We will meet again in the capital. I hope you will have modified your harsh opinion of us by then, Bryan. . . . This is Joe-Don, who will take you to a retiring room at once. Rest well."

Bormol and Creyn glided away. Almost everyone else had already left the courtyard. "Right this way, sir," Joe-Don said, his breezy aplomb equal to that of a bellman in one of the Old World's posher hostelries. "We've got a nice room ready for you. But too bad you'll miss the party."

They went off into corridors decorated in blue and gold and white. Bryan caught a glimpse of the unconscious Stein being borne away on a litter by four more human attendants.

"If there's a doctor in the house, Joe-Don, that man could use looking after. The poor chap got clobbered both physically and mentally."

"Don't worry, sir. Lady Damone—Bormol's missus—is an even better medic than Creyn. We get a lot of whacked-out specimens passing through here, the time-portal being the shock that it is. But most of the casualties get fixed up pretty good. This Tanu bunch don't have anything like the tank regeneration equipment we grew up with, but they slop on through pretty good regardless. They're mighty tough themselves and they can heal most injuries and diseases with the help of the torcs. Lady Damone'll give your pal a good veinfeed and see to his scattered marbles. Another day, he'll be as good as new. Quite a pile of muscle, isn't he? They must have him tapped for the Grand Combat."

"And what," Bryan asked quietly, "might that be?"

Joe-Don blinked, then grinned. "Kind of sports event they have a couple of months from now, around the end of October. Traditional with these folks. They're great ones for traditions... Well, here's your room, sir."

He threw open the door to an airy chamber that had white draperies billowing in front of a large window. A vertical string of sapphire lanterns hung beside a cool-looking bed. More-conventional oil lamps cast a pool of yellow radiance on a table where a simple supper had been laid out.

Joe-Don said, "If you need anything, just pull this ring beside the bed and we'll come running. I don't suppose you'll require any consoling companionship? No? Well, sweet dreams anyhow."

He whisked out and closed the door firmly behind him. Bryan didn't bother to test the lock. He gave a great sigh and began unbuttoning his shirt. Somehow, although he had not been aware of moving upward, he had come to the topmost floor of the Tanu mansion. The view from his window overlooked much of the town and gave him a distant glimpse of the city gate. Roniah lay silent and glittering, an earthbound constellation, reminding him of a Christmas display he had seen long ago on one of the more extravagant Hispanic-heritage worlds.

He wondered in a perfunctory fashion what kind of exotic cheer his companions were presently enjoying down at the Tanu party. No doubt he'd hear all about it tomorrow. Yawning, he folded the shirt . . . and felt the small bulk of the durofilm sheets tucked into the breast pocket. He took them out and there was her picture, glowing dimly with its own light.

Oh, Mercy.

Have they taken you and made you one of themselves, as they are trying to do with my friends? Thin sad woman with yearning sea-deep eyes and a smile that keeps me bound despite all reason! I have never heard you play your harp and sing; but my mind's ear creates you:

> There is a lady sweet and kind
> Was never face so pleased my mind.
> I did but see her passing by,
> And yet I love her till I die.
>
> Her gestures, motions, and her smile,
> Her wit, her voice my heart
>   beguiled,
> Beguiled my heart, I know not why,
> And yet I love her till I die.

A deep brazen note sounded, snatching him from his fatigue-drugged reverie. It was the great gong at the city gate. The portal swung open in response, seeming to admit the rising sun.

"Christ!" whispered Bryan. He watched transfixed as the Hunt came a-homing.

A rainbow poured down the main avenue of the town, taking the same route that their own party had followed not long before. Flaring and twisting, the creature of light resolved itself into a procession of splendidly mounted Tanu leaping about with the antic joy of a Novo Janeiro Mardi Gras parade. Both chalikos and riders glowed with an internal effulgence that continually shifted up and down the entire spectrum. The Hunt came closer and closer and eventually passed almost under Bryan's window. He saw that the participants, men and women alike, were arrayed in bizarre armor, apparently of gem-studded glass, adorned with spikes and knobs and other decorative excrescences that gave them the look of humanoid crustaceans fashioned out of diamonds. The chalikos were partially armored with the same material and wore shining gems on their foreheads. Both mounts and riders trailed brightly colored streamers of gossamer fabric that emitted sparks from the tapered ends.

The Hunt made a triumphant noise. The men struck their bejeweled shields with glowing glass swords to produce a musical clangor; some of the women sounded weirdly twisted glass horns with animal-head bells, and others chanted at the top of their powerful voices. Near the end of the parade were six riders glowing a uniform neonred, evidently the heroes of this particular chase. They held tall lances, upon which were mounted the night's trophies.

Severed heads.

Four of the heads had belonged to monsters—a fanged and wattled horror gleaming black and wet, a reptile with ears like batwings and a fringe of tentacles at its cheeks that still twitched, a thing having branched golden antlers and the face of a bird of prey, a nightmare simian with pure white fur and still-blinking eyes the size of apples.

The other two heads were smaller. Bryan saw them quite clearly as the procession passed by. They had belonged to an ordinary little man and woman of late middle age

11

IT WAS THE UNEXPECTED RE-CREATION OF OLD PAIN THAT finally gave Amerie her insight.

The swollen ankles chained immobile to the high stirrups, the stretched muscles on the insides of her thighs, the horde of imps twanging the spinal ganglia in the small of her back, the cramps in calves and knees—she remembered them. It had been just like this twenty-six years ago.

Her father had told the family that descending into the Grand Canyon of the Colorado on a mule would be a wonderful adventure, a trip through a cut-open layercake of planetary history that they would all look back on and savor after they'd gone out to far Multnomah. And it had started out fine. On the trail down, Amerie the child delighted in fingering the strata of colored rock that became older and older, until at the bottom she had picked up a two-billion-year-old fragment of black glittering Vishnu schist and studied it with suitable awe.

But then had come the journey back up to the Canyon's rim. And pain. That endless trip, with aching legs that finally went into spasms as she subconsciously tried to help the mule on its upward climb. Her parents were experienced trailriders and knew how to sit the slope. Her little brothers with their wire-and-plass toughness were happy to let their mounts do the work. But she, the conscientious one, had known the dreadful job that the mule was doing and had unwittingly demanded to share it. Toward the end she was crippled and weeping, and the others had sympathized with poor little Annamaria, but of course it was better to keep on riding and get to the top so that it would be over, rather than stop on the trail and delay the whole party. And Dad had urged her to be his big brave girl, and Mom had smiled pityingly, and the two little brothers had looked superior. Back on the South Rim, Dad had taken her into his arms and carried her to their room and put her to bed. She had slept for eighteen hours, and the brothers teased her for missing out on the egg ride to the Painted Desert, and she had felt guilty. That had started it all.

Mom and Dad and the boys, all gone now. But the big girl still tried to carry her load no matter how much it hurt. So there. Now you begin to understand why you have come here and all the rest of it. This pain and the remembered old ones trigger the realization. And now, just as scab-rip and toothpull and boneset can help true healing begin, now you can recover! But God, what a fool you have been. And now here you are *here* and the insight has come too late.

Amerie rode her chaliko in the Pliocene sunrise. Felice was asleep on the mount to her left, having told the nun that riding these animals was a pleasure after the half-tamed verruls of Acadie. All around the train of slumped riders, the birds of the plateau were clamoring in the dawn chorus. Should she sing her own song of praise in spite of everything? The sleep-learned Latin phrases presented themselves. Wednesday in Summer. She had forgotten Matins at midnight, so better do that before the Lauds that properly belong to dawn.

She chanted softly as the eastern sky turned from purplish gray to yellow with cirrus wisps like torn vermilion chiffon.

> Cor meum conturbatum est in me:
>> et formido mortis cecidit super me.
> Timor et tremor venerunt super me:
>> et contexerunt me tenebrae.
> Et dixit: Quis dabit mihi pennas sicut columbae,
>> et volabo, et requiescam!

Her head sank upon her breast and tears fell onto the white homespun of her habit. From the next rider ahead of her came a quiet laugh.

"Interesting that you pray in a dead language. Still, I daresay we could all do with a bit of Psalm Fifty-Five."

She looked up. It was a man in a Tyrolean hat, turned partway around in his saddle and smiling at her.

He declaimed: "'My heart is sore pained within·me! And the terrors of death are fallen upon me. Fear and trembling have seized me, and darkness has overwhelmed me. And I said: O that I had wings like a dove! For then I would fly away and be at rest.'... What's next?"

She said miserably, "'Ecce elongavi fugiens: et mansi in solitudine.'"

"Oh, yes. 'Lo, I would flee far away and live in the wilderness.'" He waved a hand at the emergent landscape. "And here it is! Magnificent. Just look at those mountains in the east. They're the Jura. Amazing the difference six million years makes in them, you know. Some of those ridges must be at three thousand meters—perhaps twice as high as the Jura of our time."

Amerie wiped her eyes on her scapular. "You knew them?"

"Oh, yes. I was very keen. Tramped and climbed all over the Earth, but liked the Alps best. I'd planned to climb them again in their juvenile aspect. My reason for coming to Exile, you see. In my last rejuv, I had my lung capacity upped twenty percent. Had the heart and large muscles fortified as well. I'd brought all kinds of special climbing gear along. D'you know— parts of the Pliocene Alps might be higher than the Himalaya we knew? Our Alps were greatly eroded by the Ice Age that'll be along in a few million years. The really high country would be farther south, around Monte Rosa on the old Swiss-Italian border, or southwest into Provence where the Dent Blanche nappe overrides Rosa's. There could be folds down there pushed above nine thousand meters. There could be a mountain higher than Everest! I hoped to spend the rest of my life climbing these Pliocene mountains. Even the Alpine Everest, if I managed to find a few kindred souls to accompany me."

"Perhaps you still will." The nun tried to force a smile.

"Not friggerty likely," he replied cheerily. "These exotics and their flunkies will put me to work hewing wood or drawing water when they find out that my only talents are classical donning and falling off alps. If I'm lucky and have any spare time after slavery, I'll tootle tunes for drinks in the local equivalent of the village pub."

He apologized for interrupting her prayers and turned forward again. In a few moments, Amerie heard the soft sounds of his flute mingling with the birdsong.

She resumed her own quiet chanting.

The caravan was on a downhill slope once more, still traveling northward parallel to the Saône. The great river was invisible, but its course was marked by a wide belt of mist-hung forest far down in the valley. The countryside beyond the woodland on the opposite bank was much flatter, a prairie dotted with trees that gradually blended into a marshy plain with many small meres and sloughs that sparkled as the sun climbed. Tributary streams twisted through the eastern swamp; but the west bank of the Saône that they traveled was several hundred meters higher, cut only by widely separated creeks and gullies, which the patient chalikos plodded across while scarcely breaking stride.

Now that it was fully light, Amerie could see the other people in the train—the soldiers and Epone riding three or four ranks ahead, the pairs of prisoners strung out behind at neatly maintained intervals. Richard and Claude were near the baggage animals and the rear guard. The outriding amphicyons galumphed stoically on either side, sometimes closing in, so that she saw their evil yellow eyes or smelled the carrion reek of their bodies. The chalikos had their own distinctive smell, odd and sulfurous, like a flatus of turnips. It must be from the roots they eat, she thought wearily. All that food that made them so big and strong and *wide*.

She groaned and tried to ease her tormented muscles. Nothing helped, not even prayer. Fac me tecum pie flere, Crucifixo condolere, donec ego vexero. Oh, shit, Lord. This isn't going to work.

"Look, Amerie! Antelopes!"

Felice was awake, pointing to the savanna on their left where a golden rise of land seemed strangely overgrown with dark stalks that waved in all directions. Then Amerie realized that the stalks were horns and the entire hillside was thick with reddish-tawny bodies. Thousands upon thousands of gazelles were grazing the dried grass. They were undisturbed by the passing caravan and raised mild black-and-white faces, seeming to nod their lyre-shaped horns at the amphicyons, which ignored them.

"Aren't they beautiful?" cried Felice. "And over there! Those little horses!"

Hipparions were even more numerous than the gazelles, roaming the uplands in huge loose herds that sometimes seemed to cover an entire square kilometer. As the party of travelers came into lower elevations where the vegetation was more lush, they saw other grazers—goatlike tragocerines with mahogany coats, larger harnessed antelopes that had thin white stripes on their fawn sides, and once in a scrubby little grove of acacias, massive gray-brown elands bearing stout spiraling horns—the bulls, with their drooping dewlaps, standing over two meters tall at the shoulder.

"All that meat on the hoof," Felice marveled. "And only a few big cats and hyenas and bear-dogs for natural enemies. A hunter would never starve in this world."

"Starving," the nun said dourly, "hardly seems to be the problem." She hoisted her skirt and began to massage her thighs by pounding them with the sides of her hands.

"Poor Amerie. Of course I know what the problem is. I've been working on it. Watch this."

As the nun stared, puzzled, Felice's chalicothere drifted casually toward her own until the sides of the two animals touched lightly. Then Felice's mount moved away, maintaining its steady pace as it trotted a good arm's length to the left of its proper position in line. After just half a minute of this aberrant movement, the beast slipped back into its normal caravan slot. It moved sedately for a few moments, then broke stride so that it decreased the distance between it and the animal ahead by a meter and a half. The chaliko continued tailgating while Amerie began to comprehend what was happening. It fell back into its usual place just as a suspicious bear-dog let out a howl.

"Mamma mia," murmured the nun. "Can the soldiers tell you're doing it?"

"Nobody's fighting my override of their control. There probably is no feedback at all, just the preset command for the entire train that keeps them moving at speed in the selected intervals. You remember when those blue partridges spooked the chalikos early last evening? The guards came back to see that we were all properly lined up again. They wouldn't have had to do that if they had feedback from our mounts."

"True. But—"

"Hang onto your wimple. Now it's your turn."

Amerie's pain and spiritual malaise were swept away in a sudden wash of hope—for her own chalicothere was now duplicating the earlier motions of Felice's animal. When the eerie solo dance had been completed, both of the creatures performed identical maneuvers in concert.

"Te deum laudamus," Amerie whispered. "You just might pull it off, child. But can you reach *them*?" She nodded in the direction of the nearest amphicvon.

"It's going to be hard. Harder than anything I ever did back in the arena on Acadie. But I'm older now." At least four months older. And it isn't a stupid game anymore with me hoping that they'd learn to care instead of only being afraid. But here she is now trusting and even the others would if only they knew. They would trust and admire. But how to test? Must not give the thing away. So hard. Which way would be best?

The bear-dog running twenty meters off Felice's left flank came slowly closer, lolling tongue dripping saliva. The brute was nearly exhausted after its long trek. Its wits were slowed and its willpower diminished. The pricking within its mind that urged it onward and kept it alert was being callused round with fatigue and hunger. The call to duty was now weak in comparison to the promise of high meat in the trough and a bed of dry grass in a shady place.

The amphicyon ranged closer and closer to Felice's chaliko. It whimpered and snorted when it realized that it had lost control of itself, shaking its ugly head as though trying to dislodge pesty insects. The heavy jaws clashed, scattering slobber; but still it came closer, pacing together with the chaliko in the dust cloud that swirled about the mount's clawed feet. The amphicyon glared in helpless rage at the small human sitting high above it—the human that was forcing, bending, compelling. It growled its fury, curling its lips above discolored teeth almost the size of Felice's fingers.

She let it go.

The effort had dimmed her vision, and her head ached abominably from the resistance of the stubborn carnivore mind. But—!

"You did that, didn't you," Amerie said.

Felice nodded. "Damn hard, though. The things aren't on light autopilot like the chalikos. It was fighting me every minute. Bear-dogs must work by training-conditioning. That's harder to crack because it's well bedded in the subconscious mind. But I think I've got it figured. Best to go after them when they're worn out, at the end of the day's travel. If I can hang onto two, or even more . . ."

Amerie gave a helpless gesture. It was incomprehensible to the nun, this direct impact of mind upon mind, this operation of a power beyond her own mental capability. What would it be like to be a metapsychic—even an imperfect one such as Felice? To manipulate other living things? To move and reform inanimate matter? What would it be like to *really* create—not merely the ghost of a hiking boot, as she had done with the aid of Epone's device, but a substantial illusion, or even matter and energy themselves? What would it be like to link in Unity with other minds? To probe brains? To enjoy angelic powers?

A bright planet shone in the east near the rising sun. Venus . . . no, call it by its other, more ancient name: Lucifer, bright angel of morning. Amerie felt a tiny frisson of fear.

Lead her not into temptation, but forgive us as we warm ourselves at Felice's fire, even as she burns . . .

The caravan marched down into the lowland, off the plateau into another river valley that opened westward through the Monts du Charolais. The scattered dwarf palmettos, pines, and locust trees of the heights gave way to maples and poplars, walnuts and oaks, and finally to a deep humid forest with sourgum, bald cypress, thickets of bamboo, and huge old tulip trees more than four meters in diameter. Lush shrubbery abounded, making the landscape seem the very exemplar of a primeval jungle. Amerie kept expecting dinosaurs or winged reptiles to appear, knowing at the same time that the notion was idiotic. The Pliocene fauna, when you came down to it, was very similar to that of the replenished Earth six million years in the future.

The riders caught glimpses of small deer with bifurcated horns, a porcupine, and a gigantic sow followed by cunning striped piglets. A troop of medium-sized monkeys swung through the upper storey of the woods, following the caravan and shrieking but never coming close enough to be seen clearly. In some places shrubs and small trees had been uprooted and stripped of green. Piles of droppings smelling of elephant identified this as the work of mastodons. A feline roar of uncanny power caused the bear-dogs to howl back defiantly. Was it machairodus, one of the leonine sabertooth cats that were the commonest large predators of the Pliocene?

After the prisonlike environment of the castle and the numbing transition of the night journey, the time-travelers now became aware of a new feeling that overcame even their fatigue and soreness and the memory of broken hopes. This forest, pierced by the slanting rays of morning sunlight, was unmistakably another world, another Earth. Here in vivid reality was the unspoiled wilderness they had all dreamed of. Blot out the soldiers and the chains and the exotic slave mistress—and this Pliocene woodland could still be apprehended as paradise.

Dew-strung giant spider webs, incredible masses of flowers, fruits and berries shining like baroque jewels in settings of many-hued green . . . cliffs with thin waterfalls dropping into pools in front of mossy grottoes . . . throngs of fearless animals . . . the beauty was real! In spite of themselves, the prisoners discovered that they were scanning the jungle for more marvels as eagerly as any pack of thrill-seeking tourists. Amerie's pain faded before visions of scarlet-and-black butterflies and gaudy treefrogs chiming like elfin bells. Even in August the birds sang their mating songs, for in a world without true winter they had not yet begun to migrate and could raise more than one brood a year. An improbable squirrel with tufted ears and patches of greenish-and-orange fur scolded from a low tree limb. Another tree was draped with a motionless python, its body as thick as a beer barrel and as gorgeously colored as a Kermanshah rug. There went a tiny hornless antelope with legs like twigs and a body no larger than a rabbit's! There flew a bird with a raucous crow voice, feathered in a splendor of violet and pink and darkest blue! By a stream stood a huge otter, poised on hind limbs and seeming to smile amiably at the prisoners riding by. Farther down the creekbed were wild chalicotheres somewhat smaller and darker than their domesticated cousins, ripping up bulrushes for breakfast and man-

aging to look dignified in spite of their mouthfuls of dripping
greenery. In the short grass beside the trail grew crowds of
mushrooms—coral, red with white spots, sky-blue with ma-
genta gills and stems. Creeping amongst them was a many-
legged millipede the size of a salami, looking as though it were
freshly enameled in oxblood-red with cream racing stripes . . .

The horn sounded its three notes.

Amerie sighed. The echoing reply set off the wild things
farther along the trail, so that the caravan met its escort in a
tangled voluntary of bird and animal voices. The forest thinned
and they came into a parklike area beside a slow-flowing river,
some western tributary of the Saône. The trail led over a lawn
beneath venerable cypresses and through the gate of a large
palisaded fort almost identical to the one they had stopped at
during the night.

"All you travelers!" Captal Waldemar bellowed, when the
last of the caravan had entered the gate and the wooden doors
were swung shut. "This is our sleeping stop. We'll rest here
until sunset. I know you're feeling pretty used up. But take
my advice and soak in the big hot-tub in your bathhouse before
you fall into the sack. And eat, even if you think you're too
tired to be hungry! Take your packs with you when you dismount. Anybody sick or gotta complaint, see me. Be ready to
remount this evening after supper when you hear the horn. You
feel like trying to escape, remember that the amphicyons are
outside and so are the sabertooth cats and a really trick orange
salamander the size of a collie dog with venom like a king
cobra. Have a nice rest. That's *all*."

A white-clad hostler helped Amerie from her saddle when
she was unable to get down on her own.

"You want to give yourself a good soak, Sister," the man
said solicitously. "It's the best thing in the world for trail
soreness. We heat the water with a solar setup on the roof, so
there's plenty."

"Thank you," she murmured. "I'll do that."

"You could do something for us here at the fort, too, Sister.
If you're not too tired and stiff, that is." He was a short, coffee-
colored man with graying kinky hair and the preoccupied air
of a minor civil servant.

Amerie felt that she could fall asleep standing up if only
there were something to lean against. But she heard herself

saying, "Of course I'll do anything I can." Her racked leg muscles spasmed in protest.

"We don't often get a priest here. Just a circuit-rider every three or four months—old Brother Anatoly out of Finiah or Sister Ruth from Goriah, way over to the west. We have maybe fifteen Catholics among the men here. We'd really appreciate it if—"

"Yes. Certainly. I suppose you'd prefer the votive Mass of St. John the Beloved Disciple."

"First your nice bath and supper." He picked up her pack, draped her arm over his shoulders, and helped her away.

As soon as Felice had dismounted, she rushed over to Richard and said, "Well? Did you get it?"

"Dead easy. And there's a second-magnitude sparkler sitting right on top of it." He looked down at her from the high back of his chaliko. "Since you're in such good shape, gimme a hand down off this brute."

"Easiest thing in the world," she said. Stepping onto the dismounting block, she put her little hands under his armpits and swung him off in one motion.

"Sweet Jesus!" exclaimed the pirate.

"I could use a little of that, too, Felice," came Claude's dry voice. The ring-hockey player went to the next chaliko and plucked the old man out of the saddle as though he were a child.

"What kinda gravity you have on Acadie, anyhow?" Richard growled.

She bestowed a condescending smile. "Point eight-eight Earth normal. Nice try, Captain Blood, but no joy."

"You mustn't try anything rash here, Felice." Claude was anxious. "I should think they'd be very alert in a place like this."

"Don't worry. I've—"

Richard hissed, "She's coming—watch it! Her nibs!"

The white chaliko bearing Epone paced majestically through the clutter of weary prisoners and their baggage.

"No dust or sweat on that one," remarked Felice bitterly, slapping at the filthy green skirts of her hockey uniform. "Looks like she's ready for the fuckin' beaux-arts ball. Must be ionized fabric in the cloak."

A few of the travelers were still astride their mounts—

among them the sturdy ginger-bearded man with the lion emblazoned on his knightly surtout. He had both elbows resting on the pommel of his saddle. His hands covered his face.

"Dougal!" Epone's voice was at once wheedling and commanding.

The knight leapt in his seat and stared at her wildly. "No! Not again. Please."

But she only signaled for hostlers to take the bridle of the knight's chaliko.

"O thou belle dame sans merci," he groaned. "Aslan. Aslan."

Epone rode away across the fort compound toward a small structure with pots of flowers hanging from its veranda roof. The hostlers led tall Dougal after her.

Claude watched them go and said, "Well, now you know, Richard. It's a good thing you're out of it. She looks like mighty rough trade."

The ex-spacer swallowed the bile that had risen in his throat at memory's slow return. "Who . . . who the hell is Aslan?" he managed to ask.

"A kind of Christ figure in an old fairy tale," the old man replied. "A magical lion who saved children from supernatural enemies in a Never-Never Land called Narnia."

Felice laughed. "I don't think his franchise extends to the Pliocene. Would either of you gentlemen care to join me in a hot tub?"

She marched off to the bathhouse, dusty feathers awave, leaving the others to limp slowly after.

12

OH, WHAT A NIGHT IT HAD BEEN!

Aiken Drum lay sprawled on snowy sheets and let his silver torc give him a replay of the high. Fizzy exotic booze. Delicious exotic food. Fun and games and music and dance and romping and stomping and flying and galloping those exotic broads with their crazy boobs down to there. Sweet houghmagandy! Hadn't he shown them that he was big enough! And hadn't he found his heart's home at last . . . Here in Exile, among these people who loved to laugh and venture as he did, he would thrive and grow and *shine*.

"Gonna be Sir Boss!" he giggled. "Gonna roj this whole fewkin' world until it yells quits! Gonna fly!"

Oh, yes. That, too.

Slowly, his naked body rose from the bed. He spread his arms wide and soared toward the ceiling where the morning sunlight shining through the drapes made ripple-bars of greeny gold. The bedroom was an aquarium and he was a swimmer in the air. Zoom! Bank! Roll! Dive! Let go and fall bouncing back to the bed shouting with delight, for it was a rare gift even among the talented Tanu, and the ladies, especially, had greeted his discovery of it with great excitement.

Wonderful silver torc!

He scrambled off the bed and went to the window. Roniah down below was awake and going about its business—human figures strolling or bustling, stately Tanu mounted on gaily caparisoned chalikos, and everywhere the little ramas at work—sweeping, gardening, fetching and carrying. Kaleidoscopic!

... Hey, Aik. Where you be, buddy?

The mental hail came to him hesitantly and garbled at first, then with increasing confidence. Raimo, of course. The surly woodsman had undergone a remarkable change of attitude as Aiken's new metafunctions became increasingly manifest at the party. Raimo left off his shit-kicking and got friendly. And why not? He could sense a winner, that one!

You there, Ray? You talking at me, Woodchopper?

Who the hell else? Hey, Aik—if this is a dream, don't wake me up.

No dream. It's realio-trulio and we are in for one helluva good time. Hey! What say we bust out and do a little sightseeing in the town?

They got me locked in, Aik.

You forgot what we learned at the party? Hang on a nanosec while I put my clothes on and I'll be right there.

Aiken threw on his golden costume, checked to be sure that no Tanu was watching, then launched himself out of his bedroom window. Hovering above the mansion like a great gleaming insect, he sent his seekersense homing in on Raimo's querulous thought pattern, then dived at the open window of his buddy and popped into the room crowing, "Tah-*dah*!"

"Damn, you really do know how, don't you?" Raimo said with some envy. "Seems I'm only good for pickin' up furniture." By way of demonstration, he caused the bed to dance and sent tables and chairs flying about the room.

"Everybody's different, Chopper. You got your talents, I got mine. You could have diddled the mechanism of the lock to escape, you know."

"Shit. Never thought of it."

Aiken grinned. "You'll be thinking of a lot of things from now on, Ray—and so will I. Last night was some kinda eye-opener, no?"

The former woodsman laughed out loud and the two of them wallowed in a mutual replay, chortling over the discomfiture of the scandalized Sukey and Elizabeth, who had retired abruptly when the members of the Hunt joined the festivities. Poor straity-ladies! No sense of humor and probably fridgies to boot. It had been good riddance when they left, and the party had gone on until dawn, featuring entertainments increasingly delightful that the two men could savor to the full, strengthened by their silver torcs. Good old metaboodly psychokinoodly!

Aiken gestured out of the window. "Come on. Let's see how the human half lives. I'm curious about the way the normals operate in this Exile setup. Don't sweat the flying bit, Ray. I can hold up the both of us."

"They'll spot us."

"I've got another metafunction. The illusion thing. Check this!"

There was a soundless snap and the small golden man disappeared. A tiger swallowtail butterfly flapped up and landed square on Raimo's nose. "Keep those paws down or I go hornet," said Aiken's voice. The butterfly vanished, and there was the practical joker again, standing in front of Raimo with one finger resting on the forester's nose.

"Hell's bells, Aik! You are *loaded*!"

"Say again, Chopper. Gimme your hand. Come on—don't be a poop. We're off!"

Two yellow butterflies flew away from the Tanu dwelling and over the town of Roniah. They swooped above the workshops of potters and rooftile makers and weavers and carpenters and metalsmiths and boatwrights and armorers and glassblowers and sculptors. They intruded upon lapidaries and painters and basketmakers and rehearsing musicians; sipped nectar from the jasmine that bloomed beside swimming pools where pregnant women lounged and laughed; flew into an open-air schoolroom where a dozen blond, lissom children pointed their fingers in amazement and a startled Tanu teacher sent a dangerous query arrowing back toward Bormol's mansion.

"To the docks!" Aiken ordered, and they flew toward the riverside. Broad flights of steps led down to a busy landing stage. Rama stevedores unloaded barges while human dockhands and boatmen, many of them naked to the waist in the morning heat, went about their jobs or loafed in shady places waiting for some other man to finish his.

The two butterflies landed atop a fat mooring bollard and

turned back into Aiken and Raimo. One dockworker gave a
shout. Seagulls rose up from the pavement and pilings, squawking an alarm. Aiken strolled off the bollard, leaving Raimo
sitting there and blinking, and struck a pose in thin air. A burly
bargee gave a shout of laughter and exclaimed, "Well—if it
ain't Peter Pan hisself! But you better send that there Tinkerbell
back for a refit!"

The dockside loafers roared. Up on the bollard, Raimo extended both of his arms to the side. His slanty-eyed Finnish
face wore a crooked grin and a look of odd concentration.
Immediately a dozen gulls fluttered down and aligned themselves from his wrists to his shoulders.

"Hey, Aik! Shootin' gallery! Zap before crap or you lose!"

The hovering little man in gold took aim with his forefinger.
"Pam!" he said. "Pam-pam-pammidy-*pam*!"

Small flashes ran along Raimo's plaid-flanneled arms. He
was engulfed in a cloud of smoke and fragmentary white feathers. The audience whistled and applauded while Raimo sneezed.
"Attaway, li'l biddy buddy!"

"And for my encore," Aiken cried, making a pass with both
hands at the bollard itself, "I give you—*shazoom*!"

There was a sharp explosion. The heavy timbers of Raimo's
perch disintegrated, leaving him suspended above the water
wearing a look of pained surprise.

"Was that nice?" the ex-forester expostulated. He floated
over to the chuckling Aiken, grasped him by the epaulets of
his golden suit, and suggested, "Maybe we should cool off
with a swim!"

The two airborne figures began to wrestle, bouncing low
over the muddy yellow waters of the Rhône among the moored
lighters and wherries and barges like wind-tossed carnival bal-
loons. The men on the docks cackled and stamped, and terrified
ramas dropped their burdens and covered their eyes.

Enough!

Creyn's mental command whipped out, hauling the two back
to the quayside and depositing them onto the pavement with a
painful jolt. Four attendants from Bormol's mansion stepped
forward to take firm hold of the still snickering miscreants.
With the fun clearly at an end, the dockworkers and boatmen
began drifting back to their jobs.

"I am programming mental restraints upon your major metapsychic functions until you have received proper training at the capital," Creyn said. "We'll have no more of this childish behavior."

Aiken waved at Elizabeth, Bryan, and Sukey, who were being escorted down the quay stairs together with Stein on his litter.

Raimo said, "Aw, Chief. How else we gonna learn what we can do?"

Aiken added, "Lord Bormol told us last night to get right into it. And did we ever!" He winked at Sukey, who glared at him.

Creyn said, "From now on, you'll do your learning in a controlled environment. Lord Bormol doesn't need you repaying his hospitality by destroying his wharf."

The little man in gold shrugged. "Don't know my own strength yet is all. You want me to try putting that thing back together again?"

Creyn's eyes, opaque blue in the sunlight, narrowed. "So you think you could? How very interesting. But I think we'll wait, Aiken Drum. It will be far safer for all of us if you stay on the leash for the time being."

Elizabeth's thought came stealing gently along...

So many wild talents you do have Aiken. What else is hidden in there? Let me look.

She sent a probe boring into him. It caromed off a hastily erected but effective barrier.

"Cut it out, Elizabeth!" Aiken cried aloud. "Quit or I'll fewkin' well zap you!"

She regarded him sadly. "Would you, really?"

"Well—" He hesitated, then gave her a lopsided smile. "Maybe not, sweetie-face. But I can't have you messing about with me, you know. Not even in fun. I'm not Stein...or Sukey, either."

Creyn said, "Our boat is waiting for us at the end of the landing stage. We must be on our way." But as they all went down the dock, the Tanu man reached out to Elizabeth on a narrow-focus mode that spoke to her mind alone:

Did you see how he did that?

Primitive/effective. Even versus me unprepared. Concerned?

Appalled actually.

How effective torcrestraint?

Adequate now while he still unuse fullpotential. Later silver never suffice will seize gold. Educators face dilemma that one. May require termination. Not my decision Tanabethanked.

Capable vastmischief even when latent. Rare old humantype uncommon in Milieu: clownmeddler.

Type not unknown among Tanu alas. Predict kid smashhit Muriah. Query Muriah survive impact.

Ironical justdeserts to your slavemasters. Humanity preyperilous.

Ah Elizabeth.

Deny? Laugh. Manipucraftylators! Desocialization/ resocialization exiles shrewdly essayed. Example: castle environment anxietyprovoke. Follows party warmthfriendshippowersexgoodies. Reinforce lesson severed heads. Crude goodguy/badguy punish/reward terror/relief mindforming. Aiken + Raimo + (Sukey?) yours. Both Hunts victorious.

How else integrate minimal delay? Some types e.g., Aiken superhazard.

More like you than you?

Perceptive Elizabeth. Angelic aloof overflyer despising pathetic exilemisfits.

!

"Ah, Elizabeth. We get to know one another better and better."

The skipper who welcomed them to the unusual boat that would take them downriver wore khaki pants and a sweat-stained T-shirt. His belly overflowed his waistband. A crinkly peppered-salt mustache and fringe-beard bracketed the jovial smile on his mahogany face. He flicked Creyn a casual salute, one finger tapping the bill of a decrepit U.S. Navy cap of twentieth-century vintage.

"Welcome aboard, milord and ladies and gents! Skipper Highjohn at your service. Take any pew you like, but the best view is up forward. Bring that stretcher over here and lash it to the tie-downs."

The human travelers came onto the strange craft and settled somewhat apprehensively into the seats, which were pneumatically cushioned and form-fitting, with elaborate harnesses that the skipper helped them to fasten.

"Is the river very rough, Captain?" Sukey inquired. She had positioned herself near Stein and kept darting uneasy glances at the sleeping giant while the attendants secured him with strong webbing.

"Don't you be concerned. I've done this Rhône-Med run for sixteen years and never lost a boat." Highjohn flipped a lid on the chair arm and revealed a hidden container. "Little barf-bucket if you need it."

Aiken piped up. "You may not have lost a boat—but how about a passenger?"

"You look like you got a strong ticker, boy. If things get too wild for you, Lord Creyn will program a calmative into your torc. Everybody set now? We'll be stopping for lunch at Feligompo Plantation around noon for any of you who have appetites. Tonight we'll be at Darask, which is below the site of the future Avignon. You know—the place with the bridge. See you later."

With a friendly wave, he went forward. The attendants from the mansion who had carried on Stein and their baggage now trooped ashore. Dockhands began scurrying about the vessel, preparing it for castoff. The passengers watched with mingled interest and unease.

The riverboat was similar in design to most of the others at the quayside, measuring about fourteen meters from its high, knife-sharp bow to its gluteally rounded stern. It was a distant cousin to the inflatable rafts and foldboats used by sportsmen and explorers on the whiter waters of the Galactic Milieu. The hull—stenciled on both sides with the name of the boat, Mojo—was a tough air-filled membrane with fat exterior corrugations and pillowlike fenders jutting out at regular intervals along the waterline. It looked as if it could be deflated and disassembled for shipment upstream via caravan. Tightly covered hatch openings fore and aft gave access to cargo holds, while the passenger accommodation was in an open area amidships that was arched over with a series of half-hoops. The dockworkers quickly covered this frame with panels of deeply tinted transparent film resembling decamole. When the last section of the bubbletop was sealed, an air blower began to operate inside the boat, providing ventilation for the occupants and rendering the water-proof canopy rigid.

Sukey turned to Elizabeth, who sat in the seat beside her.

"I didn't like the way the Captain talked. What are we getting into?"

"An interesting ride, at any rate, if the signs and portents add up. Bryan—do you know anything at all about the River Rhône?"

"It was all cut up with dams and locks and bypass channels in our time," the anthropologist replied. "The gradient is probably a lot steeper here in the Pliocene, so there are bound to be rapids. When we approach the Avignon region about a hundred-fifty kloms south of here, we'll be in an area that very likely has a deep gorge. In the twenty-second century it was stoppered by the Donzère-Mondragon Barrage, one of the largest damn projects in Europe. What we'll find down there now . . . well, it can't be too bad or they wouldn't try to navigate it, would they?"

Aiken uttered a shaky laugh. "Good question. Well, ready or not, guys, we're off to the races."

A rather stout telescoping mast was rising up behind the passenger compartment. When it reached its full height of four meters, the top section opened to disgorge a boom with a roller sail, looking for all the world like an old-fashioned portable movie screen. The sail unfurled and gave a few tentative swiveling motions. Dockhands cast off the boat's mooring warps, and vibration in the deck betokened the operation of a small auxiliary engine. The Mojo began threading in and out of the other shore traffic on its way to the mainstream, leading Bryan to deduce that it must utilize more than one rudder for maximum maneuverability.

They angled sharply away from the shore. As the current took them, the walled city of Roniah fell away astern with amazing swiftness. It was not too easy to estimate their speed, since they were a good two hundred meters from either shore; but Bryan guessed that the sediment-laden flood was racing along at a minimum of twenty knots. What would happen when this great volume of water was compressed between high rock walls farther downstream challenged the imagination of the anthropologist. His speculations were of a decidedly queasy sort.

Raimo, in the seat next to him, had found his own brand of solace. He took a pull from his replenished silver flask and offered it to Bryan rather half-heartedly. "Tanu popskull. Hardly Hudson's Bay standard, but not too bad."

"Maybe later," Bryan said, smiling. Raimo grunted and took another swallow. The euphoria of his morning adventure had faded away, leaving the ex-forester brooding and ill at ease. Bryan tried to draw Raimo out with questions about the previous night's revelry but received only the curtest replies.

"You hadda be there," Raimo said, and lapsed into silence.

For nearly an hour they moved easily through a wide bluff-sided channel—the forested foothills of the Alps on their left hand and arid tablelands rising above the near-jungle of the humid bottoms on the right. Occasionally, Creyn pointed out the location of a plantation; but the trees were so thick that it was impossible to see any details of the settlements ashore. They glimpsed smaller boats plying the shallows and once they overhauled a long covered barge riding deep in the water, baremasted and having only a small bubble over the midships steersman's cockpit. The barge greeted them with a toot from his airhorn, to which Skipper Highjohn responded with a syncopated blast of his own.

The river made a wide curve and the channel passed between a tall headland and a group of craggy islets. Small mechanical sounds announced the furling of their sail, the boom's folding, and the withdrawal of the telescoping mast back into its housing. Far from losing speed, the boat moved along faster rounding the point. It seemed to Bryan that they must be making thirty knots or more. Simultaneously he became aware of a deep vibration transmitted by the water through the sealed hull of the boat, the inflated headrest of his seat, and the very bones of his skull. The vibration increased to an audible roar as the boat came charging around a sharp bend. The walls of a canyon rose on both sides.

Sukey screamed and Raimo yelped an obscenity.

Ahead of them the narrowing Rhône slanted downhill at a one-in-five gradient, the river lashed to a foaming frenzy by the rocks of its tilted bed. The boat seemed to dive into the rapids and a great avalanche of ochre water crashed over the canopy and temporarily engulfed them. Then Mojo broke free and came to the surface, planing along among monstrous standing waves and granite boulders, rolling so steeply that yellow water climbed halfway up the watertight bubble first on one side, then on the other. The noise was almost insupportable. Raimo's mouth was wide open but his yells went unheard amidst the uproar of the cascading Rhône.

A dark mass loomed ahead. The boat heeled nearly sixty degrees to starboard as they went whipping around a tall rock pinnacle into a crooked slot between files of huge boulders. The air was so filled with flying spume that it seemed impossible that their skipper could see where he was going. Nevertheless the boat continued to zig and zag among the rocks with only an occasional bump against the pneumatic fenders.

A respite came in the form of a deep cut where the river flowed free. But the voice of Highjohn called, "One last time, folks!" and Bryan realized that they were rocketing through the defile toward a veritable fence of sharp crags, fanglike chunks of broken granite against which the yellow river waters crashed in overlapping curtains of spray. There seemed to be no way through. The stunned time-travelers gripped the arms of their seats and braced for the inevitable impact.

Mojo raced toward the tallest of the rocks, pitching violently. It crashed into the foam—but instead of hitting solid rock or sinking, it rose higher and higher on some unseen surge. There was a thrumming blow against the port side as they bounced off a rock face, completely drowned in the opaque pother. The boat seemed to roll a full 360 degrees and then wallow free to sail through the air. It landed with a bone-jarring impact, water closing again over the top of the canopy. Almost immediately it popped to the surface, floating in complete tranquillity across a broad pool that spread between low walls. Behind them was the cut they had just traversed, spewing a horsetail cataract, like the outflow of a titanic drain, into the basin thirty meters below.

"You can unfasten your safety belts now, folks," the skipper said. "That'll be all the cheap thrills for this morning. After lunch, it *really* gets rough."

He came back into the passenger compartment to check the canopy for possible leakage. "Didn't take in a drop!"

"Congratulations," whispered Bryan. With one trembling hand he fumbled with the buckles of the harness.

"Give you a hand?" suggested Highjohn, bending over to help.

Released, Bryan rose weakly to his feet. He saw that all of the others, including Creyn and Elizabeth, were motionless in their seats, eyes closed, apparently asleep.

Fists on hips, the riverman surveyed the passengers with a slow shake of his head. "Every goddamn time. These sensitive Tanu types just can't take Cameron's Sluice, being afraid of water as they mostly are. So they zonk out. And if the torc-wearing humans show any distress, the Tanu just program a zonk for them, too. Kinda disappointing—you know? Every artist likes to have an audience."

"I take your point," Bryan said.

"I don't often get a rarey like you, no torc and all and man enough to come through it without a case of the yammering fantods. This lady without the torc"—he pointed to Elizabeth—"must have just fainted away."

"Not likely," Bryan said. "She's an operant metapsychic. I dare say she just did her own calming mental exercise and napped through the excitement, just as Creyn did."

"But not you, eh, sport? I suppose you've been on rough water before."

Bryan shrugged. "Hobby sailor. North Sea, Channel, Med. The usual thing."

Highjohn clapped him on the shoulder. His eyes twinkled and he gave Bryan a comradely smile. "Tell you what. You come on forward with me and I'll show you a thing or three about driving this tub before we reach Feligompo. If you enjoy it—who knows? There's lots worse jobs you could settle into in this Exile."

"I'd enjoy riding with you in the wheelhouse," Bryan said, "but I won't be able to take you up on your offer of an apprenticeship." He grinned ruefully. "I believe the Tanu have other plans for me."

13

CLAUDE AWOKE. A COOL BREEZE BLEW THROUGH HANGING strings of wooden beads that screened all four sides of the prisoners' dormitory and kept insects from flying in. Two guards paced around and around outside the shelter, bronze helmets turning as they scanned the inmates, compound bows strung and ready, resting lightly on their shoulders where they could be drawn in an instant.

The old man tested his limbs—and by God, they worked. His field adaptation system was still Go after all the years. He sat up on his pallet and looked around. Almost all of the other prisoners were still lying as though drugged. But Felice was up, and Basil the Alpine climber, and the two Japanese ronin. Faint yapping sounds came from a closed basket next to a sleeping woman. There were snores and a few moans from the other sleepers.

Claude quietly watched Felice. She was talking in low tones with the three other men. Once one of the ronin tried to protest something she was saying. She cut him short with a fierce gesture and the Oriental warrior subsided.

It was very late in the afternoon and quite hot. The space within the walled fort was deep in green shade. A smell of cooking wafted from one of the buildings, making Claude's mouth water. Another meat stew, and something like fruit pies baking. Whatever its other flaws, the Exile society certainly ate well.

Having finished her discussion, Felice crept across the crowded floor to Claude's resting place. She looked keyed up and her brown eyes were wide. She wore the sleeveless kilt-dress that was the undergarment to her hoplite armor, but had put off the rest of the uniform with the exception of the black shin guards. The bare areas of her skin were lightly sheened with perspiration.

"Wake Richard up," she whispered peremptorily.

Claude shook the shoulder of the sleeping ex-spacer. Muttering obscenities, Richard hoisted himself onto his elbows.

"We'll probably have to do it tonight," Felice said. "One of the fort people told Amerie that by tomorrow we'll be into very heavy country where this plan of mine wouldn't have much chance of working. I need open space to see what I'm doing. What I'll do is pick a time before dawn tomorrow when it's still fairly dark and the bear-dogs are running on the dregs of their second wind."

"Now wait a minute," Richard protested. "Don't you think we'd better discuss this plan of yours first?"

She ignored him. "Those others—Yosh, Tat, Basil—they'll try to help us. I asked the Gypsies, but they're half crazy and won't take orders from a woman anyway. So this is what we do. After the midnight break, Richard changes places with Amerie and rides beside me."

"Come on, Felice! The guards'll spot the switch."

"You change clothes with her in the latrine."

"Not on your—" Richard blazed. But Felice caught him by the lapels and dragged him over the floor on his stomach until they were nose to nose.

"You shut up and listen, Captain Asshole. None of the rest of you have a hope in hell of getting out of this. Amerie pumped one of the guards after she said Mass for them this morning. These exotics have metafunctions that can zap out your brain and turn you into a lunatic or a fuckin' zombie. They can't even be *killed* with ordinary weapons! They've got some system for controlling their slave-cities that's almost perfect. Once we arrive at Finiah and they test me out and find I'm latent, they'll collar me or kill me and the rest of you'll be lucky to spend your lives shoveling shit in the chaliko barns. This is our *chance*, Richard! And you're going to do as I say!"

"Let him go, Felice," said Claude urgently. "The guards."

When she dropped him, Richard whispered, "Damn you, Felice! I didn't say I wouldn't help. But you can't treat me like a friggerty baby!"

"What else would you call a grown man who craps up his bed?" she inquired. "Who changed your dydees when you drove starships, Captain?"

Richard went white. Claude was furious. "Stop it! Both of you! . . . Richard, you were sick. A man can't help himself when he's sick. For God's sake, forget the matter. We were glad to help you. But you've got to pull yourself together now and join with the rest of us in this plan to escape. You can't let your personal feelings toward Felice wreck what may be our only chance to get out of this nightmare."

Richard glared at the little ring-hockey player, then gave her a twisted grin. "You may be the only one of us who's a match for 'em at that, sweetie-babe. Sure. I'll go along with whatever you say."

"That's fine," she told him. She reached behind the black leather of her left greave and extracted what looked like a slender golden cross. "Now the first good news is that we aren't completely weaponless . . ."

They rode away in the evening with a crescent moon shining through the cypresses. After fording the shallow tributary, the trail climbed to the Burgundian plateau and once more resumed its northerly course. Fire-beacons lit the way through deepening twilight. After a time they were able to look down on a vast heaving region of mist marking extensive swamplands where the Pliocene Saône was born from the prehistoric Lac de Bresse. The lake waters stretched northward and eastward into the distance like a sheet of black glass, drowning the entire plain below the Côte d'Or. Richard entertained the old paleontologist with descriptions of the legendary wines that would be produced in this district six million years into the future.

Later, when the stars were bright, Richard took one last sighting of Pliocene Polaris. It was the brightest star in a constellation that the two men dubbed the Big Turkey.

"That's a good job you've done," Claude said.

"The whole business may turn out to be academic if we end up dead or brain-burned . . . You think this scheme of Felice's might really work?"

"Think about this, son. Felice would be able to escape by herself fairly easily. But she's worked out this plan to give the rest of us a chance, too. You may hate the little lady's entrails, but she just might bring this thing off. I'm going to do my damnedest for her, even though I'm just an old poop one step this side of fossilization. But you're still a young man, Richard. You look like you could handle yourself in a fight. We're counting on you."

"I'm scared outa my motherin' mind," the pirate told him. "That little bitty gold knife of hers! It's nothing but a toy. How the hell am I going to do it?"

The old man said, "Try Amerie's prescription. Pray a lot."

In the forward part of the caravan, Basil the Alpinist was saluting the sinking crescent moon by playing "Au claire de la lune" on his recorder. The little butterfly dancer from Paris, who rode beside him, sang along. And amazingly enough, Epone herself joined in in a soprano voice of melting richness. The exotic woman continued to sing as Basil played several more songs; but when he began "Londonderry Air," one of the soldiers galloped back on his chaliko and said, "The Exalted Lady forbids the commonalty to sing that song."

The climber shrugged and put his flute away.

The butterfly dancer said, "The monster sings that song with her own words. I heard her, back at Castle Gateway on the first night that we were imprisoned. Isn't it odd that a monster should be musical? It's like a fairytale—and Epone is like a beautiful wicked witch."

"The witch may sing a different song before dawn," Felice said; but only the nun heard her.

The trail came closer and closer to the western shore of the great lake. The caravan would have to skirt it before heading east into the Belfort Gap between the Vosges highland and the Jura, which led to the valley of the Proto-Rhine. The lake waters were utterly calm, reflecting the brighter stars like an inky mirror. As the curve of the trail took them around a promontory, they saw a distant beacon reflected as well, a streak of orange stabbing toward them across a broad bay.

"Look—not one fire but *two*." Felice's voice held a note of anxiety. "Now what the devil do you suppose that means?"

One of the soldiers from the rear of the caravan galloped past them to confer with Captal Waldemar, then returned to his position. The chalikos slowed to a walk and finally halted altogether. Epone and Waldemar rode off the trail to the top of a small rise where they could survey the lake.

Felice gently pounded one fist into the palm of her other hand and whispered, "Shit shit shit."

"There's something out there on the water," said Amerie.

A light mist filmed the reaches of the bay. One part of it seemed to thicken and grow bright as they watched, then break into four separate, dimly shining masses, fuzzy and amorphous. As the will-o'-the-wisps approached, they grew larger and glowed in color—one faintly blue, another pale gold, and two deep red. They bounced up and down as they followed a devious path over the water to a place not far offshore from the halted caravan.

"Les lutins," said the butterfly dancer, her voice rough with fear.

The central portion of each mass now revealed a form suspended within the glow, rounded bodies with dangling appendages that flexed. They were at least twice as tall as a human being.

"Why, they look just like giant spiders!" whispered Amerie.

"Les lutins araignées," the dancer repeated. "My old Grandmère told me the ancient tales. They are the shape-shifters."

"It's an illusion," Felice decided. "Watch Epone."

The Tanu woman had risen in her stirrups so that she stood high above the back of her motionless white chaliko. The hood of her cloak dropped so that her hair was luminous in the multihued light radiating from the things out on the lake. She placed both hands at her neck and cried out a single word in the exotic language.

The flame-spiders elevated their abdomens at her. Filaments of purple light rocketed toward Epone and over the heads of the prisoners. The people exclaimed in wonderment, hardly conscious of fear. The episode was so bizarre that it seemed like a light-show performance.

The bright webbing never reached the ground. As it shimmered above them, it began shattering into a myriad of glittering fragments like dying fireworks. The outer edges of the individual spiders' haloes started to disintegrate in the same corruscating fashion, enveloping the phantoms in a cloud of swirling sparks. The glowing spiders became krakens with writhing tentacles, then monstrous disembodied human heads with Medusa hair and fiery eyes, and finally featureless balls that dwindled, dimmed, and winked out.

Only stars and the beacon fires gleamed on the lake.

Epone and the captal rode back to the trail and resumed their places at the head of the procession. The chalikos snorted and whiffled and set out again at their usual trot. One of the soldiers said something to a prisoner at the head of the column, and the word passed slowly back.

"Firvulag. Those were Firvulag."

"It was an illusion," Felice insisted. "But something sure as hell caused it. Something that doesn't like the Tanu any more than we do. That's very interesting."

"Does this mean you'll have to change your plan?" Amerie asked.

"Not bloody likely. It may even help. If the guards are on the lookout for ghoulies and ghosties and long-leggety beasties, they'll pay less attention to *us*."

The cavalcade came around the bay to the place of the double beacon, where the prisoners entered another fort for the midnight rest. Felice dismounted quickly and came to assist all three of her friends, and several other riders as well. And later, when it was time to climb back into the saddle, she was there again to help the tired people fit their feet into the stirrups just before the soldiers came around to lock on the bronze ankle chains with their enveloping leather sleeves.

"Sister Amerie isn't feeling well," the little athlete told the guard who locked her onto her own beast. "Those strange creatures out on the lake gave her a bad turn."

"Don't you worry about the Firvulag, Sister," the man told the veiled, drooping rider. "There's no way they can get you as long as the Exalted Lady is with us. She's tops as a coercer. You just ride easy."

"Bless you," came a whisper.

When the soldier moved away to tend to Basil and the dancer, Felice said, "You just try to go to sleep, Sister. That's the best thing for nerves." In a lower tone she added, "And keep your cunnilingin' trap shut like I told you!"

The poor sick nun invited Felice to take an unlikely anatomical excursion.

They went on, following the shore but still trending northward. After an hour had passed, Claude said, "I'm free. How about you, Amerie?"

The rider beside him was incongruously garbed in a starship captain's coverall and a wide-brimmed black hat with dark plumes. "My chains are broken. What an incredible child Felice is! But I can understand why she was ostracized by the other ring-hockey players. It's too freakish, all that strength in such a doll-like body."

"Her *physical* strength is something the others could live with," Claude said, leaving it at that.

Presently, Amerie asked, "How many people did she set free?"

"The two Japanese riding behind her. Basil, the fellow in the Tyrolean hat. And that poor medievalist knight, Dougal, just ahead of Basil. Dougal doesn't know that his chains have been weakened enough to be broken. Felice didn't think he was stable enough to let in on the scheme. But when the thing starts we might get him to break loose and help. Lord knows he's big and strong-looking, and maybe he hates Epone enough to snap out of his funk when he sees others in action."

"I hope Richard will be all right."

"Don't worry. I think he's ready to do his part—if only to show Felice that she's not the only one with balls."

The nun laughed. "What a collection we are! Exiles and losers all. We got just what we deserved—running away from our responsibilities. Look at me. A lot of people needed my ministry. But I had to brood and maunder about my own precious spirituality instead of getting on with my job . . . You know, Claude, most of last night was hell for me. There's something about riding that hits me in the worst way. And while I was hurting, I found I was shrinking myself. I think I finally understand the reasons why I got into this mess. Not just coming to Exile—the whole thing."

The old man said nothing.

"I think you figured it out, too, Claude. Quite a while ago."

"Well, yes," he admitted. "When we talked about your childhood that day on the mountain. But you had to find it out for yourself."

She said softly, "The firstborn daughter with the Little Mama thing in the warm Italianate family. The hard-working professional parents depending on her to help raise the cute little brothers. She loving to do it, power-tripping on the responsibility. Then the family gets ready to emigrate to a new world. Exciting! But the daughter screws up by straining some muscles and then breaking her leg in a fall."

... But just one short week in the tank, dear, and you can come out to us on the next ship. Hurry and get well, Annamaria. We're going to need your help more than ever on Multnomah, big girl!

And you hurried. But by the time you were well they were all dead—killed in a translational malfunction of their starship. So what could you do but atone? Try through all the years to show them you were sorry that you had not died along with them. Dedicate yourself to easing the passing of others as you were not able to ease theirs...

"But fighting it at the same time, Claude. I realize that now. I wasn't really a morbid person and I was glad to be alive and not dead. But that old guilt never let me go, even though it was so well sublimated in my vocation that I didn't realize how it was undermining me. I went along for years doing work that was very hard and refusing to take holidays or sabbaticals the way the others did. There was always a case that needed my special help and I was always strong enough to give it. But in the end it all became a sham. The demons weren't exorcized any more. The emotional fatigue of the job and the buried guilt all mingled and became unbearable."

The old man's voice was compassionate. "So when the contemplative orders justifiably turned you down, you scratched around and found what looked like an even better form of atonement... Can't you see that you haven't loved *yourself* enough, Amerie? This hermitage-in-Exile idea was the ultimate chair in a corner facing the wall."

Her head was averted from him so that the broad-brimmed hat hid her face. She said, "So the Exile anchoress turns out to be just as much of a fraud as the ministering nun in the hospice for the dying."

"That last bit isn't true!" Claude snapped. "Gen didn't think so and neither did I. And neither did the hundreds of other suffering people you helped. For God's sake, Amerie, try to keep a perspective! Every human being has deep motives as well as superficial ones. But the motivation doesn't invalidate the objective good we do."

"You want me to get on with my life and quit picking scabs. But, Claude—I can't go back now, even though I know the choice was wrong. I have nothing left."

"If you've got any faith remaining at all, why not believe that you're here for a reason?"

She gave him a crooked smile. "It's an interesting idea. Suppose I spend the rest of the night meditating on it."

"Good girl. I have a feeling you won't have much time for meditation later on, if Felice's plan works out... I tell you what. You meditate and I'll snooze, and we'll both do ourselves good. Wake me as soon as Basil starts playing the signal. It'll be just before dawn."

"When it's darkest," sighed the nun. "Go to sleep, Claude. Pleasant dreams."

There were no more double beacons, which seemed to have been the scouting party's warning of Firvulag in the vicinity. The caravan had come down from the plateau now and traversed open wooded slopes cut by little brooks that foamed whitely over boulders, calling for tricky footwork by the chalikos as they picked their way along in the starshine. The country became rougher and there was a tang of conifer resin in the air. As the night wore on, a breeze sprang up, ruffling the lake and making the beacon fires near the shore lean and twist. It was very quiet. Aside from the noise of the moving caravan, only owl hoots were to be heard. There were no lights of villages or farms, no sign of habitation at all. So much the better if they did manage to escape...

They came to a deep gorge lit on both sides by bonfires, where a lonely guardpost secured a suspension bridge over a cascading stream. Three torch-bearing men in bronze armor stood at attention as Epone and Captal Waldemar crossed the swaying structure. Then the soldiers led small groups of prisoners over, bracketed by amphicyons.

When they resumed their march, Richard told Felice, "It's after four. We been losing time fording the creeks."

"We'll have to wait until we get far enough away from that damn guardpost. I hadn't planned on that. There are more than three soldiers manning it, count on that. Epone will be able to send them a telepathic call for help and we've got to be sure they'll get to us too late. I want to wait another half hour at least."

"Don't cut it too fine, sweets. What if there's another post? And what about the scouts ahead who light the beacons?"

"Oh, shut up! I'm juggling factors until I'm dizzy trying to optimize this thing. Just be sure *you're* ready . . . Did you lash it firmly to your lower arm?"

"Just like you said."

Felice called out, "Basil."

"Righto."

"Would you play some lullaby tunes for a while?"

The notes of the woodwind rose softly, soothing the riders after the brief anxiety caused by the bridge-crossing. The double file of chalikos and their flanking bear-dogs now moved among titanic black conifer trunks. The trail was soft with millennia of needle duff, muffling their passage and sending even the most uncomfortable riders into a doze. The track rose gradually until it was more than a hundred meters above the Lac de Bresse, with occasional sheer drops to the water on the caravan's right. Too soon, it seemed to Felice, the eastern sky began to lighten.

She sighed and pulled down her hoplite helmet, then leaned forward in the saddle. "Basil. Now."

The Alpine climber played "All Through the Night."

When he finished it and began again, four amphicyons went charging soundlessly to the head of the procession and hamstrung Epone's chaliko with simultaneous slashes of their teeth. The exotic woman's mount uttered a heart-stopping shriek as it went down in a welter of dark bodies. The bear-dogs, with barking roars, leaped upon Epone herself. Soldiers and the front ranks of prisoners gave shouts of horror, but the Tanu slave-mistress did not cry out.

Richard thumped his free feet against his mount's neck and held tightly to the reins as the creature took off. He galloped into the midst of the quartet of soldiers trying to come to the assistance of Epone. Waldemar was shouting, "Use your lances, not the bows! Lift them off her, you stupid bastards!"

Richard's chaliko reared and crashed down upon the captal, knocking him from the saddle. A figure in white robes and a black veil leapt down as if to help the fallen officer. In the moment that Waldemar took to gasp astonishment at seeing a mustache on a nun's face, Richard slipped Felice's little dirk from its golden scabbard and pressed the steel blade home twice below the two corners of Waldemar's jaw, just above the gray metal necklet. His carotid arteries severed, the captal clutched at the false nun with a bubbling cry, gave a peculiar smile, and died.

Two riderless chalikos were thrashing together in the semi-darkness, inflicting ghastly wounds upon one another with their huge claws. Replacing the dirk in its sheath on his forearm, Richard seized the dead officer's bronze sword and backed off, cursing. There were confused shouts and a long scream of pain from the tangle of amphicyons and armed men. The two soldiers of the rear guard came pounding up to assist their comrades. One of the men charged with lance couched, spitting a small bear-dog that dashed in from the side and hoisting it high into the air. Then another hulking form came darting among the mounted guards, snapping at the heels of the enraged, screeching chalikos.

Felice sat her beast, motionless, as though she were merely a spectator to the carnage. One of the ronin, heels drumming the shoulders of his mount, rushed into the free-for-all and hauled back on his reins. The chaliko reared and brought its scimitar claws down onto the rump of a soldier's animal. The Japanese warrior, shouting an ancient battle cry, forced his own mount to ramp again and again with terrible driving blows that crushed the soldier and his chaliko into the tangled mass already on the ground. The second ronin came up on foot and grasped a lance from its scabbard on the fallen man's saddle.

"A bear-dog! Behind you, Tat!" Richard yelled.

The warrior whirled around and braced the spear on the ground as the amphicyon leaped. Transfixed through the neck, the animal body continued forward on momentum and crushed the ronin named Tat beneath its great bulk. Richard ran forward and stabbed the struggling monster in its near eye, then tried to haul it off the warrior. But someone shouted, "Here comes another one!" And Richard looked up to see a black shape with gleaming eyes not four meters away.

Felice gazed impassively at the fight, her face almost hidden within the T-shaped helmet opening.

The charging amphicyon swerved away from Richard and ran over the edge of the steep embankment, squalling in midair and striking the water with a tremendous splash. Basil and the knight Dougal rode their mounts impotently around the edge of the bedlam of noise, hesitating before the flailing bloody claws and struggling shapes. Ripping off the impeding veil and wimple, Richard picked up another lance and tossed it to Basil. Instead of stabbing with it, the climber hoisted the thing like a javelin, threw, and hit one of the soldiers high on the armor of his upper back. The point of the weapon skidded up beneath the man's kettle-helmet, penetrating the base of his skull. He fell like a bag of sand.

Felice watched.

No more bear-dogs came from the shadowy perimeter. All that were left alive were busy worrying something lying next to the body of a dead white chaliko. A single soldier stood upright among them, hacking slowly at the snarling amphicyons like some freshly painted red automaton.

"You must kill him," Felice said.

They could not find any more lances. Richard ran to the mounted knight, handed up his bronze sword, and pointed. "Take him, Dougal!"

As if in a trance, the elegant medievalist grasped the weapon and waited for a suitable moment before riding into the mass of dead and dying animals and men. He decapitated the futile chopping figure with a single blow.

There were two bear-dogs left alive as the last soldier fell. Richard found another sword and prepared to stand his ground if they came after him; but the creatures seemed seized with a kind of fit. They backed away from their prey reluctantly, giving vent to agonized howls, then turned and went leaping to their doom over the edge of the lakeside cliff.

The sky was becoming rose-colored. There were gagging sounds and hysterical sobs as the stunned prisoners, who had been herded into a compact group by Claude and Amerie during the embroilment, now came slowly forward to look. Noises from dying chalikos were cut short as the surviving ronin went about with a dispatching sword. The first morning notes of song sparrows, simple and solemn as Gregorian chant, echoed among the lofty sequoia trunks.

Felice rose up in her saddle, arms wide, fingers grasping, head in its plumed helmet thrown back as she writhed, cried out, then slumped back inertly against the high cantle.

The Japanese bent over the gory carcass of the white chaliko. He grunted and beckoned to Richard. Numbed now, feeling only curiosity, the former starship captain went stumbling into the fleshly wreckage, hindered by his incongruous nun's garb. On the ground amidst the bodies was a hideously gnawed limbless trunk swarthed in bloody rags. The face was torn to the bone all along one side, but the other was still beautiful and untouched.

An eyelid opened. A jade-green orb reached out at Richard. Epone's mind took hold of him and began to drag him down.

He screamed. His bronze sword hewed and stabbed at the thing down there but its inexorable grip held him. The dawnlight began to fade and he was being taken to a place from which he would not return.

"Iron!" the high-pitched voice of the knight called out. "Iron! Only thus may the faerie perish!"

The useless sword fell and Richard fumbled at his wrist. As he continued to sink he clutched at the instrument of redemption and sent its steely potency deep—between the heaving white-scarlet ribs without breasts to the raging heart, stilling it and quenching the body's resident spirit which took flight, releasing as it was released.

Basil and the ronin hauled Richard out of there by the arms. He was wide-eyed and still screaming but holding tight to the gold-handled knife. The three men paid no attention to the demented Dougal, who leaped from his saddle and began stomping something beneath his mailed feet.

Felice shouted a warning.

Ignoring her, the knight picked a blood-smeared golden hoop from the mess and scaled it far out over the lake, where it sank without a trace.

14

THE RIVERSIDE PALACE AT DARASK WAS IN AN UPROAR WHEN the southbound travelers broke their journey there on the second evening. The mistress of the establishment had been brought to childbed with twins and her labor was proving dangerously prolonged. Creyn went off to volunteer his medical services, leaving the prisoners in the care of a silver-torced major-domo, a black Irishman who forthrightly introduced himself as Hughie B. Kennedy VII and led them under guard to a large chamber high in one tower of the palace.

"You'll have to rough it tonight, friends," Kennedy said. "Boys and girls together here where we can keep you secure easily. We can't spare the guards tonight for single quarters, not with our poor Lady Estella-Sirone hovering on the brink and the buggerin' Firvulag gathering round, knowing what's in the wind. You'll be cool up here at any rate, and above the mosquitoes. There's a good supper out on the balcony table."

The escorting palace guards carried in Stein's litter and rolled the Viking onto one of the netting-draped bedsteads. Sukey protested. "But he needs care! He hasn't eaten or drunk all day or—anything."

"Don't fret yourself over him," Kennedy said. "When they're

235

put under with the torc"—and he fingered his own—"they're like in suspended animation. Your friend's just a hibernatin' animal, metabolism all slowed down. He'll keep until tomorrow. By then, please Jesus, all'll be well with our Lady, and we can spare some time for him." The major-domo gave Sukey a shrewd look. "Likely you'll keep a good eye on your friend."

The prisoners were allowed to take a change of clothing but nothing else from their packs, which were then removed by the guards. Kennedy apologized once more for the meagerness of their welcome and prepared to lock them in. Elizabeth came to him and said in a low voice, "I must speak privately to Creyn. It's important."

The major-domo frowned. "Ma'am, I realize that you're a privileged person, but my orders were to install all of you together here."

"Kennedy, I'm an operant metapsychic and a trained redactor. I can't get through to Creyn, but I can farsense your lady and her unborn babies and I know that right this moment they're in serious trouble. I can't help them from here, but if you take me down to the birthing room . . . there! Creyn's calling for me!"

Kennedy had heard the telepathic summons, too. "Come along, then." Taking her by one arm, he drew her into the tower corridor and slammed the door shut.

Raimo said sourly, "That was nice going. We get stuck here, but Little Red Riding Britches gets to see the fireworks."

"I never would have pegged you as an obstetrics freak," Aiken jeered.

"Didn't you hear that guy?" Raimo's pale eyes glistened and he licked his lips. "He said the Firvulag were gonna lay siege to the place! I wanna see that. Maybe get in on the fighting."

Sukey's face was twisted with scorn. "You just can't wait to join the Hunt, can you? Can't wait to get some monster's head on a pike. But you weren't so brave when we were shooting those rapids today!"

Leaving them to their bickering, Bryan and a strangely subdued Aiken Drum went out to the balcony. The promised supper had enough food for a dozen people; but all of it was cold and bore evidence of hasty preparation. Aiken picked up the leg of a roast fowl and took an uninterested bite, meanwhile inspecting the security arrangements of the balcony. It was completely enclosed in a cage of ornamental brass grillwork.

"I won't be flying out of here very quickly, will I? I suppose I could saw through the bars with one of the little vitredur gizmos I have in my pockets. But it hardly seems worthwhile trying to escape. They've got me so curious about the Tanu good life that running away seems stupid."

"I believe that's the attitude you're supposed to form," Bryan said. "You were allowed to taste just enough of your new powers to want a whole lot more. Now they've taken your metafunctions away until you submit to their training regimen down in the capital and they make you into a good little copy of themselves."

"So you think that'll happen, do you?" Aiken's golliwog grin was as wide as ever, but his black button eyes held an ugly glitter. "You don't know a fewkin' thing about me and the way my mind works. As for the metabilities, you're only a *normal*. You've never tasted the powers and you never will, so don't give me any of your high-ass professor's predictions about the way I'm going to behave!"

"They've got you collared and liking it," Bryan said mildly.

Aiken touched the silver neck-ring with a dismissive flick. "This thing! It's only put a clamp on my metafunctions. The clamp is effective now because I haven't figured how to turn it off. But I'm working on it. You think they've got me under control? What Creyn did at the very beginning was program this inhibitory thing on us. There's this little nagger in the skull that hints at horrible things happening to us if we try to escape or do anything to threaten the peace and good order of our wonderful Tanu friends. You know how much that inhibition is worth, influencing *me*? It isn't worth shit. Little Sukey and dumbo Ray in there are safe—but not Aiken Drum."

"The torcs...have you discovered how the different kinds work?"

"Not the details, but enough. One of the Tanu women at the Roniah party spilled a lot when I put it to her nicely. The old torcs are the basic article, the mental amplifiers that turn latents into operants. They're stuffed with barium chips all latticed with microscopic amounts of rare earths and bits of other junk that these jokers brought with them from their home galaxy. They handcraft the torcs and have a machine to grow and print the chips. They hardly understand how the machine functions, and most of 'em know even less about the theory behind the torcs themselves, the whole metapsychic thing. The technology of it is handled down in the capital city by some outfit called the Coercer Guild."

"Do the golden torcs have differing powers of—uh—magnification?"

"They're all exactly the same. And all they magnify is what the individual's got. If a guy's got one weakie ability latent, he becomes an operant weakie. If he's loaded with all five metafunctions in wholesale lots, he becomes operant as the Wizard of Oz. Most of the Tanu are fairly strong in just one metafunction and they tend to club up with others of the same type. The folks who have several strong powers are the real aristocrats. Just what you'd expect. It's the same sort of setup that you get in the Milieu—only on a pipsqueak scale, with everyone pretty much out for what he can get. Near as I can tell so far, there are no masterclass metas here and nothing like the Milieu's psychounion."

Bryan slowly nodded. "I'd already sensed a lack of hierarchy among these people. I wouldn't be surprised to find them still at the clan level of socialization. Fascinating—and almost unprecedented, given the high-culture trappings."

"They're barbarians," Aiken stated flatly. "That's one of the things I like about 'em! And they're not too proud to let us human latents join right in—"

"With *silver* torcs."

Aiken gave a short laugh. "Yeah. These silver collars have all the mind-expanding functions of the gold—plus control circuits. The gray torcs and the small collars of the monkeys have nothing but controls, plus a bunch of pleasure-pain circuits and a telepathic communication thing that varies a lot in its range."

Bryan peered over the edge of the balcony. "Can you get any mental clues as to what's going on around here? Quite a few alarums and excursions down there. I'm getting very curious about the Firvulag by now."

"Funny thing about those severed heads the Hunt brought in," Aiken frowned. "They weren't quite dead, some of them! And after a while they started to—how can I say it?—flicker.

The Hunters took them away, so we never really got a good look at them. But there was something subliminal about the whole scene."

Sukey and Raimo chose that moment to come out in search of dinner. Aiken asked them, "You guys *hear* anything? With your minds? I've tried, but this damn lock Creyn put on me screens out all but whispers."

Sukey closed her eyes and put her fingers in her ears. Raimo just stood there with his mouth open, finally saying, "Hell, all I hear is my stomach rumbling. Lemme at that food."

After a few minutes had passed with Aiken and Bryan watching her patiently, Sukey opened her eyes. "I get . . . eagerness. From a lot of mental sources that seem to be *different*. Broadcasting on another wavelength from humans. Even different from Tanu. I can tune them in, but it's hard. Do you understand what I mean?"

"We understand, kiddo," Aiken said.

Sukey glanced from him to Bryan anxiously. "What do you suppose it could be?"

"Nothing to bother us, I'm sure," Bryan said.

Sukey murmured something about wanting to sit with Stein and took a plate of fruit and cold meat inside. Bryan was satisfied with a roughly made sandwich and a mug of some ciderlike beverage. He stood looking over twilit Darask. In the east, the monstrous rampart of the Maritime Alps still reflected glaring sunset-pink on the highest snowfields. Extraordinary, Bryan thought. The mountains looked to be as high as the spine of the Himalaya or even the Hlithskjalf Massif on Asgard. A cool wind was coming down from the heights, spreading across the everglade flats where the Rhône finally relaxed and spread wide after its precipitate plunge from the region around unborn Lyon.

The day's journey had been something like descending a series of vast canyoned steps. They would sail peacefully for thirty or forty kilometers, then encounter savage rapids that would chute them to the next lower level at jetboat velocity. Despite Skipper Highjohn's reassurances, Bryan felt that he had survived the ordeal of a lifetime. The last stretch of rapids—occurring, as he had suspected, in the gorge area about fifty kloms above the future Pont d'Avignon—had been formidable beyond belief. The prolongation of terror had blunted his senses to the point of stupor. Aiken Drum had begged Creyn not to put him to sleep for that last rough ride, being eager for some taste of the thrills that Bryan had described. When the boat had tumbled end over end down the face of the final great cataract and fetched up in the placid Lac Provençal, Aiken's face had turned to gray-green and his bright eyes were sunken in shock.

"A fewkin' flea ride," he had moaned, "in a fewkin' food blender!"

By the time they reached Darask on the Lower Rhône, they had journeyed nearly 270 kilometers in less than ten hours. The shallowing river twined and split and braided itself into scores of channels divided by rippling grasslands and mudflats inhabited by flocks of long-legged birds and cream-and-black checkered crocodiles. Here and there islands rose from the marshy plain. Darask crowned one of them, looking for all the world like a tropical Mont-Saint-Michel towering above a sea of grass. Their boat had used its auxiliary engine to move out of the mainstream of the Rhône into a secondary channel leading to the fortified town. Darask had a small quay secured behind a limestone wall more than twelve meters high that butted against unscalable cliffs.

And now, in the town beneath the high-rising palace, ramas were lighting the small night-lamps, clambering up spindly ladders to tend those on brackets along the house roofs, working pulleys to raise long strings of lanterns up the face of the inner fortifications. Human soldiers touched off larger torches on the bastions of the town's perimeter. As Bryan and the others surveyed the scene, the peculiar Tanu-style illumination sprang into operation, outlining the spired palace in dots of red and amber that symbolized the heraldic colors of its psychokinetic lord, Cranovel.

Aiken inspected the Tanu lamps along their own balcony. They were of sturdy faceted glass resting in small niches in the stone, without wires or any other metallic attachments. They were cold.

"Bioluminescence," the little man in gold decided, shaking one. "You want to bet there are microorganisms in here? What did Creyn say—that the lights were energized by surplus meta emanations? That figures. You get some of the lower echelon torc wearers to generate a suitable waveform while they're playing checkers or drinking beer or reading in the bathtub or performing some other semi-automatic—"

Bryan was paying scant attention to Aiken's speculations. Out in the surrounding marshland, the ignes fatui were lighting their own lamps—wispy blobs of methane blue, firefly glimmerings that winked on and off in scattered synchrony, wandering pale flames gliding around the island's misty backwaters like lost elfin boats.

"I suppose those are glowing insects or marsh-gas flames out there," Sukey said, coming up behind Bryan to stare into the darkening landscape.

Raimo said, "*Now* I hear something. But not with any metafaculty. You guys catching it?"

They listened. Sukey pursed her lips in exasperation. "Frogs!"

An almost inaudible trill was building up on the breeze, swelling and finally fracturing into a complex treble chord of tinkles and peeps. An invisible batrachian maestro lowered his baton and more voices chimed in—gulps and grunts, rattling snares, pops and clicks, tunking notes as of hollow canes. Additional frog voices contributed their simulations of slowly dripping water, plucked strings, human glottal trills, buzzing drillbits, amplified guitar notes; and underriding it all was the homely *jug-o'-rum* of the common bullfrog, that durable Earth creature that would, in only six million years, accompany mankind on its colonization of the far-flung stars.

The four people on the balcony looked at one another and burst into laughter.

"We've got a front-row seat," Aiken said, "in case there's any Firvulag invasion. And this blue pitcher is full of something that's cool and definitely alcoholic. Shall we pull up chairs and fortify ourselves just in case the monsters arrive on schedule?"

"All in favor?" Bryan demanded.

"Aye!"

They held out their mugs and the little man in gold filled them, one by one.

Elizabeth pressed the back of her hand to her clammy forehead. Her eyes opened and she exhaled a long, slow breath.

Creyn and a haggard Tanu man in a rumpled yellow robe bent anxiously over her chair. Creyn's mind touched hers—supporting, querying.

Yes. I have separated them. Finally. Sorry so weak my skill rusty disuse. They will be born now.

The mind of Lord Cranovel of Darask wept gratitude. And she? Safe oh safe my darling?

Humanwomen tougher than Tanu. She recovers easily now.

He cried aloud, "Estella-Sirone!" and ran to the inner chamber.

In a few moments the querulous wail of a newborn infant came to the two who still waited. Elizabeth smiled at Creyn. The first grayness of dawn lightened the mist outside the palace windows.

Elizabeth said, "I've never handled anything quite like that before. The two unborn minds so intertwined, so mutually antagonistic. Fraternal twins, of course. But it seems incredible that genuine enmity should have been able to—"

A Tanu woman dressed all in red put her head through the curtained doorway and exclaimed, "A lovely girl! The next one is a breech, but we'll get it safely, never fear." She disappeared again.

Elizabeth got up from the chair and walked wearily to the window, letting her mind reach out beyond the birthing rooms for the first time since she had entered so many hours ago. The anomalies were outside—crowding closer and stumbling over one another in horrid eagerness—those twittering little unhuman minds, seemingly operant, changing their soulform even as she tried to grasp them for examination. They eluded her, wove disguises, faded and flared, shrunk to atomies or expanded into looming monsters that postured in the mental-physical fog swirling about the towers of the island palace.

Another baby cried.

Pierced by a terrible realization, Elizabeth's mind met that of Creyn. A slow-distilling drop of regret formed from a complex of the man's emotions. Then he slammed down an impervious screen between them.

Elizabeth ran to the door of the inner chamber and pushed the draperies aside. Several women, both human and Tanu, were attendant upon the new mother, a human wearing a golden torc. Estella-Sirone was smiling, the beautiful baby girl held to her right breast. Cranovel knelt beside her, wiping her brow.

The Tanu nurse in red brought the other baby to show to Elizabeth. It was a very small boy, weighing about two kilos, wizened as an old man and with an oversized head thickly covered with wet dark hair. Its eyes were wide open and it screeched thinly from a mouth that had a full set of tiny sharp teeth. Even as Elizabeth watched, the manikin shimmered and became furry all over its body, then shimmered again and turned to a virtual double of its plump blonde sister.

"It is a Firvulag, a shape-changer," the nurse said. "They are the shadow-brethren of the Tanu from the foundation of worlds. Ever with us, ever against us. The twin situation is fortunately rare. Most such die unborn, and the mother with them."

"What will you do with him?" Elizabeth asked. Fascinated, horrified, she sounded the small alien mentality and recognized the anomalous mode, now that it was fully separated from the more complex psychic structure of the Tanu sister.

The tall nurse shrugged. "His folk are awaiting him. And so we give him to them, as always. You would like to see it?"

Dumbly, Elizabeth nodded.

The nurse swiftly wrapped the baby in a soft towel and hurried out of the birthing room. Elizabeth had all she could do to keep up as the woman raced down flight after flight of stone stairs, all empty and echoing and lit only by the tiny ruby and amber lamps. They finally came to a cellar. A dank corridor led to the outer wall of the town and a great, locked watergate, beside which was an indoor anchorage full of deserted small boats. The gate had a wicket with a bronze bolt, which the exotic woman shot open.

"Guard your mind," she warned, and stepped outside onto the fog-obscured dock.

There were lights out there, and they converged with alarming speed, making no sound whatsoever. Then came a single deep-green glow that became a sphere some four meters across, rolling on the surface of the water and burning the mist to shreds as it approached the dock.

With great caution, Elizabeth pried apart the fabric of the illusion and looked inside. There was a boat—a punt, rather— with a dwarfish fellow poling and a round-cheeked little woman sitting in the bows with a covered basket in her lap.

So you see us, do you?

Elizabeth staggered as a barrage of lightning seemed to explode behind her eyes. Her tongue swelled as if to strangle her. The flesh of her hands blistered, blackened, burst, and cooked in a living flame.

That'll show the upstart!

"I warned you," said the Tanu woman. Elizabeth felt the tall one's arms around her, holding her up. She saw only the glowing ball receding into the mist. Her mouth was normal, her hands unhurt.

"The Firvulag are operant metapsychics of a sort. All most of them can do is farsense and spin illusions—but those can be strong enough to drive an unready mind mad. We handle them well enough—at Grand Combat time and at most other times, too. But you must not let them take you unaware."

The baby was gone. After a few seconds the green glow vanished as well, and daylight broke fitfully through rags of vapor. Far up on the battlements, a woman's voice was singing alien words to a familiar melody.

"We'll go back now," the nurse said. "My Lord and Lady will be very grateful to you. You must receive proper thanks— then refreshment and rest. There is a small family ceremony— naming the child and giving her the first tiny golden torc. They will wish you to hold the baby. It is a great honor."

"Imagine me as fairy godmother," Elizabeth murmured "What a world! Are you going to name her after me as well?"

"She already has a name. It is traditional among us to give anew the name of one who has recently passed on to Tana's peace. The baby will be called Epone—and the Goddess grant that she be more fortunate than the last who bore that name."

15

AMERIE CAME DOWN TO THE LAKESHORE WHERE THE FREED prisoners were ballasting their hastily inflated boats.

"I've had to sedate Felice. She was ready to tear the poor noddy apart."

"Not surprising," Claude growled. "Once I'd thought the matter through, I was tempted along those lines myself."

Richard was treading siphon bulbs with both feet, flooding the interstices of his and Claude's beached dinghies while the old man loaded equipment into the two small decamole craft. Richard had changed back into his pirate costume, curtly telling the nun to keep his spacer's coverall "for the duration." Now he glowered at her. "Maybe Dougal did us all a favor without knowing it. How do we know what Felice would turn into once she got hold of a golden torc?"

"There's that," Claude had to admit. "But if she'd got it, we wouldn't have to worry about any immediate danger from the soldiers. As it is, some kind of armed force is going to be breathing down our necks any minute now. We couldn't have been far from the next fort when the fight started."

Amerie said, "You two come up and help me with Felice

when you finish here. Yosh has been going through the baggage packs, retrieving some of our stuff."

"Any weapons?" Richard asked.

"They seem to have left ours back at the castle. But most of the tools are there. No maps or compasses, I'm afraid."

Claude and Richard shared a glance. The paleontologist said, "Then it's seat-of-the-pants navigation and devil take the hindmost. You go on up, Amerie. We'll be along in a few minutes."

In the aftermath of the fight, when all of the prisoners had been released, they had held a hasty conference and decided that the best chance of escape lay in taking to the water—one or two people to a decamole dinghy from the Survival Units. Only the five Gypsies had ignored Claude's warning about the dangers of riding the torc-susceptible chalikos. They had gone back to attack the suspension bridge guardpost after donning the gory armor of the slain escort and taking most of the soldiers' weaponry.

The remaining escapees had reestablished the bonding forged back at the auberge, the original Groups coming together once more to plan their collective getaway. Claude, the only person with a working knowledge of the Pliocene landscape, had suggested two possible escape routes. The one that would take them most quickly to rugged country entailed a short voyage northeast, across the narrow upper portion of the Lac de Bresse to canyons leading into the heavily forested Vosges highlands. This had the disadvantage of crossing the main trail to Finiah on the opposite shore of the lake; but if they managed to elude mounted patrols, they could reach the high country before nightfall and hole up among the rocks.

The second route would have them sailing southeast across the widest part of the lake to the shore of the Jura piedmont some sixty kilometers away, then continuing south into the mountain range itself. There seemed an excellent chance that the land in that direction was completely uninhabited, since beyond the Jura lay the Alps. On the other hand, the lakeside forts were likely to have boats of their own that could be used for pursuit. The escapees might outsail the Tanu minions; but the breeze was fitful and the nearly cloudless sky suggested that the air might go dead calm as it had the day before. If the boats were becalmed at nightfall, they might attract the attention of the Firvulag.

Basil had confidently elected for the Jura route, while Claude's conservatism inclined him to hold out for the Vosges. But the climber was most persuasive to the majority, so in the end it was decided that all of the time-travelers except the remnant of Group Green and Yosh, the surviving ronin, would go south. The prisoners had hastily unloaded their baggage from the chalikos and followed a gully down to a tiny beach below the cliff. There boats could be launched. A few of the small craft were already spreading their sails when Richard completed ballasting the two Green boats and scrambled back up the embankment in search of the others.

He discovered Claude, Amerie, and Yosh standing over Felice's unconscious body. The Japanese warrior said, "I've found Claude's woodworking tools and the knives and hatchets and saws from our Survival and Smallholder Units." He held out a hideously stained packet to Richard. "And here are also a soldier's bow and arrows that the Gypsies overlooked."

"We're grateful, Yosh," said the old man. "The bow could be very important. We have very little food except for the survival rations, and the kits have only snares and fishing gear. The people going south with Basil will have time to make new weapons if they reach the Jura shore. But our Group will be in much more danger of land pursuit. We'll have to keep moving and do our hunting on the run."

"But you should go with us, Yosh," Amerie said. "Won't you change your mind?"

"I have my own Survival Unit and Tat's lance. I'll take the rest of the tools that I scavenged down to the people on the shore. But I won't go with them, and I won't go with you." He gestured to the sky, where dark specks were already circling in the morning gold. "I have a duty here. The Reverend Sister has given my poor friend the Blessing of Departure. But Tat must not be left to the scavengers. When I've finished, I plan to head due north on foot to the River Marne. It joins the Pliocene Seine and the Seine flows into the Atlantic. I don't think the Tanu will bother to track one man."

"Well—don't hang around here too long," Richard said dubiously.

The ronin knelt swiftly beside Felice's limp form and kissed her brow. His grim eyes swept those of the others. "You must take good care of this mad child. We owe her our freedom, and if God wills she may yet accomplish her purpose. The potential rests in her."

"We know," said the nun. "Go blessed, Yoshimitsu-san."

The warrior got to his feet, bowed, and left them.

"Time for us to go, too," said Claude. He and Amerie picked up the pathetically light body of the girl while Richard gathered her helmet and pack, together with the tools and weapons.

"I can sail single-handed," the pirate said when they reached the waiting boats. "Put Felice in with me and you two follow."

They shoved off, the last to set sail, and relaxed only when they were far out from land. The lake waters were cold and of an opaque blue, fed by rivers running out of the Jura and the Vosges forest to the northeast. Amerie stared at the receding shore, where carrion birds were gradually descending.

"Claude . . . I've been thinking. Why didn't Epone die sooner from those dreadful wounds? She was literally torn to pieces before Richard and Yosh and Dougal ever got near her. She should have bled to death or died from hypovolemic shock. But she didn't."

"The people at the fort told you that the Tanu were nearly invulnerable. What did you *think* they meant?"

"I don't know—perhaps I assumed that the exotics were able to use their coercive power to fend off attackers. But I never dreamed a Tanu could survive such physical punishment. It's hard not to think of them as approximately human, given that breeding scheme Epone spoke to us about."

"Even human beings without metafunctions have been mighty tenacious of life. I've seen things in the colonies that were damn near miraculous. And when you consider the enhancement of mental powers that the Tanu achieve with the torc . . ."

"I wonder if they have regenerative facilities here in Exile?"

"I should think so, in the cities. And God knows what other kinds of technology they have. So far, we've only seen the torcs, the mind assayer, and that frisking device they used on us when we first came through the time-portal."

"Ah, yes. And that brings us to the lethal dagger."

The old man stripped off his bush jacket and pillowed his back against one of the boat seats. "I don't doubt that our anthropologist friend Bryan could tell us all about the legendary faerie antipathy toward iron. He'd probably explain it in terms of the ancient tensions between Bronze Age and Iron Age cultures . . . Be that as it may, European folklore is almost universal in believing that iron is repugnant or even deadly to the Old People."

The nun burst out, "Oh, for heaven's sake, Claude! Epone was an exotic, not some bloody elf!"

"Then you tell *me* why bear-dog bites and dismemberment and stab wounds from a bronze sword didn't finish her off, while a single thrust from a steel knife blade did."

Amerie considered. "It may be that the iron interferes in some way with the function of the torc. The blood of the Tanu is red, just like ours, and probably just as iron-rich. Their bodies and minds and the torc might operate in a delicate harmony that could be upset by the introduction of a gross mass of iron. Iron might even wonk them up if it just came near the body's intimate aura. Remember Stein and his battle-axe? None of the castle people was able to prevent him from doing terrible damage—which didn't strike me as strange at the time. But with what we know now, it seems significant."

"They frisked us thoroughly enough," Claude said. "I can understand why the guardians weren't able to pry Stein loose from his axe. But how did Felice's knife slip through?"

"I can't imagine—unless they were careless and didn't sweep her leg. Or perhaps the gold of the scabbard confused the detector. It suggests possibilities for countertactics."

Claude studied her through half-closed lids. There was an intensity about her that was new and startling. "Now you're beginning to sound like Felice! That child has no qualms about taking on the whole Tanu race. Never mind that they control the friggerty planet!"

Amerie flashed him an odd smile. "But it's *our* planet. And six million years from now, we'll be here. And they won't."

She snugged the tiller under her arm and kept the boat racing eastward, its sail taut before the freshening breeze.

They came up behind a marshy island, hauled down sails and unstepped and deflated masts and centerboards. Armloads of reeds and young willows were cut to disguise the boats. They substituted rearmounted decamole sculling oars for the sailing rudders. A person crouched low in the stern could impart a barely perceptible forward motion by wagging the oar back and forth.

Richard protested, "It'll take us two hours to travel the half klom to the shore at this rate."

"Keep your voice down," Claude warned him. "Sound travels over water." He brought his boat close to Richard's. "Somewhere on that shore is the trail—maybe even the fort where we were scheduled to stop for sleep this morning. We've got to be careful about showing ourselves until we're sure the coast is clear."

Richard laughed nervously. "The coast is clear! So that's where the cliché came from! Probably pirates—"

"Shut up, son," said the old man, weariness making his low voice harsh. "Just follow me from here on in and pretend you're a collection of flotsam."

Claude sculled so slowly that there was no wake; they seemed to drift from islet to islet, gradually approaching a low-lying shore where reeds and sedges grew more than five meters tall and long-shanked water birds with plumage of pink and blue and dazzling white stalked the shallows, jabbing at frogs and fish with their beaks.

The sun rose higher. It became excruciatingly hot and humid. Some kind of biting midge zeroed in on them, trapped as they were beneath the concealing greenery, and raised itching welts before they could find repellent in their awkwardly stowed packs. After a tedious interval of paddling, they scraped bottom on a jungly mudflat where many of the bamboos had trunks as thick as a man's thigh. Broadleaf evergreen trees perfumed the air with sickly sweet flowers. There was a game trail in the mud, heavily trampled by large flat feet. It looked as though it would lead them to higher ground.

"This is it," Claude said. "We deflate the dinghies and hike from here."

Richard extracted himself from the mass of stalks and branches in his boat and surveyed the site with disgust. "Jesus, Claude. Did you have to land us in a fuckin' swamp? Talk about your green hells! This place is probably crawling with snakes. And will you look at those footprints? Some mighty ugly mothers been cruising through here!"

"Oh, stuff it, Richard," Amerie said. "Help me get Felice ashore and I'll try to revive her while you guys—"

"Get down, everybody!" the old man whispered urgently.

They crouched low in the boats and stared in the direction from which they had come. Out beyond the marshy little islands, where the lake was deep and the breeze blew unimpeded, were a pair of seven-meter catboats that bore no resemblance to any of the craft launched by the escapees. They were slowly tacking northward.

"Well, now we know where the fort must be," Claude remarked. "South of here and most likely not very far away. They've probably got oculars on board so we'll have to stay down until they get around that point."

They waited. Sweat trickled down various body surfaces and made them itch. The frustrated midges whined and went on sorties against their unprotected eyeballs and nostrils. Claude's belly rumbled, reminding him that he had not eaten in nearly twelve hours. Richard discovered a sticky gash hidden in the hair above his left ear, and so did the local variety of blowfly. Amerie made a desultory attempt to pray; but her memory bank refused to pay out any withdrawals except the grace before meals and "Now I Lay Me Down to Sleep."

Felice moaned.

"Cover her mouth, Richard," Claude said. "Keep her quiet for just a few minutes longer."

Somewhere, ducks were quacking. Somewhere else, an animal was snuffling and slurping and breaking the giant bamboos like twigs as it sought its lunch. And elsewhere still, the silver sound of a horn sang on the limit of audibility, to be followed seconds later by a louder response farther north.

The old paleontologist sighed. "They're out of sight. Let's deflate these boats and move on."

The power-inflators, used in reverse, swiftly sucked both air and water out of the decamole membranes, reducing the boats to spheres the size of Ping-Pong balls. While Amerie revived Felice with a dose of stimulant, Claude rummaged in his pack for survival-ration biscuits and fortified candy, which he shared with the others.

Felice was listless and disoriented but seemed well enough to walk. Claude tried to get her to remove her leather cuirass, greaves, and gauntlets, which had to be acutely uncomfortable in the muggy atmosphere of the marsh; but she refused, only agreeing to keep her helmet stowed in the pack when Claude pointed out that its plumage might betray them to searchers. As a final ritual they daubed each other with camouflaging mud, then set off with Claude in the lead, Richard following, and Amerie and Felice bringing up the rear. The ring-hockey player had appropriated the bow and arrows.

They went quietly along the trail, which was wide enough for them to travel in comfort, a circumstance that pleased Richard and the women but rather alarmed the more wilderness-wise Claude. For nearly two kilometers they slogged through stands of bamboo, alder, willow, and semitropical evergreens, some trees laden with fruits of russet and purple, which Claude warned them against sampling. To their surprise, the only wildlife encountered was birds and giant leeches. The ground became higher and drier and they passed into dense forest, loud with bird and animal voices. The trees were draped in vines and the undergrowth formed a mass of impenetrable thornbushes on both sides of the trail.

At length the gloomy greenness gave way to sunlight as the trees thinned. Claude held up his hand as a signal for them to stop. "Not a peep out of you," he breathed. "I was half expecting to meet something like this."

They gazed through a thin screen of young trees into an open meadow with scattered clumps of bushes. Cropping the shrubbery was a herd of six adult and three juvenile rhinos. The full-grown specimens were about four meters in length and might have weighed two or three tons. They had two horns, piggy little eyes, and quaintly tufted ears that waggled as flies buzzed around them.

"*Dicerorhinus schliermacheri,* I'd say," Claude whispered. "This is their trail we've been using."

Felice stepped forward, nocking the razor-sharp arrow. "It's a good thing the wind is with us. Let me feel around their minds for a while and see if I can move them."

Richard said, "Meanwhile, we can hope they don't get thirsty."

Leaving Felice to experiment with her coercive power, the others withdrew back along the trail into a sunny glen at one side, where they sat down to rest. Richard planted a straight stick about as long as his arm upright in a patch of soil, marking the position of the shadow's tip with a small stone.

"Making a sundial?" Amerie inquired.

The pirate grimaced. "If we stay here long enough, we can get a fix. The tip of the shadow moves as the sun seems to travel across the sky. You wait, mark the new position of the shadow tip with another stone. Connect the two stones with a line and you got an east-west bearing. If we want to reach those highlands by the shortest route, I think we've got to bear more to the left than we've been going on this trail."

It was nearly an hour before Felice returned to tell them that it was safe to cross the meadow. They chose a new route according to Richard's aboriginal navigation; but without a convenient animal track to follow, they were forced to cross-country through the tangled, thorn-choked forest understorey. It was impossible to travel quietly and the wildlife was making a racket like feeding time at the zoo; so they threw caution to the winds and broke out the vitredur hatchets and Claude's big carpenter's axe and hacked a trail. After two exhausting hours of this, they came upon a sizable creek and were able to follow it upstream into a slightly more open section of forest.

"We're on the bench above the lake now," Claude said. "The trail to the fort must be near. Be very quiet and keep your ears open."

They crept onward, skulking in the shadows of giant conifers, cycads, and ferns. Anticlimactically, they blundered right into the trail when they had to alter course to avoid a spiderweb the size of a banquet tablecloth. The bush-constricted track was deserted.

Felice bent over a pile of chaliko dung. "Cold. They must have passed here two hours ago. See the prints heading north?"

"They'll be coming back," Claude said. "And if they have amphicyons, they'll be able to track us. Let's blot out our own prints and get out of here. Once we get higher, there should be fewer trees and easier going. We'll have to follow another stream somewhere to kill our scent."

The trees did become more widely separated as they continued upslope, but the going was hardly easy. They followed a dry water-course for most of an hour before the gentle grade above the bench steepened to a bluff studded with house-sized chunks of rock. The wind died and the heat of midafternoon smote them as they climbed.

At times when they rested, they could see out over the great lake. There were sails far to the south, apparently motionless on the water. It was impossible to tell whether they belonged to the gray-torc marines or to the escapees. They wondered out loud about the fate of Basil and his contingent, about Yosh, and about the Gypsies and their quixotic foray against the guardpost; but the trail talk dwindled as they were forced to save their breath for more difficult climbing. Hope that they would be able to cross the first high ridge began to fade after one of Richard's plass-and-fabric running shoes was slashed by a rock and he had to put on the more awkward seaboots of his original costume. Then Amerie's saddlesore legs betrayed her on a treacherous slope and she lost her footing, dislodging several large stones that tumbled down upon Claude and bruised his arm and shoulder.

"We'll never make it to the top today," Richard groused. "My left heel is one big blister and Amerie is ready to collapse."

Felice said, "It's only a couple of hundred more meters. If you can't climb, I'll carry you up! I want to get a view of the terrain we're heading into tomorrow. With luck, we might be able to see the bonfires from the fort or even trail beacons below us once it gets dark."

Claude declared he could manage on his own. Felice gave one hand to Richard and the other to the nun and hauled them up after her by main strength. It was slow going, but they were finally able to reach the top shortly after the sun descended behind the hills on the other side of the lake.

When they had regained their wind, Claude said, "Why don't we hole up on the eastern side of these big boulders? There's a nice dry shelter in there and I don't think anyone below could spot a fire if we lit one after nightfall. I could gather some wood."

"Good idea," said Felice. "I'll scout around a bit." She went off among the crags and gnarled savin junipers while the others tended their wounds, inflated decamole cots and weighted the legs with earth—because there was no water to waste—and regretfully laid out a meal of biscuits, nutrient wafers, and cheesy-tasting algiprote. By the time Claude had assembled a pile of dry branches, Felice was back, her bow resting jauntily over her shoulder, swinging three fat marmotlike animals by their hind legs.

"Hail, Diana!" chortled the old man. "I'll even skin and clean 'em!"

They lit the fire after it was completely dark and roasted the meat, devouring every gamey morsel. Then Richard and Claude collapsed onto their cots and were asleep in minutes. Amerie, her brain buzzing with fatigue, still felt obliged to shake the grease and scraps off the dinnerware, sterilize them with the power source, then shrink and stow them away. There's my big, helpful girl!

"I can see the fort," came Felice's voice from the nearby darkness.

Amerie picked her way over the rocks to where the athlete was standing. The ridge fell steeply to the southwest. The young moon hung over the lake and an incredible profusion of Pliocene stars reflected upon the water, differentiating it from the black land. Far to the south on their side of the lake was a cluster of orange specks.

"How far away is it?" the nun asked.

"At least fifteen kloms. Maybe more. As the vulture flies." Felice laughed, and Amerie was suddenly wide-awake, experiencing the same feeling of fear and fascination she had known before. The woman beside her was an indistinct silhouette in the starlight, but Amerie knew that Felice was looking at her.

"They didn't thank me," the athlete said in a low voice. "I set them free but they didn't thank me. They were afraid of me still. And that fool of a Dougal! . . . None of them—not even you—sympathized or understood why I wanted to—"

"But you couldn't *kill* Dougal! For the love of God, Felice! I had to put you out."

"Killing him would have been a comfort," said the young girl, coming closer. "I was working on my plans. Plans I never told to the rest of you. The golden arc was the key. Not only to free us, but to rescue the others—Bryan, Elizabeth, Aiken, Stein. To free all of the human slaves! Don't you see? I really could have done it! With the golden torc I could have tamed this thing inside me and *used* it."

Amerie heard herself babbling. "We're all grateful to you, Felice. Believe me. We were simply too stunned by it all to say anything after the fight. And Dougal—he was just too fast for Basil and Yosh to stop, and too crazy to realize what he was doing when he threw the torc away. He probably believed he wouldn't be safe from Epone's power until the torc was separated from her body."

Felice said nothing. After a while the nun said, "Perhaps you could get another."

There was a sigh. "They know about me now, so it will be very dangerous. But I'll have to try. Maybe waylay another caravan, or even go to Finiah. It'll be hard and I'll need help."

"We'll help."

Felice laughed softly.

"*I'll* help. I won't be retiring to any hermitage for quite some time yet."

"Ah. That's . . . good. I need your help, Amerie. I need you."

"Felice. Don't misunderstand."

"Oh, I know all about your little vow of renunciation. But that was made six million years ago in a different world. Now I think you need me as much as I need you."

"I need your protection. We all do."

"You need more than that."

Amerie backed away, tripped over a rock and fell, tearing open the scabbed cuts on her hands.

"Let me help you up," said Felice.

But the nun scrambled to her feet unaided and turned back toward the glowing remnants of the campfire where the others were sleeping. She stumbled and clenched her fingers into the lacerated palms so that her nails opened the cut even more, while behind her Felice laughed in the darkness.

16

"HE'S READY. SUKEY. YOU MUST TAKE THE FINAL DISCHARGE."

"But—can I? I could botch it again, Elizabeth."

"You won't. You'll be able to handle this aspect of his healing. He wouldn't let me—but you can do it. Don't be afraid."

"All right. Just let him come out of the torc's neural bath slowly. I'm ready."

. . . Illinois cornfields, flat as a table and stretching from horizon to horizon, with the toy farmhouse and outbuildings lonely amid the immensity. Sitting in one of the cornrows, a three-year-old boy and an Alsatian bitch. The boy, clever with his hands and mischievous, circumvents a childproof fastener and removes a beeper-trace from his jeans. He offers it to the bitch. She is pregnant and of capricious appetite, and so she swallows it. The boy rises from the ground and toddles off down the row toward an interesting noise in the far distance. The bitch, unsatisfied by her electronic snack, runs toward the farmhouse where lunch is being prepared . . .

"No! I can't go there again!"

"Hush. Easy. You're close, so close."

. . . A robot harvester, nearly as large as the farmhouse and bright orange, moves along, swallowing the corn plants in a thirty-row swath, grinding the stalks and leaves to useful pulp, shelling the ears—long as a man's forearm—and packing the rich golden kernels into containers for shipment to other farms all over the Galactic Milieu. This new maize hybrid will yield twenty cubic meters of grain to the hectare . . .

"I don't want to look. Don't make me look."

"Be calm. Be easy. Come with me. Only once more."

. . . The little boy wanders down the straight row where the black soil has baked to crumbly gray dust. Gigantic plants loom over him, tassels brown against the sky, swollen cobs jutting from the stalks ripe and ready for harvest. The boy walks on toward the noise but it is far away from him and so he must sit down and rest for a while. He leans against a cornstalk thick as the trunk of a young tree, and the broad green leaves shade him from the sun's heat. He closes his eyes. When he opens them again, the noise is very much louder and the air is full of dust . . .

"Please. Please."

"You must go there one last time. It's the only way out for you."

. . . Wonderment becomes unease becomes fear as the little boy sees an orange monster chewing toward him, its robot brain conscientiously scanning the rows ahead for signals from a beeper-trace that would trigger instant emergency shut-off. But there is no signal. The machine moves on. The boy runs ahead of it, easily outdistancing the harvester's steady one-klom-per-hour pace . . .

"She knew! She looked for me on the scanner at lunchtime and only found the dog, sending two signals instead of one there in the yard. She knew I had to be out in the fields. She called Daddy to have him stop the harvester and look for me, but there was no answer. He was outside the farm contower trying to fix a stuck rotor on one of the antennas."

"Yes. Go on. You can see her looking for you in the egg."

. . . The little boy dashes on, too inexperienced to realize that he should move to the side, out of range of the machine, instead of continuing down the row immediately ahead of it. He runs faster and a stitch comes in his side. He begins to whimper and runs more slowly. He trips, falls, gets up and staggers on with tears blinding his bright-blue eyes. Up in the air an egg-flier hovers over him. He stops and waves his arms, screaming for his mother. The harvester moves along, cutting the stalks off at ground level hauling them into its maw on a spiked conveyor, chopping, shredding, plucking the kernels from the cobs, reducing the rows of giant plants to neat packages of grain and finely ground cellulose pulp...

"No. Please, no more."

"You must. We must. Once more and then gone forever. Trust me."

...The egg lands and the child stands stock-still, waiting for his mother to save him, weeping and holding out his arms as she runs toward him, picks him up, with the noise louder and louder and the dust swirling about them in the hot sun. She holds him close to her as she pushes obliquely through the tough, impeding stalks while the great orange thing moves on, cutter beams and carrying spikes and whirling knives at work. But the fifteen meters she must traverse are too far. She gasps and lifts the boy high and throws him, so that the green corn plants and the orange machine and the blue sky all spin very slowly around him. He falls to the earth and the harvester rumbles past with the busy clanking of its machinery drowning out another noise that did not last very long...

"Oh, Jesus, I can still hear please no the machine stops and he comes and screams at me you murdering little animal Cary Cary oh my God no Daddy Daddy Mommy fell help her oh my God Cary you did it to save him and he killed you and it's his fault the murdering little animal no no what am I saying God my own little boy Steinie I'm sorry I didn't mean it oh God Cary Steinie... Daddy please keep me."

"He did, Stein."

"I know now."

"You heard it all? All that he said?"

"Yes. Poor Daddy. He couldn't help saying it. I know now. Angry and frightened and helpless. I understand. He shot the dog, though... But I don't have to be afraid. He couldn't help it. Poor Daddy. I understand. Thank you. Thank you."

Stein opened his eyes.

An unfamiliar woman's face was very near to him—sun-reddened round cheeks, a turned-up nose, intent indigo eyes set a bit too closely together. She smiled.

He said, "And I don't have to be angry at either one of us."

"No," Sukey said. "You'll be able to remember and feel sad. But you'll be able to forget it. No guilt or fear or anger about this part of your life ever again."

Stein lay without speaking, and she let her mind merge with his in a touch that admitted a sharing of his ordeal, bespoke her care for him.

"You've been helping me," he said. "Healing me. And I don't even know your name."

"I'm Sue-Gwen Davies. My friends call me Sukey. It's a silly sort of name—"

"Oh, no." He got up onto one elbow and studied her with an innocent curiosity. "You went through the auberge training program, too. I saw you, the first and second days I was there. And then you were gone. You must have passed through the gate ahead of our Group Green."

"I was in Group Yellow. I remember you, too. That Viking costume isn't easy to miss."

He grinned and shook sweat-touseled elflocks out of his eyes. "It seemed like a good idea back then. Sort of reflection of my personality . . . What are you supposed to be?"

She gave a self-conscious little laugh and toyed with the embroidered belt of her long gown. "An ancient Welsh princess. My family came from there a long time ago and I thought it might be fun. A complete break with my old life."

"What were you—a redactor?"

"Oh, no! I was a policewoman. A juvenile officer on ON-15, the last Earth colonial satellite." She touched her silver torc. "I didn't become an operant redactor until I got here. I'll have to explain about that—"

But he broke in. "I tried metapsychic treatment before. It never helped. They said I was too strong, that it would take a special kind of practitioner—one with commitment—to ever get down inside of me and root my mess out. And you did it."

She protested, "Elizabeth did all the preliminary lancing. I was trying to do it"—her eyes slipped away from his—"and I bungled the job badly. Elizabeth did a marvelous fix and drained out all the really dangerous stuff that I couldn't touch. You owe her a lot, Stein. So do I."

He looked dubious. "Back at the auberge, me and my pal Richard called her the Ice Queen. She was a very cryogenic and spooky lady. But wait—! She told us that her metafunctions were lost!"

"They returned. The shock of passing through the time-portal did it. She's a marvelous redactor, Stein. She used to be one of the top teachers and counselors in her Sector. She was masterclass. I'll never be so good—except perhaps with you."

Very carefully, he folded her in his huge arms. Her hair was long and black and very straight, with a simple grassy perfume from the Tanu soap. She lay against his bare chest, hearing his heart beating slowly, afraid to look into his mind in case the thing that she hoped for would not be found. They were alone now in the tower room. Even Elizabeth had disappeared when it became clear that the healing would be a success.

Sukey said, "There are things you have to know." She touched the silver torc about her rather plump neck. "These silver collars—your friend Aiken got one, too, and so have some other people who've passed through the portal—they make latent metafunctions operant. That's how I became a redactor... And there's an exotic race living here in the Pliocene along with us. They're called Tanu and they came here a long time ago from some galaxy light-billenia away. They're latents, too, and they wear golden collars that make them almost as powerful as the metaphysics of our Milieu. They look quite human except for being very tall and having mostly blond hair and funny eyes. The Tanu rule this place almost like the barons of the Middle Ages ruled ancient Earth."

"I'm beginning to remember," Stein said slowly. "A fight in a kind of castle... Are we still locked up in that place?"

Sukey shook her head. "They took us—you and me and a few others—down the River Rhône. We're on our way to the Tanu capital. This is a place called Darask, almost at the Mediterranean shore. We've been here for two days. Elizabeth helped the mistress of the place, who was having a hard time in childbirth, so we got to stay and fix you up and rest as a kind of reward. The river trip down here was pretty nerve-racking."

"So Elizabeth is here, and Aiken. Who else?"

"Bryan, from your Group. And another man, named Raimo

Hakkinen, who used to be a forester in British Columbia. I think he was in Group Orange. And there's a Tanu man in charge of bringing us to their capital city. His name is Creyn and he seems to be some kind of exotic physician when he's not acting as a prisoner-escort. He healed all of the wounds you got in the fight, by the way—and without using any regen-tank, either, just something like plass wrapping and mind-power. The rest of your friends and the other people who were being kept prisoner in the castle were sent to another place hundreds of kloms north of here."

"What are they planning to do with us?"

"Well, Elizabeth is special, obviously, because it seems she's the only human in all of Exile who is operant without a torc. I suppose they plan to make her Queen of the World if she'll stand for it."

"Jesus H. Christ!"

"And Bryan—he's another special case. No torc on him, either. I haven't discovered why, but the Tanu appear to think that they need an anthropologist to explain what all of us humans have done to their Pliocene society. Coming through the time-gate, you see. It's very complicated, but . . . well, silver-torc wearers like Aiken and me and Raimo, the ones with latent metabilities made operant, we have a chance to join the aris-tocracy of the Tanu if we behave ourselves. Ordinary people who aren't latent don't seem to be enslaved or anything—the exotics have some kind of small ape to do the rough work. The ordinaries that we saw were working at various arts and crafts."

Stein raised his hands to touch his own torc, then tried to undo it by twisting and pulling. "Can't get the damn thing off. You say it'll turn on my latent metafunctions?"

Sukey looked stricken. "Stein . . . your torc . . . it isn't silver. It's some gray metal. You're not a latent."

A dangerous gleam came into the bright-blue eyes. "Then what's my torc for?"

Her lower lip caught between her teeth. She reached out one hand to the metal around his neck. In a voice that was scarcely more than a whisper, she said, "It controls you. It gives pleasure or pain. The Tanu can use it to communicate with you telepathically, or they can use it to locate you if you run away. They can put you to sleep, and soothe your anxieties, and program hypnotic suggestions and do other things, probably, that I don't know about yet."

She explained more about the operation of the torcs as she knew it. Stein sat, ominously quiet, on the edge of the bed. When she had finished he said, "So the ones who wear gray mostly do jobs that are essential or potentially vital to the exotics. Soldiers. Gate guardians. This boatman taking us down a dangerous river. And they do their jobs without rebelling, even though they're not turned into zombies by the damn torc."

"Most of the gray-wearers that we've met behaved normally and seemed happy enough. Our boat skipper said he loved his job. One of the palace people that I talked to here said that the Tanu are kind and generous unless you go against their orders. I—I expect that after a time, you simply do as they expect you to without any coercion at all. You're conditioned and loyal. It's really the same sort of socialization that takes place in any tight group—but the loyalty is guaranteed."

Very quietly, Stein said, "I won't be a goddamn flunky for some exotic slavemaster. I came through the time-gate and gave up everything I owned to get away from all that. To be a natural man, free to do as I pleased! I can't live any other way. I won't! They'll have to burn out my brain first."

Eyes swimming, Sukey let her fingers stray to his cheek. Her mind slipped beneath his surface consciousness and saw that he was telling the simple truth. The obstinacy that had shut out every healer save the one who had loved him now stood unyielding before any notion of adaptation, totally rejecting the thought of making the best of a difficult situation. Stein would never bend to the Tanu. He would break. If they dominated him at all, they would dominate only his mindless shell.

Tears spilled, splashing onto the bedsheets and the wolfskin kilt that Stein still wore. He took both of her hands. She said, "It didn't turn out to be the world that any of us dreamed about, did it? I was going to find the tunnel leading to the hollow Earth paradise, to Agharta. Creyn said that the legends had to refer to the paradise his people founded here. But that can't be true, can it? Agharta was a land of perfect peace and happiness and justice. This can't be the same place. Not if it— makes you miserable."

He laughed. "I'm a hard case, Sukey. Things'll be different for you. You'll get to join the high life. Be a Pliocene princess instead of just a Welsh one."

She pulled away from him. "I forgot one other important thing about this Exile world. Human women . . . the Tanu undo our salpingzaptomy and restore our fertility. Their own women don't reproduce very well on Earth, and so . . . they use us, too. Some human women become Tanu wives, like the lady of this palace that we're in right now. But a lot are just used as—as—"

Stein drew her close to him again and wiped her tears away with a corner of the bedclothes. "Oh, no. Not you, Sukey. It won't happen to you."

Incredulously, she raised her face. He said, "Go ahead. Look deep inside. As long as it's you, I don't mind."

She took a shuddering breath and plunged into the new place, and could not help crying out when she found that what she hoped for did exist, all new and strong.

After he had hushed her and the pledge was sealed in both their minds, they completed the healing of each other in their own way.

17

CLAUDE AND RICHARD AND AMERIE COULD HAVE SLEPT FOR days, but with the sunrise came a distant howling of amphicyons angling up the ridge from the south, and they realized that the Tanu were going to do their utmost to prevent the escape of Felice, whose role in the massacre had doubtless been betrayed by some recaptured prisoner. The remnant of Group Green didn't waste any time trying to destroy traces of their camp but marched on not long after dawn, deflating their equipment and eating a scratch breakfast as they went. Claude had attempted to relinquish leadership to Felice, but she refused to hear of it.

"You've had experience in this kind of travel. I haven't. Just get us off this ridge as quickly as you can and down into thick woodland with a good-sized river. Then I think we'll be able to shake off the trackers."

They skidded and tramped and once even rappelled over a small cliff in their downhill flight, making better time when they found a dry wash that turned into a thin rivulet in the lower elevations. Trees crowded together and became taller, roofing over the widening stream and shading them from some of the sun's heat. As they splashed down the rock-clogged watercourse they startled big brown trout and fishing weasels that resembled pale minks. They took to the stream bank, first on one side, then on the other, in an attempt to confuse pursuit. Claude had them tramp an obvious trail up a tributary creek, relieve themselves to enhance the spoor, then double back in the water and continue wading down the original stream. It was becoming dangerously deep in places, broken with short pouroffs and stretches of white water.

Claude called a halt in midmorning. He and Felice were in good shape, but Richard and the nun sagged with weary gratitude. They rested on half-submerged rocks out in a backwater pool, straining their ears for sounds of pursuit. They heard nothing but an explosive *splat*! a short distance downstream.

"If I didn't know better," Amerie remarked, "I'd say that was a beaver."

"Quite likely," Claude said. "Might be our old friend Castor, but it's more likely Steneofiber, a more primitive type that didn't go in much for dams but just dug holes in the—"

"Shhh," Felice hissed. "Listen."

Rushing water, birdsong, the occasional screeches of what Claude had told them was an arboreal ape, a small squirrel chattering its annoyance.

And something large clearing its throat.

They froze on their rocks and instinctively drew up their legs, which they had been dangling in the water. The noise was a guttural cough, unlike anything they had heard before in the Pliocene. The bushes on the left bank swayed slightly as an animal passed through and came down to the stream to drink. It was a cat, massive as an African lion but with large canine teeth protruding like daggers below its closed jaws. It muttered to itself like a dyspeptic gourmet after an overly lavish feast and took a few desultory laps. Its upper body was decorated with marbled polygons of russet edged with tan and black; these merged into dark stripes about the animal's face, and black spots on its underparts and lower limbs. It had whiskers of heroic proportions.

The breeze shifted and carried the scent of the humans to the drinking sabertooth. It raised its head, stared directly at them with yellow eyes and snarled, exuding the studied restraint of a creature in complete command of an awkward situation.

Felice met its gaze.

The others were immobile with horror, waiting for the cat

to spring into the water. But it did no such thing. Its belly was full and its cubs were waiting, and Felice's mind stroked its feline vanity and told it that the scrawny prey crouching on the rocks was scarcely worth a ducking. So the machairodus lapped and glared at them and wrinkled the bridge of its nose in a contemptuous one-sided snort, and at last withdrew into the undergrowth.

"It will take me five minutes," Amerie whispered, "to offer a Mass of Thanksgiving. And long overdue."

Felice shook her head with an enigmatic smile and Richard turned away looking superior, but Claude came to Amerie's rock and shared the gold thimble of wine and the flake of dried bread from the Mass kit she carried in the pocket of Richard's uniform. And when that was over they went on their way again, chopping a path on the bank opposite from that claimed by the sabertooth.

"It was so incredibly beautiful," the nun said to Claude. "But why does it need those teeth? The big cats of our time got along nicely with shorter ones."

"Our lions and tigers didn't try to kill elephants."

Richard exclaimed, "You mean those monstrous hoe-tuskers they tried to frighten us with in the auberge Tri-D's? Here?"

"More likely the smaller mastodons in these uplands. Gomphotherium angustidens is probably the common sort. Hardly half the size of those rhinos we dodged yesterday. We won't run into deinotherium until we have to cross a swamp or a large river bottomland."

"Kaleidoscopic," the pirate growled. "Pardon me for asking, but do any of you aces have a destination in mind? Or are we just running?"

Claude said softly, "We're just running. When we've shaken off the soldiers and the bear-dogs, then there'll be time enough to make strategic decisions. Or don't you agree, son?"

"Aw, shit," said Richard, and began hacking at the streamside shrubbery once more.

At last the brook merged with a large turbulent river flowing in a southerly direction. Claude thought it might be the upper Saône. "We won't follow this river," he told the rest of the Group. "It probably curves around to the southwest and empties into the lake forty or fifty kloms downstream. We'll have to cross over, and that means the decamole bridges."

Each Survival Unit was equipped with three bridge sections that could be married to produce a narrow, self-supporting span twenty meters in length that resembled a ladder with close-set rungs. Moving up the river to a point where the torrent narrowed between two craggy shelves of rock, they inflated and ballasted the sections, joined them, and swung the bridge over to the opposite bank.

"Looks kinda flimsy," Richard remarked uneasily. "Funny— when we practiced with it back at the auberge it seemed a lot wider."

The bridge was a good third of a meter in width and steady as a rock. However, they had used it to cross a still pond in the auberge's cavern, while here surging rapids and sharp rocks awaited below.

"We could inflate another bridge and lash the two side by side if it would make you feel safer," Amerie suggested. But the pirate bristled indignantly at the suggestion, hoisted his pack, and lurched across like an apprentice tightrope walker.

"You next, Amerie," said Claude.

The nun stepped confidently onto the span. How many hundreds of logs had she walked over, crossing the mountain streams of the Oregon Cascades? The bridge rungs were less than a handspan apart, impossible to fall through. All that was necessary was a firm step, balanced posture, and keep the eyes on the opposite bank and not on the foaming chute six meters below—

Her right thigh muscle went into spasm. She teetered, caught herself, then overbalanced on the opposite side and went feet-first into the river.

"Dump your pack!" Felice screamed. Moving so fast that her hands were blurred, she dropped the bow and arrows, unfastened her own backpack, slapped the quick-release buckles of her cuirass and greaves, and jumped in after Amerie.

Richard gaped from the other side, but the old man ran back the way he had come, to the relative calm of the smaller stream's outspate. Two heads bobbed in the rapids. The leading one fetched momentarily against a humpbacked boulder and disappeared. The second one swept up to the rock and also went under, but after a long minute both women reappeared and floated toward Claude. He seized a stout piece of driftwood and held it out. Felice caught hold with one hand and he was able to pull her in. Her other hand had the fingers entwined in Amerie's hair.

Claude waded out and dragged the nun onto the bank. Felice rested on hands and knees in the shallows, spewing and coughing. He lifted Amerie's sodden body in a jackknife bend to empty the lungs of water, then filled them with his own warm air.

Breathe, child, he begged her. Live, daughter.

There was a sound of gagging, a first halting expansion of the chest beneath the soaked and torn starship captain's uniform. One last kiss of shared breath, and she returned.

Amerie's eyes opened and she stared wildly at Claude, then at the smiling Felice. A choked sob rose in her throat and she buried her head in the old man's breast. He had Felice pull the warm Orcadian sweater from his pack and wrapped the nun in it; but when he tried to pick Amerie up and carry her across the bridge she was much too heavy for him. So it was the little athlete who had to assist the nun, while the paleontologist toted his own and Felice's gear.

Amerie's pack with its medical supplies was lost, swept far downstream. They had to set her broken arm with the meager first-aid equipment from the individual Survival Units, following steps outlined in a laconic plaque entitled *Common Medical Emergencies*. The injury was a simple fracture of the left humerus, easily reduced even by amateur medics; but by the time Amerie was treated and sedated, the afternoon was well advanced. Richard convinced Claude and Felice that it would be useless to try to press on farther, regardless of possible pursuit. They went a short distance from the river into a concealing grove of massive oaks. There Richard erected two decamole cabins while Felice went out and shot a big fat roebuck and Claude grubbed nourishing cattail tubers from a boggy spot.

With their stomachs full, cots set on maximum soft, and critter-proof screendoors latched, they fell asleep even before night fell. They never heard the owls and nightingales and treefrogs singing, nor the fading howls of bear-dogs raging on a cold and futile trail far to the south. They did not see the mist start to rise from the rapids as the stars brightened. And they never saw the glowing grotesqueries of the Firvulag, who came and danced on the opposite bank of the river until the stars paled with the coming of dawn.

* * *

The following morning Amerie was feverish and weak. By common consent they dosed her with their limited store of medication, made her comfortable in one hut, and withdrew to the other so that she could sleep and mend. They all stood in need of recuperation, and there seemed little danger that any pursuit party could cross the crag-bordered torrent without their being aware of it.

Felice was confident that they had eluded the trackers altogether. "They might even find equipment from Amerie's pack downstream and decide that we've drowned in the river."

So they slept, lunched on cold venison and algiprote, and then sat in the shade of an ancient oak, sipping small cups of precious instant coffee and trying to decide what to do next.

"I've been working on a new plan," said Felice. "I've considered different possibilities and decided that the best place to get another torc would be near Finiah, where there are plenty of Tanu. They might even have a storehouse or a factory for the things. What we have to do is hide out until Amerie is healed, cross the Vosges, then hole up outside the city. We can rustle supplies from caravans or outlying settlements."

Richard choked on his coffee.

Felice went on serenely, "And then, after we've analyzed their defenses and learned more about the actual technology of the torcs, we can work out plans for the strike."

Richard set his little cup down on a tree root with great care. "Kid, you've conned us and bullied us into going along with your plans so far, and I'm not saying you didn't do a damned good job getting us away from Epone and her stooges. But there is no way you're gonna force me into a four-man invasion of a whole city full of exotic mind mashers!"

"You'd prefer to hide in the woods until they hunt you down?" she sneered. "They won't stop searching, you know. And the Tanu will be coming out themselves instead of just sending human slavies. If we follow my plan—if *I* get a golden torc—I'll be a match for any of them!"

"That's what *you* say. How do we know you'll be able to get it up? And what's in it for us? Do we get to be your loyal spear carriers while you're playing Madam Commander? No friggerty golden torcs are going to do the rest of us poor normals any good. Sure as shit some of us'd get chopped by these freaks before your private guerrilla war was over, win *or* lose. You want to know what my plans are, bull-dolly?"

She sipped her drink, eyes hooded.

"I'll tell you!" Richard blustered. "I'm gonna rest up here for another day or two and repair my footgear, and then I'm heading north to the big rivers and the ocean, just like Yosh did. A little luck and I might even meet up with him. When I get to the Atlantic I'm sailing southward along the coast. While you're doing your bandit-princess routine, I'll be getting pissed on good wine and bouncing broads in my pirate shack in Bordeaux."

"And the rest of us?" Claude kept his tone neutral.

"Come with me! Why not? I'll be marching easy, not breaking my butt climbing to hell and gone over the Vosges. Listen, Claude—you and Amerie stick with me and I'll help you find some nice peaceful place the Tanu never heard of. You're kinda old to get mixed up in this crazy kid's battles. And what life would it be for a nun, for God's sake? *This* one kills people for fun."

Felice said, "You're wrong, Richard," and drank coffee.

The old paleontologist turned from one to the other, then shook his head. "I've got to think about this. And there's something else I've been meaning to do. If you don't mind, I'll just go a little farther into this grove of oak trees and spend some time alone." He got to his feet, felt briefly in the big pocket of his bush jacket, and walked off.

"Take as long as you like, Claude," Felice called. "I'll see to Amerie. And keep a lookout, too."

"Don't get lost," Richard added. Felice muttered an expletive under her breath.

Claude wandered along, automatically noting landmarks as he had done for so many years on freshly tamed planets. An oak with two massively drooping branches like ogre arms. A reddish pinnacle standing out amidst the gray granite. A dry meadow with a maple, one branch turned anomalously golden too early in the season. A little pool dotted with pink waterlilies, with a pair of ordinary mallard ducks swimming lackadaisically about. A spring issuing from the rocks, adorned with lacy ferns and shaded by a magnificent beech.

"How's this, Gen?" the old man inquired.

He knelt down and held out his palms to the trickle, drank, then laved his forehead and the sunburnt back of his neck. Asperges me, Domine, hyssopo, et mundabor. Lavabis me, et super nivem dealbabor.

"Yes, I think this will do very well."

He took a thin flat stone from the basin of the spring and went to the foot of the beech tree. After carefully removing a pad of moss, he dug a hole, set the carved wooden box into it, and replaced the soil and plants, patting them firm. He marked her resting place with no stone nor cross; those who cared about her knew where her dust lay. When he was finished he went back to the spring for a handful of water to refresh the disturbed moss, then sat down with his back against the tree trunk and closed his eyes.

When he awoke it was late afternoon. Something crouched at the spring and watched him with a wary light-green gaze.

Claude held his breath. It was one of the most beautiful little animals he had ever seen, its graceful and sinuous body not much longer than his hand, with a slender tail adding another twenty centimeters to its length. Its underparts were pale orange and the upper fur tan with subtle black shading rather like a kit fox. The feline face was full of intelligence, mild and unthreatening, for all that it resembled that of a miniaturized cougar.

It had to be Felis zitteli, one of the earliest of the true cats. Claude pursed his lips and whistled a soft, undulating call. The animal's large ears cupped toward the sound. With infinite slowness, Claude slipped his hand into his pocket and withdrew a small piece of cheeselike algiprote.

"Pss-pss-pss," he invited, placing the food on the mossy sward beside him.

Calmly, the little cat came to him, nostrils quivering, white whiskers pointing forward. It sniffed the food discreetly, tested it with a dainty pink tongue, and ate it. Eyes proportionally larger than those of a domestic cat and outlined in black looked at Claude in an unmistakably friendly fashion. There was a faint humming sound. Felis zitteli was purring.

The old man gave it more food, then ventured to touch it. The cat accepted his stroking, arching its back and curling its black-tipped tail into an interrogative curve. It came closer to Claude and butted its forehead against the side of his leg.

"Oh, you are a cutie, aren't you? Tiny little teeth. Do you eat insects and little rock critters, or do you fish for minnows?" The cat tilted its head and bestowed a melting glance, then leaped into his lap, where it settled down with every evidence of familiarity. Claude petted the pretty thing and spoke softly to it while shadows purpled and a chill breeze stole through the grove.

"I'll have to be going," he said reluctantly, slipping one hand beneath the warm little belly and lifting the cat to the ground. He got to his feet, expecting the animal to take fright at the movement and flee. But it only sat down and watched him, and when he moved away, it followed.

He chuckled and said, "Shoo," but it persisted. "Are you an instant domestic?" he asked it, and then thought of Amerie, who would face a long stint of convalescence with him and Richard on their way north. If they left Felice behind (and there seemed no alternative), the nun would fret about her as well as brood over her own guilts. Perhaps this charming little cat would be a distraction.

"Will you ride in my pocket? Or do you prefer shoulders?" He picked it up and inserted it into the bellowslike pocket of his jacket. It turned about several times and then settled down with its head out, still purring.

"That's that, then." The old man lengthened his stride, passing from landmark to landmark until he came back into the open part of the oak grove where they had set up camp.

The two decamole cabins were gone.

Throat constricted, heart racing, Claude staggered back behind a huge tree bole, leaning with his back to the trunk until his pulse slowed. He peered cautiously out, studying the clearing where the camp had been. It was empty of their equipment. Even the fire trench and the remains of the roasted deer were gone. There were no footprints, no broken ferns or shrubs to indicate a scuffle (take *Felice* without a fight?), nothing to show there had ever been human beings among the big old trees.

Claude left his place of concealment and did a more careful search. The site had been cleaned up by persons who knew their woodcraft, but there remained a few clues. One dusty place bore parallel sweep marks from the branch that had been used to obliterate footprints. And down by the torrent, on a faint game trail that led upstream, was a piece of emerald-green fluff stuck to the resiny trunk of a pine.

A bit of green feather. Dyed green.

Claude nodded as the puzzle began to resolve itself. They had found three people and three packs and taken them this way. Who? Certainly not the minions of the Tanu, who would not care about concealing their presence. Then—? Firvulag?

Claude's heart leaped again and he pinched his nostrils shut and exhaled gently. The adrenalin flood was stemmed and the pounding in his chest eased. There was nothing to do but follow. And if they caught him ... well at least he had fulfilled part of what he had come here to do.

"You're sure you don't want to get off?" he whispered to the cat, crouching and pulling open the pocket to afford an easy egress. But the animal only blinked its big eyes sleepily and cuddled down out of sight.

"It's us versus them, then," Claude said, sighing. He set a good pace and hiked up the noisy river until it was nearly dark. Then he smelled smoke and followed his nose into a stand of sequoias on a rocky slope above the river. There was a sizable fire, surrounded by many dark figures who were laughing and talking.

Claude lurked among the shadows, but he was evidently expected. Completely against his will, he found himself walking up to the fire with his hands above his head, drawn by the same irresistible compulsion he had known in the examining chamber of the Lady Epone.

"It's an old one!" somebody said as he came into the fire-light.

"Not such an alter kocker, though," a hulking shape remarked. "He might be good for something."

"Acting more reasonable than his friends, anyhow."

There were perhaps a dozen tough-looking human men and women seated on the ground around the flames. They were dressed in dark buckskin and oddments of ragged costume, eating the last bits of Felice's venison and turning a long spit crowded with spatchcocked birds.

One desperado arose and came over to Claude. It was a middle-aged woman of medium height with dark hair graying at the temples and eyes that displayed a fanatic sparkle in the firelight. Her thin lips tightened critically as she studied the old man. She lifted the fine beak of her nose in a proud gesture and Claude could see a golden torc nestled beneath the collar of her doeskin cloak.

"What do you call yourself?" she asked sternly.

"I'm Claude Majewski. What have you done with my friends? Who are you?"

The mind-grip gentled and the woman looked at him with astringent humor. "Your friends are safe enough, Claude Majewski. As for myself, I am Angélique Guderian. You may call me Madame."

18

THE RIVER RHÔNE FLOWED SLOW AND WIDE. THE BOAT, even with its sail fully spread and its small engine working, was a long time leaving the Isle of Darask behind. The watery plains of the Camargue shimmered with a golden haze that blurred regions a kilometer or so away into an indistinct scrim backdrop. Later, as the boat traveled farther south, the passengers caught sight of mountains on their left and the tops of occasional rock outcroppings in the swamp; but there was no sign of the sea. Handsome little orange-and-blue reedlings and red-headed buntings teetered on the tall papyrus growing beside the river's main channel. The bubbletop was off all morning and the passengers watched, fascinated, as crocodiles and dugongs cruised around them. Once there was a shoal of marvelous watersnakes, nearly transparent and shining like undulant rainbows beneath the hazy sun.

Around noon they pulled in to another island where more than twenty boats were gathered—cargo craft, small yachts conveying brightly garbed Tanu, larger vessels crowded with silent little ramas sitting five abreast on rows of benches like small unchained galley slaves who had lost their oars. The island had only a few low buildings. Skipper Highjohn explained that they would not disembark here, only stop long enough to reinstall the bubble panels.

"Not another damn shoot-the-chutes!" groaned Raimo. He pulled out his flask.

"The very last," Highjohn soothed him, "and not rough, even though it's a bit steep. One of the unreconstructed gorfs who piloted Tanu barges through here back in the earliest days of the time-portal named the thing la Glissade Formidable. Sounds classier than the Dreadful Slide, so that's what we call it today, too."

Stein, sitting in a seat beside Sukey, looked puzzled. "But we should be in the Rhône delta now. Bang on the Mediterranean shore. What kind of gradient can there be?"

"You're in for a surprise," Bryan told him. "I couldn't believe it myself when the skipper explained it to me. I used to sail the Med, too, you'll remember. What it adds up to, Stein, is a slight miscalculation on the part of the boffins who drew up our Pliocene maps."

The workman installing the transparent panels gave the last one a smack and said, "You're off, Cap'n!"

"Belt in, everyone," Highjohn ordered. "You come forward, Bryan. You're gonna love this one."

A light wind sprang up as they puttered away from the moorage, following in the wake of a thirty-meter barge loaded with metal ingots. The vapors that had obscured their view finally dissipated, and they looked to the south for a first glimpse of the sea.

They saw a cloud.

"What the *hell* is that?" Stein wondered. "Looks like a plass factory on fire or a big volcano vent. Friggerty cloud goes clear to the tropopause."

The mast of the riverboat folded and withdrew, and the auxiliary engine cut out. They began to pick up speed. The clumps of marshgrass were more widely spaced now, and the boat followed a marked channel that trended southeastward, close beneath a rounded head-land on their left that jutted into the flats as an outlier of the alpine foothills. They were heading directly toward the towering white cloud, picking up speed every minute.

And then Elizabeth said, "Dear Lord. The Mediterranean is gone."

The barge that was traveling about half a kilometer ahead of them dropped out of sight. To the east and west along the horizon were low points of land—but between them was only a line of water meeting milky sky, having a shallow dip in the center. And there was a sound, a swelling rumble with a hissing component that grew to deafening proportions as they swept closer and closer to la Glissade Formidable, where the wide expanse of the Rhône ended at the continental brink.

Creyn's mental voice rang in the brains of all the torc-wearers. "Shall I program oblivion?" But they all replied, "No!" for their curiosity was greater than any terror of what lay ahead.

The boat raced over the edge and started down, borne on muddy waters cascading over a steep fan of sediment, plunging at eighty kilometers an hour into the depths of the Empty Sea.

They came to the end of the Glissade after four hours and floated in the pale waters of a great bitter lake. All around them were the many-colored rocks of the continental roots and glistening, fantastically eroded shapes of salt and anhydrite and gypsum. With its bubble panels stowed away, the boat spread its sail and raced along toward the southwest, for it was there that Creyn told them that the capital city of Muriah lay—at the tip of the Balearic Peninsula, which the Tanu called Aven, above the perfect flat of the White Silver Plain.

They traveled for one more day, overcome by the strangeness and the beauty and hardly able to talk about it except for endless exclamations in both the vocal and mental speech, to which Creyn responded, "Yes, it is wonderful. And more to come, more splendid than you can imagine."

In the late evening of the sixth day after they had departed from Castle Gateway they arrived. The high peninsula of Aven stretched away into the west, green and rolling, with a single peak near its tip and other eminences half-hidden in haze. A team of helladotheria in glowing trappings of rainbow fabric pulled the boat up a long rollered way while chaliko-riders dressed in gauzy robes and glass armor, bearing lights, animal-headed horns and banners, followed along the steep towpath. The welcoming Tanu sang all the way to the blazing city high above the salt. Their song had a haunting melody that seemed strangely familiar to Bryan; but those human beings who wore the torc were able to understand the alien words:

Li gan nol po'kône niési,
'Kône o lan li pred néar,
U taynel compri la neyn,
Ni blepan algar dedône.
 Shompri pône, a gabrinel,
 Shal u car metan presi,
Nar metan u bor taynel o pogekône,
Car metan sed gône mori.

There is a land that shines through life and time,
A comely land through the length of the world's
 age,
And many-colored blossoms fall on it,
From the old trees where the birds are singing.
 Every color glows there, delight is
 commonplace,
 Music abounds on the Silver Plain,
On the Gentle-Voiced Plain of the Many-
 Colored Land,
On the White Silver Plain to the south.

There is no weeping, no treachery, no grief,
There is no sickness, no weakness, no death.
There are riches, treasures of many colors,
Sweet music to hear, the best of wine to drink.
 Golden chariots contend on the Plain of Sports
 Many-colored steeds run in days of lasting
 weather.
Neither death nor the ebbing of the tide
Will come to those of the Many-Colored Land.

PART III

THE ALLIANCE

1

THE GIANT SEQUOIA HAD ENDURED FOR 10,000 YEARS. STANDING amidst a grove of lesser specimens high in the Vosges, it was hollowed by ancient wildfire and rot. In millennia past lightning had sheared its top, so that the Tree was only about 100 meters in height; the trunk nearest the ground spanned fully a fourth of that distance, giving the sequoia the appearance of a huge truncated pylon. That it lived at all was evidenced only by sparse branches writhing at the broken crown, their small needles seemingly incapable of photosynthesizing enough sugar to nourish such a monument.

The sequoia was host to a family of fire-backed eagles and several million carpenter ants. Since early in the afternoon it had also harbored a band of freeliving humans who were accustomed to use the great hollow trunk as a safe-house in times of particular danger.

A thin rain fell. In another hour it would be dark. A woman in a water-stained doeskin cloak stood beside one buttress of the great bole; her eyes shut, her fingertips pressed to her throat. After five minutes had passed, she opened her eyes and wiped some of the moisture from her forehead. Stooping, she pulled aside the fronds of a large fern and entered an inconspicuous opening, a nearly healed fissure that led into the interior of the Tree.

Someone helped her out of the sodden cloak. She nodded her thanks. All around the inner perimeter of the trunk small fires burned on low stone platforms, their smoke plumes plaiting together with that of a larger central blaze and rising toward the natural chimney high above. The main fire was laid on a great X-shaped hearth. Its flames towered at the center and diminished to a comfortable cooking height at the ends of the arms. People were gathered around the central fire in great numbers; smaller groups huddled near the subsidiary fireplaces. The place smelt of steaming clothing spread before the flames, of baking ash-bread and pots of hot spiced wine, and of simmering meat stew.

Richard hovered over the stew kettle, snarling at the cooks and occasionally adding dried herbs from a collection of crocks at his feet. Claude and Felice sat together nearby, and Amerie was using her good arm to lay out medical supplies on a clean blanket. The nun's tiny wildcat watched with keen interest, having learned quickly that the drug doses, dressings, and instruments were not playthings or prey.

Angélique Guderian came to this side of the fire and extended her hands to the warmth. She said to Amerie, "It's a good thing, ma Soeur, that Fitharn and the other Firvulag were able to retrieve your pack. We are always short of medical supplies, and we will have great need of your secular skills as well as your spiritual ones. There are no professional healers among us, since all such persons are subjected to the bondage of the gray torc as soon as their expertise is discovered. We can only presume that your own torcless state is the result of a Tanu error."

"And there's no escape for the gray-torcs, once they're collared?"

"They may escape, certainly. But should a wearer of either the gray or silver torc come within the sphere of influence of a coercive Tanu, the human will be compelled to serve the exotic—even to giving up his life. This is why there can be no torc wearers among us."

"Except yourself," said Felice softly. "But those who wear gold are free, aren't they?"

Claude was whittling a new rosary for Amerie, his vitredur

knife gleaming like sapphire in the firelight. He asked, "Can't the torcs be cut off?"

"Not while the person lives," Madame replied. "We have tried, of course. It is not that the metal is so durable, but rather that the torc somehow becomes bonded to the life-force of the wearer. This bonding is accomplished after the torc has been worn for an hour or so. Once a person has adapted, to unfasten or sunder the device brings death in convulsions. The mortal agony is similar to that inflicted by certain perverted redactors among the Tanu."

Felice leaned closer to the fire. She had finally taken off her armor after the thirty-six-hour forced march to the Tree, and the wet cloth of her green dress clung to her slight body. Her legs and upper arms, where they had not been protected by gauntlets and greaves, were a mass of scratches and deep bruises. News that the Tanu Hunt had invaded the Vosges sent Madame and her scouting party, together with the remnant of Group Green, fleeing toward the Tree refuge, where they had been met by other human renegades.

Felice tried hard to be casual. "So there is no way that you can remove your own torc, Madame?"

The old woman gazed at the girl athlete for a long moment. At last she said, "You must not allow yourself to fall into temptation, my child. This golden torc remains a part of me until my death."

Felice gave a light laugh. "There's no need for you to be afraid of me. Just look into my mind and see."

"I cannot read your mind, Felice. You know that. I am no redactor, and your strong latencies shield you. But many years at the auberge gave me an insight into the personalities of others such as yourself. And limited though my own metafunctions may be, I am in the confidence of the Firvulag . . . and *they* read you like a child's primer."

"So that's it," Felice remarked obscurely. "I felt something."

"The Firvulag have watched you almost from the beginning," the old woman said. "They always follow the caravans, the Little People, hoping for some contretemps that will put the travelers into their power. So they behold you on the shore of the Lac de Bresse in your bid for freedom. They even aided you—did you realize that?—by adding images of confusion to the minds of the chalikos and the soldiers, so that you and your friends were able to triumph. Ah, the Firvulag were impressed by you, Felice! They saw your potential. But they also feared you—and quite rightly. And so Fitharn, wisest among those who were following, caused a vivid illusion to seize the mind of one of your confrères—"

"Dougal!" Felice cried, springing to her feet.

"C'est ça."

Richard gave an ironic cackle. "Crafty spooks! I'll bet they could get that golden torc back out of the lake if they wanted to."

A chaotic mix of emotions played over the girl's face. She began to speak, but Madame held up her hand.

"The Firvulag bestow their gifts only as they choose, not as we demand. You will have to be patient."

Claude said, "So the Firvulag followed us all the way. Don't tell me that they clouded the minds of our pursuers as well?"

"Certainly," Madame Guderian replied. "Would not the boatful of gray-torc marines have seen some trace of your own wake? Would not the tracking soldiers have found you in the forest, in spite of your pathetic attempts to throw them off the scent? But of course the Firvulag helped! And Fitharn also notified us of your presence in our Vosges forest, and so we came for you. His people also warned us of the Hunt, which does not usually penetrate deeply into the mountains."

Richard tasted the stew again and grimaced. "Now that we're here in a safe place, what happens? I'll be damned if I'm going to spend the rest of my life hiding out."

"We do not enjoy it, either. You have caused us a good deal of trouble by escaping into the Vosges. Ordinarily, the Tanu are inclined to let us be, and our free people reside in small homesteads or in secret villages. I myself live in Hidden Springs, which is near the future site of Plombières-les-Bains. But now Lord Velteyn of Finiah is wild over the killing of Epone. You must understand that no Tanu has ever before been killed by a mere bareneck human. Velteyn's Flying Hunt will now search out even the most remote of our settlements, hoping to find Felice. There will be gray-torc patrols everywhere—at least until the Tanu become distracted by the preparations for the Grand Combat . . . As to what shall be done with you, we will discuss that when Peo and his warriors return. I have already perceived their approach."

Claude rolled one of the large rosary beads toward the little cat. The animal patted it toward Amerie, then arched its back in appreciation of its own cleverness. The nun picked up the cat and stroked it as it tried to nestle into her sling. "Do you have any news of the other escapees? The people in the boats? Our friend Yosh? The Gypsies?"

"Two of the Gypsies survived their encounter at the ravine bridge. They will be guided here. There has been no word at all about the Japanese. The Firvulag in the northern regions are savage and not inclined to respect the alliance that their High King has formed with us. Your friend's chance of survival is not good. As to those in the boats—most were recaptured by gray-torc marines from the lake forts. They are now imprisoned in Finiah. Six escapees who reached the Jura shore are presently in the care of friendly Firvulag and will be taken to a free-human refuge in the high mountains. Seven more"— Madame shook her head—"were taken by les Criards, the malign Firvulag known as Howlers."

"What will happen to them?" Amerie asked.

Madame lifted her shoulders and the golden torc reflected the flames. "These exotics! Ah, ma Soeur, they are barbaric, even the best of them. And the worst—! Who shall even speak of their enormities? Firvulag and Tanu are members of the same species. En vérité, they actually constitute a dimorphic race with a most peculiar genetic pattern. On their home planet, this led to an ancient antagonism between the two forms—the one tall and metapsychically latent, the other mostly short in stature and with limited operancy. You must understand that the exotics came to Earth in order to be free to pursue certain barbarous customs, holdovers from their archaic culture, that were justly proscribed by the civilized ones of their galactic confederation. Some of their cruel games are physical—the Hunt, the Grand Combat, of which you will learn more later. But others are jeux d'esprit—games of the mind. The Tanu, with their wide-ranging latent metafunctions, do not favor this subtle jousting so much. It is more commonly the province of the torcless Firvulag. The Little People possess some farsensing power, plus one highly developed operant metafunction—that of creativity. They are masters of illusion. But what illusions they make! They are capable of driving humans, even the weaker among the Tanu, insane with terror or anguish. Sensitive persons may even be killed outright from psychic shock. Firvulag can take the shape of monsters, devils, whirlwinds, conflagrations. They insinuate their delusions into more helpless minds and trigger suicide or self-mutilation. The latter is of great amusement to the worst of them, the so-called Howling Ones, since they are themselves deformed mutants. The weapons of the Firvulag are our own nightmares and fever-dreams, the fears and phantoms that assault one's imagination in dark places. They take a sadistic delight in destroying."

"But they haven't destroyed *you*," Felice said. "They gave you a golden torc. Why?"

"Because they hope to use me, of course. I am to be a tool—a weapon, c'est-à-dire—against their most deadly foe: the Tanu, their brothers."

Amerie said, "And now you hope to use us."

Madame's thin lips lifted in a small smile. "It is obvious, is it not, ma Soeur? You do not know how poor we are, what odds we have faced. The Tanu call us Lowlives . . . and we have assumed the name proudly. Over many years our people have managed to escape from captivity and were hardly thought to be worth pursuing. Most of us have no special talents that can be used against the exotics. But you in your Group are different. The Tanu would take revenge upon you—but we Lowlives see you as invaluable allies. You must join us! Felice, even without a torc, can control animals, even influence certain humans. She is physically strong and an experienced gameplaying tactician. You, Amerie, are a doctor and a priest. My people have struggled for years without either. Richard is a navigator, a former commander of starships. For him there may be a key role in the liberation of humanity—"

"Now just a damn minute!" bellowed the pirate, waving his soup ladle.

Claude flipped bits of wood into the fire. "Don't forget me. As an old fossil hunter, I can tell you exactly what Pliocene beast will be cracking your bones for the marrow after the Tanu and Firvulag get finished with you."

"You are quick with a jest, Monsieur le Professeur," said

Madame tartly. "Perhaps the old fossil hunter will tell us his age?"

"A hundred and thirty-three."

"Then you are two years my senior," she retorted, "and I will expect you to render good advice to our company as a result of your vast experience. As I lay before you my grand design, the plan for the liberation of humanity, give us your invaluable counsel. Correct any youthful impulsiveness that I may show."

"Gotcha, Claude," Richard said, snickering. "Say . . . if anybody cares, this vat of slumgullion is as ready as it will ever be."

"Then we will eat," said Madame, "and shortly Peo and the fighters will join us." She raised her voice. "Mes enfants! You will all come to supper!"

Slowly, all of the people from the smaller fires approached, carrying bowls and drinking vessels. The total number of Lowlives included perhaps two hundred, far more men than women, with a handful of children as quiet and alert as the adults. Most of the people were dressed in buckskin or homespun peasant garb. They did not seem to be outstanding physical specimens, nor were any of them decked out in the wildly eccentric fashion of certain timefarers in the Finiah caravan. The Lowlives did not look beaten or desperate or fanatical. In spite of the fact that they had just fled for their lives at Madame's mental alarm, they did not seem afraid. They saluted the old woman gravely or cheerfully, and many of them had a smile or even a joke for Richard and the other cooks dishing out the hastily prepared fare. If one word could be used to describe the guerrilla contingent, it might be "ordinary."

Amerie searched the faces of these free people, wondering what had inspired this relative handful to defy the exotics. Here were exiles whose dream had come alive again. Was it possible that this small nucleus could grow—even prevail?

"Good friends," Madame was saying, "we have among us newcomers whom all of you have seen but few as yet have met. It is on their account that we have had to gather here. But we may hope, with their help, to reach our precious goal that much sooner." She paused and looked about the company. There was no sound except the snap and sizzle of the firelogs.

"As we eat, I will ask these new arrivals to tell us how they came from the prison of Castle Gateway to this free place." Turning to the remnant of Group Green, she asked, "Who will be your speaker?"

"Who else?" Richard said, pointing the ladle at Claude.

The old man rose to his feet. He spoke for nearly a quarter of an hour without interruption until his narrative reached the point where Felice was about to initiate the attack upon Epone. Then there was a loud hiss. Amerie's little cat sprang from her arms and struck a stiff pose, facing the door of the Tree like a miniature puma at bay.

"It is Peo," said Madame.

Ten people, all heavily armed with bows and blades, came stamping and dripping into the shelter. They were led by a gigantic middle-aged man nearly as massive as Stein who wore the shell ornaments and fringed deerskin clothing of a Native American. Claude held off continuing his tale until these people were served with food and given a place close to the big fire. Then the paleontologist resumed and told the story to the end. He sat down and Madame handed him a cup of hot wine.

Nobody spoke until the gray-haired Native American said, "And it was iron—*iron* that killed the Lady Epone?"

"Nothing but," Richard declared. "She was chewed to pieces and I let her have a couple of good ones with the bronze sword—but she still just about nailed me. Then something made me try Felice's little dagger."

The red man turned to the girl and demanded, "Give it to me."

"And who the hell do you think you are?" she said coolly.

He roared with laughter and the sound of it boomed in the hollow trunk of the Tree as in an empty cathedral. "I'm Peopeo Moxmox Burke, last chief of the Wallawalla tribe and former justice of the Washington State Supreme Court. I'm also the one-time leader of this gang of paskudnyaks and its present Sergeant at Arms and Warlord in Chief. Now may I please examine your dagger?"

He smiled at Felice and held out a great hand. She smacked the golden scabbard into it smartly. Burke drew out the leaf-shaped little blade and held it up in the firelight.

"Stainless steel alloy with an eversharp edge," the girl said. "A common toy on Acadie, useful for picking teeth, cutting sandwiches, pricking out transponders from rustled cattle, and putting out the lights of casual assaulters."

"It seems quite ordinary except for the gold of the hilt," Burke said.

"Amerie has a theory about it," Claude said. "Tell him, child."

Burke listened thoughtfully as the nun set forth her hypothesis on the possible deadly effect of iron on torc-bearing exotics, then murmured, "It could be. The iron disrupting the life-force almost like a neural poison."

"I wonder . . ." Felice began, staring at Madame with an innocent expression.

The old woman went to Chief Burke and took the knife from him. As the assembled crowd gasped, she held it to her own throat below the golden neck-ring and pricked the skin. A pearl-sized drop of dark blood appeared. She handed the dagger back to Burke.

"It seems," Felice said gently, "that Madame is made of sterner stuff than the Tanu."

"Sans doute," was the old woman's dry reply.

Burke mused over the small blade. "It's incredible that we never thought to try iron against them. But vitredur and bronze weapons were so easily available. And we never tumbled to the reasons why they confiscated steel items back at the Castle . . . Khalid Khan!"

One of the crowd, a gaunt man with burning eyes, a scraggly beard, and an immaculate white turban, got to his feet. "I can smelt iron as readily as copper, Peo. All you have to do is furnish the ore. The religious prohibition that the Tanu put on ironwork among their human subjects simply led us to carry on with copper and bronze out of sheer inertia."

"Who knows where iron ore might be found?" Madame asked of the company. There was silence until Claude said, "I might help you there. We old fossil hunters know a little geology, too. About a hundred kloms northwest of here, down the Moselle River, should be an accessible deposit. Even primitive men worked it. It'll be near the site of the future city of Nancy."

Khalid Khan said, "We'd have to do the refining work up there. Arrowheads would be best to begin with. Some lance tips. A few smaller blades."

"There's another experiment you might try," Amerie said, "once you have a strong iron chisel."

"What's that, Sister?" asked the turbaned metalsmith.

"Try removing gray torcs with it."

"By damn!" exclaimed Peopeo Moxmox Burke.

"Iron might short out the linkage between the brains of the torc wearers and the slave-circuitry," the nun went on. "We must find *some* way of freeing those people!"

One of Burke's fighters, a hefty fellow puffing a meerschaum, said, "To be sure. But what about those who don't wish to be freed? Perhaps you don't realize, Sister, that a good many humans are quite content in their filthy symbiosis with the exotics. The soldiers, especially. How many of them are sadistic misfits, delighting in the rôles given them by the Tanu?"

Madame Guderian said, "It is true, what Uwe Guldenzopf says. And even among those of goodwill, even among the barenecks, there are many who are happy in bondage. It is because of them that the expiation of my guilt cannot be a simple matter."

"Now don't start that again, Madame." Burke was firm. "Your plan, as it stands, is a good one. With the addition of iron weapons, we can shtup it forward that much faster. By the time we've located the Ship's Grave, we'll have enough of an armory to give the scheme a reasonable chance of success."

"I'm not going to wait weeks or months for you people to hatch your plot," Felice declared. "If my dirk killed one Tanu, it can kill others." She held out her hand to Burke. "Give it back."

"They'd get you, Felice," The Native American said. "They're expecting you. Do you think all of the Tanu are as weak as Epone? She was small fry—fairly powerful as coercers go, but her redact function wasn't worth much or she'd have smelled you out back at the Castle, even without using the mind-assay machine. The leaders among the Tanu can detect people like you in the same way that they detect Firvulag. You're going to have to keep out of the way until you get your golden torc."

She exploded. "And when will that be, dammit?"

Madame said, "When we manage to obtain one for you. Or when the Firvulag choose to give you one."

The girl replied with a volley of obscenities. Claude went up to her, took her by the shoulders, and sat her down on the soft wood-dust of the floor. "Now that's enough of that." Turning to Burke and Madame Guderian, he said, "Both of you have referred to a plan of action that you seem to expect us to participate in. Let's hear it."

Madame uttered a deep sigh. "Very well. First, you must know what we are up against. The Tanu seem to be invulnerable, immortal, but they are not. They can be killed by Firvulag brainstorms, the weaker ones—and even a powerful coercer-redactor may be overwhelmed if many Firvulag all project together or if one of their great heroes, such as Pallol or Sharn-Mes, chooses to fight."

"What is this bad vibes thing?" Richard asked her. "Can you do it?"

She shook her head. "My latent abilities include the far-sensing function in moderation, a somewhat less powerful coercive ability, and an aspect of creativity that may spin certain illusions. I can coerce ordinary humans, and grays who are not under direct compulsion from a Tanu. I cannot coerce the exotics or humans wearing gold or silver torcs—except with subliminal suggestions, which they may or may not follow. My farsense permits me to eavesdrop upon the so-called declamatory or command mode of the mental speech. I can hear the golds, silvers, and grays when they call out to one another over moderate distances, but I cannot detect more subtle narrow-focus communication unless it is directed at me. On rare occasions I have perceived messages coming from far away."

"And can you farspeak back?" Claude asked in an excited tone.

"To whom would I speak?" the old woman inquired. "All around us are enemies!"

Amerie exclaimed, "Elizabeth!"

Claude explained. "One of our companions. An operant farspeaker. She was taken south to the capital." He told what he knew of Elizabeth's former life and her regained metafunctions.

Madame frowned in preoccupation. "So it was *she* that I heard! But I did not know. And so I suspected a Tanu trick and withdrew at once from the touch."

"Could you contact her?" Claude asked.

"The Tanu would hear me," the old woman said, shaking her head. "I seldom project, except to sound the alarm to our people. Rarely to call to our Firvulag allies. I have not the skill to use the narrow focus that is undetectable except to the intended receptor."

Felice broke in rudely, "The plan! Get on with it!"

Madame pursed her lips and lifted her chin. "Eh bien. Let us continue to speak of the potential vulnerability of the Tanu. They kill one another by decapitation during their ritual combats. In theory a human could accomplish this, too, if it were possible to get close enough. However, the Tanu with coercive or redactive functions defend themselves mentally, while the creators and the psychokinetics are capable of physical asault. The weaker among them remain within the protective sphere of their more powerful fellows or else have bodyguards of armed silvers or grays. There are two other ways in which a Tanu may meet death—both very rare. The Firvulag told me of a very young Tanu who died by fire. He panicked when burning lamp oil spilled upon him and in fleeing, fell off a wall. His human guardians were unable to reach him before he was incinerated. If they had rescued him before his brain burned, they could have restored him to health in the usual Tanu fashion."

"Which is?" Amerie asked.

Chief Burke said, "They have a psychoactive substance that they call Skin. It looks like a thin plass membrane. Tanu healers with a certain combination of PK and redact are able to work through this stuff in some metapsychic way. They just wrap the patient up and start cogitating. They get results comparable to our best regeneration-tank therapy back in the Milieu, but with no hardware. Skin works on human beings, too, but it's worthless without the Tanu operator."

"Do the Firvulag use Skin?" asked the nun.

Burke shook his huge head. "Just old-fashioned frontier-doctoring. But they're tough little devils."

Felice laughed. "So are we."

"The last way that the exotics may die," Madame resumed, "is by drowning. The Firvulag are excellent swimmers. However, most of the Tanu are rather more sensitive than humans to the injurious effects of immersion. Still, death by drowning is very rare among them and seems to take mostly certain careless sportsmen of Goriah in Brittany, who are accustomed to carry their Hunt to the sea. Sometimes they are swallowed or carried into the depths by the enraged leviathans that they prey upon."

Felice grunted. "Well, there's not much chance we'll be able to hold the bastards' heads under water. So how *do* you plan to get the drop on 'em?"

"The plan is complex, involving several phases. It requires the co-operation of the Firvulag, with whom we have a very precarious alliance. Briefly, we would hope to attack and over-run Finiah aided by the forces of the Little People, who would be able to wreak havoc once they penetrated the city walls. Finiah is a strategic target of prime importance and it is isolated from the other Tanu population centers. Within its environs and protected by its defenses is the only barium mine in the Exile world. The element is extracted with great difficulty from a meager ore by rama workers. It is vital to the manufacture of torcs. *All* torcs. If we eliminate the supply of barium by destroying the mine, the entire socioeconomy of the Tanu would be undercut."

"Kinda long-range for a disaster, isn't it?" Richard remarked. "I should think they'd have stockpiles of the stuff stashed away."

"I have said that the matter is complex," Madame responded in some irritation. "We will also have to find a way of stopping the flow of time-travelers. As you will see, it is the coming of humanity to the Pliocene that has enabled the Tanu to dominate the era. In the days before I began my meddling, there was a virtual balance of power between Tanu and Firvulag. This was destroyed by the human advent."

"I get it," said Richard, the old intriguer. "The Firvulag are willing to help you and your bunch in hopes of restoring the good old days. But what makes you think the little spooks won't turn on *us* once they get what they want?"

"It is a matter still requiring some reflection," said Madame in a low voice.

Richard gave a derisive snort.

"There's more to the plan," said Peopeo Moxmox Burke. "And don't kick it in the head until you've heard the whole thing. Now down south in the capital—"

The little cat growled.

All of them looked toward the entrance crevice. There stood a short, broad-shouldered figure in a dripping, mucky cloak. His high-crowned hat leaned lugubriously over one ear from an accumulation of moisture. He grinned at the company through a mask of mud in which eyes and teeth were the only bright points.

"Pegleg!" exclaimed Burke. "For God's sake, bubi—what have you been up to?"

"Had to go to ground. Bear-dogs on my trail."

As he came stumping toward the fire, Madame whispered, "Not a word of the iron."

The new arrival was something under a meter and a half in height, with a barrel chest and a visage that was rosy-cheeked and long-nosed, once the filth had been wiped away. He had lost one leg below the knee, but walked about agilely enough with the aid of a singular prosthesis fashioned of wood. Seating himself by the fire, he swabbed at the peg with a damp rag, revealing carvings of snakes and weasels and other creatures twining about the artificial limb. They had inset jewels for eyes.

"What news?" Burke inquired.

"Oh, they're out there, all right," Pegleg replied. Somebody passed food and drink, which the little man attacked with gusto, simultaneously talking with his mouth full. "Some of the lads drew off a large patrol coming up the Onion River. Finished a good half dozen and sent the rest off with their tails between their legs screeching for Daddy Velteyn. No sign of the Exalted Cocksman himself yet, Té be thanked. Probably doesn't want to get his lovely glass armor all wet in the rain. I had a bad moment when some bear-dogs all from the squad that we finished began tracking me unawares. Could've nailed me, the sneaky turdlings, but I happened on a nice stinking bog and hid in it until they tired of waiting."

The little man held out his mug to the nun for a refill of wine. Amerie's cat had not returned to her, even though she snapped her fingers in a way that usually brought the animal running. Two baleful glowing eyes watched Pegleg from a dark pile of baggage far from the central fire. The cat continued to utter high-pitched, quavering growls.

"We must introduce our new companions to you," Madame said graciously. "You have seen them, of course. The Reverend

Sister Amerie, Professor Claude, Captain Richard . . . and Felice."

"May the Good Goddess smile on you," the little man said. "I'm Fitharn. But you can call me Pegleg."

Richard goggled. "Christ! *You're* a Firvulag?"

The one-legged man laughed and climbed to his feet. There beside the fire stood a tall, dead-black apparition with coiling tentacles for arms, slitted red eyes, and a mouth full of shark's teeth that slavered foul saliva.

Amerie's little cat let out a spitting screech. The monster vanished and Pegleg resumed his seat by the fire, nonchalantly drinking his wine.

"Impressive," said Felice. "Can you do others?"

The Firvulag's eyes twinkled. "We have our favorites, little one. The visions-of-the-eye are the least of it, you understand."

"I do," said Felice. "Since you had to flee the amphicyons, I conclude that they're not affected by your powers."

The exotic sighed. "A perverse species. We have to watch out for the hyaenids, too—but at least *they* can't be tamed by the Foe."

"I can control bear-dogs," Felice said in soft persuasion. "If I had a golden torc, I could help win this war of yours. Why won't you give me what you've already given Madame Guderian?"

"Earn it," said the Firvulag, licking his lips.

Felice clenched her fists. She forced a smile. "You're afraid. But I wouldn't use my metafunctions against any of you. I swear it!"

"Prove it."

"Damn you!" She started toward the little man, her doll-like face twisted with rage. "How? How?"

Madame intervened. "Felice, compose yourself. Be seated."

Fitharn stretched out his peg and groaned. "More wood for the fire! I'm chilled to the bone and my leg-long-gone torments me with phantom pain."

Amerie said, "I have a medication . . . if you're certain that your protoplasm is near-humanoid."

He gave her a broad grin and nodded, extending the stump. As she applied a minidoser he cried, "Ah, better, better! Té's blessing, if you can use such a thing, Sister."

"Masculine, feminine, only aspects of the One. Our races are closer than you think, Fitharn of the Firvulag."

"Perhaps." The little man stared morosely into his winecup.

Madame said, "When you arrived, Fitharn, I was explaining to the newcomers my plan. Perhaps you will be good enough to assist me. Tell them, if you will, the story of the Ship's Grave."

Once again, the exotic's cup was filled with wine. "Very well. Come close and listen. This is Brede's Tale, which was told to me by my own grandfather, gone these five hundred years to Té's dark womb until the great rebirth, when Té and Tana shall be sisters no more, but One, and Firvulag and Tanu cease at last their contention in the truce that shall have no end . . ."

He was silent for a long while, holding the cup to his lips and closing his eyes against the hot wine's rich fumes. Finally he set the vessel beside him, folded his hands in his lap, and told the tale in an oddly cadenced singsong:

"When Brede's Ship, through Té's compassion, brought us here, its mighty striving drained its heart and strength and mind—and so it died that we might live. When we left the Ship our flyers spread their curving wings, and people sang the Song together, friend with foe. We made our weeping way to where the Grave would be. We saw the Ship come burning from the east. We saw it coming through the high air and the low. It howled its agony. As the rising of a planet's sun dismisses night, so did the flaming of our Ship transform the very day, and make the Earth-star dim.

"The passing of the Ship devoured the air. The forests and the eastern mountains fell and thunder rolled around the world. The waters steamed within the brackish eastern seas. No living thing survived along the westward-trending path of death, but we watched sorrowing until the end. The Ship cried out aloud, it burst, it yielded up its soul. Its falling made the planet moan. The air, the waters, planet-crust, and Ship had merged into a glowing holocaust of stormy wound. But we stayed, singing there until the fire was quenched by rain and tears of Brede, and then we flew away.

"Then Pallol, Medor, Sharn, and Yeochee, Kuhsarn the Wise and Lady Klahnino, the Thagdal, Boanda, Mayvar, and Dionket, Lugonn the Shining One and Leyr the Brave—the best of Tanu and of Firvulag—went forth into the setting sun to find a living-place while still the Truce prevailed and none should fight. The Tanu chose Finiah on the riverside; but we, far wiser, took High Vrazel on the fogbound mountain crag. This being done, one task alone remained—to consecrate the Grave.

"In final flight the aircraft took to air. We rode within them to the place, and all embarked to stand upon a rim of land above a cup of liquid sky too wide to see across, while all around the land lay scorched and still. We watched a Great Ordeal, the first upon this world, with Sharn contending for the Firvulag and for the Tanu, bright Lugonn. With Sword and Spear they smote until their armor blazed and birds fell from the sky and heedless watchers lost their eyes. They battled for a month of hours and longer still, until the folk who watched screamed out as one, transfigured in the glory that redounded to the Ship and solemnized its death.

"At last, brave Sharn could bear no more. He fell with Sword in hand, steadfast until the end. The victory was won by bright Lugonn, whose Spear had caused the crater's lake to boil and liquefied the rocks and conjured sparkling dew that merged its tears with ours. And thus the votive offerings of Man and Blade were chosen for the consecration of the Grave. We marched away, the voices of our minds raised up in Song for one last time in honor of the Ship and also him who there was offered up to captain it upon its voyage to the healing dark. There, comforted within the Goddess's womb, they wait the coming of the light . . ."

The Firvulag raised his cup and drained it. He stretched his arms with a pop and crackle of ligaments and sat staring at Felice with a whimsical expression.

Madame Guderian said, "Within this ancient tale are certain pieces of information that repay our study. You will have noted the reference to aircraft. These are clearly machines of some sophistication, since they were able to leave the moribund Ship prior to its entrance into Earth's atmosphere. Given the advanced technology implied by the encapsulation of the passengers within the intergalactic organism, one can hardly assume the smaller craft to be simple reaction-engine fuelers. It is more likely that they were gravo-magnetically powered, like our own eggs and subluminal spaceships. And if so—"

Richard interrupted, wide-eyed. "They'd probably still be operational! And Pegleg said his people *marched* away from the Grave, so they must have left the aircraft there. Son of a bitch!"

"Where are they?" cried Felice. "Where's this Grave?"

The little Firvulag said, "When a person dies among us, the remains are taken by the family or friends to a secret place, one that none of the mourners has ever seen before. After the interment ceremony, the grave is never visited again. Its very location is blotted from the mind lest the remains be disturbed by the Foe or by irreverent rascals who would steal the funerary offerings."

"Quaint customs," Richard said.

Felice wailed, "Then you don't know where the Ship's Grave is?"

"It's been a thousand years," the little man replied.

Richard flung the ladle into the stewpot with a clang. "But, dammit, it's gotta be a whackin' great crater! What'd he say—? 'A cup of liquid sky too wide to see across.' And it lies east of Finiah."

"We have been searching," Madame said. "Ever since I first heard the tale three years ago and conceived the plan, we have looked for the Ship's Grave as best we could. But understand the terrain, Richard! The Black Forest lies beyond the Rhine to the east. In our day it was a minor range, a picturesque parkland full of hikers and carvers of cuckoo clocks. But now the Schwarzwald mountains are younger and higher. There are portions well above twenty-five hundred meters, rugged and dangerous to cross and a notorious haunt of les Criards—the Howling Ones."

"And do you know who *they* are?" inquired the Firvulag, smirking at Richard. "They're the people like me who don't like people like you. The snotty ones who won't let King Yeochee or anyone else tell 'em who their enemies are."

Madame said, "We have, over the past years, done a precarious exploration of the middle portion of the Black Forest range, north of Finiah. Even with the help of friendly Firvulag such as our good friend Fitharn, the project has been fraught with peril. Ten of our people have been killed and three driven mad. Five more vanished without a trace."

"And we lost some of our lads to the Hunt, too," Pegleg added. "Guiding humans just isn't healthy work."

Madame went on, "Forty or fifty kilometers east of the Black Forest begins the Swabian Alb, a part of the Jura. It is said to be full of caves inhabited by monstrous hyenas. Not even the malign Firvulag care to dwell in this territory—although it is rumored that a handful of grotesque mutants eke out a pathetic livelihood in sheltered valleys. Yet it is in this inhospitable country that the Ship's Grave is most likely to be found. And with it, not only workable flying machines but perhaps other ancient treasures as well."

"Would there be weapons in the aircraft?" Felice asked.

"Only one," said the Firvulag Fitharn, staring into the fire. "The Spear. But it would be enough, if you could get your hands on it."

Scowling, Richard said, "But I thought the Spear belonged to the guy named Lugonn—and he was the *winner* of the fight!"

"The winner received the privilege of sacrificing himself," Madame explained. "Lugonn, Shining Hero of the Tanu, raised the visor of his golden glass helmet and accepted the thrust of his own Spear through his eyes. His body was left at the crater, together with the weapon."

"But what the hell good would this Spear do us?" Richard asked.

Fitharn spoke softly. "It isn't the kind of weapon you might think. Any more than the Sword of our late hero, Sharn the Atrocious—which the obscene Nodonn has had in his thieving clutches in Goriah for forty years—is any kind of ordinary sword."

"They are both photonic weapons," Madame said. "The only two that the exotics brought from their home galaxy. They were to be used only by the great heroes—to defend the Ship in case of pursuit or, later, in the most exalted forms of ritual fighting."

"Nowadays," said Chief Burke, "the Sword only serves as the trophy of the Grand Combat. Nodonn's had it so long because the Tanu have won the contest for forty years running. Needless to say, there's little chance we'd ever be able to get our hands on the Sword. But the Spear is another matter."

"Christ!" Richard spat in disgust. "So to make Madame's

plan work, all we have to do is mount a blind search over two-three thousand square kloms crawling with man-eating spooks and giant hyenas and find this antique zapper. Probably clutched in some Tanu skeleton's hand."

"And around his neck," Felice said, "is a golden torc."

"We will find the Ship's Grave," Madame stated. "We will search until we do."

Old Claude hauled himself to his feet with some difficulty, limped over to the pile of dry wood, and picked up an armful. "I don't think any more blind hunting will be necessary," he said, tossing the sticks onto the blaze. A great cloud of sparks soared into the Tree's black height.

Everybody stared at him.

Chief Burke asked, "Do you know where this crater might be?"

"I know where it *has* to be. Only one astrobleme in Europe fits the bill. The Ries."

The stout fighter with the pipe smacked his own forehead and exclaimed, "Das Rieskessel bei Nördlingen! Natürlich! What a bunch of stupid pricks we've been! Hansi! Gert! We read about it in kindergarten!"

"Hell, yes," sang out another man from the crowd. And a third Lowlife added, "But you gotta remember, Uwe, they told us kids a meteorite made the thing."

"The Ship's Grave!" one of the women cried out. "If it's not just a myth, then there's a chance for us! We really might be able to free humanity from these bastards!" An exultant shout went up from the rest of the crowd.

"Be silent, for the love of God!" Madame implored them. Her hands were clasped before her breast almost prayerfully as she addressed Claude. "You are certain? You are positive that this—this Ries must be the Ship's Grave?"

The old paleontologist picked up a branch from the wood-pile. Scuffing an area of dust flat, he drew a vertical row of X's.

"There are the Vosges Mountains. We're on the western flank, about here." He poked, then slashed a line parallel to, and east of, the range. "Here's the Rhine, flowing roughly south to north through a wide rift valley. Finiah is here on the eastern bank." More X's were drawn behind the Tanu city. "Here's the Black Forest range, trending north-south just like the Vosges. Same basic geology. And beyond it, slanting off to the northeast, the Swabian Jura. This line I'm drawing under the Jura is the River Danube. It flows off east into the Panonian Lagoon in Hungary, someplace over under the woodpile. And right about *here*—"

The entire company was on its feet, straining to see and holding its collective breath as the old man stabbed his branch down.

"—is the Ries astrobleme. A few kloms north of the Danube, at the site of the future city of Nördlingen, maybe three hundred kloms east of here. And sure as God made little green apples, that's your Ship's Grave. It's a crater more than twenty-five kloms in diameter. The largest in Europe."

There was an uproar among the Lowlife folk. People crowded in to congratulate Claude and get refills of wine. Someone got out a reed flute and began to play a sprightly tune. Others laughed and danced about. The day that had begun in panicked flight from exotic enemies showed signs of ending as a celebration.

Ignoring the merrymakers, Madame whispered to Chief Burke. She and the Native American beckoned to the remnant of Group Green and withdrew into a deeply shadowed part of the hollow sequoia.

"It may be possible," Madame said, "just barely possible, to implement the plan yet this year. But we will have to set out at once. You must lead, Peo. And I must also go to detect and repel the Howling Ones. We will require your help to find the crater, Claude, and that of Felice to coerce hostile animals. Richard must come to pilot a flying machine, if we should indeed find any to be operational. We will take also Martha, who was a highly skilled engineer and who may help decipher the operation of the exotic devices as well as repair them. Also Stefanko, who tested egg transports. He can assist Richard if need be, and perhaps he might be able to pilot a second aircraft."

Chief Burke said, "Seven people. Two of them old, and Martha's not strong. Awkward, Madame. Too few for strength, too many for speed. Even with Felice and me for muscle, it'll be a rough trip."

Felice said, "I want Amerie to come. We could need a doctor."

The nun lifted her good shoulder in a hesitant gesture. "I'm willing—but I think I'd be more trouble than help."

"There is no question of your accompanying us, ma Soeur," said the old woman, giving Felice a sharp glance. "You can do the most good by remaining here, recovering your strength, and ministering to the people. We have some stolen medications, but many of them are unsuited to lay administration. There are any number of debilities you can allay—poorly knit fractures, fungus afflictions, internal parasites. When this present emergency has passed, Uwe Guldenzopf and Tadanori Kawai will take you to our village at Hidden Springs northwest of here. You will live in my own cottage and the people will come to you."

Chief Burke said, "Khalid Khan can take charge of the iron-smelting party. Say, ten strong men. Claude can tell Khalid what to look for, and if the boys locate the ore and get to work, they might have a fair number of weapons ready by the time we return."

"*If* we return!" Richard exclaimed. "Chrissake, why does everybody just take it for granted that I'm willing to go along with this scheme? Forget it! As soon as the heat's off from the Tanu, I'm blasting outa here."

"You can't weasel out," Felice said. "We need you!"

"Let that other sucker—the egg driver—be the pilot. I don't fight other people's wars."

Madame reached out one hand and touched the black velvet doublet of Richard's costume. "Der fliegende Hollander, is it not? I saw it performed many times in Lyon...Oh, Richard! This need not be your destiny. Do not run away. We need you! Help the rest of us to become free and thereby find your own peace. Stefanko's flight experience is very limited. You know how automated our egg-craft were. But you! You have boasted of how you flew the most advanced starships, orbital landers— even primitive aeroplanes. If any among us can operate the exotic craft and bring back the Spear of Lugonn it is you."

Her mind seemed to embrace him—suppressing his objections, calming all fear. And in spite of himself, Richard felt his resolution waver. He knew the damn woman was coercing him, playing her own tune on his superego, bending his will-power; but the more he struggled to get away, the more compelling her mental hold became...

Richard! Dear son, don't I know you? I—the mother of one hundred thousand wretched wayfarers who came to me as their last hope? You have always been alone, always self-centered and fearful of opening yourself to other persons, for to do so is to risk rejection and pain. But it is a risk we are born to take, we humans. We cannot live alone, cannot find happiness or peace alone, cannot love alone. The person alone must always be fleeing, always searching. He flees from the loneliness without end. He searches, whether he will or not, for another who will fill his emptiness . . .

Richard backed away from the terrible old woman until he was trapped against the ancient wood of the Tree, trying to defend himself against the thrust of her need and hope and—damn her!—the genuine compassion flowing out from her like healing water bathing his cracked and shitty soul.

Aloud, she said, "Come with us, Richard. Help us—all of us who need you. I cannot truly coerce you. Not beyond the passing moment. You must choose freely to help us. And in the giving you will receive what you have hungered for."

"Damn you!" he whispered.

My poor flawed little one. You have been mortally selfish and paid for your folly. The Milieu forced you to pay. But the sin remains, as does my own, and its true expiation must be in the same coin as that unjustly used. The loss of your starship, of your livelihood, was not enough and you know it! You must give of yourself, and then you will no longer despise yourself. Help us. Help your friends who need you.

"Damn—" He blinked away the mist that had risen in his eyes.

Save.

His words were barely audible. "All right." The others were all looking at him, but he could not see their eyes. "I'll go with you. I'll fly the aircraft back here if I can. But that's all I can promise."

"It is enough," Madame said.

Back at the central fire, the singing and laughing were more subdued. People drifted away to the smaller hearths to prepare for sleep. A small figure hobbled toward Madame, silhouetted against the dying bonfire.

"I've been thinking on your expedition to the Ship's Grave," said Fitharn. "You're going to need the help of our people."

"To find the Danube quickly," Claude agreed. "Do you have any idea of the best way to reach it? In our time, its headwaters were in the Black Forest. God knows where the river begins nowadays. The Alps—even some super version of Lake Constance."

"There is only one person with the authority to help you," the Firvulag said. "You're going to have to visit the King."

2

YEOCHEE IV, HIGH KING OF THE FIRVULAG, CAME TIPTOEING into the main audience hall of his mountain fortress, his seeker-sense probing the dim recesses of the great cavern.

"Lulo, my little pomegranate! Where are you hiding?"

There was a sound like the jingling of tiny bells mixed with laughter. A shadow fluttered among the red-and-cream stalactites, the hanging tapestries, the tatty fringed trophy banners from Grand Combats forty years gone. Leaving a musky scent in its wake, something glided like a huge moth into a cul-de-sac chamber at one side of the hall.

Yeochee rushed in pursuit. "Now I've got you trapped! There's no way out of the crystal grotto except past me!"

The alcove was lit by candles in a single golden sconce. The flames struck glints from an incredible profusion of quartz prisms that encrusted the walls, sparkling pink and purple and white like the interior of a giant geode. Heaps of dark furs made inviting mounds on the floor. One of these heaps quivered.

"So there you are!"

Yeochee bounded into the grotto and lifted the concealing rug with tantalizing slowness. A cobra with a body as thick as his arm reared up and hissed at him.

"Now, Lulo! Is that a way to welcome your King?"

The serpent shimmered and acquired a woman's head. Her hair was varicolored like the snakeskin, her eyes a teasing amber. The tongue that stole from her smiling lips was forked.

With a cry of delight, the King threw open his arms. The snake-woman grew a neck, shoulders, soft arms with clever boneless fingers, a marvelously formed upper torso. "Stop right there for a moment," Yeochee suggested, "and we'll explore a few possibilities." They fell onto the bed of furs with an élan that made the candle flames gutter.

A trumpet sounded far away.

"Oh, damn," groaned the King. The concubine Lulo whimpered and uncoiled but her forked tongue continued to dart hopefully.

The trumpet blatted again, nearer this time, and there was a booming of gongs that made the mountain vibrate in sympathy. The stalactites just outside the crystal grotto hummed like tuning forks.

Yeochee sat up, his once jolly face a mask of dismay. "That stupid contingent of Lowlives. The ones who think they're onto a secret weapon against the Tanu. I promised Pallol I'd check 'em out."

The alluring lamia wavered, melted, and became a plump little naked woman with apple cheeks and a blonde Dutch bob. Pouting, she pulled a mink rug over herself and said, "Well, if this is going to take a while, for Té's sake at least get me something to eat. All this chasing about has got me starving to death. No bat fritters, mind you! And none of that awful broiled salamander, either."

Yeochee tied his slightly shabby cloth-of-gold dressing gown and ran his fingers, comb-fashion, through his tangled yellow hair and beard. "I'll order you something lovely," he promised. "We caught us a new human cook the other day who has a marvelous way with cheese-and-meat pastry." The King smacked his lips. "This business won't take long. Then we'll have a picnic right here, and for dessert—"

The trumpet sounded a third time, just outside the hall.

"You're on," said Lulo, snuggling down under the mink. "Hurry back."

King Yeochee stepped outside the grotto, took a deep breath, and transformed himself from one hundred sixty to two hundred sixty centimeters in height. The old robe became a great trailing cloak of garnet-colored velvet. He acquired a splendid suit of gold-chased obsidian parade armor, its open helm surmounted by a tall crown sprouting two curling members like golden ram's horns and a beaklike extension jutting over the forehead that threw his upper face into deep shadow. He turned on his eyes so that they gleamed with sinister chatoyance. Making a run for it, he assumed the throne without a moment to spare.

The trumpet sounded for the last time.

Yeochee raised one mailed hand and several dozen illusory courtiers and men-at-arms winked into being about the throne dais. The rocks of the mountain hall began to glow with rich colors. Rippling music, as from a marimba of glass, filled the room as six Firvulag of the palace guard escorted the humans and Fitharn Pegleg into the royal presence.

One of the quasi courtiers stepped forward. Using Standard English for the sake of the Lowlives, he declaimed: "Let all pay homage to His Appalling Highness Yeochee IV, Sovereign Lord of the Heights and Depths, Monarch of the Infernal Infinite, Father of All Firvulag, and Undoubted Ruler of the Known World!"

An organlike peal of deafening intensity stopped the approaching visitors in their tracks. The King arose and seemed to grow taller and taller before their eyes until he loomed among the stalactites like some gigantic idol with emerald eyes.

Fitharn doffed his tall hat briefly. "How do, King."

"You have our leave to approach!" boomed the apparition.

Fitharn stumped forward, the seven humans trailing after him. Yeochee noted with regret that only two of the Lowlives— a sharp-featured fellow with a big black mustache and a younger woman, hollow-cheeked and thin, with fair hair pulled into an unflattering knot—seemed genuinely impressed by his monstrous guise. The rest of the human party regarded His Appalling Highness with either scientific interest or amusement. Old Madame Guderian even betrayed a trace of Gallic ennui. Oh, what the hell. Why not relax?

"We shall condescend to assume a gentler aspect!" Yeochee decreed. He shrank down to his ordinary self—gold dressing gown, bare feet, and all, with his coronet set askew as usual. "Now what's all this?" he inquired of Fitharn.

"Madame Guderian's plot against the Tanu seems to've

taken a quantum leap, King. Better let her tell it."

Yeochee sighed. Madame reminded him disconcertingly of his late grandmother, a lady who always knew when he had been up to childish mischief. Despite the old Frenchwoman's talent for political intrigue, Yeochee had long since bitterly regretted giving her a golden torc. Madame's schemes always seemed to end up benefiting the Lowlife humans, with only minimal gain to the Firvulag. He should have followed his first instinct and blasted her to flinders with his psychoenergies in those early days when she first had the temerity to step through her own time-gate. Indirectly, after all, she was the author of the present Firvulag degradation!

The old woman, dressed now in the dappled deerskin garments favored by forest prowlers of her race, stepped boldly to the throne and gave the King a perfunctory bob of her head.

"You're looking well, Monseigneur. Plenty of healthy exercise, one trusts."

Yeochee frowned. But at least the old trout had jogged his memory in regard to Lulo's promised snack. He reached out and pulled a bellrope. "Pallol tells me you may have discovered the location of the Ship's Grave."

"It is true." She gestured toward a silver-haired man among the humans. "One of our new compatriots, Professor Claude, believes he has identified the locale. It was known to him through his scientific studies in the world of the future."

"Still known six million years from now?" The King beckoned to the paleontologist, who came closer. "You there, Claude. Tell me—in the future, did your people have any recollections of *us*?"

Claude smiled at the little exotic and let his gaze wander about the fantastic hall that lay within the heart of the Vosges' highest mountain.

"Your Majesty, right this minute humanity's direct ancestors are small apes cowering in the forest. They have no language, and so there is no way they can pass on to their descendants any memories whatsoever. Primitive human beings having the power of speech won't evolve for another two or three million years or so, and they won't develop reliable oral traditions until—oh, say, eight or nine thousand years before my time. Wouldn't you agree that it was highly unlikely for future humanity to have retained any recollections of a race of small shape-changing exotic people who live in underground dwellings?"

The King shrugged. "It was only a thought . . . So you know where the Ship's Grave is, eh?"

Claude said, "I believe so. And you have no moral objections to our plundering it to our mutual benefit?"

Yeochee's beady green eyes flashed dangerously. "Be careful, old Claude. You won't be robbing the Ship of anything that can't be returned in good time—with interest—when the unfair advantage that the despicable Foe has seized is equalized."

Madame said, "We will help you to accomplish this end, Monseigneur. I have sworn it as part of my expiation! When humans can no longer be enslaved by the Tanu, the status quo between your two races will be restored. And our first strike will be against Finiah—using an aircraft and the Spear from the Ship's Grave."

The King twisted his beard into golden ropes. "The time factor! It's only three weeks to the equinox—then another week and a half and we're into the Truce for the Grand Combat ingathering. H'mm. Our forces would need at least a week to prepare for an attack against the Tanu. Is there a chance that you can get back here with the flyer and the Spear before the Truce begins? We'd be willing to join you in an attack if there was a real hope of knocking off Velteyn and his flying circus. If we were successful against Finiah, the morale of our lads and lasses would be at zenith going into the Games this year."

The old woman turned to Claude. "Is it possible for us to get to the Ries and back inside of a month?"

"We might barely manage it. But only if we obtain a guide who can take us by the shortest route to the head of small-boat navigation on the Danube. This would be some place beyond the Black Forest in a kind of sediment-filled basin—the molassic foredeep between the Swabian Jura and the Alps. The river would likely flow as gently through the molasse as the Sweet Afton. We could sail to the Ries easily and fly back."

"Within the month?" the King persisted.

"If you use your good offices to get us a guide, it's feasible."

Fitharn stepped forward. "The mighty Sharn-Mes suggested that one Sugoll might be made to assist the expedition. A bad-tempered joker, even for a Howler, and not any too loyal. But he claims to rule the Feldberg country, even the Water Caves beyond the Paradise Gorge. Sharn-Mes thought that if anyone knew of this river, Sugoll would. I can take these people to his lair if you'll authorize Madame to impress his service."

"Oh, very well," grumbled the King. He crouched down and began groping under the throne, presently hauling out a small coffer that looked as if it was carved from black onyx. After fumbling with its golden catch, he flung it open, rummaged around, and came up with a Parker pen of twenty-second-century vintage and a much-creased, stained piece of vellum. Still kneeling on the floor he scrawled several emphatic ideographs and appended the royal signature.

"That should do it." He replaced the writing materials and the chest and handed the missive to Madame. "It's the best I can do. Freely translated, it says: *Help these people or it's your ass.* You have our royal leave to coerce this Sugoll into slime-mold if he gives you a hard time."

Madame gave a gracious nod and tucked the note away.

A bowlegged little fellow in a belted red smock came trotting into the audience hall and saluted the King. "You rang, Appalling One?"

"We hunger and thirst," said the Monarch of the Infernal Infinite. He turned abruptly from the steward and shot a question at Madame. "You really think this expedition has a chance of success?"

"It does," she affirmed solemnly. "Captain Richard, here, was a master of starships. He will be able to pilot one of the flyers spoken of in your legends, if they have not been destroyed by the elements. Martha and Stefanko possess technical knowledge that will enable us to make both the aircraft and the Spear operational. Chief Burke and Felice will defend us against natural perils en route. I myself will use my metafunctions to confound inimical members of your own race, as well as such Tanu that may venture to pursue us. Professor Claude will lead us to the crater once we are safely on the river. As to success—" She ventured a wintry smile. "That remains in the hands of le bon dieu, n'est-ce pas?"

Yeochee glowered at her. "Why can't you speak English like a regular human being? Don't I have enough trouble with you? Oh—I admit the plan sounds good. But so did the scheme for tunneling under the Finiah wall and setting off that damned guano explosive your people cooked up. And at the last minute Velteyn let the Rhine into the diggings! A hundred and eighty-three Firvulag stalwarts swimming for their lives in a soup of bird shit!"

"This time it will be different, Monseigneur."

Yeochee beckoned to the steward. "Bring me some of the best ale. And have that new human cook, Mariposa—the one with the nose—bake up one of those big flat open-face tarts with the melted chamois cheese and tomato sauce and the new sausage."

The steward bowed low and ran off.

"We have your leave, then, to pursue the expedition immediately?" Madame asked.

"Oh, yes, yes." The King's growl was petulant. He drew his golden bathrobe around himself. "We command it, in fact. And now you are dismissed . . . Fitharn, you stay here. I've got something to talk over with you."

The palace guards, who had stood immobile in their black-glass armor during the interview, now thumped short lances on the floor and prepared to escort the human visitors out. But the smallest female, the one with the cloud of pale hair who was scarcely as tall as a Firvulag woman, had the boldness to call out.

"Your Majesty! One more word."

"Oh, very well," sighed the King. "I know who *you* are. I suppose you still think we ought to give you a golden torc."

"Don't make me wait!" Felice fixed him with a gaze even more penetrating than Madame's. "With a golden torc I could insure that the expedition would be a success."

The King vouchsafed what he hoped was a suave smile. "I know all about your extraordinary abilities. You'll be rewarded with your heart's desire in good time. But not yet! First, help your friends get the Spear and the flyer. If you should happen to find Lugonn's torc there at the crater, take it! If not, we'll see what can be done when you return. Deliver the goods and then we'll talk about presents."

He waved his hand in dismissal and the guards ushered the humans out.

"Are they gone?" Yeochee whispered, jumping down off the dais to peer into the gloom.

"Gone, King," Fitharn confirmed. He sat on the edge of the

regal platform, pulled off one boot, and tipped a pebble from it. "Ah, you little bastard!"

"Show some respect," growled Yeochee.

"Speaking to the stone in my shoe, Appalling One . . . Well? What do you think?"

"Risky, risky." The King paced up and down, hands clasped behind his back. "If only we could do without these damned middlemen! Pull off the whole thing ourselves!"

Fitharn said, "The despicable torc wearers must often entertain the same thoughts. They, too, are dangerously dependent upon humanity. But there is no other way for us, Appalling One. The humans are smarter than we are, stronger in other ways as well. Could we ever hope to operate a flyer after all this time? Or put the Spear into working order? We've had forty years to think of ways to bring down the Foe—and all we've done is cry in our beer. I don't like the redoubtable Guderian any more than you do, King. But she's a most formidable person. Like her or lump her, she can help us."

"But we can't *trust* humans!" howled Yeochee. "Did you feel that blast of hostility from Felice while she was saying 'pretty please'? Give that one a golden torc—? I'd sooner try to plug a lava dike with my royal swizzle stick!"

"We can control Felice. Pallol and Sharn-Mes have been giving the matter thought. Even if she finds a torc at the Ship's Grave, she can't learn to use it overnight. They'll fly back here right away and Felice will be wild to get into the fight against Finiah. We'll put her in the care of our Warrior Ogresses—"

"Té's titties!" blasphemed the King.

"—and Ayfa or Skathe can put her down at the least hint of treachery. If Felice survives the assault on Finiah we can get rid of her by sending her south to the Combat. That will seem to fit right in with the second phase of Guderian's famous plan. Don't worry, King. We'll use Felice and the rest of them to our advantage . . . and then Sharn and Pallol will engineer a suitably heroic demise for our noble human allies. If we play this right, the Firvulag can end up with both the Spear *and* the Sword—on top of the Tanu torcers and the Lowlives, too! And you can really mean it when you call yourself Undoubted Ruler of the Known World."

Yeochee gave him an awful look. "Just wait until it's *your* turn in the king barrel! We'll see how well you—"

The steward came skipping out of the passage, carrying a large steaming tray and a glass flagon of tawny liquid. "It's ready, Appalling One! Hot-hot-hot! And not with ordinary salamander sausage, either, but with a new kind! The cook Mariposa says it'll frizzle your cojones!"

Yeochee bent over the tray to savor the fragrance of the wheel-shaped open pie. It was cut into wedges, each one oozing delectable layers of creamy white and red.

"Beggin' your pardon, King," Fitharn ventured, "but what the hell is that?"

The King took the platter and the bottle of ale and began to trudge happily toward the crystal grotto. "The special dish of one Señora Mariposa de Sanchez, late of Krelix Plantation, earlier of Chichen-Itza Pizza Parlor in Merida, Mexico... Leave us, Fitharn. Go with those damned Lowlives and watch 'em."

"As you command, Appalling One."

At last, the great cavern was quiet once more. Yeochee poked his head around the entrance to the geode chamber. The candles burned low and two fascinating eyes peered at him from the stack of dark furs.

"Yoo-hoo!" he caroled. "Goody time!"

Lulo came bouncing toward him in the most charming way. "Grrum! Yumyumyum!"

He gave a delighted speech. "Let go! Let me put it down first, you mad succubus, you! Oh, you're going to love this. It's my newest favorite. Half cheese, half axolotl!"

3

"THE UNICORN! THE UNICORN! THE UNICORN!"

Martha keened the word unceasingly as she wept over the torn body of Stefanko lying in the middle of the marsh trail. Great cypresses reared up from pools of brown water on either side. Where the morning sunlight shone through the trees there were clouds of dancing midges and scarlet dragonflies hawking among them. A lobster-sized crayfish, perhaps attracted by the blood dripping into the water, scrabbled slowly up the shallow embankment that raised the trail above the Rhine bottomland.

Peopeo Moxmox Burke sat propped against a mossy trunk, groaning as Claude and Madame Guderian cut away his deerskin shirt and one leg of his pants.

"The horn seems only to have grazed your ribs, mon petit peau-rouge. However, I will have to sew. Claude, administer a narcotic."

"See to Steffi," the Chief pleaded through clenched teeth.

Claude only shook his head. He took a herendorf bleb from the medical kit Amerie had prepared for them and applied the dose to Burke's temple.

"Oh, God. That's better. How is the leg? I could feel the bugger's teeth fress me to the bone."

Claude said, "Your calf muscle is all slashed to hell. And

316

you can bet those tusks were poison-filthy to boot. There's no way we can patch this out here, Peo. Your only chance is professional care back with Amerie."

Cursing softly, Burke rested his huge gray head against the cypress and let his eyes close. "My own fault. Stupid schmuck— I was concentrating on covering our scent by taking us through that patch of stinking pitcher plants. Watching for hoe-tusker sign, traces of bear-dogs . . . and we get ambushed by a god-damn *hog!*"

"Silence, child," Madame ordered. "You derange my stitching."

"It was no ordinary porker," Claude said. He wrapped the chief's leg in porofilm after packing the wound with antibiotic floc. The decamole leg splint was already inflated and ready to be fastened in place. "I think the beast that did this job on you was none other than Kubanochoerus, the giant one-horned Caucasian boar. It was supposed to've been extinct by the Pliocene."

"Huh! Tell that to Steffi, poor faygeleh."

Madame said, "I will finish tending Peo, Claude. See to Martha."

The paleontologist went over to the hysterical engineer, studied her swaying, wild-eyed actions for a moment, and saw what had to be done. He grasped her by one wrist and yanked her roughly to her feet. "Will you shut up, girl? Your stupid bawling will bring the soldiers on us! Do you think Steffi would want that?"

Martha choked in outraged astonishment and drew back one arm to slap the old man's face. "How do you know what Steffi would want? You didn't know him! But I did, and he was gentle and good and he took care of me when my damn guts were—when I was sick. And now look at him. *Look* at him!" Her ravaged, once beautiful face crumpled in fresh sobs. Martha's momentary fury at Claude dissolved and her arm fell. "Steffi, oh, Steffi," she whispered, then fell against the sturdy old man. "One minute he was walking along and smiling over his shoulder at me, and the next—"

The gray monster had burst without warning from a thick stand of reeds and charged the middle of the line of hikers, tossing Stefanko into the air and then savaging him. It had switched its attack to Peo when the chief drew his machete and tried to stop the animal's awful gobbling. Fitharn had burst into illusory flame, driving the boar off the natural causeway into the swamp shallows. Felice and Richard followed the fireball with drawn bows, leaving the others to help the wounded. But there was no helping Stefanko.

Claude held the shuddering Martha in his arms, then pulled out the tail of his bush shirt and used it to wipe her streaming eyes. He led her to the mossy hollow where Madame was working on Burke and made her sit down. The knees of the engineer's buckskin trousers were stained with dark blood and muck, but there were also bright scarlet patches down around both ankles.

"You'd better have a look at her, Madame," Claude said. "I'll take care of Steffi."

He got a mylar blanket from his own pack and went to the body, fighting to control his own rage and revulsion. He had known Stefanko only four days; but the ready competence of the man and the warmth of his personality had made him a congenial trail-mate on the trek from High Vrazel to the Rhine bottomland. Now Claude could only do his best to smooth the contorted face back into its accustomed smooth lineaments. No need to look so surprised any more, Steffi boy. Just relax and rest. Rest in peace.

A horde of flies had descended upon the ripped mass of intestines and moved only with sluggish reluctance as Claude rolled Stefanko's body onto the metallic sheet. Using the heat-beam of his powerpack, the old man welded the edges of the mylar into a bag. The job was nearly finished when Fitharn, Richard, and Felice came squelching back out of the jungle.

Felice held up a ridged yellowish object like an ivory marlinspike. "We got the fuckard for what good it does."

Richard shook his head in awe. "A pig the size of a goddam ox! Musta weighed eight hundred kilos. Took five arrows to finish it off after Pegleg trapped it in a thicket. I still can't figure how anything that big could have snuck up on us unawares."

"They're intelligent devils," Fitharn growled. "It must have followed us downwind. If I'd had my wits about me I'd have sensed it. But I was thinking about how we'd have to hurry to cross the river before the morning mist lifted."

"Well, we're stuck here now that it's broad daylight," Felice said. She held up the trophy horn. "This fellow saw to that."

"Now what?" Richard wanted to know.

Felice had unclipped the arrows from the holder on her compound bow and she now knelt to dip the stained glassy heads in the water beside the trail. "We'll have to hide out on this side until sundown and then cross. The moon's nearly full tonight. We could probably get over the narrow strip of east-bank lowland in a couple of hours and then bivouac among the rocks at the foot of the Black Forest scarp for the rest of the night."

The Firvulag gave an exclamation. "You're not thinking of going on?"

She glared at him. "*You're* not thinking of turning back?"

Claude said, "Steffi's dead. Peo's in a bad way. He's going to have to be taken back to Amerie by one of us, or he'll lose his leg—or worse."

"That still leaves five of us," Felice said. She frowned, tapping the boar horn against her buckskin-clad thigh. "Pegleg could go back with the Chief. He could get help from his people along the way. And before you leave," she said to the little man, "tell us how to get to the stronghold of this guy Sugoll."

"It won't be easy." The Firvulag wagged his head. "The Black Forest is a lot more rugged than the Vosges. Sugoll's place is up on the northeastern slope of the Feldberg, where the Paradise River comes off the snowfields. Bad country."

"The Tanu won't be looking for us on the other side of the Rhine," she said. "Once we're across, we probably won't have to worry about any more gray-torc patrols."

"There are still Howlers," Fitharn said. "And at night, the Hunt. Airborne, if Velteyn leads it. If the Hunt spots you in the open, you're finished."

"Can't we travel mostly by day?" Richard suggested. "Madame Guderian's metafunctions can warn us of hostile Firvulag."

The old woman had come up to the group, an expression of deep concern upon her face. "I am not so worried about les Criards as about Sugoll himself. Without his help, we may never locate the Danube in time. But if Fitharn does not accompany us, Sugoll may feel that he can ignore the King's directive with impunity. And there is another matter for grave concern . . . Martha. She has begun to hemorrhage from the shock. Among the Tanu, she was forced to give birth to four children in quick succession and her female organs—"

"Oh, for God's sake," said Felice impatiently. "If she rests, she'll pull out of it. And we'll take our chances with Sugoll."

"Martha is greatly weakened," the old woman persisted. "She will become worse before she is better. This has happened before. It would be best if she returns with Peo and Fitharn."

Richard looked dubious. "But now that Stefanko's gone, she's the only technician we've got. Without her help, God knows how long it might take me to trace the circuits on that exotic aircraft. And if the zapper needs work, I wouldn't have a prayer of fixing it."

"The expedition could be postponed," Fitharn said.

"That would mean waiting a whole year!" Felice blazed. "I won't do it! I'll go get the damn Spear all by myself!"

Back at the cypress, Martha cried out to them, "We can't postpone the search, Madame. Anything could happen in a year. I'll be all right in a day or two. If I get a little help, I know I can make it."

"We could rig a litter from one of the cots," Claude suggested.

Felice brightened. "And in the rough spots, I could carry her on my back. She's right about anything being likely to happen if we delay." Her eyes strayed to the Firvulag, who looked back at her with bland objectivity. "Others could find the Ship's Grave ahead of us."

"It would be wisest to turn back," Fitharn said. "However, the decision will have to be that of Madame Guderian."

"Dieu me secourait," the old woman murmured. "One of us has already given his life." She took a few slow steps toward the mylar-wrapped bundle lying on the trail. "If we could ask him his opinion, we know very well what he would say."

She turned back to them, lifting her chin with the familiar gesture. "Alors . . . Fitharn, you will turn back with Peo. The rest of us will go on."

They concealed themselves for the rest of the day in a dense taxodium grove hard by the western bank of the Rhine. The gnarled, low-growing branches made comfortable perches. Curtained by festoons of lichens and flowering epiphytes, they could safely observe the river traffic and at the same time be secure from the crocodiles, hoe-tuskers, and other potentially dangerous wildlife that infested the bottomland.

It became very hot as the sun climbed. Food was no problem, for there were plenty of turtles whose meat could be roasted with the power-beams, as well as palms with edible hearts and an abundance of honey-sweet grapes the size of golf balls that drove Richard into raptures of oenological speculation. But as morning dragged into afternoon, boredom and reaction from the dawn violence made the younger members of the party drowsy. Richard, Felice, and Martha stripped off most of their clothing, tied themselves to upper limbs of the big tree, and slept—leaving Claude and Madame on branches below keeping watch over the broad river. Only a few supply barges from upstream plantations drifted past their hiding place. Finiah itself lay about twenty kilometers to the north on the opposite bank, where the short Paradise River tributary tumbled out of a deep gorge that almost bisected the Black Forest massif.

"Later," Madame told Claude, "when it is dark, we will be able to see Finiah's lights against the northern sky. It stands on a promontory jutting into the Rhine. It is not a large city, but it is the oldest of all the Tanu settlements and they have illuminated it with great splendor."

"Why did they migrate southward, out of this area?" Claude asked. "From what I've been told, most of the Tanu cities are down around the Mediterranean, with this northern country left pretty much to the Firvulag."

"A very warm climate is more to the Tanu taste. I believe that the division of territory between the two groups reflects a very ancient pattern, perhaps one that goes back to the origins of the dimorphic race. One might imagine a world of singular ruggedness where highland and lowland forms evolved—perhaps interdependent yet antagonistic. With the coming of high civilization and the eventual migration of the race to other worlds in their galaxy, these ancient tensions would be sublimated. But it would seem that Tanu and Firvulag genes never blended completely. From time to time during the history of these people the old rivalries would be resurrected."

"And crushed by the high-tech majority," Claude said. "Until this one group of barbarian throwbacks found a perfect refuge instead of coming to the usual quixotic end."

She nodded her agreement. "It was perfect for the exiles, our Pliocene Earth . . . except for the irony that equally quixotic humans should also have desired to dwell on it."

She pointed to a pneumatic barge far out on the river. "There goes one of the products of the human advent. Before the humans came, the Tanu had simple rafts of wood. They had little river commerce because of their dislike of water. They supervised their own plantations and even did honest work because there were not so many rama slaves. The torcs for the little apes formerly had to be made by hand in the same manner as their own golden torcs."

"Do you mean that human know-how enabled mass production?"

"For the ape torcs, yes. And the entire silver and gray system, with its linkage to the golden torcs of the Tanu rulers, was devised by a human psychobiologist. They made him a demigod and he still lives in Muriah—Sebi-Gomnol the Lord Coercer! But I remember the pinched little self-hating man who came to my auberge forty years ago. Then he was called Eusebio Gomez-Nolan."

"So a human being is responsible for this slave setup—? Sweet Lord. Why do we screw things up, wherever we go?"

She gave a short bitter laugh. With her hair straggling in sweat curls about her ears and forehead, she seemed to be scarcely forty-five years old. "Gomnol is not the only traitor to our race. There was a Turkish man of the circus, one of my earliest clients, named Iskender Karabekir. His fondest wish, as he told me, was to train sabertooth tigers to do his bidding. But I have discovered that in this Exile world he devoted himself instead to the domestication of chalikos and helladotheria and amphicyons—which became pivotal in the subsequent Tanu domination of society. The ancient Hunt and Grand Combat were fought by Tanu and Firvulag afoot. The groups were evenly matched, for what the Firvulag lacked in finesse and sophisticated metafunctions they made up in sheer numbers and a more rugged physique. But a mounted Tanu Hunt was a different matter. And a Grand Combat with Tanu and torced human warriors on chalikoback and Firvulag afoot has become an annual massacre."

Claude stroked his chin. "Still, there was the Battle of Agincourt—if you'll pardon my mentioning it."

"Bof!" said Angélique Guderian. "Longbows will not conquer the Tanu, nor will gunpowder. Not while perverse members of our own human race betray their fellows! Who taught the Tanu physicians how to reverse the human sterilizations? A gynecologist from the planet Astrakhan. A human woman! Not only our talents but our very genes have been placed in the service of these exotics—and many, such as Martha, choose death rather than the degradation of becoming brood stock. Do you know how Martha came to us?"

Claude shook his head.

"She threw herself into the Rhine, hoping to drown herself in the spring flood rather than submit to a fifth impregnation. But she was cast ashore, dieu merci, and Steffi found her and restored her. There are many others like Martha among us. Knowing them, loving them—and knowing also that I am the one ultimately responsible for their pain—you will understand why I cannot rest until the power of the Tanu is broken."

The river was turning from shining pewter to gold. On the Black Forest side, the heights of the Feldberg to the south became luminous with the sinking sun, tinted primrose and purple. In order to reach Sugoll, they would have to go up into that high country and cross at least seventy kilometers of mountain forest—and all this before even beginning their search for the Danube.

"Quixotic," Claude said. He was smiling.

"Are you sorry you agreed to help me? You are an enigma to me, Claude. I can understand Felice, Richard, Martha—the strong-willed ones of our company such as Chief Burke. But I have not yet been able to understand you. I cannot see why you came to the Pliocene at all, much less why you agreed to go on this quest for the Ship's Grave. You are too sensible, too self-possessed, too—débonaire!"

He laughed. "You have to understand the Polish character, Angélique. It breeds true, even in a Polish-American like me. We were speaking of battles. Do you know which one we Polacks are proudest of? It happened at the beginning of the Second World War. Hitler's Panzer tanks were rolling into the northern part of Poland and there was no modern weaponry to stop them. So the Pomeranian Cavalry Brigade charged the tanks on horseback, and they were wiped out, man and beast. It was madness, but it was glorious . . . and very, very Polish.

And now suppose you tell me why *you* decided to come to the Pliocene."

"It was not because of romanticism," she said. There was no more of the accustomed asperity in her tone, not even grief. She told her story flatly, as though it were the scenario of a stage play that she had been forced to attend too many times— or even an act of confession.

"In the beginning, when I was only greedy for money, I did not care what kind of world lay on the other side of the time-portal. But later, when my heart was finally touched, it became very different. I attempted to have the travelers send messages back to me, reassuring me about the nature of the Pliocene land. Time and again I gave to sensible-seeming persons materials that I felt certain would survive the reversal of the temporal field. Very early tests by my late husband had shown that amber was best, and so my envelopes were pieces of this material, carefully sliced in half, with little wafers of ceramic to insert. These could be written upon with an ordinary graphite pencil, then sealed in the amber with natural balsam cement. I instructed certain travelers to study the ancient scene, write down their considered judgment of it, then return to the vicinity of the time-gate where the translations invariably took place at dawn. You see, Professor Guderian had long ago established that solar time in the ancient epoch was the same as that of the modern world we lived in. I had wished to give the new arrivals maximum daylight to adjust to the new environment, so I always sent them at sunup. Malheureusement, this unvarying program made it most convenient for the minions of the Tanu to control the portal! Long before it occurred to me to try the amber message holders, the exotics had built Castle Gateway and taken steps to seize all time-travelers immediately upon their arrival."

"So you never got any messages from the past?"

"Nothing. In later years, we tried more sophisticated techniques for mechanical retrieval of information, but nothing worked. We could get no pictures, no sounds from the Pliocene. The devices always returned to us in a useless condition. Of course, it is easy to see why!"

"And yet you kept sending people through."

Her face was haunted. "I was tempted again and again to

shut down the operation—but the pathetic ones would implore me, and so I continued. Then there came the time when my fearful conscience could no longer be denied. I took the amber materials, constructed a simple trip-lever device to operate the switch of the machine, and came to see for myself this world six million years distant from our own."

"But—" Claude began.

"In order to elude my devoted staff, who would surely have stopped me, I made the translation at midnight."

"Ah."

"I found myself enveloped in a terrible dust storm, a hell of choking wind that threw me to the ground and rolled me as easily as a Russian thistle across the arid plateau. I had taken cuttings of my beloved roses, and in my fright I clung to them as the hurricane tumbled and battered me. I was blown to the lip of a dry watercourse and precipitated into its rocky depths, where I lay unconscious until dawn, badly bruised but otherwise unhurt. By the time the sun rose the sirocco was gone. I spied the Castle and had just made up my mind to go to it for aid when the attendants came trooping out to wait for the morning's arrivals."

She paused and a slow smile stole over her lips. "No time-travelers came that day. My staff was too much in a tumult, you understand. The people from the Castle became very agitated and rushed back inside. Not long thereafter a troop of soldiers came galloping posthaste out of the barbican and rushed off to the east, passing not thirty meters from the bushy cleft where I lay hidden. At the head of the train was an enormously tall exotic man dressed in robes of purple and gold.

"You will understand that I was in great pain from my battering. I crawled into a kind of shallow cave beneath the roots of an acacia tree that grew on the rim of the dry ravine. As the sun climbed, my thirst became dreadful. But this torment was as nothing compared to my agony of soul. Back in the auberge, I had imagined many possible derangements of the Pliocene world—fierce beasts, inhospitable terrain, exploitation of newcomers by the earlier arrivals among the time-farers—even a malfunction of the translational field that would cast the poor travelers into oblivion. But never had I imagined that the ancient epoch would see our planet in thrall to a nonhuman race. All unwitting, I had sent my pathetic, hopeful people into slavery. I turned my face into the dust and asked God to grant me death."

"Oh, Angélique."

She did not seem to see or hear him. Her voice was very quiet, barely audible among the rising evening clamor of the Rhineland birds and insects.

"When I finally stopped weeping, I saw a round object half-buried in the dust not an arm's length away on the ravine floor. It was a melon. The rind was thick and it had not been broken by its rolling across the plateau in the windstorm. When I cut into it with my small couteau de poche I found it sweet and laden with water. And so my thirst was quenched and I lived through the day.

"Very late in the afternoon there came a procession of carts drawn by strange animals. I know now that these were hellads, large giraffes with short necks used for draft purposes. The carts had human drivers and contained vegetables resembling large beetroots—fodder for the Castle chalikos. The carts entered the fortress by the postern gate and after a time returned laden with manure. As they journeyed back into the lowlands I followed at a far distance. Just before nightfall we came to a kind of farm with the buildings secure behind a stockade. I hid myself in bushes and tried to decide what to do. If I revealed myself to the farm people they would surely recognize me. And was it not possible that they would exact retribution for my betrayal of their dreams? I would accept this punishment if God willed. But I had already begun to suspect that a different rôle had been ordained to me. So I did not approach the gate of the farm but went instead into a dense forest adjacent to it. I found a spring, ate a small amount of the food in my Survival Unit, and prepared to spend the night in a great cork tree—even as we have sheltered ourselves in this cypress today . . ."

The other three members of the expedition had wakened on their perches among the higher branches. Now they swung down as slowly and quietly as sloths to take places next to Claude and listen. The old woman, sitting far out from the trunk with her legs dangling, did not seem to notice them.

"Very late in the night, after the moon went down, the monsters came. At first there was a great silence, with all of the jungle noises falling still as though a switch had been cut.

I heard a sound of horns and a distant baying. And then it seemed as though the moon were rising again over a ridge of land just north of my tree. There was light of many colors coming from some flaming thing twisting in and out of the trees. It raced down the slope toward me. I heard a noise like a tornado, at once terrible and musical. The fiery apparition became an elfin cavalcade—the Hunt!—and it glowed as it raged downhill. It was chasing something. That I saw when the whirlwind of jeweled riders came into a small glen some two hundred meters away from me. By the bright starlight I saw the prey shambling along—a huge creature, black as ink, with coiling arms like those of a devilfish springing from its shoulders and eyes like great red lamps."

"Fitharn!" Richard hissed. Claude gave him an elbow in the ribs. Madame paid no attention to the interruption.

"The black monster dodged among the trees on the slope below me, coming ever closer, with the Hunt in hot pursuit. I have never in my life known such terror. My very soul seemed to shriek with it, although I uttered no sound. With all of my will I prayed for deliverance, clinging to the large branch of my cork tree with eyes tightly shut. There was a noise of carillons and thunderbolts, a buffeting wind, blinding flashes of light that penetrated my closed lids, smells of ordure and ozone and cloying perfume. Every nerve end of mine seemed assaulted and overloaded—but still I willed myself to be safe.

"And the Hunt passed by. I knew that I was fainting, but my fingernails dug deeply into the soft cork bark and kept me from falling. There was darkness and I knew nothing. When I awoke... a little man in a tall hat stood beneath my tree looking up at me with starlight shining on his round cheeks and pointed nose. He called out, 'Well done, woman, you hid the both of us!'"

Claude and the others had to laugh. Madame looked from one to the other in a kind of surprise, then shook her head and allowed herself a small smile. "Fitharn took me in charge and we went to the underground home of one of his confrères, where we were safe from further harassment. Later, when I had recovered my wits, I had long conversations with the Little People and learned the true situation here in the Pliocene world. Because I am who I am, and because of the brief flash of strong metafunction I had shown in concealing us, Fitharn brought

me at length to the Firvulag Court at High Vrazel in the Vosges.
I proposed that the Firvulag take humans as their allies rather
than bedevil them, as had been their custom since the opening
of the time-gate. I contacted the soi-disant Lowlife humans of
the region in turn and convinced them of the wisdom of the
alliance. We engineered several encounters with the gray-torcs
to the Firvulag advantage, and the entente was confirmed. King
Yeochee bestowed the golden torc upon me after our spies
enabled his warriors to ambush and kill Iskender-Kernonn, the
Lord of Animals—that same Turk who had earlier used his
perverted talents in the service of the Tanu. After that, there
were minor triumphs and major failures, refinements of planning, advances and setbacks. But always in my mind I have
cherished the hope that one day I would be able to help undo
the evil I have done."

There was a harsh little laugh from the dimness on the other
side of the cypress trunk. Martha sat apart from the others in
a forked branch. "How noble of you, Madame, to take all of
our guilt upon yourself. And the atonement as well."

The old woman did not reply. She raised one hand to her
neck and passed two fingers behind the golden collar as though
trying to loosen it. Her deepset eyes were glittering; but as
always, the tears did not fall.

From the mudflats upstream came the basso bellowing of
deinotherium elephants. Closer to the tree-refuge some other
creature began reiterating a plaintive *hoo-ah-hooo, hoo-ah-
hooo*. Large bats zipped among the palms that clustered on the
high ground. Over the backwaters, patches of mist had already
coalesced and now extended thickening feelers toward the
mainstream of the Rhine.

"Let's get out of here," Felice said abruptly. "It's dark
enough now. We've got to be across the river before the moon
shows over those mountains."

"Right," said Claude. "You and Richard help Martha down."

He held out his own hand to Angélique Guderian. Together
they climbed from the tree and made their way to the water's
edge.

4

THE BLACK FOREST OF ELDER EARTH WAS A THOROUGHLY tamed woodland. When seen from a distance its firs and pines did appear dark; but within the twenty-second-century forest itself all was green and pleasant, with manicured pathways that tempted even the laziest hikers to indulge wanderlust without the threat of inconvenience. Only in the southernmost part of the range, around the Feldberg and its sister peaks, did the terrain rise above a thousand meters. In the twenty-second century the Schwarzwald was thickly peppered with quaint resorts, restored castles, Kurhäuser, and mountain villages where outworld visitors were welcome by costumed inhabitants and mouthwatering Kirschtorten.

The Pliocene Schwarzwald was something else altogether.

Before the erosive action of small Pleistocene glaciers wore the range down, it was higher and more sinister. Facing the rift valley of the Proto-Rhine was an escarpment that rose sheerly for almost a kilometer and a half, broken only by occasional narrow gorges cut by torrents from the highlands. Foot-travelers approaching the Black Forest from the river had to climb up one of these clefts, following precipitate game trails or scrabbling over great blocks of granite sheathed in rampant greenery, kept moist even during the dry season by mists rising from chains of cascades. Able-bodied Firvulag hikers were known to have ascended the escarpment in eight hours. It took Madame Guderian and her crippled party three days.

Above the rim of the eastern horst the true Black Forest began. Nearest the river, where strong winds blew down the trough from the Alps, the spruces and firs grew contorted into fantastic shapes. Some of the trunks resembled dragon coils or writhing brown pythons, or even humanoid giants frozen forever in agony, their upper limbs woven together into a roof twenty or thirty meters above the ground.

Farther east, this Twisted Forest calmed and straightened. The land of the southern Schwarzwald rose rapidly toward a culminating crest more than two thousand meters high, with three eminences. On the flanks of the western slope were conifers of climactic proportions, white firs and Norway spruces seventy meters tall growing in ranks so dense that when one tree died, it could hardly find room to fall, but instead leaned against supportive neighbors until it decayed and fell to bits. Only rarely was there a break in the forest canopy that allowed Richard to plot their course from the sun or the North Star. They could find no obvious trail, so the ex-spacer had to lay one out—moving from landmark to tedious landmark, never able to get a line of sight more than fifteen or twenty meters long because of the denseness of the trees.

The understorey of this evergreen expanse received very little sun. Its dreary bluish twilight supported almost no low-growing green plants—only saprophytes nourished by the detritus of the great trees. Some of the things that battened on decomposition were degenerate flowering plants, pale stalks with nodding ghostly blooms of livid white, maroon, or speckled yellow; but paramount among the eaters of the dead were the myxomycetes and the fungi. To the five humans traveling through the Pliocene Black Forest it seemed that these, and not the towering conifers, were the dominant form of life.

There were quivering sheets of orange or white or dusty translucent jelly that crept slowly over the duff of needles and decaying wood like giant amoebae. There were bracket fungi—from delicate pink ones resembling baby ears to stiff jumbos that jutted from the trunks like stair treads and were capable of bearing a man's weight. There were spongy masses of mottled black and white that enveloped several square meters of forest floor as though veiling some unspeakable atrocity. There were airy filaments, pale blue and ivory and scarlet, that hung from rotting limbs like tattered lacework. The forest harbored puff-ball globes two and a half meters in diameter, and others as small as pearls from a broken string. One variety of fungus cloaked decaying shapes in brittle husks resembling colored popcorn. There were obscene things resembling cancerous organs; graceful ranks of upright fans; counterfeit slabs of raw meat; handsome polished shapes like ebony stars; oozing diseased purple phalluses; faerie parasols blown inside out; furry sausages; and mushrooms and toadstools in varieties that seemed to be without number.

At night, they were phosphorescent.

It took the foot-travelers another eight days to traverse the Fungus Forest. During this time they saw no animal larger than an insect; but they would never cease to feel that invisible watchers lurked just outside their field of vision. Madame Guderian assured her companions again and again that the region was safe despite its ominous aspect. There was no source of food for predatory animals in the fungoid realm of life-in-death, much less support for Firvulag, who were notorious trencher-folk. The thickly matted upper branches made it impossible for the Flying Hunt to see anyone moving below. Other Lowlife scouting parties that had penetrated similar forests farther north in the range had reported them empty except for the trees, the triumphant fungi, and their parasites.

But still there was the feeling.

They suffered and grumbled all through the ghastly woods, wading through soft growths that concealed treacherous, ankle-trapping holes. Richard declared that the spores in the air were choking him. Martha drooped in anemic silence after pestering Madame one time too many with a report that something was prowling among the giant toadstools. Claude caught a fierce case of jock itch that crept all the way up to his armpits. Even Felice was ready to scream out loud at the endless trek; she was sure that something was growing in her ears.

When they finally broke free of the Fungus Forest, all of them—even Madame—shouted with relief. They came into a brilliantly sunny alpine meadow that stretched north and south along the slope of an undulating crest. One bald tor rose from a ridge on their left; to the right were two more barren gray domes. Ahead of them and farther east was the rounded height of the Feldberg.

"Blue sky!" cried Martha. "Green grass!" Heedless of her disability, she went bounding over the flower-dotted alp and scrambled to the top of the eastern ridge, leaving the others to follow more slowly. "There's a little lake down there, not half a klom away!" she called. "And lovely *normal* trees! I'm going to soak and scrub myself and lie in the sun until I'm cooked to a frazzle. And I never want to see another mushroom again for as long as I live."

"Say again, sweetie," Richard agreed. "Not even a truffle."

They descended to the beautiful little tarn, icy cold in its depths but sun-warmed in shallower little pools around its rocky perimeter, and gave themselves up to the luxury of becoming clean again. Their filthy buckskins were left to soak in a tiny brook that ran from the lake down into the eastern valley. Shrieking like children, they went splashing and diving and swimming and wallowing.

Never since he had entered the Pliocene had Richard been so happy. First he swam to the other side of the tarn and back again. (It was only about fifty meters across.) He found a shallow pothole with the water warmed to precisely the right temperature and floated with the sun glaring redly behind his shut eyelids. Dark sand, scintillating like mica, floored his little pool. He took handfuls of it and rubbed his entire body, even his scalp. Then one last dash across the lake and out onto a hot granite slab to dry.

"You should have tried out for the Polity Olympics," Martha said.

He crept up a little higher on his rock and peered over the far edge. She was below him, lying flat on her stomach on a sheltered hollow and looking at him with one eye. Bright pink flowers grew in the crevices around her.

"How you feeling now?" Richard inquired. And he thought: Hey! She looked so different. Clean, relaxed, smiling with one corner of her mouth tilted higher than the other.

"I'm much better," she said. "Why don't you come down?"

*   *   *

On the opposite shore of the lake, Claude and Madame Guderian lay side by side on decamole cots among the gentians and asters and harebells, baking the miseries out of their old bones and munching bilberries from the low-growing bushes that grew everywhere on the alpine meadow. A stone's throw away, Felice's pale-skinned form was bending in rhythmic exertions. There was a regular slapping sound as she beat their soiled clothing against the rocks of the little brook.

"Oh, to be young and energetic again," said Madame, a lazy smile upon her lips. "She has such enthusiasm for this mad expedition of ours, that little one. And what strength and patience she has shown with poor Martha. It is hard for me to credit your ominous assessment of Felice's character, mon vieux."

Claude grunted. "Just a little angle of mercy . . . Angélique, I've been doing some calculating."

"Sans blague?"

"This isn't funny. It's been fifteen days since we left Yeochee's court at High Vrazel. We took eleven of those days just to travel the thirty kloms from the Rhine to the crest of the Schwarzwald. I don't think we have a hope in hell of getting to the Ries inside of the four weeks' limit—even if we do contact Sugoll. There's probably another forty or fifty kloms of land travel ahead of us before we even reach the Danube. Then damn near two hundred kloms down the river to the Ries."

She sighed. "Probably you are right. But Martha is strong enough to keep up with the rest of us now, so we will press on nevertheless. If we are not back before the Truce begins, we will have to wait until another time to attack Finiah."

"We can't do it during the Truce?"

"Not if we hope for the assistance of the Firvulag. This Truce, which covers periods of a month prior to *and* following the Grand Combat week, is deeply sacred to both exotic races. Nothing will induce them to fight each other during Truce time. It is the time when all of their warriors and Great Ones go to and from the ritual battle, which is held on the White Silver Plain near the Tanu capital. Of course, in olden times, when Firvulag sometimes triumphed in the yearly contest, the Little People might host the games on their own Field of Gold. It lies somewhere in the Paris Basin, near a large Firvulag city named Nionel. Since the Tanu expansion, the place has been virtually abandoned. It has not hosted the Combat in forty years."

"I should think it would be good tactics to go after the mine when the Tanu are out of town. Do we really need the Firvulag?"

"We do," she said starkly. "There are only a handful of us and the ruler of Finiah never leaves the mine completely undefended. There are always silvers and grays there, and some of the silvers can fly.

". . . But the real reason for the matter of timing has to do with my grand design. Strategy—not tactics—must guide us. We do not aim simply to destroy the mine—but rather the entire human-Tanu coalition. There are three steps in the master plan: first, the Finiah action; second, an infiltration of the capital, Muriah, in which the torc factory itself would be destroyed; and third, the closing of the time-portal at Castle Gateway. Originally we had thought to instigate guerrilla warfare against the Tanu after the threefold plan was accomplished. Now, with the iron, we will be in a position to demand a genuine armistice and the emancipation of all humans who do not serve the Tanu willingly."

"When do you see the implementation of phases two and three? During the Truce?"

"Exactly. For these, we do not require Firvulag help. At Truce time the capital is filled with strangers—even Firvulag go there with impunity! A penetration of the torc factory would be greatly simplified then. As for the time-gate—"

Felice came running up as lightly as a mountain sprite. "I can see flashes over to the east, on the flank of the Feldberg!"

The two old people sprang to their feet. Madame shaded her eyes and followed the girl's pointing finger. A series of short double flashes came from a high wooded slope.

"It is the interrogation signal, as Fitharn warned us. Somehow, Sugoll has become aware of us entering his domain. Quickly, Felice. The mirror!"

The athlete ran back to the brook where the packs lay and returned in a few seconds with a square of thin mylar mounted on a folding frame. Madame sighted through its central aperture and flashed the response Fitharn had taught them: seven long slow flashes, then six, then five, then four-three-two-one.

They waited.

The reply came. One-two-three-four. Five. Six. Seven. Eight.

They relaxed. Claude said, "Well, they won't come gunning for us now, at any rate."

"No," Madame agreed. Her voice held a touch of sarcasm. "At least Sugoll will meet with us face to face before deciding whether or not to burn out our minds . . . Eh bien." She handed the mirror back to Felice. "How long do you think it will take us to reach the foot of the Feldberg? That valley we must cross—it is not too deep, but there are woodlands and meadows where les Criards may lurk, probably a river to cross, and the terrain will be rougher than that of the Fungus Forest."

"We'll count on Sugoll keeping his friends and relations under control," Claude said. "And good solid ground instead of that spongy muck will let us keep moving right along, even if it is a bit steep in places. Barring any unforeseen balls-up, we might make it to the mountain in a dozen hours."

"Our clothes are drying on the hot rocks," Felice said. "Give 'em an hour or so. Then we can march on until sundown."

Madame nodded in agreement.

"Meanwhile, I'll hunt lunch!" the girl declared brightly. Taking her bow, she went running naked toward a cluster of nearby crags.

"Artemis!" exclaimed Madame in admiration.

"One of our old Group Green companions, an anthropologist, used to call her that, too. The Virgin Huntress, goddess of the bow and the crescent moon. Benevolent—if you kept her happy with the occasional human sacrifice."

"Allons donc! You have a one-track mind, Claude, seeing the child always as a menace. And yet see how perfect she is for this Pliocene wilderness! If only she could be content to live here as a natural woman."

"She'll never settle for that." The paleontologist's usually kindly face was as hard as the granite around him. "Not so long as there's one golden torc left in the Exile world."

"Thank you, Richard," Martha said, smiling into his eyes, and with his vision still dimmed, she was beautiful enough and it had been very good between them.

"I wasn't sure you really meant it," he said. "I didn't want to—hurt you."

Her gentle laugh was reassuring. "I'm not completely ruined, even though strong men have been known to blanch at the sight of my little white body. The fourth birth was a cae-sarian, and these donks never heard of a transverse. Just slice 'er open down the middle, grab the precious kid, and pass the catgut and darning needle. It didn't heal properly. A fifth preg-nancy probably would have been the end of me."

"The filthy swine! No wonder you—uh—I'm sorry. You probably don't want to talk about it."

"I don't mind. Not any more. D'you know? You're the first man since *them*. Before this, I couldn't even bear the thought of it."

"But Steffi—" he began hesitantly.

"A dear gay friend. We loved each other, Richard, and he took care of me for months when I was really bad, just as though I were his little sister. I miss him dreadfully. But I'm glad you're here. All the way through that horrid forest... I watched you. You're a fine navigator, Richard. You're a good man. I hoped that you wouldn't be—revolted by me."

He pulled himself up into a sitting position, back resting against a great hot boulder. She lay again on her stomach, chin on clasped hands. With her scarred belly and pitifully shrunken breasts hidden, she looked almost normal; but her ribs and shoulder blades were prominent and her skin had a translucency that revealed too many of the blue blood vessels beneath. There were smudgy shadows around her eyes. Her lips were purplish rather than pink as they continued to smile at him. But she had loved him with marvelous passion, this wreck of a handsome woman, and when something within him said: *She will die,* he felt his heart contract with an amazing, unprecedented pain.

"Why are you here, Richard?" she asked. And without knowing why, he told her the whole story without sparing himself—the dumb sibling rivalry thing, the greedy maneu-vering and betrayals that had made him master of his own starship, the ruthlessness resulting in wealth and prestige, the ultimate crime and its punishment.

"I might have guessed," she said. "We have a lot in com-mon, you and I."

She had been a Deputy Supervising Engineer on Manapouri, one of the two "New Zealand" planets, where extensive marine mining made up an important part of the economy. A contract had been let for the sigma-field energy-dome of a new township to be built six kilometers beneath the planet's South Polar Sea. An Old World company sent its people to install the dome generator; approval of each phase of the work was subject to personal inspections by Martha and her staff. She had worked with the offworld technicians for nearly six months, and she and the project head had become lovers. Then, with the generator complex three-quarters completed, she discovered that the contractor had substituted certain structural components when a shipment from Earth went astray. The substitutions were rated at ninety-three percent of the capacity of those called for in the original specs. And everybody knew how ridiculously high those standards had been set, for Manapouri had originally been surveyed by the ultrapicky Krondaku. Her lover had pleaded with her. To dismantle the thing and make replacements would lose them months of time, put the job into the red, and probably get him the sack for authorizing the sneetch in the first place. Ninety-three percent! That dome generator would keep running in anything short of a Class Four tectonic incident. On this stable-crust world, the chances of that were one in twenty thousand.

And so she had given in to him.

The sigma-field generator complex was completed on time and within budget. A hemispheric bubble of force flowed out from it and pushed back the seawater for a radius of three kilometers. A mining village of fourteen hundred and fifty-three souls sprang up within its security, down beneath the frigid waters near Manapouri's South Pole. Eleven months later there was a Class Four . . . 4.18, to be exact. The dome generator failed, the waters reclaimed their hegemony, and two-thirds of the people were drowned.

"The worst thing about it," she added, "was that nobody ever blamed me. It was right on the knife-edge for the original specs, with that 4.18. *I* knew that the thing would have held if we hadn't sneetched, but nobody else thought to question it. It was a borderliner, a tossup, and the thing had crapped out. Tough. The generator complex was so smashed up by the quake and turbidity currents that they didn't bother with much of a fail-analysis. There was more important work to be done on Manapouri than dredge through half a klom of sediment looking for broken parts."

"What about *him*?"

"He had been killed a few months earlier at a job on Pelon-su-Kadafiron, a Poltroyan world. I thought of killing myself but I couldn't. Not then. I came here instead, looking for God knows what. Punishment, probably. My executive mind-set was all wiped out and I was completely switch-off. You know—take me, stomp me, use me, just don't make me have to think . . . The stud farm setup I landed in after the trip from Castle Gateway seemed like a mad dream. They only take the best of the women for breeding stock. Those under forty, natural or rejuvenated, those who aren't too ugly. The rejects are kept sterile and made available to the gray torcs and the bareneck males. But us keepers had fertility restored by Tanu physicians, and then we were sent to the Finiah pleasure dome. Would you believe there were lots of dopey broads like me who just lay there and took it? I mean, if a dame didn't mind the basic shabbiness of being used, it was a hotsheet paradise. I understand that the Tanu women are better than the men when it comes to incendiary sex—but the men left no chime unrung as far as I was concerned. The first few weeks were a nympho's delight. And then I got pregnant.

"All the little expectant moms are treated like royalty by the Tanu. My first baby was blond and adorable. And I'd never had any, and they let me nurse him for eight months. I loved him so much I almost came up sane. But when they took him away, I went back on psycho-line and wallowed around the pleasure dome with all the rest of the screwed-silly tarts. The next pregnancy was awful and the baby turned out Firvulag. The Tanu sire them one time in seven on humans and one time in three on their own women; but Firvulag parents never have Tanu children. At any rate, they didn't let me nurse the poor little spook—just took him out and left him in the traditional spot in the woods. I hadn't even recovered from him when they were trying to knock me up again. But by then, all the fun had gone out of it. I was sobering up, maybe. It's bad to be too sane in the pleasure dome . . . whether you're a human female *or* a human male. Too many of those Tanu blasts and you start hurting instead of skyrocketing. It happens sooner with some than with others—but if you're the average human, after a while Tanu sex starts killing you."

"Yeah," said Richard.

She looked at him quizzically. He gave a small humiliated nod. She said, "Welcome to the club . . . Well—I had another blond baby and then a fourth. The last was the caesarian—four and a half kilos of lovely fat girl-child, they said. But I was delirious for a week, so they farmed her out to a wet nurse and gave me six whole months of peace to pull my poor old bod back in shape. They even gave me a treatment with their Skin, which is a kind of poor man's regen-tank, but it didn't do much good. The practitioner said my mind-tone was wrong for it, just as it was wrong for a gray torc. But I knew that I just didn't want to get well and have more babies. I wanted to die. So one lovely night I slipped quietly into the river."

He could think of no words to comfort her. The uniquely feminine abasement was a horror beyond his understanding—although he pitied her and raged inwardly against the ones who had used her, planted a half-human parasite inside of her that fed on her, kicked against her internal organs and belly wall, then violated her again as it burst out into the open air. God! And she'd said that she loved the first baby! How was it possible? (*He* would have strangled the little bastards before they drew their first breath.) But she'd loved one, and would have loved the others, likely as not, if they hadn't been taken away. She'd loved those paingivers, those unworthy children. Could a man ever make sense of the ways of women?

And you'd think she'd never want to look at another male. But somehow she'd fathomed his own need and—yes!—needed him as well. She might even like him a little. Was she as generous as all that?

Almost as though she read his thoughts, she gave a sensuous little chuckle and beckoned him back to her. "We still have time. If you're the man I think you are."

"Not if it would hurt you," he found himself saying even as he came back to life. "Never if it would hurt you." But she only laughed again and pulled him down. Women were amazing.

Off in a remote little nook of his brain, something was typing out a message to him, a conviction that grew to enormous, almost frightening, proportions as the exquisite tension built to its culmination. This person was not "women." She was not, as all the others had been to him, an abstraction of feminine sexuality, a comforter, a receptacle for physical release. She was different. She was Martha.

The message was hard to understand, but any minute now, he was going to figure it out.

5

It had been Martha who gave the Bogle his title.

He had been there, sitting on a boulder and regarding them with a misanthropic glare, when they awoke early the next morning in their camp below the southern flank of the Feldberg. After brusquely identifying himself as an emissary from Sugoll, he had ordered them to pack up without even waiting to let Richard make breakfast. The pace he set up a spur ridge of the mountain was deliberately trying and he would have raced them uphill without a rest if Madame had not occasionally demanded that they stop to catch their breath. Plainly, the dwarfish creature was feeling ill-used at having to serve as a guide and had decided to wreak his own petty revenge.

The Bogle was much shorter than any Firvulag they had ever seen before—and much uglier, with a tubby little torso and skinny arms and legs. His skull was grotesquely compressed to the point of being birdlike. Large black eyes with overlapping pouches were set close together above his toucanish nose. Prominent ears drooped flaccidly at the upper margins. His skin shone greasy reddish brown, and his sparse hair twisted into strands like a string mop. The Bogle's clothing, belying his physical repulsiveness, was neat and even beautiful:

341

polished boots and a wide belt of carved black leather, wine-red breeches and shirt, and a long vest embroidered in flamelike patterns and studded with semiprecious stones. He wore a kind of Phrygian bonnet with a large brooch positioned just above his scraggly brows, which were knit in what seemed to be a permanent scowl.

Following their trollish guide, the five travelers skirted the mountain ravines, following a tiny but very distinct trail, and passed through a part of the Black Forest that had nearly as many broadleaf trees as conifers. Wherever the Feldberg brooks slowed enough to pool there were bosky dingles clogged with tall ferns and alders, creeping clematis vines, and fall-blooming primroses with poisonously bright blossoms. They came to a hollow where the waters of a hot spring bubbled to the surface. Lush and unhealthy-looking vegetation crowded the steamy swale. A flock of ravens croaked a sardonic greeting from the half-eaten carcass of a small deer that lay near the edge of a mineral-encrusted puddle. More bones—some clean, some furred with thick moss—were strewn about the undergrowth.

Farther east, the rock formations began to change. Colored limestone outcroppings intruded amongst the granite. "Cave country," Claude remarked to Madame. They were walking side by side now, the path widening as they passed below a wooded cliff. The sun was warm; nevertheless, the paleontologist felt a subterranean chill. In the few places where the rock face was visible, they saw scarlet and blue swallows with long forked tails darting in and out of pocks in the limestone. Spiny-ribbed elephant-ears grew in dense patches beneath the trees. They sheltered clumps of distinctive mushrooms, white-stemmed, red caps flecked in white.

"They are here," the old woman said abruptly. "All around us! Can you not feel them? So many! And all . . . deformed."

For a moment, he failed to catch the significance of what she was saying. But it fit—fit with the undercurrent of anxiety that had lurked at the edge of his consciousness ever since early morning. Fit with the surliness of the Bogle, whom Claude had mistaken for an ordinary Firvulag.

"Les Criards," Madame said. "They follow us. One of them leads us. The Howling Ones."

The path led uphill at an easy slope, entirely free of debris. The swallows flickered among the firs and beeches. Great bars of golden light slanted down into the forest as if through open windows.

The old woman said, "Such a beautiful place. But there is desolation here, mon vieux, a wretchedness of spirit that at once touches my heart and disgusts me. And it grows stronger."

He lent her his arm, for she was faltering, apparently for no physical reason. Her face had gone dead white. "We could ask the Bogle to stop," Claude suggested.

Her voice was dulled. "No. It is necessary to go on . . . Ah, Claude! You should thank God for not making you sensitive to the emanations of other minds! All sentient beings have their secret thoughts, those that remain hidden except to the good God. But there are other thoughts as well, pitched, as it were, on different psychic levels—the nonvocal speech, the currents and storms of emotion. This latter is what I am enveloped in now. It is a most profound enmity, a malevolence that can come only from the most distorted personalities. The Howling Ones! They hate other beings but they hate themselves so much more. And their howling fills my mind . . ."

"Can't you shut it out? Defend yourself as you did against the Hunt?"

"If I had been properly trained," she said forlornly. "But all that I know I have taught myself. I do not know how to counter this horde. They don't offer any concrete threat that I can seize upon." Her expression was very near panic. "All they do is hate. With all their strength . . . they hate."

"Do they seem to be more powerful than ordinary Firvulag?"

"I cannot be sure of that. But they are different in some unnatural way. That is why I called them deformed. With the Firvulag, and even with the Tanu, human metapsychics can feel a certain mental kinship. It is no matter that the exotic is an enemy. But never could I be akin to these Criards! I have never before been so close to so many of them. Only rarely did we encounter them in our little enclave within the Vosges, and there they were wary. But these—!"

Her voice broke off, harsh and too high-pitched. Her right fingers stroked the golden torc with a feverish urgency while those of her left hand dug painfully into Claude's arm. She kept darting her eyes from side to side, scanning the crags. There was nothing unusual to be seen.

Felice, who had been at the tail end of the line behind them, now closed the distance and announced, "I don't like this place at all. For the past half hour or so I've had the damnedest feeling. Nothing at all like those nervous fantods we got in the Fungus Forest, either. This time, there bloody well *is* something to be afraid of! Come on, Madame—what's going on?"

"The malign Firvulag—the Howlers—are all around us. Their mental projections are so powerful that even you, in your latent state, can perceive them."

The blonde athlete's mouth tightened to a straight line and her eyes flashed. In her unaccustomed buckskin garb, she looked like a schoolgirl playing at Red Indians. She asked Madame, "Are they getting ready to attack?"

"They will do nothing," the old woman replied, "without the permission of their ruler, Sugoll."

"Only mental intimidation, damn their eyes! Well, they don't scare me!" Felice unstrapped the bow from her pack and checked the arrows expertly without losing stride. The cliff had now become a crazy jumble of blocks and pinnacles with the rising of the land. The trees thinned. They could see far out over the intermontane valleys. Even the distant Alps were barely visible to the south. The Feldberg itself reared up another thousand meters above them, chopped off in a sheer precipice on its southeastern face as though some Titan had taken an axe to it, mutilating the symmetry of the smoothly rounded crown.

Up at the head of the line, the Bogle was holding up one hand. They had arrived at an alpine park, a meadow surrounded on all sides by steep rocks. Precisely in the center of the area was a haystack-shaped knoll of velvety black stone, veined with a weblike tracery of bright yellow.

"This is it," said the Bogle. "And here I gladly leave you."

He folded his arms and, scowling, faded from sight. The scowl lasted longer than the rest of him.

"Well, that's a hell of a—" Richard began.

"Silence!" Madame exclaimed.

Without knowing why, the other four drew close to her. Her brow was dewed with sweat and she clutched at the torc as if it had suddenly become too small for her. Above the little bowl of flower-tufted gravel was a cloudless sky; but the air seemed to be thickening into a liquid in which uncanny trans- parent whorls and streamings formed and reformed faster than the eye could follow. It became impossible to see clearly beyond the encircling rocks. The upper slopes of the mountain shimmered and flowed and broke into fluid masses of constantly changing shape. The black knoll, on the other hand, assumed a pristine clarity. It was obviously the center of whatever activity was pending.

Madame gripped Claude's arm in mortal desperation. "So many, doux Jésus! Can you not feel them?"

Richard ventured to say, "*I* sure as hell feel something. It feels like a sigma force-shield bombardment, for God's sake! Hostile minds against us—is that it?"

The aura of foreboding was building to an unbearable crescendo. There was a low-cycle vibration in the rock underfoot as well, amplified in slow spurts, almost like the treading of invisible feet inside the mountain.

And things howled.

The atmospheric whirlings intensified. A new sound began—a mad ensemble of tremolo notes that wailed up and down at a hundred different intervals, each voice with a tempo of its own. The humans clapped their hands over their ears. The avalanche of sound forced them to scream in a futile effort to neutralize it before it overwhelmed them.

And then it stopped, and the Howlers appeared.

The five travelers stood like a group of statuary, eyes wide and mouths still agape. The rocks surrounding the alpine clearing were crowded with beings. There seemed to be hundreds of them, perhaps even thousands; they sat atop one another, dangled from overhanging formations or from one another's lower limbs, peered out of crevices and clambered agilely over the heads and bodies of their fellows in an effort to get a front-row view.

They were the folk of nightmares.

Most of them were very small, under a meter in height, with the rounded torso and skinny limbs of the Bogle. Many had disproportionately large hands and feet. Some of the bodies seemed twisted, as with spinal deformities; others had asymmetric bulges under well-made garments, hinting of tumorous growths or even concealed extra limbs. The heads were grotesque: pointed, flattened, ridged like tree bark, crested, even horn-bearing. Some were too large or too small for the supporting body, or monstrously ill-suited as the tiny female head with the lustrous curls and lovely features that sat incongruously on the hunched form of a young chimpanzee. Almost all of the faces were hideous, warped or swollen or stretched beyond any semblance of humanoid normality. There were faces covered with red and blue wattles, with hair, with saurian scales, with weeping scabs, with cheeselike exudate. There were eyes bulbous, beady, stalked, misplaced, superfluous. Some of the creatures had mouths so wide as to be froglike; others lacked lips altogether, so that the stumps of rotted teeth were exposed in perpetual ghastly grins. Those mouths ranged from animal muzzles grafted onto otherwise normal skulls to improbable vertical slits, coiled trunks, and parrot beaks. They opened to show fat tusks, close-set narrow fangs, drooling gums, and tongues that might be black or fringed or even double or triple.

Very gently, the misbegotten throng howled again.

On the black rock now sat a fairly tall bald-headed man. His face was beautiful and his body, clad from neck to heel in a tight-fitting purple garment, that of a superbly muscled humanoid.

The howling ceased abruptly. The man said, "I am Sugoll, the lord of these mountains. Say why you come."

"We bring," Madame said in a barely audible voice, "a letter from Yeochee, High King of the Firvulag."

The bald man smiled tolerantly and held out one hand. Claude had to support Madame Guderian as she approached the rock.

"You are afraid of us," Sugoll observed as he perused the piece of vellum. "Are we so disgusting to human eyes?"

"We fear what your minds project," Madame said. "Your bodies can only stir our compassion."

"Mine is an illusion, of course," said Sugoll. "As the greatest of all these"—he swept one arm to encompass the quivering mass of creatures—"I must naturally be their superior in all things, even in physical abomination. Would you like to see me as I really am?"

Claude said, "Mighty Sugoll, this woman has been severely affected by your mental emanations. I was once a life-scientist, a paleobiologist. Show yourself to me and spare my friends."

The bald man laughed. "A paleobiologist! See if you can classify me, then." He stood upright on his rock. Richard came and took Madame back, leaving Claude standing alone.

There was a brief flash and all of the humans except the

old man were momentarily blinded.

"What am I? What am I?" Sugoll cried out. "You'll never guess, human! You can't tell us and we can't tell you because none of us knows!" Peal after peal of mocking laughter rang out.

The handsome figure in purple was once again seated on his rock. Claude stood with feet widely planted, his head down on his breast and his lungs pumping. A trickle of blood oozed from his bitten lower lip. Slowly, he raised his eyes to meet Sugoll's.

"I do know what you are."

"What's that you say?" The goblin ruler hitched forward. In one lithe movement he vaulted to the ground and sprang close to Claude.

"I know what you are," the paleontologist repeated. "What all of you are. You are members of a race that is abnormally sensitive to the background radiation of the planet Earth. Even the Tanu and Firvulag who live in other regions have suffered reproductive anomalies because of this radiation. But you—you have compounded the problem by living *here*. I daresay you've drunk from the deep springs, with their juvenile water, as well as from the shallower fountains and the brooks of melted snow. You've probably made your homes in caverns"—he pointed to the yellow-streaked knoll—"full of attractive black rocks like that one."

"It is so."

"Unless I miss my guess and my old memory bank's fritzed out, that rock is nivenite, an ore containing uranium and radium. The deep springs are likely to be radioactive, too. During the years that you people have lived in this region, you've exposed your genes to many times the radiation dose experienced by your fellow Firvulag. This is why you're mutated, why you've changed into . . . what you are."

Sugoll turned and stared at the velvet-black rock. Then he threw back his beautifully formed illusionary skull and howled. All of his troll and bogle subjects joined in. This time the sound was not terrifying to the humans, only unbearably poignant.

At length, the Howling Ones ceased their racial dirge. Sugoll said, "On this planet, with only primitive genotechnology, there can be no hope for us."

"There *is* hope for generations unborn if you move away

from here—say, into more northerly regions where there are no concentrations of dangerous minerals. For those of you alive today . . . well, you have your powers of illusion-making."

"Yes," the exotic ruler agreed, his voice flat. "We have our illusions." But then the implications of what Claude had said began to reveal their true import to him. He cried out, "But can it be true? What you said about our children?"

The old man said, "You need advice from an experienced geneticist. Any human with that background has probably been enslaved by the Tanu. All I can tell you is a few basic generalizations. Get out of this area to put a stop to new mutations. The worst of you are probably sterile. The fertile people will likely have recessives for normality. Inbreed the most normal among you to fix the alleles. Bring normal germ plasm into the population by mending your fences with the other Firvulag—the normal ones. You'll have to use your illusion-making powers to make yourselves attractive as potential mates, and you'll have to be socially compatible to encourage the mixing. That means no more bogey-man mentality."

Sugoll gave a bark of ironic laughter. "Your presumption passes belief! Emigrate from our traditional lands! Give up our mating traditions! Make friends with our old enemies! Marry them!"

"If you want to change your genetic pattern, that's the way to start. There's a long shot, too . . . if we should ever manage to liberate humanity from the Tanu. There just might happen to be a human genetic engineer among the time-travelers. I don't know exactly how the Tanu Skin works, but it may be possible to utilize it to alter your grossly mutated bodies back into a more normal form. We were able to do this in some cases, using the regeneration-tanks of the future world that I came from."

"You have given us much to ponder." Sugoll was more subdued. "Some of the intelligence is bitter indeed, but we will think on it. Eventually, we will make our decision."

Madame Guderian now stepped forward and resumed her rôle of leader. Her voice was firm; her color had returned. "Mighty Sugoll, there is still the matter of our mission. Our request of you."

The exotic clenched his fist, which still held Yeochee's

message. The vellum crackled. "Ah—your request! This royal command was useless, you know. Yeochee has no power here, but doubtless he did not care to admit it to you. I allowed you to enter our territory on a whim, curious as to the extremity that would make you take such a risk. We had planned to amuse ourselves with you before finally permitting you to die . . .".

"And now?" Madame inquired.

"What do you ask of us?"

"We seek a river. A very large one, rising in this area, which flows eastward until it reaches the great half-salty lagoons of the Lac Mer hundreds of kilometers from here. We hoped to travel upon this river to the site of the Ship's Grave."

There was a surprised chorus of howls.

"We know the river," Sugoll said. "It is the Ystroll, a truly mighty flood. We have a few legends of the Ship. Early in the history of our people on this world, we broke away from the main body of the Firvulag and sought independence in these mountains, away from the Hunting and the senseless annual slaughter of the Grand Combat."

Madame had to explain carefully the human complicity in the recent rise to dominance of the Tanu, as well as her own scheme to restore the old balance of power while freeing humanity. "But to do this, we must obtain certain ancient items from the crater of the Ship's Grave. If you will furnish us with a guide to the river, we believe that we will be able to locate the crater."

"And this plan—when will you put it into effect? When might the human scientists be free of the Tanu yoke and able— if Téah wills—to help us?"

"We had hoped to implement the scheme this year, before the start of the Grand Combat Truce. But there is scant hope of this now. Only twelve days remain. The Ship's Grave lies at least two hundred kilometers from here. It will doubtless take us half of the remaining time just to walk to the head of navigation on the river."

"That is not so," Sugoll said. He called out, "Kalipin!"

The Bogle stepped forth from the throng. His formerly surly face was transfigured by a broad smile. "Master?"

"I do not understand these kilometers. Tell the humans how it is with the Ystroll."

"Below these mountains," the Bogle said, "are the caverns where we make our homes. But at other levels—some deeper, some shallower—are the Water Caves. They are a maze of springs, bottomless pools and streams flowing through the blackness. Several rivers have their sources in the Water Caves. The Paradise, which flows past Finiah to the northwest, is one. But the mightiest torrent born beneath our mountains is the Ystroll."

Claude exclaimed, "He could be right! There were underground tributaries to the Danube even in our own time. Some said they came from Lake Constance. Others postulated a connection to the Rhine."

The Bogle said, "The Ystroll emerges as a full-grown river into a great lowland to the northeast. If you enter the Water Caves at Alliky's Shaft via the lift buckets, you can pick up the Dark Ystroll not two hours' march from here. Then it is a subterranean water-journey of but a single day to the Bright Ystroll, that which flows beneath the open sky."

Madame asked Sugoll, "Would your boatmen guide us along the underground section?"

Sugoll did not speak. He lifted his eyes to the surrounding crowd of monstrosities. There was a musical chorus of howls. The goblin shapes began to shift and change, and the terrible swirling pattern of the sky calmed. The mental energies of the little people relaxed from the projection of undisciplined hatred and self-loathing and began to weave gentler illusions. The dreadful deformities faded; a throng of miniature men and women took the place of the nightmares.

"Send them," sighed the Howling Ones.

Sugoll bowed his head in acknowledgment. "It will be done."

He arose and lifted his hand. All of the small people repeated the gesture. They became as tenuous as mountain mist burning away in the noon sunlight.

"Remember us," they said as they vanished. "Remember us."

"We will," Madame whispered.

The Bogle went trotting away, beckoning for them to follow. Claude took Madame Guderian's arm, and Richard, Martha, and Felice came trailing behind.

"Only one thing," the old woman said to Claude in a low tone. "What did he *really* look like, this Sugoll?"

"You can't read my mind, Angélique?"

"You know I cannot."

"Then you'll never know. And I wish to God," the old man added, "that I didn't."

6

LATE IN THE EVENING, WHEN THE GIANT HAWKMOTHS AND the flying squirrels played their aerial games above the wooded canyon of Hidden Springs Village, seven men bearing six heavy sacks came home to the Lowlife settlement, led by Khalid Khan. They sought Uwe Guldenzopf, but his hut was empty. Calistro the goat-boy, bringing his animals home from their browsing, informed the seven that Uwe was at the community bathhouse with Chief Burke.

"The Chief is here?" Khalid exclaimed in consternation. "Then the expedition to the Ship's Grave was a failure?"

Calistro shook his head. He was about five years old, sober and responsible enough to know something of the great plans that were afoot. "The Chief was hurt, so he came back. Sister Amerie fixed his wounded leg, but he still must soak it many times each day . . . What do you have in the sacks?"

The men laughed. Khalid dropped his load on the ground with a loud clanging sound.

"Treasure!" The speaker was a wiry, shock-haired individual standing just behind Khalid, the only one of the seven not burdened down. The stump of his left arm was wrapped in a wad of dark-stained cloth.

"Let me see!" begged the child. But the men were already

352

on their way up the flat-floored canyon. Calistro hurried his
animals into their night pen and rushed to follow.

White starlight shone on a small area of open grass near the
banks of the brook that was born of the hot and cold springs'
mingling; however, most of the village lay concealed in deep
shadow, the homes and community buildings sheltered beneath
tall pines or spreading ever-green oaks that hid them from
Finiah's Tanu sky-searchers. The bathhouse, a large log structure with a low-eaved roof overgrown with vines, was built
against one of the canyon walls. Its windows were closely
shuttered, and a U-shaped passage kept torchlight from the
interior from shining out the open door.

Khalid and his men entered into a scene of steamy cheer-
fulness. It seemed that half the village had gathered in here on
this rather chilly evening. Men, women, and a few children
splashed in stone-lined hot or cold pools, lolled in hollow-log
soaking tubs, or simply lounged about gossiping or playing
backgammon or card games.

Uwe Guldenzopf's voice rang out over the communal din.
"Hoy! Look who's back home again!" And the Lowlives raised
a shout of welcome. Somebody yelled, "Beer!" And one of
Khalid's grimy contingent appended a heartfelt, "Food!" The
boy Calistro was sent to roust out the village victualers while
the new arrivals pushed through a gabbling, laughing mob
toward an isolated tub where Peopeo Moxmox Burke sat, his
long graying hair stringy in the bathhouse vapors and his craggy
face atwitch as he suppressed a delighted grin.

"How," quoth he.

"Beats me," the Pakistani metalsmith replied. "But we did
it." He dropped his sack on the stone floor and opened it,
taking out a lance-head rough from the casting mold. "Secret
weapon, Mark I." Turning to one of the other men, he groped
in his sack and produced a handful of smaller objects, approximately leaf-shaped. "Mark II. You sharpen 'em, they're arrowheads. We've got about two hundred and twenty kilos of
iron all told—some of it cast like these, some in bars for
miscellanea, ready for forging. What we have here is medium-
carbon steel, smelted in the best antique style. We built us a
forced-draft furnace fueled with charcoal and drafted with six
skin bellows hooked up to decamole tuyères. Carbon from

charred bulrushes. We buried the furnace so we can go back and make more iron when we've a mind to."

Burke's eyes glistened. "Ah, mechaieh! Well done, Khalid! And all the rest of you, too—Sigmund, Denny, Langstone, Gert, Smokey, Homi. Well done, all of you. This could be the breakthrough we've all been dreaming of—praying for! Whether or not the others succeed at the Ship's Grave, this iron will give us a fighting chance against the Tanu for the first time."

Uwe stood sucking his meerschaum, his gaze wandering over the tattered and soot-stained smelters. "And what happened," he inquired, "to the other three of you?"

The grins of the men disappeared. Khalid said, "Bob and Vrenti stayed too long one evening at the ore pit. When we came to check up on them, they were gone. We never saw a trace of them again. Prince Francesco was off hunting for the pot when the Howlers nailed him."

"They let us have *him* back, though," said the skinny hatchet-faced man named Smokey. "Day later, poor Frankie came staggerin' back into camp starkers. They'd blinded and gelded him and cut off his hands—and then really got down to business with hot pitch. His mind was gone, o' course. Small hope the Howlers blunked him before they had their fuckin' fun 'n' games."

"Suffering Christ," growled Uwe.

"We got a bit back," Denny offered. His black face flashed a wry smile.

"You did," said the bandy-legged little Singhalese named Homi. He explained to Chief Burke, "On our way home, a Howler came at us in broad daylight—oh, maybe forty kloms down the Moselle from here. All dressed up in his bloody monster suit like a great winged naga with two heads. Denny let him have an iron-tipped arrow in the guts and he went down like a rotten willow tree. And would y'believe? All that was left was this hunchbacked dwarf with a face like a stoat!"

The men grunted in reminiscence and a couple of them whacked Denny on the back. The latter said, "At least we know now that the iron works on both kinds of exotics—right? I mean, the Howlers are nothing but screwed-up Firvulag. So if our noble spook allies ever forget who their friends are . . ."

There were murmurs of agreement and a few quiet laughs.

Chief Burke said, "It's a point to keep in mind—although

God knows we need Firvulag help to bring off Madame's plan against Finiah. The Little people were agreeable to the original scheme. But I'm afraid adding iron to the equation might give them second thoughts."

"Just wait'll they see us take out some Tanu with the iron," Smokey said confidently. "Just wait'll we equalize things with them dog-collar sumbitches! Why—the damn Firvulag'll kiss our feet! Or bums! Or somethin'."

Everybody roared.

An excited young voice from among the crowd of villagers shouted, "Why should we hold back on the Tanu until Finiah? There's a caravan going to Castle Gateway in two days. Let's sharpen up some arrows and bag us an Exalted One right away!"

A few of the others yelled approval. But Chief Burke hauled himself out of his bath like an enraged bull alligator and yelled, "Simmer down, you turkey-turd shlangers! *Nobody* touches this iron without permission from me! It has to be kept secret. Do you want the whole Tanu chivalry on our necks? Velteyn would send out a screech like a goosed moose if we tipped our hand. He might bring in Nodonn—even call for reinforcements from the south!"

They mumbled at this. The aggressive youngster called out, "When we use iron in the Finiah attack, they'll know. Why not now?"

"Because," Burke drawled, in the sarcastic tone he had once used to freeze the collops of inept fledgling advocates, "the attack on Finiah will come just prior to the Truce for the Grand Combat. None of the other Tanu will pay much attention to Velteyn's troubles then. You know the way these exotics' minds work. Nothing, but *nothing*, gets in the way of preparations for the glorious shemozzle. Two or three days before Truce— when we hope to strike—not a Tanu on Earth will come to the aid of Finiah. Not even to help their pals, not even to save their barium mine, not even to beat back humans armed with iron. They'll all be hot to head south to the big game."

The crowd fell back to palaver over the amazing single-mindedness of the exotic sportsmen, and Burke began to get dressed. Uwe waggishly suggested that the Tanu were nearly as bad as the Irish for loving a fight without considering the long-view consequences. There was universal laughter at this and not a single son nor daughter of Erin's Isle rose to defend the racial honor. The thought flashed into Burke's mind that there was a reason for this, and he ought to know what it was; but at the same moment Khalid Khan caught sight of the red man's healing wound.

"Mashallah, Peo! You did scratch yourself up a bit, didn't you?"

Burke's left leg was hideously indented at the calf by a purplish-red scar over twenty cents in length. He grunted. "Souvenir of a one-horned chozzer. It killed Steffi and damn near did for me by the time Pegleg shlepped me back here to Amerie. Galloping septicemia. But she caught it. Looks like hell, but I can walk—even run, if I care to pay the price."

Uwe reminded him, "The meeting of the Steering Committee. Tonight. Khalid should come."

"Right. But first we have to see to the needs of this gang. How about it, men? Food and drink's on the way—but is there anything else we can do for you now?"

Khalid said, "Sigmund's hand. Aside from our three deaders, he's the only casualty."

"What happened?" Burke asked.

Sigmund sheepishly hid his stump. "Aw. I was stupid. Giant salamander sprang at me, fanged me right in the palm. You know there's only one thing to do, the way their venom works . . ."

"Sig was bringing up the rear," Denny said. "All of a sudden we missed him. When we went back to investigate, there he was putting on a tourniquet cool as you please, with his vitredur axe and his mitt lying on the ground beside him."

"You come along with us to Amerie's place," the Chief said. "We'll have her check it out."

"Aw, it's all right, Chief. We put plenty of AB and progan on it."

"Shut your pisk and come along." The Chief turned to the others. "The rest of you boys relax and eat and have a couple of days' sleep. There'll be a big council of war—a contingent one, anyhow—inside of a week, when the volunteers from the other settlements start showing up. We'll need you to work on this iron when we get the blacksmith shop set up some place where the Firvulag won't spot it. Till then, I'll take charge of the stuff. Put it out of temptation's reach."

Then Burke raised his voice so that the entire bathhouse could hear him. "All of you! If you value your own lives, and if you give a damn about the liberty of humans who are still enslaved, forget about what you've seen and heard here tonight."

A breath of assent rose from the assemblage. The Chief nodded and hoisted two of the heavy sacks. Khalid and Uwe dragged away the other four and they moved out of the bathhouse, trailed by Sigmund.

"The meeting is at Madame's cottage as usual," Burke told the metalsmith as he limped along. "Amerie's living there now. We put her on the committee by acclamation."

Uwe said, "That nunnie is some medic. She shrank Maxl so we don't have to keep him locked up anymore. And poor Sandra—no more suicidal threats now that the fungus is cured. Then there's Chaim's eyelid, all rebuilt, and she healed that big mother of an ulcer on Old Man Kawai's foot."

"That'll make for quieter meetings," Khalid remarked. "One less thing for the old boy to complain about. This nun sounds like a handy lady to have around."

The Chief chuckled. "I didn't even mention the way she cleaned up sixteen cases of worms and almost all the jungle rot. Madame might have to do some fancy politicking in the next election if she wants to hold on to the freeleadership of this gang of outlaws."

"It never struck me that she relished the honor." Khalid was acerbic. "Any more than you did when you were in the hot seat."

They plodded along, making almost no sound on the path that wound beneath the sheltering trees. The long canyon had many little dead-end tributaries from which the numerous springs debouched. Most of the cottages had been built close to these natural water supplies. There were some thirty homes altogether, in which dwelt the eighty-five human beings who made up the largest Lowlife settlement in the known Pliocene world.

The four men crossed a rill on stepping-stones and headed up one of the rocky clefts to where a distinctive little house stood under a huge pine. The cottage was not built like the others of prosaic logs or wattle and daub, but of neatly mortared stone, washed white with lime and reinforced with dark half-timbering. It was eerily evocative of a certain elder-world dwelling in the hills above Lyon. Madame's rose cuttings, nourished by the manure of mastodons, had burgeoned into rampant climbers that all but smothered the thatched roof in blossoms. The night air was heavy with their perfume.

The men came up the path, then halted. Standing in their way was a tiny animal. Stiff-legged, its oversized eyes gleaming, it growled.

"Hey, Deej!" Burke laughed. "It's just us, pupikeh. Friends!"

The little cat growled louder, the low rumble moving up the scale to become a threatening howl. It stood its ground.

Chief Burke put down his burden and knelt with one hand out-stretched. Khalid Khan stepped behind Sigmund, a memory and a terrible suspicion crowding to the fore of his mind. A memory of a rainy night inside a Tree when the cat had growled like this before. A suspicion of a valued companion who had been too good a woodsman to be surprised by the relatively sluggish attack of a giant salamander . . .

Khalid slipped open the mouth of his sack just as the cottage door swung wide to show Amerie's veiled figure silhouetted against dim lamplight.

"Dejah?" the nun called, rattling her rosary beads in what was evidently some signal. She caught sight of the men. "Oh, it's you, Chief. And Khalid! You're back! But what—"

The turbaned metalsmith seized the hair of the one they had called Sigmund. With his other hand he pressed something gray and hard against the man's throat.

"Do not move, soor kabaj, or you are dead, even as your brother before you."

Amerie screamed and Uwe uttered an obscenity—for Khalid was suddenly struggling with a gorgon. Instead of hair, the Pakistani clutched writhing little vipers growing from Sigmund's scalp. These struck, sinking tiny fangs into flesh that puffed up, throbbed, as quasi-deadly venom flooded the blood vessels and went racing toward Khalid's heart.

"Stop, I say!" roared the anguished smith. Involuntarily, his right arm tightened, driving the dull point of the iron lance-blank into the soft hollow below the monster's voicebox.

The thing emitted a gurgling squeal and went limp. Khalid sprang away from the falling body, dropping the iron. It hit the earth with a dull thud and came to rest close beside the dead shape-changer. Amerie and the three men stared down at the creature, which could have weighed no more than twenty or thirty kilos. Flattened little dugs identified it as a female.

Its bald cranium was monstrously compressed just above the eyes and elongated backward into a triangular bony collar. It had a mere hole for a nose and a massive lower jaw with loose, peglike teeth. The body was almost globular, the limbs spiderishly thin, with the left forepaw missing.

"It's not . . . a Firvulag," Amerie managed to say.

"A Howler," Burke told her. "Some biologists believe they're a Firvulag mutation. Each one is supposed to have a different true shape. All hideous."

"You see what she was trying to do, don't you?" Khalid's voice was shaking from reaction and chagrin. He felt his left hand, which was now completely normal. "She saw us kill her mate with iron, and had to find out what the new weapon was. So she must have crept up on Sigmund as he marched at the end of the line and . . . she took his place. Cut off her hand so she wouldn't have to carry the iron."

"But they've never masqueraded as humans!" Uwe exclaimed. "What could have been its motive?"

"Look at her—dressed in rags," Amerie said. She knelt down in the light from the doorway to examine the goblin body. One of the Howler's crude skin boots had dropped off in the struggle, exposing a humanoid foot—miniaturized but as perfectly formed as that of a child. There was a pathetic blister at the heel; evidently the little being had had to hurry to keep pace with the faster humans.

The nun replaced the boot, straightened the pipestem legs, closed the glazed eyes. "She was very poor. Perhaps she hoped to discover information valuable enough to sell."

"To the normal Firvulag?" Burke suggested.

"Or to the Tanu." The nun got up and dusted the front of her white habit.

Khalid said, "There might be others. Others who watched us at the smeltery. If this one could change to human shape, how will we ever be sure—"

Burke picked up the iron blade, grasped the metalsmith's arm, and drew the rough lancehead across the skin. A few drops of dark blood sprang from the abrasion. "You're real enough, anyhow. I'll go test the rest of the crew right away. Later, we'll work out something a little less crude. Pinprick, maybe."

He limped away toward the bathhouse. Uwe and Khalid

hauled the precious bags of iron into the rose-covered cottage, then returned to where Amerie stood over the body. She held the cat, which was still gently growling.

"What shall we do with her, Sister?" Khalid inquired.

Amerie sighed. "I have a large basket. Perhaps you can put her in the springhouse for me. I'm afraid I'll have to dissect her tomorrow."

As the Steering Committee waited for Chief Burke to return to the cottage, the Victualer in Chief offered samples of a new beverage. "We took some of that lousy raw wine of Perkin's and steeped this little forest wildflower in it."

Everybody sipped. Amerie said, "That's nice, Marialena."

Uwe said something in German under his breath. "You know what you've done, woman? You've reinvented Maiwein!"

"That's it! That's it!" Old Man Kawai piped. He was only eighty-six; but since he had declined rejuvenation on a matter of principle, he resembled an unwrapped Oriental mummy. "Most refreshing, my dear. Now if we can only produce a decent saké . . ."

The cottage door opened and Peopeo Moxmox Burke stooped to enter. The other committee members sat stark still until the red man gave a nod. "They were all kosher. I tested not only the smelters, but all the rest of the folks in the bathhouse as well."

"Thank heaven," said the Architect in Chief. "What a thought—shape-changers infiltrating *our people!*" He wagged his neatly trimmed muttonchops, managing to look like an accountant who had discovered that a valued client was cooking the books.

"Neither Firvulag nor Howlers had any reason to try this trick before," the Chief warned. "But now, with the attack coming up and the iron as a maybe not-so-secret weapon, we're going to have to be alert for other attempts. When the volunteers start arriving, every single one must be tested. And we'll test all participants before every important meeting or briefing."

"My responsibility," said Uwe, who was Hunting and Public Safety. "Whip me up some needles, Khalid?"

"As soon as I can get the forge hot tomorrow."

The Chief took his place with the other seven committee members around the table.

"All right, let's get this over as quickly as possible so Khalid can get some rest. As Deputy Freeleader, I call this meeting of the Steering Committee to order. Old business. Structures. Let's have it, Philemon."

"The huts at the Rhine staging area have been completed," said the architect. "Everything is ready there except the main shelter pavilion. The boys will have our Hidden Springs visitor dorm ready in another two or three days."

"Good," said the Chief. "Public Works. Vanda-Jo."

A taffy-haired woman with the face of a madonna and the voice of a drill sergeant spoke up. "We've finished the masked trail from here to the staging area. A hundred and six bloody kilometers, invisible from the air. Corduroyed the last two kloms through the swamp—and don't think that wasn't a bitch! Still putting up the thorn boma around the staging camp to keep most of the critters out and the recruits in."

"How about the launching ramps?"

"Decided on pontoons. Inflated skins and boarding. Put 'em up at the last minute. Pegleg and his lads are contributing the skins."

"Good. Hunting and Public Safety."

"Nothing much new from me," Uwe said. "Most of my people are working with Vanda-Jo or Phil. I've liaised with the commissary at High Vrazel to help with quantities of game and staples when the extra bods start arriving. And we've set up a procedure for processing new arrivals here at Hidden Springs before sending them to the river."

"Sounds okay. Domestics."

Old Man Kawai pursed his scored lips. "There is *no* way we can come up with more than a hundred boiled-leather hard hats and chest guards by D-Day. You know how long it takes to shape and dry that stuff—even with the forms filled with hot sand. The volunteers are just going to have to go mostly bare-ass unless you want our people deprived. Do shimasho? I've done my best, but I'm no miracle man."

"The shortage can't be helped," Burke said soothingly. "How about the camouflage nets?"

"We'll be putting the big one in position tomorrow, just in case they get back early with the exotic flyer." The wizened ancient threw an anxious glance at the Chief. "Do you really think they've got a chance, Peo?"

"Not much of one," Burke admitted. "But we won't give up hope until the last hour before the Truce...Human Services."

"Linen bandages ready," Amerie said. "We're assembling stores of oil and alcohol and all of the AB we can scrape up. Fifteen fighters have been rough-trained as front-line medics." She paused, her face furrowed with determination. "I want you to change your mind about having me accompany the fighters, Peo. For the love of God—when will they need me *more* than in a battle?"

The Native American shook his head. "You're the only doctor we have. Probably the only one in the Lowlife world. We can't have you at risk. There's the future to think about. If we do liberate Finiah, we may be able to de-torc other medical people. If we fail and the troops come across the Rhine to our staging area...it may be a long time until the next war. Our fighters will tend their own injuries. You stay here."

The nun sighed.

"Industry," said Burke.

"We brought back two hundred and twenty kilos of iron," Khalid said. "Four of our men died. We have enough experienced people left to begin final work on the weapons as soon as we get some sleep."

There were somber congratulations all around.

"Provisioning."

We've enough stored here to feed five hundred people for two weeks," Marialena said. "That does not include the five tons of instant rations we'll distribute to fighters going down to camp. You don't want any cooking going on down by the Rhine where the Tanu might spot the smoke." She pulled a handkerchief from the sleeve of her pink and yellow gown and mopped her ample brow. "Those poor souls are going to curse pemmican and parched bulrush roots before this thing is over."

"If that's all they curse," Burke said, "they'll be lucky. All right, that leaves my report. Warlord in Chief. I've received word from Pallol, the Firvulag generalissimo, that his forces will hold themselves combat-ready for the last three days in September. Under optimal circumstances we'll mount the attack before dawn on the twenty-ninth, which will give us nearly two full fighting days before the Truce officially begins on October first at sunrise. After that, we humans'll be on our own—and Finiah better be ready for mop-up. I'll have more details on plans of attack at the war council later. Okay? Now—new business. We'll consider the matter of the Howler spy as already introduced and sent to Public Safety for action."

"The final preparation of the iron weapons," Khalid said. "My men will soundproof one of the vented caves and turn it into a smithy. I'll need some help from Phil's people."

"More new business?"

"We will need more alcoholic drink," Marialena said. "Mead or beer from the Firvulag. I can't have the volunteers swilling our young wines."

Burke chuckled. "Perish the thought. Uwe—will you sound out the High Vrazel people on that?"

"Check."

"Any more new business?"

Amerie hesitated. "Perhaps it's too soon to bring this up. But there is the matter of the second phase of Madame's plan."

"Hai!" cried Old Man Kawai. "If Finiah is a success, Madame will want to send others south immediately!"

Philemon was uneasy. "We'll do well to accomplish even a small part of the first phase of Madame's plan—much less the other two. I say, leave this to Madame to work out when she returns. It's *her* scheme. Perhaps she and that wild little person, Felice, will have worked something out."

"Caracoles," grumbled Marialena. "I must consider the later phases, even if the rest of you shirk your responsibility. If our people must go south without proper provisions, it is I who receive the cow-chip bouquet! Ahhh—I'll do what I can."

"Thank you, querida," the Chief said peaceably. "I'll talk with you tomorrow about a possible division of rations. But I think that's the best we can do for now on Phase Two or Three planning. There are too many unknown factors—"

"Such as who will survive Finiah!" wailed Old Man Kawai. "Or, if we even mount the Finiah attack in the first place!"

Vanda-Jo slapped one hand on the table. "Tails up! No defeatism allowed! We're going to hit those high-pocket bastards like they've never been hit before. And, Khalid—I've got dibbies on one iron arrowhead, if you please. There's a certain Tanu stud on the other side of the Rhine whose ass belongs to me."

"If you're sure that one will do it," the metalsmith laughed.

"Order," Burke muttered. "Chair will entertain a motion to table strategy planning for the Grand Combat."

"So move," said Amerie. It was quickly affirmed and seconded.

"Any more new business?" the Chief asked. Silence.

"Move adjournment," said Old Man Kawai. "Past my bedtime."

"Second," said Uwe, and the Steering Committee meeting came to an end. Everyone except Chief Burke bade Amerie goodnight and slipped away into the shadows. The quondam judge stretched out his wounded leg for the nun to examine.

At length she said, "There's nothing more I can do for you, Peo. Hot soaks and moderate exercise to keep the muscles from tightening. I can give you a herendorf to block the pain on D-Day."

He waved a deprecating hand. "We'll save it for somebody who really needs it."

"As you like."

They went outside, where the village was quiet except for faint insect noises. It was nearly midnight and the moon was still down. Burke craned his neck and studied the starry vault of the sky.

"There it is, just above the rim of the canyon," he said, pointing.

"What?" she inquired.

"Ah—I forgot you were a newcomer, Amerie. The constellation we call the Trumpet. See the triangular bell, the four bright stars forming the straight tube? Take special note of the mouthpiece star. It's the most important one in all the sky— at least to the Tanu and Firvulag. On the day when it culminates at midnight over Finiah and High Vrazel—those are the oldest exotic settlements, remember—it will mark the opening of the five-day Grand Combat."

"The date?"

"By our Milieu calendar, around October 31 or November 1."

"You're kidding!"

"It's true. And the noon culmination that takes place exactly six months later comes around May Day. The exotics have another big show then, which Tanu and Firvulag celebrate separately—the Grand Love Feast. Most popular with the females of the species, it's said."

"That's really very odd," Amerie said. "I'm no folklorist, but those two dates . . ."

"I know. Only in our time, there was no good explanation—in astronomy or anything else—for the ritualization of those days rather than any others occurring about the same times."

"It's ridiculous to assume a correlation."

"Oh, certainly." The Native American's face was inscrutable in the starlight.

"I mean—six million years."

"Do you know the significance of the mouthpiece star? It's a marker. Their home galaxy lies almost directly behind the star."

"Oh, Peo. How many light years?"

"A hell of a lot more than six million. So in one way, they've come even farther away from home than we have, poor devils."

He gave her a brief salute and limped away, leaving her standing beneath the stars.

7

"BUT IT ISN'T BLUE!" FELICE PROTESTED. "IT'S BROWN."

Madame changed the course of their dinghy to avoid a stranded snag. "The color brown—it lacks that certain cachet. The composer wished to evoke the river's beauty."

The girl gave a contemptuous snort as she studied the terrain. "This place would never win any prizes. Too dry. It looks like it hasn't rained for months." She knelt upright in the bow of the little boat and scanned the open dun-colored slopes with the aid of Madame Guderian's little monocular. Only in the arroyos and in the flats nearest the Danube were there areas of green. The widely scattered groves of trees had a dusty bluish look.

"I can see a few small herds of hipparions and antelopes," the girl said after a time. "Nothing else seems to be alive in those uplands on the left bank. No sign of the crater. Nothing distinctive at all except that little volcano yesterday. You don't think we could have passed it by, do you? This damn river really *rolls*."

"Richard will tell us at noon."

The old woman and the athlete had shared one decamole boat since the party had emerged from the Water Caves nearly two days ago. Claude, Martha, and Richard occupied a second boat that drifted a few dozen meters ahead of them on the swift current of the Bright Ystroll. In spite of the drought they had made splendid time, since the flood received most of its water from the Alps, which shone white in the far south. On the previous night they had pulled up on a wooded gravel bar to sleep, the Bogle having warned them against camping on shore. They were grateful for their isolation when they were awakened later by the cries of hyenas. Claude told them that some of the Pliocene species attained the bulk of large bears and were active predators as well as scavengers.

For navigation, they had one precious map. Back at the Tree, Richard had traced pertinent portions from the fading plass of a venerable Kummerley + Frey Strassenkarte von Europa (Zweitausendjährige Ausgabe), which a nostalgic Low-life treasured as his dearest memento of times to come. The old road map was dim and difficult to decipher, and Claude had warned Richard that the watershed of the Pliocene Danube was going to be greatly altered during the coming Ice Age by volumes of glacial till washing down from the Alps. The tributary streams of the upper Danube that were shown on the map would likely occupy different positions during the Pliocene; and the bed of the great river itself would lie farther south, twisted all out of recognition. The travelers could not hope to follow Galactic Age landmarks to the Ries crater. But there was one precious bit of data from the old map that would have retained its validity over six million years; the exact longitudinal component in kilometers between the meridian of High Vrazel peak (alias Grand Ballon) and that of the Ries (symbolized on the map by the future city of Nordlingen, which lay within what would be a mere ringwall plain on the Elder Earth). No matter how the Ystroll wandered, it was still bound to cross the Ries meridian. As nearly as Richard had been able to determine from the decrepit plass of the road map, the linear distance was 260 kilometers—three and one-half degrees of longitude east of the "prime meridian" of High Vrazel.

Richard had set his accurate wrist chronometer for precisely noon at High Vrazel and had carefully improvised a quadrant to measure the solar angle. Every clear day, the quadrant could be used to tell them local noontime—and the difference between this and P.M. noon shown on the watch could be used to calculate the longitude. When they reached the Ries meridian on the Danube, all they had to do was march due north to reach the crater . . .

One of the figures in the lead boat raised an arm. The craft pulled in to shore.

"There's a little break in the northern highlands there," Felice said. "Maybe Richard has decided it's our best bet." When they had beached their boat next to the other one, she asked, "What d'you think, guys? Is this it?"

"Pretty close, anyhow," Richard said. "And it doesn't look like too bad a hike, for all it's uphill. I calculate thirty kilometers north should hit the lower rim. Even if I'm a little off, we should be able to see the thing from the crest of those northern hills. Damn crater's supposed to be more than twenty kloms wide, after all. How about lunch, while I set up one more sun shot?"

"I've got fish," Martha said, raising a string of silvery-brown shapes. "Richard's excused for his navigating chores, and that leaves you two to dig the perishin' bulrushes while Madame and I get these to grilling."

"Right," sighed Claude and Felice.

They made their fire in a well-shaded spot near the edge of a large grove. Clear water came trickling down a limestone ledge to disappear into a muddy depression that swarmed with little yellow butterflies. After fifteen minutes or so, the delectable smell of roasting young salmon came wafting to the tuber grubbers.

"Come on, Claude," Felice said, sloshing a net full of lumps up and down in the water to rinse them. "We've got enough of these things."

The paleontologist stood quietly, up to his knees in the river among the tall stalks. "I thought I heard something. Probably beavers."

They waded back to the bank where they had left their boots. Both pairs were still there, but something—or someone—had been messing about with them.

"Look here," said Claude, studying the surrounding mud.

"*Baby* footprints!" Felice exclaimed. "Screw me blind! Could there be Howlers or Firvulag in this country?"

They hurried back to the fire with the tubers. Madame used

her far-sensing metafunction to scan the area and professed to sense no exotic beings.

"It is doubtless some animal," she said, "with prints that mimic those of children. A small bear, perhaps."

"Bears were very rare during the early Pliocene," Claude said. "More likely—ah, well. Whatever it is, it's too small to do us any harm."

Richard came back to the group and tucked map, note-plaque, and quadrant back into his pack. "We're near as damn all," he said. "If we really hump this afternoon, we might get there fairly early tomorrow."

"Sit down and have some fish," Martha said. "Doesn't the aroma drive you wild? They say that salmon is just about the only fish that's nutritionally complete enough to serve as a as a steady diet. Because it has fat as well as protein, you see." She licked her lips—then gave a strangled squeak. "Don't ... turn ... around." Her eyes were wide. The rest of them were sitting on the side of the fire opposite her. "Right behind you there's a wild rama."

"No, Felice!" Claude hissed, as the athlete's muscles automatically tensed. "It's harmless. Everybody turn very slowly."

Martha said, "It's carrying something."

The little creature, its body covered with golden-tan fur, stood a short distance back among the trees, trembling noticeably but with an expression of what could only be called determination upon its face. It was about the size of a six-year-old child and had fully humanoid hands and feet. It carried two large warty fruits, greenish bronze streaked with dull orange. As the five travelers regarded it with astonishment, the ramapithecine stepped forward, placed the fruits on the ground, then drew back.

With infinite caution, Claude rose to his feet. The little ape backed up a few paces. Claude said softly, "Well, hullo there, Mrs. Thing. We're glad you could stop by for lunch. How's the husband and kiddies? All well? A little hungry in this drought? I'm not surprised. Fruit is nice, but there's nothing like a bit of protein and fat to keep body and soul together. And the mice and squirrels and locusts have mostly migrated into the upper valleys, haven't they? Too bad you didn't go along with them."

He stooped and picked up the fruits. What were they? Melons? Some kind of papaw? He carried them back to the fire and took two of the larger salmon and wrapped them in an elephant-ear leaf. He put the fish down in the exact spot where the fruit had been and withdrew to his place by the fire.

The ramapithecus stared at the bundle. She reached out, touched a greasy fishhead, and put the finger into her mouth. Giving a low crooning call, she everted her upper lip.

Felice grinned back. She drew her dirk, hefted one of the fruits, and sliced it open. A mouth-watering sweet smell arose from the yellowish-pink flesh. Felice cut off a tiny slice and took a bite of it. "Yum!"

The rama clucked. She picked up the package of fish, everted her lips over her small teeth once again, and ran into the trees.

Felice called out, "Give our regards to King Kong!"

"That was the damnedest thing," Richard said. "Smart, aren't they?"

"Our direct hominid ancestors." Claude stirred up the tubers.

"We had them for servants in Finiah," Martha said. "They were very gentle and cleanly little things. Timid—but they would work conscientiously at the tasks given them by torc wearers."

"How were they cared for?" Claude asked, curious. "Like little people?"

"Not really," Martha said. "They had a kind of barn adjacent to the house, where they lived in partitioned stalls—almost like small cave rooms filled with straw. They were monogamous, you see, and each family had to have its own apartment. There were community areas, too, and dormitory nooks for the singletons. The childless adults worked for about twelve hours, then came home to eat and sleep. The mothers would care for their young for three years, and then put them in charge of 'aunties'—old females who acted for all the world like schoolteachers. The aunties and other very old males and females played with the children and cared for them when the parents were absent. You could see that the parents were unhappy at having to leave the little ones, but the call of the torc couldn't be denied. Still—the rama-keepers told me that the auntie system was a variant of one used by the creatures in the wild. It generally produced well-adjusted individuals. The Tanu have raised ramas in captivity for as long as they've lived on this planet."

"Those sounds they make," Claude said. "Could ordinary bare-necked people such as yourself communicate with them?"

Martha shook her head. "They answered to their names, and there were perhaps a dozen simple voice commands they'd respond to. But the principal means of communicating with them was through the torc. They could grasp very complex *mental* commands. And of course they were trained with the pleasure-pain circuitry so that they required little supervision for routine tasks such as housework."

Madame shook her head slowly. "So close to humanity, and yet so far away from us. Their life span is only fourteen or fifteen years in captivity. Probably less in the wild. So fragile, so helpless-seeming! How did they ever survive the hyenas, the bear-dogs, the sabertooth cats, and other monsters?"

"Brains," Richard said. "Look at that one who came to us. Her family won't be hungry tonight. There's natural selection working right in front of us. That little ape is a survivor."

Felice looked at him with a wicked expression. "I thought I noticed a family resemblance . . . Here you go, Captain Blood. Have some of your great-great-et-cetera grandmother's fruit for desert."

They left the Danube behind them and walked. It felt like the temperature was over forty in the September sun, but their adapted bodies could take it. Over the sunburnt grass, through thickets of brittle maquis, over boulders in the dry watercourses they walked. Richard had set their goal—the notch between two long hills that lay due north beyond slowly rising land with hardly a patch of shade and no water at all. They stripped to shorts, backpacks, and broadbrimmed hats. Madame passed a precious squeeze-bottle of sunburn cream. Richard led and Felice took the rear, the athlete ranging out tirelessly to be sure that no animal stalked them and to search—without luck, as it turned out—for some spring or other source of water. Between the two marched Claude and Madame, supporting Martha between them. The engineer became weaker as the hot hours of hiking accumulated; but she refused to let them slow down. None of them wanted to stop, in spite of the fact that there seemed to be nothing ahead of them but the dry stubbly upland reaching to the undulating horizon. Above it hung a pale-yellow, pitiless sky.

At last the sun dropped low and the sky turned to a light green. Madame called a halt near a rock-choked ravine where they could at least relieve themselves in privacy. Madame led Martha off and when the two returned, the old woman's face was grim.

"She is hemorrhaging again," she told Claude. "Shall we stop here? Or shall we make again a litter from one of the cots?"

They decided upon the litter. While there was still daylight, they wanted to press on. Just a few kilometers farther and they would reach the brow of the hills.

They continued on as they had done earlier in the journey, one at each corner of the modified cot. Martha lay with her lower lip clamped between her teeth, twin spots of bright rose on her pale cheeks the badges of her mortification. But she said nothing. The heavens turned to ultramarine and then to indigo, and the first stars appeared. However, they could still see well enough to walk and so they kept going—higher and higher, closer to the notch.

At last they were at the summit. The four of them set the litter down and helped Martha to her feet so that she could stand with them and look northward. About five kilometers away and just slightly below the pass where they rested was a long rampart. It reared up from the countryside behind the line of hills in a virtual jungle of spiny maquis scrub and curved away on both sides in a great arc that eventually melted into the northern horizon. The bare lip of the crater gleamed pale in the dusk.

Felice took Richard's head between her hands and kissed his mouth, standing on tiptoe. "You did it! Right on the nose, buccaneer-baby—you did it!"

"Well, I'll be damned," said the pirate.

"I don't think so." Claude's broad Slavic face wore an exultant smile.

"Oh, Madame. The Ship's Grave!" Martha's voice broke; her eyes spilled tears. "And now—now—"

"Now we will make camp," the Frenchwoman said practically. "We will rest well and recover our strength. For to-morrow, our work really begins."

The skeleton had been laid out in state in the belly compartment of the fifth flyer that they inspected.

Unlike the other craft, which had had their hatches closed, the sepulchre of Lugonn was wide open to the elements. For long years the mammals, birds, and insects of the maquis had made free with it. Felice had, as always, been first up the boarding ladder of the exotic craft. Her cry of triumph at finally finding the remains of the Tanu hero was followed by a tortured howl that raised the neck hairs of the other four members of the expedition.

"He has no torc! *No torc!*"

"Angélique!" Claude shouted in alarm. "Reach out and stop her doing any harm in there!"

"No . . . torc!" A shriek of diabolic rage echoed within the flying machine and there was a thudding sound. As Richard and Claude clambered up the ladder, Madame Guderian stood beneath the shadow of the metal bird's wings, eyes wide, mouth drawn into a strained grimace, both hands clenching the gold at her throat. It took every bit of her coercive metafunction to restrain Felice, to force the girl to back off from the instinctive urge to destroy the source of her frustration. Driven by furious disappointment, the athlete's latencies trembled on the brink of operancy. The old woman felt her own ultrasenses being tested to the limit. She held, pressed the volcanic thing that writhed within her mind-grasp while at the same time her telepathic voice cried: Wait! Wait! We will all search! Wait!

Felice let go her opposition so abruptly that Madame Guderian staggered backward and collapsed into Martha's frail arms.

"Okay!" Richard shouted from above. "I popped her one. She's out cold!"

"But did she ruin anything?" Martha called, easing Madame to the dusty ground.

"Doesn't look like it," Richard replied. "Get up here, Marty, and have a look at this frigger yourself. Like something out of a goddam fairy tale."

Felice lay in a heap on the far side of the flyer's belly compartment, which measured about three by six. She had managed to seize Lugonn's helmeted skull and dash it to the deck in a paroxysm of rage; but the interior of the ancient craft was so deep in dust, animal droppings, and other organic trash that the relic had come to no harm. Claude knelt down and restored the head to its place. Resting on his haunches, he studied the legend laid out before him.

Lugonn's armor, heavily jeweled and filmed with gold, was now so dimmed and crusted that his bones could barely be discerned within the articulated plates and scales of glass. The crystalline helmet, crested with a peculiar heraldic animal, was a baroque and incredibly intricate piece of craftsmanship—so gorgeous, even coated with grime, that one forgot that it had a utilitarian purpose: to deflect photonic beams. Carefully, Claude raised the visor and unfastened the overlapping gorget plates and hinged cheekpieces. Lugonn's skull was mutilated by a great wound, perfectly circular and a full twelve centimeters in diameter, which drilled through the naso-orbital region and obliterated the rear of the skull opposite the eyes.

"So that much of the tale was true," the old man murmured.

He could not resist inspecting the skull for nonhuman attributes. Most of the differences were subtle; but the Tanu had possessed only thirty teeth and he had been notably longheaded as well as massively built. Aside from anomalies in the positions of some cranial sutures and the mental foramina, the Tanu skull seemed almost completely humanoid.

Richard stared about the compartment, noting the adobe wasp nests that crusted almost every surface, the shredded bulkhead insulation, the exposed ceram framework of once luxurious cabin appointments. There was even a beehive in one of the open forward lockers.

"Well, we don't have a prayer of getting this sucker off the ground. We'll have to go back to one of the others."

Martha was digging in the mounds of rubbish on the left side of the skeleton in armor. She gave a satisfied cry. "Look here! Help me get it out of the garbage, Richard!"

"The Spear!" He helped her push away the moldy mess. In a few minutes the two of them had laid bare a slender instrument nearly a meter taller than the great skeleton, connected by a cable near the butt to a large jeweled box that had once been worn at Lugonn's waist. The box straps had now disintegrated, but the glassy surface of the box and the Spear itself did not seem to be corroded.

Martha wiped hands on hips. "That's it, all right. Zapper and powerpack. Careful of those studs there on the upper arm-rest, lovie. Even cruddled up as they are, they might still trigger the thing."

"But how," Claude marveled softly, "how did he ever pull the trigger on himself?"

"Oh, for chrissake," said Richard. "Forget that and help us get the thing outside before our little butch Goldilocks wakes up and goes bonkers again."

"I am awake," Felice said. She massaged the point of her chin, where a bruise was forming. "I'm sorry about that. I won't lose control again. And no hard feelings for the love-tap, Captain Blood."

Madame Guderian came slowly up the boarding ladder. Her eyes rested briefly on the glass-armored skeleton and then passed to Felice. "Ah, ma petite. What are we going to do with you?" A sadness weighted her voice.

The girl got up and displayed a gamine grin. "I didn't really spoil anything with my little temper fit. And I guarantee it won't happen again. Let's forget it." She prowled about the flyer interior, kicking at the trash. "I expect the torc's around here someplace. Maybe some critter carried it away from the skeleton and stashed it in another part of the ship."

Claude took up the pack and started to descend the ladder while Richard and Martha followed with the still-tethered weapon, not wanting to risk disconnecting the cable.

Madame regarded the skeleton. "So here you lie, Shining Lugonn. Dead before the adventures of your exiled people had scarcely begun. Your tomb defiled by the little vermin of Earth— and now by us." Shaking her head, she turned to descend the ladder. Felice sprang to the old woman's assistance.

"I've a wonderful idea, Madame! I won't be any use working on the aircraft or the Spear. So when I'm not needed for camp chores or hunting, I'll come back here and clean this place out. I'll make it all neat again and polish his golden glass armor— and when we leave, we can close the hatch."

"Yes." Madame Guderian nodded. "It would be a fitting work."

"I'd have to move all this rubbish anyway," Felice added, "when I was looking for the torc. It must be here somewhere. No Tanu or Firvulag would have dared to take it. I know I'll find it."

Standing on the ground now, Madame looked up at Felice— so small, so winsome, so dangerous. "Perhaps you will. But if you don't? What then?"

The girl was calm. "Why, then I'll have to hold King Yeochee to his promise, that's all."

Richard said, "How about getting down here and giving us a hand, kid? You can moon around with your ancient astronaut all you want when we get a work camp set up. Come on— we're going to move back to the last bird in line. See if you can carry this whole Spear rig by yourself, will you? She's an awkward bitch for a two-man tote."

Felice dropped lightly down from the belly hatch, hoisted the eighty-kilo powerpack in one arm, and stood while Claude and Richard balanced the long weapon on her opposite shoulder.

"I can manage," she said. "But God knows how that old boy ever used this gadget in a running fight. He must have been quite a lad! Just wait till I find his torc."

Claude and Madame looked at each other wordlessly for a moment, then helped Martha gather up their things. They began the half-kilometer trudge back along the crater lip to the Number Four Aircraft.

Madame said, "We have been fortunate, finding the Spear so readily. But there is another factor that may preclude an attack on Finiah this year."

"And that is?" Claude inquired.

"The matter of who shall fly the ancient craft during the actual firefight." She looked back over her shoulder at Richard, who was supporting Martha. "You will recall that he agreed merely to fly the machine back to the Vosges. If we must train another pilot for the battle—"

Martha had heard every word, of course. She turned to the ex-spacer with a stricken expression.

Richard gave a terse little bark of laughter. "Madame, you prove it again and again. You're no mind reader. D'you really think I'd miss our little war?"

Martha clutched him tighter and whispered something to

him. Madame said nothing—but as she turned away from them to resume the march along the rim trail, she smiled.

After a while, Richard said, "There's something else we ought to think about, though. Wouldn't it be best if we concentrate first on fixing up the flyer and hold off on the Spear until we get back home? Today is September twenty-second and the little King said that the Truce begins on October first. We're cutting things *damn* short if the spooks are gonna need a week to mobilize. And what about getting your people ready, Madame? And working out the tactics for the iron weapons— if they got 'em? Seems to me, the faster we get outa here, the more time'll be left for organizing. And back at your village, Martha can get proper medical care from Amerie. Maybe somebody like Khalid Khan could help out with the Spear repairs, too."

It was Martha who demurred. "Don't forget we've got to *test* the Spear. We must get it working, then install it in the aircraft somehow and try it out from the air. If this zapper is as powerful as I think it is, every Tanu with a microgram of farsense would be able to detect its atmospherics if we shot it off within a hundred kloms of the Vosges."

"God, yes," Richard said, crestfallen. "I forgot about that."

Madame said, "We must do the best we can to put both flyer and Spear in working order before we leave this place. As for those back home, we will trust Peo to have everything in readiness. He knows every nuance of the plan against Finiah. If we have even one day remaining before the start of the Truce, we will still mount the attack."

"Well, let's get hopping then!" Felice said. She broke into a brisk trot, leaving the rest of them straggling far behind. They saw her wave at them briefly from the vicinity of the neighboring flyer, then vanish down the outside of the crater into the scrub. When they reached the great metal bird, they found the Spear placed carefully in the shadow of its wings. Beside it, scratched in the dust, was a message: GONE HUNTING.

"For what?" Richard wondered cynically. Then he and Martha climbed up the ladder of the undisturbed aircraft, opened the simple hatch lock, and disappeared inside.

8

IT TOOK THREE DAYS TO GET THE FLYER AIRBORNE.

Richard had known that these exotic craft were gravo-magnetic the moment he had looked inside the first specimen. The flight deck and passenger compartment of the thirty-meter bird had simple easyseats—not acceleration couches. Ergo, "inertialess" drive, the universal propulsion system for aircraft and subluminal spaceships of the Galactic Milieu, which enabled almost instantaneous acceleration or deceleration in apparent defiance of gravity-inertia. The odds seemed good that the exotics had tapped the key forces of the universe in much the same "cablecar" fashion as the engineers of the Milieu. Richard and Martha had warily opened one of the sixteen power-modules of what they hoped was the flux-tap generator, using the flyer's own tools. They found to their relief that the liquid within *was* water. No matter that the thingummies generating the rho-field reticula were concentric spheres within spheres instead of the stacked crystalline blades of the analogous Milieu device; the principle, and the basic operation, had to be the same. When the generator was fueled with good old aqua pura, this exotic bird would very likely go.

Claude rigged up a still and tended the ever-bubbling de-camole pot while Richard and Martha traced the control circuitry and made sense of the quaint in-ship environmental system, which was capable of recharging itself once they got a little water into the powerplant. After one day of fiddling with the alien controls, Richard felt confident enough to carry on with the analysis alone, letting Martha transfer her efforts to the Spear. For safety's sake, on the off chance that the flyer might blow during one of the groundside tests, they transferred the work camp to a shelf-like clearing in the maquis several kloms downslope from the aircraft, where a spring gushed through the crater wall.

On the evening of the third day, as they gathered around the campfire, Richard announced that the ancient machine was ready for its first flight test.

"I've scraped most of the lichen off and dug all the bird and bug nests out of the vents. She seems damn near good as new, for all her thousand years of squatting."

"How about the controls?" Claude asked. "Are you sure you've figured them out?"

"I turned off all the audibles, of course, since they weren't speaking my language. But the flight instrumentation is mostly graphic, so I can get by. Can't read the altimeter, but there's a terrain-clearance and position monitor that shows a nice picture—and eyeballs were made before digitals anyhow. Numeralwise, the engine cluster is hopeless. But each reader is equipped with three idiot lights—cyan, amber, and violet for go, watch-it, and bye-bye. So I should do all right there, too. My big problem is going to be the wings. Putting wings on a gravo-mag aircraft is weird! They must be a cultural relic. Maybe these folks just *enjoyed* gliding!"

"Richard," Martha said breathlessly. "Take me with you tomorrow."

"Oh, Marty-babe—" he began.

Madame intervened. "You may not, Martha. There is a risk, even though Richard is confident."

"She's right," he said, taking Martha's hand. It was cold in spite of the warm evening. The firelight threw cruel shadows on the engineer's sunken cheeks and eyes. "Once I've checked her out—then we'll go for a spin. Promise. We can't let anything happen to you, kid . . . Who'd put that damn zapper back together?"

Martha moved closer to Richard and stared into the fire. "I think the Spear will work. The powerpack shows half-charge, which is really remarkable, and none of the tiny little internal components of the lance unit seems to have been damaged. The main difficulties have been cleaning out the barrel and replacing the chewed-up cable. It was lucky that the flyer had some stuff that seemed compatible. I'll need one more day to finish and reassemble, and then we can test it and begin practice."

"How powerful do you think it will be?" Claude asked.

"There are several options, I believe," the engineer said. "The lowest setting is the only one lacking a caplock, so they might have used that for their ritual fighting. I'd guess its power to be within lightpistol range. The four higher settings under the lock must have been for special purposes. At the top of the line, we could have us a portable photon cannon."

Richard whistled.

"I don't think we dare test it on max unless we want to risk draining the powerpack," Martha said.

"No chance of recharging?" asked Richard.

"I can't get the pack open," she admitted. "It takes a special tool and I was afraid to kark around with it. We'll just have to save our big zap for the war."

The gnarled branches of the maquis burned with a pungent resinous odor, snapping and throwing sparks that had to be smacked out. Only a few insects buzzed in the drought-stricken jungle. When it was full dark, the remaining birds and small mammals in the area would come to the spring to drink, and Felice and her bow would glean food for tomorrow.

The blonde athlete said, "I have Lugonn's place nearly clean now. There's no sign of the torc."

Only Martha was able to voice a regret.

Richard said, "Should be plenty of the things lying around if we make good at Finiah. You won't have to beg the little King for one. Just reach down on the battlefield and grab."

"Yes," sighed Felice.

"How have you planned to mount the Spear, Richard?" Claude asked. "I can't see how we could rig up a pilot-operated trigger given the short time we have left."

"There's really only one way to handle it. I hover the aircraft and somebody else shoots the zapper out the open belly hatch.

I suppose we could trust one of Chief Burke's bullyboys to—"

The old man said softly, "Every exopaleontologist knows how to handle big zappers. How do you think we cut the rocks to get the specimens out? I've carved up a few cliffs in my day—even moved a mountain now and then to get at some really choice fossils."

Richard chortled. "I'll be damned. Okay, you're hired. We'll be a two-man crew."

"Three," said Madame. "You will need me to provide a metapsychic screen for the flyer."

"Angélique!" Claude protested.

"There is no helping it," she said. "Vel:?yn and his Flying Hunt would see you hovering there."

"You're not going!" the old man stormed. "Not a chance! We'll come over Finiah at high altitude, then drop down vertically and take 'em by surprise."

"You won't." Madame was implacable. "They will detect you hovering. We can only hope to surprise them if I conceal the vessel metapsychically during its initial maneuvers. I must go. There is nothing more to be said."

Claude got to his feet and stood hulking over her. "The hell there isn't. Do you think I'd let you fly into the middle of a fire-fight? Richard and I have one chance in a hundred of getting out with whole skins. We're going to need every grain of concentration to do the job and then get out. We can't afford to be worrying about you."

"Tchah! Worry about yourself. Radoteur! Who is the leader of this group? C'est moi! Whose plan is it, de toute façon, for the entire attack? Mine! I go!"

"I won't let you, you stubborn old she-gorf!"

"Try to stop me, senile Yankee-Polack vieillard!"

"Shrew!"

"Salaud!"

"Ball-breaking old bat!"

"Espèce de con!"

"Shut the hell up!" thundered Felice. "The pair of you are as bad as Richard and Martha!"

The pirate grinned and Martha turned away, nibbling her lip to suppress laughter. Claude's face blackened with embarrassed rage, and Madame was stunned out of her hauteur.

Richard said, "You two listen to me. The rho-field of the

fluxtapper will prevent any of the Tanu Hunt from touching the aircraft. It'll probably deflect lances and arrows and whatnot, too. So all we really have to worry about is mental attack. For countering that, our only hope is Madame's metapsychic screen."

"If I had a torc . . ." Felice muttered.

Richard asked Madame, "How long can you hold out against a bunch of 'em?"

"I don't know," she admitted. "We will be disguised as vapor until we direct the first blasts at the city wall. Then they will know an enemy is there, and many minds will be brought to bear upon my little screen. It is certain to be pierced. We can hope that this will happen after we strike at the mine. Once this is done, we can flee at top speed."

"How fast can Velteyn's outfit fly, anyhow?" Richard asked.

"Not much faster than a chaliko at full gallop. The mind of this Tanu champion is able to levitate his own steed and those of twenty-one warriors through PK, psychokinesis. There is only one other who is capable of such a feat and that is Nodonn, the Tanu Battlemaster and Lord of Goriah in Brittany. He can support fifty. There are others who can levitate themselves individually and a few who can carry one or two other persons. But none is strong enough to support many riders save these two."

"If I had a torc!" Felice wailed. "Oh, wait! Just wait!"

"We'll leave 'em in the dust," Richard scoffed. "A couple of zaps to take out the wall on either end of the city, maybe one for the Tanu quarter to demoralize the opposition, then the big zorch for the mine. If that Spear really is a portable cannon, we can melt the place to a slag heap."

"And come home safely ourselves," Claude said, staring into the fire. "While our friends fight it out on the ground."

"Velteyn will try to defend his realm," Madame warned them. "He is exceptionally strong in creativity, and there are strong coercers in his company. We will be in great danger. Nevertheless, we will go. And we will succeed." There was a loud snap and an ember flew through the air like a meteor, landing in front of the old woman. She got up and stamped upon it with great thoroughness. "I believe it is time for us to retire. We will want to get up early for Richard's test flight."

Martha rose from her place and said to Richard, "Come for a little walk with me before we settle down "

"Conserve your strength, chérie," Madame warned.

"We'll just go a little way," Richard said.

He slipped one arm around the engineer's waist to steady her. They went out of the pool of firelight, leaving the others still talking, and walked to the far side of the camp clearing. Only stars illumined the tangle of maquis, for the new moon had gone down. Above them was the overgrown slope with its narrow trail leading to the crater rim. They could not see the refurbished flyer, but they knew it was up there waiting.

"We've been happy, Richard. Can you figure it? A pair like us."

"Two of a kind, Marty. I love you, babe. I never thought it could happen."

"All you needed was a good old-fashioned sexy girl."

"Fool," he said, and kissed her eyes and cold lips.

"When it's all over, do you think we could come back?"

"Back?" he repeated stupidly.

"After the Finiah attack. You know we're going to have to teach others how to fly the machine and maintain it so that they can carry out the other two phases of Madame's plan. But you and I needn't worry about those. We'll have paid our dues. We can have them fly us back here, and then—"

She turned to him and he held her. Too frail and racked by cramps and hemorrhage to endure any further intercourse, she had still insisted upon consoling him. They spent every night in each other's arms, sharing one of the decamole huts.

"Don't worry, Marty. Amerie will know how to fix you up for good. We'll come back here somehow and get a flyer just for ourselves and find us a good place to live. No more Tanu, no more Firvulag or Howlers, no more people at all. Just you and me. We'll find a place. I promise."

"I love you, Richard," she said. "Whatever happens, we've had this."

In the morning, Richard waved goodbye to the others and went up to where the bird stood. It still looked pretty scruffy in spite of the scraping, but he'd soon fix that.

He settled into the pilot's seat and patted the console in the manner of an equestrian soothing a skittish mount. "Oh, you beautiful, droop-snoot, swivel-winged thing. You wouldn't badass the old Cap'n, would you? Course not. We're gonna fly today!"

He lit her up and went through the checklist. A familiar sweet hum of rho-field generators came to him there on the flight deck and he grinned at the thought of microscopic thermo-nuclear reactions hitting nicely on all sixteen, ready to weave a net of subtle forces that would free the metal bird from gravity's domain. All of the engine idiot lights gleamed cyan-for-go. Keeping her firmly latched to Earth, he fed juice to the external web. The bird's scabby skin glowed faintly purplish in the bright sunshine as the rho-field reticula clothed it lightly. All the crud that he'd been unable to remove sizzled away, leaving the surface a smooth cerametal black—just what you'd expect for an aircraft with orbiter capability.

He cut in the environmental system. Oh, yeah—little bluey-green lights telling him that no matter where the ship carried him, his life would be duly supported. Ease off on the field-web runup. Crank back the wings to minimum area until he got used to them. No use risking overcontrol on his maiden flight, wallowing all over the sky like a shot duck. Gotta do this with class, Cap'n Voorhees.

Okay . . . okay . . . and *upsy* daisy!

Straight up and dead level and hold at squiggle-hundred meters according to the readout on the indecipherable altimeter display. Call it 400. Down below, the Ries crater was a great blue cup with little spread-winged birds strung around its western lip, politely waiting for permission to drink. There were forty-two of them, with one missing where a section of the rim had collapsed in a landslide, and one empty slot for his own aircraft.

Damn those wings when the wind caught him at hover! He'd better move. Slowly . . . slowly . . . bank and zoom. Figure eight and vertical five and stop and start and swoop and glide and pendulum arc and—hot damn, he was doing it!

Down on the ground, four small figures were jumping up and down. He did a creditable imitation of a wing-waggle to let them know that he had seen them, then laughed out loud.

"And now, my friends, fare thee well, for I must leave you!

We'll save the touch-and-goes for later. Now the old Cap'n is gonna give himself a few lessons in how to drive this here flying machine!"

He slammed the rho-field into full inertialess web, stuck a burr under her tail, and took off vertically for the ionosphere.

9

WOULD VOLUNTEERS COME?

As the days of September dwindled and the preparations at Hidden Springs were completed, this question was paramount among the followers of Madame Guderian. Her influence—and indeed, the benefits of her Firvulag-Human Entente—did not extend much farther than the tiny settlements of the Vosges and the upper Saône wilderness, a region that would be able to muster not more than 100 fighters. Communication with other Lowlife enclaves was minimal because of the danger from Hunts, gray-torc patrols, Howlers, and even nominal subjects of King Yeochee who were reluctant to give up their human-harassing ways.

Before leaving High Vrazel, Madame and Chief Burke had discussed this problem with the shrewd old Battlemaster of the shape-changers, Pallol One-Eye. It had been agreed that the only hope for recruitment of more distant humans lay in the hands of the Firvulag. Only the illusion-spinners could hope to shepherd groups of Lowlife fighters from the far villages to Hidden Springs in time for the Finiah attack; but it was clearly going to take more than a simple call to arms to budge skeptical humans from their swamps or mountain fastnesses—especially if the invitation to the war was delivered by the little exotics.

Madame and Peo had recorded joint appeals on AV letter-plaques and left these with Pallol; however, the Firvulag messengers would have to establish credibility for the enterprise, and to this end a certain stratagem proposed by the Battlemaster was ultimately agreed upon. At the same time that Madame's expedition left High Vrazel for the Ship's Grave, picked Firvulag teams, including King Yeochee's most tactful Grand Combat referees, had set out on journeys to the south and west to summon all of the Lowlives in the known world to participate in the strike against Finiah.

The Little People went laden with gifts. And it happened that lonely huddles of cabins tucked away among the volcanoes of the Massif Central were visited at night by benevolent pixies. Bags of finely milled flour, flagons of honey and wine, luscious cheeses, candy, and other rare dainties appeared mysteriously on human doorsteps. Missing geese and sheep unaccountably found their way back to their pens; even lost children were guided home safely by butterflies or will-o'-the-wisps. On the mountain slopes of the Jura, a poorly tanned deerskin pegged to the wall of a Lowlife hovel might disappear, and in its place the delighted inhabitants would discover well-cobbled boots, fur jerkins, and butter-soft suede garments. Deep in the swamps of the Paris basin, the fen-dwellers would find that rotting punts were exchanged for new decamole dinghies stolen from Tanu caravans; great nets of waterfowl were left where outlaw human hunters could find them; plass containers of Survival Unit insect-repellent, more precious than rubies, appeared on the windowsills of the stilt-legged marshland houses where no passerby could possibly have reached. In scores of Lowlife settlements, humans were amazed when odd jobs were done by invisible helpers. Sick folks were nursed by elfin women who vanished with the dawn; broken things were mended; empty larders were filled; and always there were gifts, gifts, gifts.

Finally, when the Firvulag messengers ventured to appear en clair and present the awesome plan of Madame Guderian (who was, of course, known to all of the fugitives), the Lowlives were at least willing to listen. Fewer numbers agreed to respond to the appeal for fighting volunteers, for there were many emotional burn-outs and physical cripples among them, as well as a sizable percentage who cared only for their own

skins. But the bolder, the healthier, and the more idealistic
spirits were fired by the notion of striking a blow against the
hated Tanu, while others agreed to participate in the attacks
when the subject of loot was delicately broached. So the Firvulag emissaries began to return, and those at Hidden Springs
exulted because they brought with them a total of nearly 400
men and women recruited from places as far away as Bordeaux
and Albion and the tidal estuaries of the Anversian Sea. These
were welcomed in the name of Free Humanity, briefly trained,
and equipped with weapons of bronze and vitredur. None of
the newcomers, it had been agreed, would be told of the iron
until the very day of the attack; and only the most competent
of the volunteer fighters would be armed with the precious
metal.

The secret staging area in the Rhineland bottoms opposite
Finiah was in a state of full readiness by the middle of the last
week in September. Lowlife warriors and a contingent of crack
Firvulag stalwarts were poised to cross the river in sailing
lighters belonging to the Little People. The boats would be
disguised as blobs of mist for as long as the most powerful
Tanu did not consciously seek to penetrate them. Another Firvulag force was concealed farther upstream in a second camp,
primed to strike at the second break in the city wall, which
was supposed to be made roughly opposite to the main thrust.

Tactics and targets had been decided upon and logistic preparations were complete. All that remained was the arrival of
the Spear of Lugonn.

"The Hunt flies tonight, Peopeo Moxmox Burke."

It was very dark in the cypress swamp, for the moon was
down. Chief Burke focused his night ocular on the activity
across the river. The high, narrow-necked peninsula upon which
the Tanu city perched was, as always, ablaze with an incredible
display of colored lights. The much sharper vision of Pallol
One-Eye had already discerned what the Chief now viewed
through his scope: a glowing procession rising from the topmost
parapet of House Velteyn. It spiraled slowly toward the zenith,
the figures of the Flying Hunt distinct even at a distance of
two kilometers. Tanu riders whose faceted armor flashed every
color of the rainbow mounted upward on great white chalikos.
The legs of the steeds pumped in unison as they galloped into

the airy darkness. There were twenty-one knights in the train and another who forged ahead to lead them, his billowing cloak streaming back like a comet tail of vaporous silver. From the distance came the faint notes of a horn.

"They're turning south, Battlemaster," said Burke.

Beside him, Pallol One-Eye nodded, he who had seen 600 winters upon his own far world and more than a thousand orbits of the nearly seasonless Pliocene Earth. He was taller than the Native American and nearly twice as massive, and he moved as fluidly as the black man-sized otters of the riverine jungle whose form, three times magnified, he often adopted. His right eye was a great orb of gold with an iris colored deep red; the left eye was hidden by a jeweled black leather patch. It was whispered that when he lifted that patch in battle, his glance was more deadly than a thunderbolt—which is to say that the destructive potential of his right-brain's creativity was second to none among the Firvulag and the Tanu. But Pallol One-Eye was an irascible ancient now, and he had not deigned to soil his obsidian armor at a Grand Combat for more than twenty years, unable to bear his people's annual humiliation. He had found Madame Guderian's plan against Finiah to be mildly amusing, and he had acquiesced in a Firvulag rôle when both Yeochee and the young champion, Sharn-Mes, decided to support the Lowlives. Pallol declared that he would lend the effort his good advice, and he had done so; but it was unthinkable that he should participate personally in what he termed "Madame's little war." More likely than not, the assault would be indefinitely postponed when the lady failed to return with the vital metériel. And even if she did bring back the Spear, how could mere humans hope to wield it effectively against the bravos of Velteyn? It was a weapon for a hero! And it was all too true that heroes were in short supply among this effete younger generation.

"Now they're crossing the Rhine—heading west into the Belfort Gap," Burke said. "No doubt planning to convoy the last caravan from Castle Gateway before the Truce."

Still Pallol only nodded.

"The Tanu can't have any inkling of our preparations, Battlemaster. We've carried it off without a flaw."

This time Pallol laughed, a grating sound like the chafing of lava blocks. "Finiah shines bright across the river, Leader of Humans. Save your self-congratulation for its snuffing. Madame Guderian will not return and all of this scheming against the torc-wearing Foe will be for nothing."

"Perhaps so, Battlemaster. But even if we don't fight, we've accomplished things that we never dared dream of before. Nearly five hundred Lowlives have been brought together in a common cause. Only a month ago, that would have been an idle fancy. We were scattered and afraid, mostly without hope. But not any more. We know that there *is* a chance that we can break the Tanu domination of humanity. If you Firvulag help us, we can do it sooner. But even if you break off the alliance, even if Madame fails to bring back the Spear this year, we'll return to fight again. After this, humans will never go back to the old timid ways. Others of us will go searching for the Ship's Grave if Madame fails. We'll find that ancient weapon and make it work again—something your people could never do. And if the Spear is gone—if we never find it—we'll use other weapons until the Tanu slavers are defeated."

"You mean you will use the blood-metal," said Pallol.

Chief Burke was silent for a dozen seconds. "You know about the iron."

"The senses of the torc-wearers may be so puny that they require machines to sniff the deadly metal out—but not those of the Firvulag! Your camp reeks of iron."

"We will not use it against our friends. Unless you plan betrayal, you have nothing to fear. The Firvulag are our allies, our brothers-in-arms."

"The Tanu Foe are our true brothers and yet we are fated to contend with them eternally. Could it be otherwise between Firvulag and humanity? This Earth is destined to belong to you, and you know it. I do not believe that humanity will be satisfied in allowing us to share. You will never call us brothers. You will call us interlopers and try to destroy us."

"I can speak only for myself," Burke said, "since my tribe, the Wallawalla, becomes extinct upon my death. But there will be no treachery by human against friendly Firvulag as long as I am the general of the Lowlives, Pallol One-Eye. I swear it on my blood—which is as red as your own. As for our never being brothers... this is a matter I'm still pondering. There are many different degrees of kinship."

"So thought our Ship," sighed the old champion. "It brought

us here." He tilted his huge head toward the sky. "But why? With so many other yellow stars in the universe, so many possible planets—why here, with you? The Ship was instructed to find the *best*."

"Perhaps," said Peopeo Moxmox Burke, "the Ship took a longer view than you."

All day long the birds of prey had circled.

They rode thermals above the Vosges woodland in a neat stack, holding most of the time at altitudes appropriate to their species. Lowest was a wheeling flock of small swallow-tailed kites; above them soared a mated pair of bronze buzzards; the fire-backed eagles came next, and then a lone lammergeier vulture, mightiest of the bone crackers. Most lofty of all the circling birds was the one that had initiated the day-long vigil and attracted all of the others. On motionless wings, it orbited at a height so remote that it was barely visible to watchers on the ground.

Sister Amerie watched the birds through the sparse branches of a stone pine, her tawny cat resting in her arms. "'Wherever the body is, there will the eagles be gathered together.'"

"You quote the Christian scriptures," said Old Man Kawai, who was shading his eyes with a tremulous hand. "Do you think the birds are truly clairvoyant? Or do they only hope, as we do? It is late—so late!"

"Calm yourself, Kawai-san. If they get here tonight, there'll be a whole twenty-four-hour day for the Firvulag to join in the assault. That should be enough. Even if our allies withdraw at sunrise day after tomorrow, we can still win with the help of the iron."

The ancient continued to fret. "What can be keeping Madame? It was such a slim hope. And such hard work we have done here in expectation that the hope would be fulfilled!"

Amerie stroked the cat. "If they arrive before dawn tomorrow, the attack can still proceed according to the second alternative."

"*If* they arrive. Have you considered the navigation problem? Richard must come first to Hidden Springs. But how will he find it? Surely these tiny mountain valleys must look much alike from the air, and ours is hidden because of the Hunt. Richard will not be able to distinguish our canyon, even in daylight, if he approaches at a high altitude. And he does not dare to fly a low-level search, lest the enemy observe him."

Amerie was patient. "Madame will conceal the ship mentally, of course. Calm yourself! This constant worry is bad for your health. Here—pet the cat. It's very soothing. When you stroke the fur, you generate negative ions."

"Ah so desu ka?"

"We can hope that the flyer would be equipped with an infrared scanner for night flight, just as our eggs of the twenty-second century were. Even with all of our fighters gone, there are still more than thirty warm bodies here in Hidden Springs. Richard will sniff us out."

Old Man Kawai sucked in his breath. A horrible thought of a new sort crossed his mind. "The metapsychic concealment of the aircraft! If its volume is more than about ten cubic meters, Madame will be unable to render it invisible! She will only be able to disguise it somehow and hope that the Tanu do not concentrate their perceptive powers too closely upon it. What if the machine is so large that her faculties are insufficient to invest it with a plausible illusion?"

"She'll think of something."

"It is a great danger," he moaned. The little cat gave him a long-suffering glance as his hand essayed a few nervous pats. "The Flying Hunt could even discover the aircraft while it rests here! All that is needed is for Velteyn to descend for a close look at my poor camouflage nets. They are pathetic things."

"Adequate for night concealment. Velteyn has no infrared, thank God. And he almost never comes this far west nowadays. Stop your fussing! You'll stew yourself into cardiac arrest. Where's your jiriki?"

"I am a foolish, useless old man. I would not be here in the first place if I were able to rule myself through Zen . . . The nets—if they fail their purpose, the fault will be my own! The dishonor!"

Amerie gave an exasperated sigh. She thrust the cat at Kawai. "Take Deej into Madame's cottage and give her some leftover fish. Then hold her on your lap and close your eyes and pet her and think of all those lovely Tri-D's that used to come rolling off your assembly lines in Osaka."

The old man giggled. "A substitute for counting sheep? Yatte mimasu! It may serve to tranquilize me, at that. As you say, there is still time to mount the attack . . . Come, kitty. You will share your valued negative ions with me."

He pottered off, but turned after a few steps to say with a sly grin, "However, one incongruity remains. Forgive my flaunting of the obsolete technology, Amerie-san—but even the lowliest electronicist knows that it is quite impossible for negative ions to be cat-ions!"

"You get out of here, Old Man!"

Tittering, he disappeared into the cottage.

Amerie walked down the canyon past the huts and cottages, nodding and waving to the few people who, like herself, could not resist watching the sky while they waited and prayed. The last of the able-bodied men and women had marched off under Uwe's command three days ago, and the deadline for the optimal two-day assault had come and gone. But there was still time to execute the one-day attack. At dawn tomorrow, it could be that human beings would unite together for the first time on this Exile world to challenge their oppressors.

Oh, Lord, let it happen. Let Madame and the rest of them get here in time!

It was getting cooler as the sun descended, and soon the thermals—those buoyant upwellings of heated air—would fade away completely and the soaring raptors would have to come back to earth. Amerie came to her secret place beneath a low but open-armed juniper and lay down, face to the sky, to pray. It had been such a wonderful month! Her arm had healed quickly and the people . . . ah, Lord, what a fool she had been to think of becoming a hermit. Hidden Springs folk and the other Lowlife outlaws of the region had needed her as a physician and counselor and friend. Among them she had done the work she had been trained for. And what had become of the burnt-out case with the self-punishing compulsion to flee into a haven of solitary penitence? Here she could even pray her Divine Office, contemplate in the forest stillness; but when the people needed her, she was there ready to help. And they were there to help. And he was there in the midst of them. It was her dream fulfilled, even in its changing—only now the language that she prayed in was a living one.

I put my trust in the Lord! How dare you say
to my soul:

fly away like a sparrow to the mountains,
for lo—the wicked draw their bows and aim
　　their arrows,
to shoot in the dark the upright of heart;
and they have destroyed the good things
while just people let the evil happen!

But the Lord tests both the just and the wicked;
he hates the lawless ones, the evil-lovers.
Flaming coals and burning sulfur will he pour
　　on them!
A fiery whirlwind shall be their punishment . . .

The lammergeier flew away to his lair among the high crags and the eagles descended to their roosting trees an hour before the sun set. The kites scattered, having to satisfy their appetites with insects, and even the buzzards disappeared at last, perhaps wondering what had prompted all of them to waste time waiting in the futile hope of sharing the great newcomer's prey. He alone still circled aloof in the high air, completely disdainful of the vanished thermals.

And Amerie watched him, lying under the tree, watched that distant speck endlessly wheeling that had drawn all the others and then disappointed them. That bird with motionless wings.

Heart pounding, she scrambled to her feet and ran back up the canyon to rout everybody out.

"Stand back! Don't touch it until the field's off, for God's sake!" someone shouted.

The huge thing, still glowing faintly purple, seemed to fill the whole lower end of the canyon. It had descended just as soon as the sky was fully dark, subsonic by a whisker but still shoving a hurricane blast ahead of it that tore bundles of thatch from the roofs and sent poor old Peppino's geese tumbling like leaves in a gale. It had come to a dead halt no more than two meters above the highest trees, its drooping nose, gull wings, and fan-shaped tail bathed in a crawling network of nearly ultravisible fire. Old Man Kawai, composed now and curtly efficient, had sent several youngsters for wet sacks and ordered the rest of the villagers to stand by the rolls of camouflage netting.

They all watched, awe-struck as the hovering thing folded its great wings back against its thirty-meter fuselage and delicately felt its way down. It nosed obliquely between a pair of tall firs where there was a minimum of undergrowth, hesitated just barely off the ground, and then let its long legs settle. There was a loud hiss; a few bushes began to smolder and wisps of smoke curled up around the footpads. The skin of the bird went dead black.

Then the people, who had stood as though paralyzed, broke into wild cheers. A number sobbed aloud as they rushed to follow Kawai's orders, beating out the little fires that had been set by the rho-field and hustling to set up poles and guy-ropes for the nets.

The belly hatch opened and the ladder extruded. Slowly, Madame Guderian came down.

Amerie said, "Welcome home."

"We have brought it," said Madame.

"Everything is ready. Exactly as your plan specified."

Lame Miz Cheryl-Ann, who was two hundred and three and nearly blind, seized one of Madame's hands and kissed it; but the Frenchwoman hardly seemed to notice. Up above, a word of warning came from within the flyer. A litter was lowered from the hatch by Felice and Richard.

Madame said only, "You are needed, ma Soeur." And then she turned and walked as in a daze toward her cottage. Amerie knelt down and took one of Martha's bony wrists. Richard stood there in his ruffled pirate shirt and battered buckskins with fists clenched and tears running down his dirty sun-scorched cheeks.

"She wouldn't let us come back until the Spear was working right. And now she's damn near bled to death. Help her, Amerie."

"Follow me," said the nun, and they rushed off after Madame, carrying the litter with them, leaving Claude to see that the big black bird of prey was safely bedded down for the night.

10

BEFORE DAWN THERE WAS THE BATTLE MASS, AND THEN MAdame exerted her farspeech power to transmit an enigmatic "we come" to Pallol, insuring that the invasion fleet would be poised to exploit the bombardment of Finiah's wall. Sunrise was less than an hour away and if past performance was any criterion, Lord Velteyn and the members of his Flying Hunt would be back at their stronghold after the night's foray.

Claude strode along nearly at the end of the procession heading for the flyer and wished Felice would shut up. She was once again attired in her black leather ring-hockey armor, which had been beautifully refurbished by Old Man Kawai's artisans, and she was wild with anxiety lest she would miss the war.

"I wouldn't take up any room. And I *swear* I won't say a word during the flight! Claude, you've got to let me come with you. I *can't* wait for you to come back after the strike. What if you don't make it?"

"If Velteyn nails the flyer, you'd go down with us."

"But if you get away, you could put me down right outside Finiah! Say, at the breach in the wall on the land side of the

396

peninsula. I could go in with the Firvulag on the second wave! Please, Claude!"

"The Hunt could have spotted us by then. Landing could be suicide—and that's not what this fight is all about. Not for me and Madame Guderian, at any rate. Finiah is just the beginning of our war. And Richard's got Martha to live for now."

Up ahead, villagers were pulling the nets from the black bird. A few candles gleamed in the mist where Amerie was blessing the aircraft.

Felice said, "I could help you with the Spear, Claude. You know what an awkward big bastard it is. I could be useful." She clutched at the old man's bush shirt and he stopped abruptly and took her by the shoulders.

"Listen to me, girl! Richard is all strung up. He hasn't slept for more than twenty-four hours and he's half-crazy with worry because of Martha. Even with the transfusions, Amerie gives her less than a fifty-fifty chance. And now Richard has to fly a combat mission in an exotic aircraft with a couple of old crocks and the future of Pliocene humanity riding on his tail! You know how he feels about you. Having you in the flyer during the mission could be the last straw. You say that you'd keep out of the way. But *I* know you couldn't help asserting yourself once the heat was on. So you're staying here, and that's that. We'll do our job and then run for home—and with luck we'll leave Velteyn completely mystified about where we've gone. We'll come back and pick you up. I promise you that if we make it, we'll get you to the battle not more than an hour or so after the main assault begins."

"Claude . . . Claude . . . ." Her face peered through the T-shaped opening in the black hoplite helmet, panic and fury and some other more alien emotion at war with reason. Claude waited, praying that she wouldn't jump him. But he was so steeped in fatigue that he almost didn't give a damn whether or not she knocked him cold and forced the others to let her take his place. It was in her mind, all right; but she also knew that he was by far the better shot.

"Oh, *Claude*." The blazing brown eyes closed. Tears poured behind the cheekpieces of her helmet and the green plumes flattened as she wrenched away from him and fled back toward Madame's cottage.

He let out a long breath. "Be ready when we get back!" he called, and then hurried to where the others were waiting.

The great bird crept furtively from its hiding place. When it was in the clear, it mounted the predawn sky like a violet spark going up an invisible chimney, attaining an altitude of 5000 meters in a thunderclap inertialess surge. Angélique Guderian stood beside Richard, clutching the back of his seat with one hand and her golden torc with the other. Richard had changed into his old spacer's coverall.

"You got us hidden, Madame?" he asked.

"Yes," she replied faintly. She had said hardly a word since their safe return.

"Claude! You ready?"

"Whenever you give the word, son."

"We're on our way!"

A split second later, the belly hatch rolled smoothly back. They hovered motionless above a patch of microscopic jewels, shaped roughly like a tadpole with its tail joined to the eastern bank of the Rhine.

"Why, it's on the Kaiserstuhl," Claude said to himself.

The patch grew, spread, its star-cluster blur clarifying into twinkling lights as the flyer dropped—subsonically this time— and stopped dead in the air about 200 meters above the highest eminence of the Tanu city.

"Give it to 'em," said Richard.

Claude horsed the great Spear into position and took a bead on the line of fiery dots marking the Rhineside wall. Somewhere in the graying mists of the river waited a flotilla of Firvulag boats loaded with human and exotic troops.

Keep her depressed, old man! You don't want to boil your own folks out of the water!

He raised the caplock and swung it aside. There—right there. Touch the second stud.

A thin bar of green-white lanced without sound.

Down below, a tiny orange flower bloomed—but the line of dots atop the wall remained unbroken.

"Shit!" Richard exclaimed. "You missed! Elevate!"

Calmly, Claude took aim once again, pressed the stud. This time there was no burst of orange fire, only a dull-red glow.

Perhaps a dozen of the rampart lamps were swallowed by it.

"Hee-*yow*! Gotcha!" screeched the pirate. "Making a one-eighty, Claudsie-boy! Ready for the back door!"

The flyer spun on its vertical axis and Claude found himself aiming at a point near the base of the shining tadpole's tail. He fired and missed...high. He fired and missed again...low.

"Jesus, hurry up!" urged Richard.

The third time, the blast struck the wall squarely, melting it at a point where the causeway of the peninsular neck met the extinct volcanic mass of the Kaiserstuhl proper.

Madame moaned. Claude felt dragon talons grip his guts.

"Are they coming?" Richard demanded. "Hang on, Madame! Sweet Christ, Claude—get on with it! Never mind zapping the Tanu buildings. Go for the mine!"

The old man wrestled the Spear around, a sudden burst of sweat greasing his hands and making them slip on the weapon's glassy butt. His used-up muscles trembled as he tried to bring the weapon to bear upon the small blue constellation that marked the mine workings. He could not depress the Spear sufficiently to bring the target into range. "Quick, Richard! Take her a couple of hundred meters south!"

"Aye," growled the pirate. The flyer changed position in the twinkle of an eye. "That better?"

"Wait...yes! I've just about got her. Have to do this right the first time. Only have one blast at full zap—"

"Merde alors," Madame whispered.

The old woman staggered away from Richard to crash against the right bulkhead. Fists pressed to her temples, she began to scream. Claude had never heard such a sound from a human throat, such a distillation of anguish, horror, and despair.

At the same moment, something flashed past the flight deck port. It glowed neon-red and was shaped like a mounted knight.

"Oh, God," said Richard flatly. Madame's screams cut off and she fell senseless to the deck.

"How many?" asked Claude. He tried to get a grip on himself, tried to steady the heavy Spear on target, prayed that his damned old body wouldn't betray him at this last extremity. They had almost done it! Almost...

"I make it twenty-two." Richard's calm voice seemed to come from a considerable distance. "The whole Round Table circling us like Sioux around a wagon train. All scarlet except the leader, and I'd put his spectral class somewhere in the B0 range—look out!"

One of the figures, the blue-white one, soared down and took a position immediately below the flyer. He drew his glassy sword and thrust it upward. Three Roman-candle globes of ball lightning left the tip and soared rather slowly toward the open belly hatch. Claude dodged, pulling the Spear out of the way, and the things flew into the aircraft, where they began caroming off the panels and decking, hissing and emitting a fearful smell of ozone.

"Shoot!" shrieked Richard. "For God's sake, shoot!"

Claude took one deep breath. He said, "Steady, son," and aimed, depressing the fifth stud of the Spear of Lugonn just as the little blue lights centered themselves in the weapon's sight.

An emerald bar jabbed once at the spangled earth. Where it struck, the rock went white, yellow, orange, roiling crimson like a flame-armed starfish. Claude fell sideways and the Spear clanged to the deck. The belly hatch started to close.

Lightning balls bounced and crackled. The old men felt one of them strike him in the back, rolling up his spine from buttocks to the base of his neck, burning all the way. The interior of the flyer was filled with smoke and a smell of burnt flesh and fabric. There were sounds, too, Claude discovered, as he studied the scene from afar—a sizzle as the remaining two energy balls sought their targets, curses and then a thin scream from Richard, a whimpering sob from Angélique as she tried to creep toward him over the smeared deck, someone breathing in and out in harsh, rhythmic persistence.

"Get it away from me!" a frantic voice cried. "I can't see to land! Ah—dammit, *no!*"

A jarring crash and a slow tilt to one side. Claude felt a breeze (amazing the way it seared his back) and the hatch opened. A peculiarly angled surface of grassy ground, gray and dim in the first light of morning. Richard sobbing and cursing. Angélique making no sound. Voices shouting. Heads poking up through the hatch—again at that odd angle. Wails from that silly youngster, Old Man Kawai. Amerie's familiar tones: "Go easy. Go easy." Felice spitting obscenities when somebody said she was going to get her armor all messed up.

"Put him over my shoulder. I can carry him. Stop your

wiggling, Claude. Silly old fart! Now I'm going to have to walk all the way to the war."

He laughed. Poor Felice. And then his face was upside down among her green skirts and he was jouncing up and down and he screamed. But after a little bit the movement stopped, and they laid him on his stomach and something touched his temple, making the pain and the rest of it grow muzzy.

He said, "Angélique? Richard?"

Unseen, Amerie replied, "They'll recover. You all will. You did it, Claude. Sleep now."

Well, how about that? And for a moment he saw the fiery starfish again, but with crimson and gold limbs expanding, branching out among the hapless helpless firefly patterns of Finiah streets in the instant before the hatch of the flyer slammed shut. How about that . . . and if the lava kept oozing out of the old Kaiserstuhl volcano for even a little while, it was going to be a long, long time before they mined any more barium in the regions around there.

"Don't worry about it, Claude," Felice said.

And so he stopped.

11

HALF-DOZING IN THE DEAD HOUR BEFORE DAWN, MOE MARSHAK and the other human troops on duty in Finiah had mistaken the first blast of the photon weapon for a lightning stroke. The thin green beam had lanced out of the stars, barely missing the Rhineside wall that the gray-torc garrison manned and demolishing an adjacent mess hall inside the compound. Marshak was still gaping at the flames consuming the wreckage when Claude's second shot struck the Number Ten bastion squarely, breaching the fortification not a dozen meters from Marshak's station. Great blocks of granite flew in all directions and the air boiled with smoke and dust. Oil tubs that held the watch fires spilled in the concussion and sent blazing rivulets racing down the cracked walkway.

When Marshak was able to get a grip on himself, he rushed to look through one of the embrasures. There in the fog-blurred waters below were the boats.

"Alert!" he shouted aloud; and then his mind sent the alarm on the declamatory mode, amplified by his gray torc.

MARSHAK: Invasion viaRhine! Wallbreach StationTen!
CAPTAL WANG: Howthehellmany be there Moe? Howmany boats?
MARSHAK: Wholefuckin river FULL!! Eightyhundred who can

402

count damnfog bastards everywhere Firvulagboats but let-
mesee *yes*! LOWLIVES TOO! Repeat Lowlives + Foe
invading. Landings! Rocks swarming damnfuckers penetrating breach estimate hole maybeninemeters max.

CORNET FORMBY: All troopsofwatch to StationTen. General
alert RhineGarrison to arms. Dutyobservers scan/report.
Defensiveunits   to   wallstations . . . CANCELCANCEL-
CANCEL! Defensiveunits to garrisoncompound! Invader
penetration compound!

COMMANDER SEABORG: Lord Velteyn. Alert. Firvulag and human invasion force has penetrated the city fortifications at
breached Number Ten Station. Countering.

LORD VELTEYN OF FINIAH: Kinfolk arise and defend! Flyers to
saddle! Na bardito! Na bardito taynel o pogekône!

Chief Burke and Uwe Guldenzopf led the mob of Vosges
Lowlives and outland volunteers up the steep rampart and across
the tumbled rubble of the breakthrough. Vitredur arrows and
crossbow bolts rained down from the battlements, but until the
defenders could redeploy at ground level, the invaders would
have a brief advantage. As bad luck would have it, the breach
was within the grounds of the principal Finiah garrison. In
addition to the confusion caused by the mess hall conflagration,
which was spreading to adjoining structures, a chaliko stable
had been broken open by falling debris and numbers of the
great animals were loose.

Three soldiers ran from the guardhouse at the compound
gate. "Take 'em," yelled Burke, and howling desperados fell
upon the little force and cut it to pieces. "Out of here! Into the
city streets! And get this gate off the hinges!"

Troops were pouring from the barracks, some with their
armor only half strapped on. Free-for-all clashes erupted everywhere in the murk as invaders scrambled through the broken
wall while the human minions of the Tanu strove to press them
back. The irregulars trying to unhinge the gates were attacked
and overwhelmed, and soldiers swung the heavy metal grille
shut, locking it.

"We're sealed in!" Chief Burke jumped on top of an over-
turned feed wagon. His face and upper torso were painted in

the old war patterns and he had the wing feather of a fire-eagle thrust into his knotted, iron-colored hair. "Hit the sonsabitches! Get that gate back open! This way!"

He saw Uwe fall beneath a sword-wielding gray-torc and leaped down, brandishing the wide tomahawk Khalid Khan had forged for him. The blade sank into the soldier's crested bronze kettle-helmet as though it were made of pasteboard. Burke hauled the body off to find Guldenzopf lying flat on his back, one hand clutching his breast and an expression of agony on his bearded face.

Burke knelt. "Did he nail you, bubi?"

Struggling up on one elbow, Uwe groped inside his buckskin shirt. Bone-colored bits gleamed in the lurid light. "Only my second-best meerschaum, dammit."

The Lowlives remained hemmed in, unable to break out of the area in the immediate vicinity of the garrison complex. Those crowded in the breach were pressed both by the defenders and by their own comrades coming up from the beachhead. A wail of panic arose. Some invaders fell and were trampled. A garrison officer wearing a silver torc and full blue-glass body armor directed a unit of halberdiers that advanced upon the stalled irregulars. Sweeping crystal blades mowed down the packed, shrieking throng.

And then the monsters came to the rescue.

High on the steep slope of rubble shone the wavering nightmare shape of a three-meter albino scorpion—the illusionary aspect of Sharn the Younger, general of the Firvulag. From the minds of the exotics came a mighty wave of terror and dread that overloaded the telepathic circuits of the gray torcs and sent their wearers writhing into madness. Sharn himself could smite the enemy at a range of nearly twenty-five meters; others of his advancing company might not have auras so formidable, but woe to the Foe who fell into their clutches!

Hideous trolls, spectres, manticores, shambling dark presences seized the soldiers in spine-crunching embraces, sank fangs into unarmored throats, even rent men limb from limb. Some of the exotics were capable of flinging bolts of psychoenergy that broiled troops in their bronze cuirasses like lobsters in the shell. Other Firvulag harassed with sheets of astral fire, streams of nauseating ichor, or brain-crippling illusions. The great hero Nukalavee the Skinless, wearing his aspect of a flayed centaur with blazing eyes, howled until enemy soldiers fell writhing to the ground, eardrums split and minds reduced to near-idiocy. Another champion, Bles Four-Fang, invaded the headquarters of the garrison, caught up the silver commander named Seaborg, and appeared to devour him—armor and all—while the dying officer calmly broadcast final telepathic orders to his subordinates directing the troops now making a last stand at the gate opening into the inner city. Seaborg's aides blunted their vitredur weapons against Bles's scaly illusory hide, only to be eaten alive in turn for their temerity. By the time the monster had downed the last adjutant, the headquarters building was afire and the invasion force swarmed in Finiah's streets. So Bles withdrew in good order, picking his teeth with a silver spur. His appetite had only been whetted, and the morning was young.

Vanda-Jo was still overseeing the last wave of volunteers embarking from the staging area when Lord Velteyn and the Flying Hunt took to the air. Shouts of fear came from the crowd as they saw the glowing knights mount up from the city across the water. One man yelled, "The bleeders're coming for *us*!" and jumped into the Rhine. A fiasco was averted when Vanda-Jo tongue-lashed the outlanders for their cowardice, pointing out that the Hunt was circling high above Finiah, bent on some more urgent objective.

"So into the boats and quit farting around!" she bellowed. "You don't have to be afraid of Velteyn and his flying circus any more! Did you forget our secret weapon? We've got iron! You can kill Tanu now—even easier than you can kill those traitor human torcers that do their dirty work!"

Eyeballs rolled anxiously in the half-light. The Firvulag skipper in the two-masted shallop nearest Vanda-Jo glowered in dwarfish impatience. "Hurry it up, spiritless earthworms, or we'll sail to the war without you!"

Suddenly a column of emerald light stabbed down from apparently empty sky in the axis of the wheeling Hunt, striking a low knoll within the city across the Rhine. Orange-and-white fire fountained up at the point of impact, and seconds later, the sound of a rolling detonation sped over the river.

"The mine!" somebody shouted. "The barium mine's blowing up! God—it looks like a volcano erupting in there!"

As if the bombardment had been a signal, another gout of flame belched up from the farthest reaches of Finiah, back where the peninsula narrowed to a small neck connecting the city to the mainland.

"See that?" Vanda-Jo was exultant. "The second wave of spooks have landed opposite our main beachhead! That female Firvulag general named Ayfa is attacking from the Black Forest side. *Now* will you shitheads get a move on?"

The men and women on the dock hoisted their iron-tipped spears into the air and yelled. They pounded down the spindly gangplanks into the waiting boats so eagerly that the small craft rocked and nearly swamped.

On the other side of the Rhine, flames made a scarlet track on the dark water. The faerie lamps of blue and green and silver and gold that had outlined the splendid Tanu City of Lights began to wink out.

Velteyn, Lord of Finiah, pulled up the reins of his chaliko and hung in midair, shining like a magnesium flare. The nobles of his Flying Hunt, eighteen male and three female knights, all glowing red, drew in their mounts to surround him. His thought-thrust was nearly incoherent with frustration and rage:

Gone! The flying machine is gone . . . and yet my lightnings surely penetrated its belly. Kamilda! Send your farsense seeking it.

. . . It recedes from us Exalted Lord. Ah Tana at a speed unprecedented! It drops behind the brow of the Vosges and beyond my perception. My Lord if I ascend to a great height—

Stay Kamilda! More urgent threats confront us below. Look all of you! Look what the Foe has done! O the shame the pain the havoc! Down to the ground all of you. Each to command a mounted party of chivalry in defense of our City of Lights! Na bardito!

Na bardito taynel o pogekône!

The fighting moved steadily inland from the Rhineside break. Two hours after dawn, the western front was strung through the gardens of the pleasure dome, on the very outskirts of the Tanu quarter.

Moe Marshak had reloaded his quiver several times from

those of fallen comrades. He had wrenched the gaudy crest of his bronze helmet early on and then rolled in filth to camouflage the shine of his cuirass. Unlike certain of his luckless fellows, he had deduced quickly that the Firvulag would be able to detect the telepathic communication, and so he made no attempt to contact his officers for orders. Maintaining a quiet mind, he went his lone way, keeping out of monster range as he skulked Finiah's byways, potting Lowlives with cool economy while dodging hysterical ramas and noncombatants. Marshak had already taken out at least fifteen of the enemy, plus two bare-neck civilians he had caught looting a gray-torc corpse of its weaponry.

Now Marshak slipped into the long porch that formed the perimeter of the pleasure dome. Hearing one of the distinctive Lowlife yodels, he concealed himself behind thick ornamental shrubs and nocked one of the serrated war arrows in his compound bow.

In the next instant an unexpected diversion came from within the building. The stained glass from a pair of French doors perhaps five meters away from the soldier shivered to atoms from the impact of some heavy object. There were screams and a rumbling sound. Long hands all adorned with rings fumbled with the jammed catch. Other hands shook the bent framework. The angle was such that Marshak could not clearly see the people trapped inside, but their cries of terror and dismay reached both his mind and ears, as did the uncanny warbling of the thing pursuing them.

"Help! The door's stuck! And it's coming!"

Help us! *Helphelphelp us!* HELP US!

The blanket coercive summons of a Tanu overlord clutched at Marshak's consciousness. His gray torc compelled obedience. Forsaking his hiding place, he ran to the door. On the other side, pressed against the mangled copper fretwork, were three female denizens of the pleasure dome and their tall Tanu client, whose handsome violet and gold robes proclaimed him an official of the Farsensor Guild. He presumably lacked the coercive or psychokinetic potential to fend off the apparition that was now poised in an inner doorway, ready to strike.

The Firvulag wore the appearance of a gigantic hellgrammite, a larval water insect with clashing razor-sharp mandibles.

The brute's head was nearly a meter wide, while the long segmented body, slick with some stinking secretion, seemed to fill the corridor behind it.

"Tana be thanked!" cried the Tanu. "Quickly, my man! Aim for its neck!"

Marshak raised his bow, shifted position to avoid the struggling women, and let fly. The glass-tipped shaft sank for most of its length between chitinous plates behind the creature's scissoring jaws. Marshak heard the Firvulag utter a telepathic bellow. Without hurrying, he drew two more arrows and sent them into the hellgrammite's glittering orange eyes. The insectile form wavered, became insubstantial . . . and then the awful thing was gone and a dwarf in black obsidian armor lay dead on the floor, throat and eyesockets transfixed.

The soldier used his vitredur short sword to pry open the ruined latch. Pleasure surges engendered by the grateful exotic throbbed along his pelvic nerves in the sweet, familiar reward. When the nobleman and his disheveled companions were freed, Marshak saluted, right fist pressed against his heart.

"I am at your service, Exalted Lord."

But the farsensor dithered. "Where are we to *go*? The route to House Velteyn is cut off!" His abstracted expression showed that he was scanning about with his mind's eye.

"Well, we can't go back inside," said the most petite of the pleasure dome inmates, a black woman of exquisite contours and sharp voice. "The damn muffers are crawling out of the woodwork!"

"Oh, Lord Koliteyr," squealed a teary blonde. "Save us!"

"Silence!" commanded the Tanu. "I'm attempting to—but no one will respond to my summons!"

The third woman, thin and empty-eyed, her provocative attire half torn from her bony shoulders, sank down on the pavement and began to laugh.

Koliteyr gasped. "The dome is surrounded! I call—but Lord Velteyn's knights are in the thick of battle! . . . . Hah! The invaders cringe and retreat before the coercive might of Tanu chivalry! The Goddess be thanked, there are many more powerful than I!"

A great jarring thump came from inside the pleasure dome. Distant cries became louder. More glass broke and a rhythmic pounding began.

"They're coming! The monsters are coming!" Once again, the blonde burst into hysterical tears.

"Soldier, you must lead us—" The Tanu scowled, shook his head as if to clear it. "Lead us to the Northern Watergate! There may be a boat—"

But it was too late. Across the garden, trampling flowerbeds and hurtling through the bushes came a force of twenty-odd Lowlife humans led by a half-naked red man of heroic stature.

Marshak's hand poised above his quiver, frozen. Most of the invaders had compound bows as good as his own held at the ready.

"Surrender!" shouted Peopeo Moxmox Burke. "Amnesty for all humans who yield freely to us!"

"Stand back!" cried the Tanu farsensor. "I—I will burn out your minds! Strike you mad!"

Chief Burke smiled, and his painted face, framed in straggling gray hair, was more menacing than the Firvulag phantasm had ever been. The exotic man knew that his bluff was useless, just as he knew there would be no amnesty for those of his race.

Commanding Marshak to defend to the death, Koliteyr tried to flee. The iron tomahawk spun and split the exotic's skull before he had taken two steps.

Marshak relaxed. He let the bow and arrow fall to the flagstones and watched the approaching Lowlives in numb silence.

The strategic importance of the barium mine had been made clear to Sharn-Mes at the Lowlife briefing session prior to the invasion. Humiliation of the hated Foe, the Firvulag general was made to understand, must take second place to the complete destruction of the mine and its trained personnel. It was vital to Madame Guderian's grand design that the supply of the precious element, indispensable in the manufacture of torcs, be cut off.

Shortly before noon, when Sharn was taking a breather with Bles and Nukalavee in a makeshift command post well supplied with liberated beer, a Firvulag scout arrived with important news. The Mighty Ayfa and her Warrior Ogresses had made a successful thrust from the eastern breach and now invested the sector around the mine workings. They had ascertained that molten rock, triggered by Claude's blast from the Spear, had plugged the mine entrance, buried the main refinery and the complex that housed the human and rama workers, and flowed some distance into the streets of the upper city before congealing. However, the mine administration building with its store of purified barium stood firm. The place was completely surrounded by black and steaming lava—now sheathed in a clinkery skin of cooled rock except where cracks revealed the red glowing interior. There were still Tanu engineers in the building, and among them a creator of the first rank. Ayfa and her force had gleaned this intelligence when an unexpected bolt of psychoenergy zapped one of the investigating ogresses to a cinder, narrowly missing the Dreadful Skathe. She of the snaggle-teeth and dripping talons had spun a psychic shield over the survivors that sufficed for a disorderly retreat out of mindbolt range.

"And so the Mighty Ayfa," the scout concluded, "now awaits your suggestions, Great Captain."

Bles uttered a hoarse bleat of ironic laughter. He tipped half a barrelful of bear into his maw. "Ahh—let's go help the poor little ladies save their honor."

"Honor, my left testicle!" hissed Nukalavee. "If the Foeman's creative force strained the defense of Skathe, then he is a worthy antagonist to any of us at a distance. We would expend our mind-power simply in the erection of screens and have little left for offense."

"Even the approach is fraught with danger," Sharn noted. "The crust of cooling lava, as this scout says, is fragile and may crack under the weight of a stalwart. You know our minds cannot penetrate dense rock deeply enough to strengthen the crust. And to fall through into the magma below is certain doom." He addressed himself to the dwarf messenger. "Pliktharn—how broad is the expanse of lava that would have to be crossed?"

"At least fivescore giant steps, Great Captain." Pliktharn's face became eager. "The crust would bear *my* weight easily!"

"You could send me and Nukalavee to mind-guard him, along with Ayfa and Skathe," Bles suggested. "The four of us working together have the range."

"And what happens when our brave gnomish brother reaches the mine building?" Nukalavee sneered. "How will he attack the Foe *through our own mental screens*? Four-Fang, you've worn that reptile suit so long that your wits are shrinking to fit your illusory brainpan!"

"The Great Captain Ayfa," cautioned the scout, "has perceived that the Tanu engineers are calling upon Lord Velteyn for help."

Sharn smacked a great hand onto the table. "Té's tonsils! And when he responds, he'll airlift them out, barium and all! We can't take that chance. I hate like hell to resort to Lowlife tactics—but there's only one way to handle this."

"Easy does it, lads!" Ayfa called out. "Don't lose your nerve now that you're almost there."

Homi, the little Singhalese iron-smelter, clutched Pliktharn's neck tighter. The lava crust bent as the Firvulag approached the lee of the mine building. There the flow was thicker and had held heat longer, which meant that the skin of cooled rock might crack and let them fall through to the magma at any moment.

About the incongruous pick-a-back figures shone a radiant hemisphere, the mental screen conjured by the joint power of Ayfa, Skathe, Bles, and Nukalavee. The four heroes, and most of the force of Warrior Ogresses, were concealed behind the sturdy walls of burntout townhouses, well back from the edge of the lava flow and a full 200 meters from the mine headquarters. Energy bolts flung by the trapped Tanu creator blazed from an upper-storey window, disintegrating into a web of lightnings as they were neutralized by the screen's potential. At length, Pliktharn and Homi reached a lower window and climbed inside. Ayfa, who was strong in the farsensing talent, observed what happened next.

"The three Foemen descend to the lower chamber, armed with vitredur geology picks! One of them has considerable coercive power. He's trying to force Pliktharn to lower the screen—but that won't work, of course. The mindbolt flinger now gathers his strength for one mighty thrust at point-blank range! He uses steady pressure rather than abrupt projection. Our screen wavers! It goes spectral—into the blue! The yellow! It will surely fail—! But now the Lowlife has his arbalest ready and aims at the creator. Ah! The missile of blood-metal passes through our weakening shield as through a curtain of rain! The Foeman falls! A second shot, and a third—and all of the Foe are downed!"

The four heroes leapt and the Warrior Ogresses whooped with joy in the triumph. All of their minds, even at the great distance, felt the death-flare of first one Tanu mind, then a second.

But the mindbolt flinger was strong even in the dying. Amplified, agonized, his thought thundered in the aether:

The Goddess will avenge us. Accursed through the world's age be those who resort to the blood-metal. A bloody tide will overwhelm them.

An instant later, his soul flickered out.

The Lowlife named Homi, having retrieved the three iron quarrels for reuse in his crossbow, appeared at the window and waved. Then he and Pliktharn set to work chipping and prying at the heavy limestone windowsill until its mortar gave way. The stone smashed the thin lava crust beneath the window, sending up a gush of smoke and flame. Before the fresh rift could heal, the human and the Firvulag were seen to toss certain small containers into the pit of molten rock, after which they climbed out a different window and made their way carefully back the way they had come.

A young girl clad in shiny black jogged in apparent tirelessness along the narrow Vosges jungle trail. Shadows grew deeper and a cool wind swept from the heights into the ravine that the footpath followed. Treefrogs were beginning their evening songs. Before long, the predators would awaken. After nightfall, there would be so many hostile creatures on the prowl that Felice would be unable to fend them off with her coercive power. She would be forced to bivouac and wait until dawn.

"And I'll be too late! The Truce starts at sunup and the war in Finiah will be over!"

How far had she come? Perhaps two-thirds of the 106 kilometers that lay between Hidden Springs and the western bank of the Rhine? She had lost so much time this morning before getting started, and the sun went down at eighteen hundred hours . . .

"Damn Richard! Damn him for getting hurt!"

She should have insisted on going with them in the flyer. She could have done *something*. Helped old Claude steady the Spear. Assisted Madame's mental defense. Even deflected the

globe of ball lightning that had blinded Richard in one eye and
caused him to crash the flyer.

"Damn him! Damn him! The Firvulag will quit fighting
when the Truce begins and our people will have to withdraw.
I'll be too late to get my golden torc! Too late!"

She splashed heedlessly across a small stream. Ravens, disturbed in their feeding upon some otter's leftovers, rose
squawking into the vinehung forest canopy. A hyena mocked
her, its mad laugh echoing from the ravine wall.

Too late.

The glass carnyx of a fighting Tanu woman sounded the
charge. Armored chalikos, bearing knights who coruscated each
in a different jewel-color, galloped down the corpse-strewn
boulevard toward the barricade where the contingent of Lowlives was making its stand.

"Na bardito! Na bardito!"

There were no Firvulag allies at hand to dampen the mental
assault. Images of brain-searing intensity whipped and stabbed
at the humans. The night was fraught with unspeakable menace
and pain. Plunging exotics in their sparkling harness seemed
to be coming from all directions, gorgeous and invulnerable.
The humans loosed iron-tipped arrows, but skillful psychokinetics among the Tanu turned most of the fusillade aside, while
the rest clattered harmlessly against the plates of the glass
armor.

"The spooks! Where are the spooks?" howled a despairing
Lowlife. A moment later one of the knights crashed upon him,
impaling his claw-torn body with a sapphire lance.

Of the sixty-three human beings who had made their stand
in that street, only five escaped into the narrow alleys where
hanging awnings, lines of washing, and crowded ranks of rubbish carts abandoned by panicked rama sanitary workers made
it impossible for the mounted Tanu to follow.

A mammoth bonfire was ablaze in the Central Plaza of
Finiah. Jubilant phantoms in a hundred hideous guises capered
around it, waving battle standards festooned with strings of
freshly psychogilded skulls.

Khalid Khan protested. "They're wasting time, Mighty

Sharn! Our people are taking a terrible beating when they meet the Tanu unsupported by Firvulag mind-cover. Even the mounted gray-torcs can cut right through our infantry. We've got to work together! And we must find some way to counter those chaliko-riders."

The great luminous scorpion bent over the turbaned Pakistani, multicolored organs within its translucent body throbbing to the rhythm of the exotic war chant.

"It has been many years since we had cause for celebration." The unhuman voice clanged in Khalid's brain. "For too long the Foe has lurked safely behind stout city walls, despising us. You do not understand how it has been with us—the humiliation our race has suffered, draining our valor and driving even the most powerful of us to hopeless inaction. But behold! Look upon the trophy skulls, and these only a small proportion of the total!"

"And how many of them belong to Tanu? Dammit, Sharn—most of the enemy casualties have been among the torced and bareneck humans! The noncombatant Tanu are all holed up in House Velteyn where we can't reach them, and only a handful of their mounted knights have been killed!"

"The Tanu chivalry"—the eerie voice hesitated and then made reluctant admission—"presents a formidable challenge to us. Armored war steeds with their minds held in thrall by the riders are not intimidated by our horrific illusions or shape-shifting. We must contend against them physically, and not all of the Firvulag company are of heroic frame. Our obsidian weapons—our swords, halberds, chain-flails, and throwing spears—are not often effective against the chaliko cavalry in the Grand Combat. And the same obtains in this battle."

"You need a change in tactics. There are ways for foot soldiers to put down charging horsemen." The metalsmith's teeth glittered in a brief grin. "My ancestors, Pathan hillmen, knew how!"

The response of the Firvulag general was cool. "Our battle customs are fixed by sacred tradition."

"No wonder you're losers! The Tanu weren't afraid to innovate, to take advantage of human science. Now you Firvulag have human allies on your side—and you stick one timid little toe into the battlefield and then mess about singing and dancing instead of going for the prize!"

"Beware lest I punish your insolence, Lowlife!" But the furious retort lacked conviction.

Khalid said softly, "Would you help *us* if we try a new tactic? Would you shield our minds while we try to knock those long-shanked bastards out of the saddle?"

"Yes . . . we would do that."

"Then pay close attention."

The monster scorpion metamorphosed into a handsome young ogre wearing a thoughtful scowl. After a few minutes the hobgoblins left off their madcap dancing, changed into gnomish warriors, and crowded in to listen.

Converting Sharn's lieutenants proved to be more difficult. Khalid had to engineer a demonstration. He rounded up ten volunteer Lowlives equipped with iron-tipped javelins and led them to the approaches of House Velteyn, where gray-torc and Tanu riders guarded the ultimate sanctuary. The paved avenue was lit by widely spaced torchères. No other invaders were to be seen because of the heavy concentration of defenders. Sharn and six of his Great Ones lurked in the shelter of a deserted mansion while Khalid deliberately led his squad of spearmen into plain sight of a patrolling gray troop.

The human leader, fully armored in blue glass, drew his vitredur blade and led a charge at the gallop down the cobblestone street. Instead of scattering, the Lowlives drew closely together, forming a tight phalanx bristling with four-meter spears.

The patrol swerved to the right at the last instant to avoid crashing into the iron porcupine, individual troopers reining up and wheeling their mounts about so that they could strike with longsword or battleaxe. They were plainly nonplussed, since almost all of the antagonists they had encountered thus far had emulated the Firvulag maneuver of tossing their pole-arms and then fleeing. This pack of innovators stood their ground until the animals were off balance in the turn, then stabbed deep into the unarmored bellies of the huge clawed beasts.

The hideous pain of disembowelment overrode the mind-control exerted by each rider upon his mount. Wounded chalikos stumbled and fell—or went careening off in a frenzy while the troopers hung on for their lives. Khalid's warriors pounced upon the unhorsed, dispatching them with spear or blade. Five

minutes after the initiation of the attack, every member of the
gray troop was either dead or had fled.

"But will it work on the Foe?" inquired Betularn of the
White Hand skeptically. With Pallol Battlemaster a nonparti-
cipant, he was the doyen of Firvulag stalwarts, and his opinion
counted for much.

Khalid grinned at the beetle-browed giant while one of his
comrades tried to staunch bleeding arm and leg wounds with
torn strips of the dead captal's cloak. "It will work on the Tanu,
providing we take them by surprise. We must assemble as many
Lowlives and Firvulag as possible for a massed thrust against
House Velteyn. Those of our people who don't have spears
will improvise them from bamboo awning poles. We needn't
use iron to gut the chalikos—but each human fighter will have
to have an iron weapon to use against downed Tanu riders.
And *your* people will have to be right in the thick of things
beside ours, handling mind-defense and getting in whatever
licks they can."

The venerable warrior shook his head slowly. He said to
Sharn, "This is contrary to our Way, as you know, Great
Captain. But the Foe has defied tradition for more than forty
years." The other five Great Ones growled assent. "We have
prayed to the Goddess for a chance to recoup our honor. And
so I say . . . let us essay the Lowlife tactic. And her will be
done."

Long after midnight, with smoke from the burning city
blotting out the stars and the untended torchères guttering low,
Lowlives and Little People gathered for the grand assault. In
a rare display of cooperative virtuosity, the best of the Firvulag
illusion-spinners wove a curtain of confusion to decieve the
farsensing Foe. The Tanu besieged within House Velteyn knew
that the enemy was up to something, but the nature of the
assault remained in doubt.

The Lord of Finiah himself, aloft once again with several
of his most trusted tacticians, made pass after pass at low
altitude, attempting to discern the plan of the invaders; but the
metapsychic shimmer was just dense enough to defeat his far-
sight. He beheld the Foe massed opposite the main portal of
his palace. There were to be no feints, no multipronged storm-
ing of the several entrances—that much was self-evident. With

typical Firvulag singlemindedness, Sharn seemed to be gambling everything on a last great frontal assault.

Velteyn sent the telepathic order on the intimate mode to each knight commander, and these in turn transmitted the Lord's words to their subordinates:

"To the forecourt! Let all the noble Tanu battle company, all of our adopted kinfolk of the gold and silver torc, all loyal and valiant gray soldiery attend! The Foemen gather for their final push. Let us destroy them body and soul! Na bardito! Forward, fighters of the Many-Colored Land!"

All aglow and exalted with battle ardor, the Tanu chivalry charged in a mass against the indistinct, dense groups of advancing Foe. The screens of confusion snapped off in the last seconds before contact to reveal the deadly pincushions of spears—many of them iron. With mental weapons all but neutralized by the Firvulag, the Tanu unshipped their pennoned lances and sent their mounts caracoling about the flanks of the hedgehog formations, alert for the expected rain of flung spears. And thus the treacherous novelty caught them completely unawares.

Velteyn, from his vantage point in the sky, could only farwatch aghast in those early minutes of slaughter. Then he dove his mount down, bombarding the enemy with all the psychoenergy he could muster. His mind and voice rallied the shattered ranks.

"Abandon your animals! Let all fight afoot! Creators and psychokinetics—raise shields for your fellows! Coercers—compel all grays and silvers to stand fast! Beware the blood-metal!"

The vast courtyard and immediate palace grounds were now a surging mass of bodies. Dull-red flashes signaled Firvulag and Tanu mindscreens interfacing in mutual collapse, after which the antagonists might fight hand to hand —with perfidious Lowlives attacking with the iron at every opportunity. The merest prick from the blood-metal meant death to a Tanu. Human gold-torcs, of course, could be wounded by the blood-metal, but not mortally poisoned. Velteyn's heart warmed at the bravery shown by the gold adoptees, many of whom seized iron weapons and turned them against the Firvulag.

Unfortunately, it was otherwise with the grays and silvers. The discipline of the torc faded in the face of diminished coercion from beleaguered Tanu overlords. The lower echelons among the human levies were unmanned by the demoralizing sight of Tanu knights falling to the iron. Both Firvulag and Lowlives seized the advantage and decimated the ranks of the terror-stricken troops.

For three hours, Velteyn hovered above the battlefield, invisible except to his own forces, directing the ultimate defense of his City of Lights. If they could only hold out until dawn—until the start of the Truce! But as the sky beyond the Black Forest massif paled, two powerful bodies of the Foe, spearheaded by Bles Four-Fang and Nukalavee, made a great press and reached the palace gate.

"Fall back!" Velteyn cried. "Stand and defend the portal!"

The jewel-armored knights did their utmost, wreaking a fearful toll of dwarfs and humanity as they laid about with their glowing two-handed swords. Sooner or later, however, an iron dart would find a chink of vulnerability at groin or armpit or the back of a knee—and another brave warrior would attain Tana's peace.

Velteyn groaned aloud, overwhelmed by sorrow and rage. The doors of his palace were giving way. There was no course left but the evacuation of the noncombatants via the roof with the help of the sadeyed little human PK adept, Sullivan-Tonn. By Tana's grace, the two of them might save most of the nearly 700 trapped Tanu civilians while the knights staved off the invading horde in the stronghold corridors.

If only he could die with them! But that release was forbidden to the humiliated Lord of Finiah. He was going to live on, and he was going to have to explain all of this to the King.

Peopeo Moxmox Burke slumped against the roof parapet of House Velteyn, letting fatigue and reaction sweep over him. Gert and Hansi and a few other Lowlives beat the bushes of the roof garden and searched the ornate penthouse for hidden Tanu. But they found only the discarded baggage the fugitives had left behind—spilled pouches of jewelry, heavy embroidered cloaks and fantastic headgear, broken flagons of perfume, a single ruby-glass gauntlet.

"No sign of 'em, Chief," Hansi said. "Ganz ausgeflogen. They've flown the coop."

"Get back downstairs, then," Burke ordered. "See that all

the rooms are checked out—and the dungeons, too. If you see Uwe or Black Denny, send them to me. We'll have to coordinate the looting."

"Check, Chief." The men clattered away down the broad marble stairway. Burke raised one leg of his buckskin trousers and kneaded the puckered flesh around the healing scar. With the anesthetic of battle fury worn off, it hurt like hell; and there was a long cut on his bare back and about forty-seven bruises and abrasions that were also making themselves known. But he was in pretty good shape, for all that. The rest of the Lowlife army should be so lucky.

One of the fleeing evacuees had left behind a basket with wine and breadrolls. Sighing, the Chief began to eat and drink. In the streets below, Firvulag were gathering their wounded and their dead and forming long processions on their way to the Rhine watergates. Bobbing lanterns out on the river marked the position of small boats that had already begun the withdrawal in anticipation of the dawn. Here and there among the burning ruins stubborn human loyalists continued a futile resistance. Madame Guderian had warned Burke that the humans living in Finiah might prove less than grateful for their liberation. She had been right, as usual. There were interesting times ahead, damn it.

Sighing once again, he finished the wine, gave his stiffening muscles a stretch, then took up a discarded Tanu shawl to wipe off his warpaint.

Moe Marshak shuffled a few steps forward in line.

"Quit crowding, big boy," snarled the lovely dark-skinned woman from the pleasure dome. The other two inmates had not worn gray torcs and were long gone, led away to the sailing lighters that shuttled back and forth between Finiah and the Vosges shore. The promise of amnesty was being kept by the Lowlives. But if you were a human torc wearer, there was a catch.

Marshak knew all about the activity of the drumhead tribunal, of course. He was in telepathic communion with all of the grays within his range who had not deliberately shut him out—as the black woman had. The Tanu, givers of delight and power, were gone. As they had wafted away to the east, they had reached out in poignant farewell, caressing and commis-

erating and sending a final warm surge flooding the neutral
networks of those who had been faithful, so that the gray-torc
prisoners had an illusion of celebration in place of grief and
despair. Even now, at the end, they could comfort one another.
The kinship remained. None of them was alone—except by
choice.

The black woman stood before the judges, her eyes bright.
When the question came, she almost screamed her reply: "Yes!
Yes, by God! Do it! Give me back my self again!"

Lowlife guards led her through a door to the right of the
tribunal. The rest of the grays, mourning the sister's defection
but respecting her choice, reached out one last time. She defied
them all, placed her head on the block. The great mallet smote
the iron chisel and there was overpowering pain. And silence.

Now Marshak's turn came. As a man dreaming, he told the
Lowlife judges his name, his former occupation in the Milieu,
the date of his passage through the time-portal. The oldest of
the judges pronounced the formula.

"Moe Marshak, as a wearer of the gray torc, you have been
held in bondage by an exotic race and compelled to abet the
enslavement of humanity. Your Tanu overlords have been defeated by the Alliance of Freeliving Humans and Firvulag. As
a prisoner of war, you are entitled to amnesty, provided that
you agree to the removal of the torc. If you do not agree, you
will be executed. Please make your choice."

He chose.

Every nerve in his body seemed to ignite. Kindred minds
sang as they gave consolation. Steadfast, he reaffirmed the
unity and a great rejoicing flare obliterated all other sensation:
the sight of the hollow-eyed judges, the pressure of hands that
gripped and dragged him away, the penetration of his heart by
the long blade, and the final cold embrace of the River Rhine.

Richard stood in the dim little log chapel in Hidden Springs
village where they had laid Martha out, seeing her in a swimming reddish haze even though Amerie had tried to reassure
him that his right eye was virtually undamaged.

He wasn't angry. Disappointed, that was all, because Marty
had promised to wait. Hadn't they planned it all together?
Hadn't they loved each other? It wasn't like her to let him
down after all they'd been through together.

Well, he would work something out.

Wincing a little from the bandaged burns, he gathered her into his arms. So light, so white. All gowned in white. He almost fell as he pushed the door open. No depth perception with only one eye. "Doesn't matter," he told her. "I can wear a patch like a real pirate. Just you hang on."

He went lurching toward the place where the flyer stood, covered by camouflage netting, one landing strut broken and one wing partly crushed by his prang-in. But a gravo-mag ship didn't need wings to fly. It was still in good enough shape to take both of them where they wanted to go.

Amerie spotted him just as he was lifting Martha inside. She came running, her nun's veil and robes billowing. "Richard! Stop!"

Oh, no you don't, he thought. I did what I promised. Now it's you guys who owe *me*.

With the flyer tilted, it was tricky to maneuver Martha. He made her comfortable and tossed the Spear out, powerpack and all. Maybe some wisehead would figure out how to recharge it some day. Then Madame Guderian could get another flyer and go zap all the rest of the Tanu cities and make Pliocene Earth safe for good old humanity.

"Just don't call me to drive the bus," he muttered. "I've got other plans."

"Richard!" the nun shouted again.

He waved to her from the flight deck port and sat down in the charred seat. Close hatch. Light up. Juice to the external web. Camouflage netting burning away. Oh-oh. Environmental system in the amber. Shorted by the lightning, maybe. Well . . . it would last long enough.

The soothing hum filled his brain as he brought the ship up level. He glanced back at Marty to be sure that she was still safe. Her form wavered, seemed to go red. But in a moment it was all right, and he told her, "I'll take us up nice and slow. We've got all the time in the world."

Amerie watched the broken-winged bird rise vertically into the golden morning sky, following the first component of the sign she traced. The mist was gone now and it was going to be a beautiful day. Over in the east the smoke cloud was thickening, but upper-level winds carried it in the opposite direction.

The aircraft ascended until it was a mere speck. Amerie blinked, and the speck became invisible against the bright vault of the heavens.

THE END

*Volume II of The Saga of Pliocene Exile,
entitled* THE GOLDEN TORC, *tells of the
adventures of the other four members of
Group Green in the Tanu capital city, and
of their reunion with the northerners in an
attempt to accomplish the final phases of
Madame Guderian's plan to liberate
Pliocene humanity.*

APPENDIXES

SOME NOTES ON "THE TANU SONG"

THE ENGLISH WORDS TO THE TANU SONG, APPEARING ON page 279 of this volume, are freely adapted from *Gods and Fighting Men: The Story of the Tuatha de Danaan and of the Fianna of Ireland*, a compendium of Celtic myth translated and "arranged" by Lady Augusta Gregory (New York: Charles Scribner's Sons, 1904). She tells some of the adventures of a race of heroic faeries or gods, the People of Dana or Men of Dea, who were said to have come to Ireland "from the north" in times implied to be late pre-Christian or early Christian. Her tales are part of the greater body of Celtic mythology originally engendered on continental Europe at a much earlier date.

One section of Lady Gregory's book tells the adventures of the god Manannan the Proud, who was said to have established other members of his race in Ireland, after which he himself disappeared—only to pop up again from time to time, playing tricks and making sweet music. Chapter 10 of *Gods and Fighting Men* tells how Manannan sent a faerie woman to summon one Bran, son of Febal, to his current abode in the Land of Women, also called Emhain (Aven) of Many-Colored Hospitality. The woman sings the following song to Bran:

425

I bring a branch of the apple-tree from Emhain, from the far
island around which are the shining horses of the Son of Lir
[Manannan]. A delight of the eyes is the plain where the hosts
hold their games; curragh racing against chariot in the White
Silver Plain to the south.

There are feet of white bronze under it, shining through life
and time; a comely level land through the length of the world's
age, and many blossoms falling on it.

There is an old tree there with blossoms, and birds calling from
among them; every color is shining there, delight is common,
and music, in the Gentle-Voiced Plain, in the Silver Cloud
Plain to the south.

Keening is not used, or treachery, in the tilled familiar land;
there is nothing hard or rough, but sweet music striking on the
ear.

To be without grief, without sorrow, without death, without
any sickness, without weakness; that is the sign of Emhain; it
is not common wonder that is.

There is nothing to liken its mists to; the sea washes the wave
against the land; brightness falls from its hair.

There are riches, there are treasures of every color in the Gentle
Land, the Bountiful Land. Sweet music to be listening to; the
best of wine to drink.

Golden chariots in the Plain of the Sea, rising up to the sun
with the tide; silver chariots and bronze chariots on the Plain
of Sports.

Gold-yellow horses on the strand, and crimson horses, and
others with wool on their backs, blue like the color of the sky.

It is a day of lasting weather, silver is dropping on the land; a
pure white cliff on the edge of the sea, getting its warmth from
the sun.

The host race over the Plain of Sports; it is beautiful and not
weak their game is; death or the ebbing of the tide will not
come to them in the Many-Colored Land.

There will come at sunrise a fair man, lighting up the level lands; he rides upon the plain that is beaten by the waves, he stirs the sea till it is like blood.

An army will come over the clear sea, rowing to the stone that is in sight, that a hundred sounds of music come from.

It sings a song to the army; it is not sad through the length of time; it increases music with hundreds singing together; they do not look for death or the ebb-tide . . .

From this felicitous fragment (which unfortunately continues with the rather dull adventures of Bran and his comrades in Emhain, where they ultimately meet disaster), and from the first three paragraphs of Lady Gregory's first chapter, which list the names and attributes of the principal Celtic gods, I derived a fragile skeleton for *The Many-Colored Land* and *The Golden Torc*, its culminating sequel. The actual plot of the saga, needless to say, has no basis in folklore; but students of mythology will recognize elements borrowed not only from the Celts but also from the fairy tales of nearly a dozen other European nations. The exotic people are all given names derived from those of the heroic faeries, with attributes that may or may not match the originals; the archetypal human characters Aiken Drum, Felice Landry, and Mercy Lamballe are also out of Celtica, via Jung and Joseph Campbell, among others. Folkloric bits purveyed by the character Bryan Grenfell are all authentic; especially noteworthy is the almost universal theme of the anima-menace—the faerie woman who snatches mortal men and wreaks her passionate will on them until they are drained husks. She shows up in tales from the Balearics to Russia.

The musical setting for The Tanu Song, which follows, is my own simplified adaptation of that mysterious melody, "Londonderry Air," which is purportedly of faerie authorship. This version, arranged for four human voices (SATB wtih divisi), varies somewhat from that which the exotics would sing. Their voices possessed richer overtones than those of humanity; and they were fond of dissonances and "violations" of human harmonic theory that sound weird, to say the least, when essayed by a human chorus. Only a few of these musical oddities have been included in the arrangement.

Among the Tanu, The Song was sung as a solo or in double chorus. On the rare occasions when Tanu and Firvulag sang together, such as the Grand Combat featured in *The Golden Torc*, the full grandeur of the exotic music was made manifest. The Little People used different words in their own dialect; and more important, they used different phrasing and at least four separate contrapuntal melody lines, which twined and writhed through the fabric of the basic Tanu harmonies in a richly complex polychoral effect. I must leave to more skilled hands the transcription of The Firvulag Song proper, as well as its musical marriage with the version sung by the Tanu.

The traditional "Londonderry Air" has perhaps the most eccentric history of any Irish melody. It does not fit any known Irish meter, and its history, as detailed by Anne G. Gilchrist in *English Folk Dance and Song Society Journal* (December 1932, p. 115), is a cloudy one. The air was first published in 1855 by George Petrie in *Ancient Music of Ireland*, noted "name unknown" and having no words. After the song appeared in Petrie's collection, its striking beauty led many arrangers to try to fit words to it. The best-known and most adequate version is "Danny Boy" (1913), with lyrics by Frederick E. Weatherly. Most public-domain songbooks use turgid lyrics composed by Katharine Tynan Hinkson (b. 1861) beginning: "Would God I were the tender apple blossom/That floats and falls from off the twisted bough,/To lie and faint within your silken bosom,/Within your silken bosom, as that does now." An equally unsingable version with slightly more dignity is "Emer's Farewell to Cucullain" (1882), with words by Alfred Percival Graves in a setting by C. Villiers Stanford. This begins: "O might a maid confess her secret longing/To one who dearly loves but may not speak!/Alas! I had not hidden to thy wronging/A bleeding heart beneath a smiling cheek."

The original melody in Petrie's collection came from a Miss Jane Ross of Limavady in the Northern Irish country of Londonderry. The lady arranged it for the piano herself and simply commented to Dr. Petrie that it was "very old." Unfortunately, later researchers were unable to find any trace of its origins, nor were there any Gaelic words to it. The fact that its meter was "wrong" for Irish folksong made it even more suspect, and some denied that it was a traditional melody at all.

Gilchrist tracked down relatives of Miss Ross and established that she was indeed a serious student of folksong, dedicated and honest. She collected some melodies herself, and others came from her brother, who fished in neighboring County Donegal. Both regions are known for preserving ancient bits of Irish culture.

It would seem, then, that we can discount the possibility of Miss Ross's palming off one of her own compositions as a traditional air. The problem of the atypical meter is ingeniously attacked by Gilchrist, who suggests that Miss Ross might have erroneously transcribed the tune in common (4/4) time rather than in the 3/4 or 6/8 rhythm of the majority of old Gaelic songs. If the rhythm is thus changed, and certain prolonged notes shortened, one does indeed get a typical Irish ditty of rather appalling banality. Gilchrist claims to see affinities between the transmogrification and two other songs, "The Colleen Rue" and "An Beanuasal Og."

If Miss Ross did err, we can only bless her for the inadvertent modification that brought musical immortality to what would have otherwise been a forgettable jig. If, on the other hand, she did record the air faithfully, then its provenance is a mystery still. We can only fall back upon the whimsical opinion that ascribes the haunting song to faerie folk—whoever they might have been.

The Tanu Song

WORDS BY JULIAN MAY

FOR FOUR LOW VOICES

Ancient Celtic Melody
Adapted and Arranged by
JULIAN MAY

ALBION

NORTH

PENEP

GULF OF ARMORICA

ⴰAu
Cu

ARMO

ⴰSn

Strait of Redon

RICA

Sn ⴰAu
Gorsh ■
[Belle Île]
R. Laar

N

■ Rocilan [Île de Ré]

PARIS
BASIN

GULF OF AQUITAINE

BORDEAUX

Garonne

MT-DORE

MAS

CANTAL

CEN

ⴰAg
■ Sasaran

PYRENEES

Black Crag ■

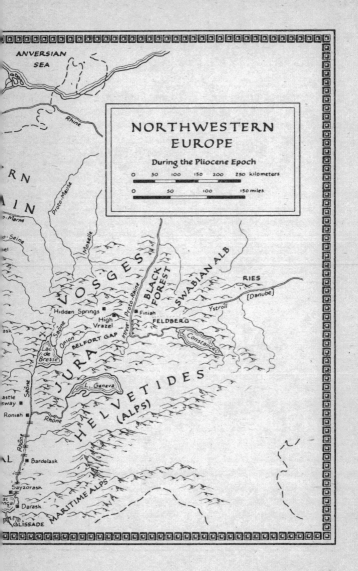

NORTHWESTERN
EUROPE

During the Pliocene Epoch

0   50   100   150   200   250 kilometers

0   50   100   150 miles

ANVERSIAN
SEA

Rhine

Proto-Meuse

o-Marne

o-Seine

sel

Moselle

VOSGES

BLACK
FOREST

SWABIAN ALB

RIES

(Danube)

Hidden Springs

High
Vrazel

Finiah

Proto-Rhine

FELDBERG

Ystroll

Saône

Onion

BELFORT GAP

Lac
de
Bresse

JURA

Constance

L. Geneva

HELVETIDES

(ALPS)

astle
eway

Ronish

Rhône

Saône

Rhône

AL

Bardelask

Sayzorask

ac
ngal

Darask

GLISSADE

MARITIME ALPS

ABOUT THE AUTHOR

JULIAN MAY's short science fiction novel, *Dune Roller*, was published by John W. Campbell in 1951 and has now become a minor classic of the genre. It was produced on American television and on the BBC, became a movie, and has frequently been anthologized. Julian May lives in the state of Washington.

Dear Reader,

Your opinions are very important to us so please take a few moments to tell us your thoughts. It will help us give you more enjoyable DEL REY Books in the future.

1. Where did you obtain this book?

Bookstore	☐1	Department Store ☐4	Airport	☐7	5
Supermarket	☐2	Drug Store ☐5	From A Friend ☐8	
Variety/Discount Store ☐3		Newsstand ☐6	Other_____	

(Write In)

2. On an overall basis, how would you rate this book?

Excellent ☐1   Very Good ☐2   Good ☐3   Fair ☐4   Poor ☐5   6

3. What is the main reason that you purchased this book?

| Author | ☐1 | It Was Recommended To Me ☐3 | 7 |
| Like The Cover ☐2 | | Other_____ | |

(Write In)

4. In the same subject category as this book, who are your *two* favorite authors?

_____ 8
_____ 9
_____ 10
                                            11

5. Which of the following categories of paperback books have you purchased in the past 3 months?

Adventure/		Biography	☐4	Horror/		Science	
Suspense	☐12-1	Classics	☐5	Terror	☐8	Fiction	☐x
Bestselling		Fantasy	☐6	Mystery	☐9	Self-Help	☐y
Fiction	☐2	Historical		Romance	☐0	War	☐13-
Bestselling		Romance	☐7			Westerns	☐2
Non-Fiction ☐3							

6. What magazines do you subscribe to, or read regularly, that is, 3 out of every 4 issues?

_____ 14
_____ 15
_____ 16
                                            17

7. Are you: Male ☐1   Female ☐2   18

8. Please indicate your age group.

| Under 18 | ☐1 | 25-34 | ☐3 | 50 or older ☐5 | 19 |
| 18-24 | ☐2 | 35-49 | ☐4 | | |

9. What is the highest level of education that you have completed?

Post Graduate Degree ☐1	College Graduate ☐3	Some High	20
Some Post Graduate	1-3 Years College ☐4	School	
Schooling ☐2	High School	or Less ☐6	
	Graduate ☐5		

(Optional)

If you would like to learn about future publications and participate in future surveys, please fill in your name and address.

NAME_____

ADDRESS_____

CITY _____ STATE_____ ZIP_____ 21

Please mail to: Ballantine Books
                   DEL REY Research, Dept.
                   516 Fifth Avenue — Suite 606
                   New York, N.Y. 10036

F-9